ZHIA DIVA

Karen Ann Ferrell

Stone
Tooth
Press

Published by Stone Tooth Press
Powder Springs, Georgia
www.stonetoothpress.com

Copyright 2021 © Karen Ann Ferrell

Cover: Terry Rydberg, Fine Print Design

First Printing: May 2021
Printed in the United States of America

For more information or to contact the author, visit stonetoothpress.com

Library of Congress Control Number: 2021906380

ISBN 978-1-7369744-0-7

Stone
Tooth
Press

Dedication

To my sister Terry and
her daughter Victoria,
for making dreams come true.

Note to reader:
The "zh" in Zhia, and all other proper names in this story in which it
occurs, is the sound in the middle of the word 'vision.'"

PROLOGUE

He hesitated in the doorway, wondering if he were doing the right thing. His heart urged him on, but his head…

This is going to be harder than I thought. Not even the greenest newcomer to a Singers' Hall would consider using such outworn words. But were I to set sentiments even as tired as those to a good tune, the nobodies—non-Singers—would eat up the story and ask for more. It has all the right elements: love found and lost and found again, lust, intrigue, danger…and even a happy ending. But before I return to that moment when I was hesitating in the doorway, torn between my heart and my head—Nia Diva, daemon of music, pardon that cliché and any other banalities I fail to catch!—let me explain how I came to be standing there.

Chapter One

As may be inferred, I am a Singer. My name is Rois, a sensible, everyday name. My stage name is Golden Throat, a moniker which I didn't choose and which I disliked from the start. I didn't like it any better after some self-appointed herald of hurtful news told me that when my father first heard it—likely from the same person who decided to ruin my day—he laughed himself hoarse. Justly so. I would be the first to agree that, in his prime as a Singer, Father deserved the name far more than I ever will; but I was the one stuck with it.

When this story begins I had just been chosen Champion of the Singers' Festival. I was the first from my Hall to win the prize, and at twenty-two—or maybe twenty-three; the wheel of the stars has turned more than thirty times since that first victory and my memory is not as good as it was—the youngest Singer to do so. (That distinction is now claimed by a girl of eighteen).

As is customary, I used most of the pleasantly heavy purse that was part of the prize to throw a party. Well, a bash. All right, an orgy. Wine, women, song…(Considering it was a Singer's celebration, there wasn't much singing, and what we were drinking was quite a bit more potent than wine. There were, however, plenty of women.) Everyone got drunk and enjoyed themselves immensely. I fell madly in love with a delightful young woman, Eia by name, whose charms would have been hard to resist had I been sober. Since from the moment the party started I had been working diligently to overcome that condition, and had succeeded only too well, when Eia whispered a suggestion to me and went out a door that led into a garden, I followed without a second thought.

I woke in the garden, alone, soaked, and chilled to the bone. I had been so drunk that not even the heavy evening rain had roused me. My throat was raw. I didn't know if it was from what I had been drinking or if I was catching a cold. I hoped it was the former; the Hall Master would have my hide if my stupidity got me sick. I managed to get to my feet and went inside. Both Singers and the women whose profession is pleasure favor bright clothing; my bleary eyes were assailed with color. Wincing, avoiding not-yet-conscious revelers, some of whom were lying in puddles of vomit, I made my distinctly unsteady way through the rented party room.

The revelry had reduced it to shambles. The previous evening, when the lights had been dim and my be-liquored eyesight even dimmer, I hadn't noticed the mess. In the gray pre-dawn, it looked like the aftermath of a raider attack.

Ignoring the little voice in my aching head that told me I wouldn't get my damage deposit back, I went in search of Eia. I remember I was hoping for a goodbye kiss, if not something more pleasant. She was nowhere to be seen. When I realized that my stomach was none too steady, either, and that the reek in the room was doing nothing to settle it, I quit looking and headed for the Singers' Hall. The just-rising sun made my eyes water and worsened my headache.

The Master was waiting—"lying in wait" is probably more accurate—just outside my cubicle. I remember being glad that, by custom, Masters wear only black. With the Master was the owner of the place my little celebration had trashed. Clad as he was in clothing that was the same dull brown as the stone of the wall, I wouldn't have seen him had his face not been crimson with indignation. The greedy so-and-so wouldn't agree not to go to the magistrates until I handed over not only what little remained from my prize purse, but also the tiny gold cup on a chain—a cup just big enough to hold the ritual two sips of wine for Nia Diva—that was the Champion's cherished trophy.

Throughout this proceeding, the Master had been looking at me. When the appeased owner was gone, he said "Congratulations" in a tone that contradicted the word and cuffed the side of my head. I think he added "idiot" as he walked away. I didn't care. All I wanted was to take off my wet clothes and snuggle into bed. I was so miserable it didn't even occur to me to wish that Eia was there to warm me.

When I woke, the sun was westering. My headache was worse but my throat was better. My stomach would have been better had it not been so empty. To avoid any digestion-related additions to the music, few Singers eat more than bread and water before a performance. Since the Festival had started in the early afternoon, I'd had little lunch. Food had been conspicuously absent from the party. I had slept through two of this day's meals, and it was too early for the evening repast. I would have to wait.

"Idiot," I muttered to myself as I got out of bed. The cold spell was not long over, but the wooden shutters with their heavy curtains were open. Shivering, I turned my back on the blinding orange brilliance my window framed, splashed cold water from the basin onto my face and under my arms, dried myself with the coverlet (I couldn't find a towel), and drew on the least colorful of my clothes. The shadow of the rumpled bedding which the sun's oblique rays cast on the stone of the wall looked like a shapely woman lying on her side. I remembered what I could of Eia.

As a Singer will, I tried to turn my thoughts into a song. I got stuck almost at once, as I couldn't think of a word that rhymed with "Eia". Between my hangover and my hunger, my mind was so unfocused that the only descriptions I could dredge up were painfully bad. "Hair of gold, eyes like the sky..."

True, but trite. To be satisfied with that drivel I would have to be drunk. Or a nobody.

My stomach complained, loudly. "Shut up," I said aloud, though not loudly. I didn't fear being overheard; nearly all the Singers from my Hall had been at the party. Some were probably still sleeping off the carouse. Though as a group Singers are known to be eccentric, talking to one's stomach is a bit odd even for a Singer. Last night in the garden, I had been talking to other body parts. Eia hadn't seemed to find it odd.

I began improvising, something along the lines of, "One kiss, my love, would be a feast. One glance would ease my pain. Come to me now, my love, and let me feast again."

"That song needs work." The voice that came from outside my door startled me.

That the voice was a woman's didn't surprise me. The wheel of stars had turned fourteen times since the first woman was admitted to a Singers' Hall. Being at that time only a child and not knowing I would end up at a Singers' Hall, I'd thought nothing about it. I knew that girls were good for nothing but pushing into mud puddles or frightening with crawly things. But my father—then a well-known Singer at the pinnacle of his career, who didn't share my interest in mud puddles or crawly things—had thought about it quite a bit, and had said even more. In fact, he was loudly and repetitively indignant. His ranting got so bad that my mother, who usually deferred to my father in all things, forbade him to raise the subject at meals.

What surprised me was that I didn't recognize the woman's voice. Singers know one another's voices like nobodies know one another's faces. I glanced at the speaker. My first thought was that she was a mediocrity on two legs. She was neither old nor young, neither short nor tall, neither slim nor fat (though way too round for my taste), neither beautiful nor ugly. I suppose some people, if they noticed her at all, would describe her as comely; to me she was nothing but an intrusion, and an untimely one, at that.

Then I saw she was holding a broom and realized she was just another starstruck female, one of the not-worth-counting horde of entirely forgettable women who seek employment at a Singers' Hall so they can be close to their favorite idol. These females—I use that term not to be rude but because it includes all ages; some of the worst behaved are well past their youth—are frequently so infatuated they're willing to do anything. Apparently some of them are not aware that magistrates long ago ruled that any issue from such encounters was the responsibility of the mother. Only the mother.

This woman didn't appear to be either as predatory or as vacuous as some I'd seen. She looked like she might actually know how to use that broom. Still, she was a nobody. That she might prove less tedious than many of her ilk didn't make her presence more welcome or her unsolicited critique less annoying.

I was in a foul mood from hunger for food, hunger for Eia, and a hangover headache that was making it hard to think at all, let alone well. I hoped this woman would try offering herself to me as a way of making amends for her unwelcome remark so I could reject her. I looked at her again and decided to just get rid of her. If I couldn't have Eia, I didn't want even an offer from anyone else.

The problem is, entirely too many nobodies mistake being moved by a song for being in love with the Singer. Some are too shy to do more than adore from afar, which is pathetic; others make nuisances of themselves by hovering and even pursuing. Each Singer develops his or her own way of dealing with the latter bunch of pests. My way, while not exactly kind, is invariably effective.

Though standing would have allowed me to look down on the woman, I sat on the bed because I was somewhat dizzy. I gave her a long, measuring look—a rudeness I compounded by making no attempt to hide it—before remarking, "I don't suppose someone of your bulk can run faster than her brothers."

If she was startled or disconcerted, she hid it well. After the briefest of pauses she replied, "Thank you for your concern for my virtue. I have no brothers."

"That's a mercy. Then is it your father you must outstrip, or didn't your mother know who he was?"

"My parents are dead." Her voice was devoid of emotion. She might have been telling me the sky was blue.

I can't say the disclosure didn't affect me. By then, I had realized that the woman was younger than I; it wasn't likely that her parents had died of old age. That she spoke so calmly about a probably tragic and almost certainly untimely loss suggested either that she hadn't cared about her parents, or that she had been so deeply hurt by their deaths that she hadn't yet recovered. I didn't want to continue to bait her; but it was clear she hadn't the sense to realize I was telling her that her presence wasn't welcome.

Feeling sorry for a nobody was, for me, a wholly unfamiliar exercise; one for which I told myself I had neither time nor patience. (My pride insisted on this fiction. It was less embarrassing than admitting that feeling compassion made me uncomfortable.) I found it easy to be sarcastic. "Oh, you're an orphan, with no one in the world to turn to, so you're reduced to drudgery, surviving by eating crumbs from tables until a dashing hero comes to sweep you off your feet and take you away from all of this." I gave her time to writhe in my ridicule before adding, "If you're looking for someone to rescue you, you've come to the wrong place. I'm not your hero."

"You've made that quite clear."

I was congratulating myself on finally getting it through her thick skull that I was telling her to leave when I realized that her response was open to another, much less flattering, interpretation. No inflection of the woman's voice told me which she intended; the look on her face left me with no doubts.

I was so affronted I was momentarily speechless. With just five words, the woman had handed me the most thorough, demoralizing slam I had ever received. Worse, I hadn't immediately realized it. What made my cup of wrath overflow was that I could think of no retort. I finally retaliated with "What kind of rock did you crawl out from under?", knowing even as I spoke how feeble a rejoinder it was.

She didn't laugh; I was relieved. She didn't have to laugh; far more potent weapons remained in her arsenal. "One quite a bit classier than yours."

As a put down, it wasn't the equal of the first one. Coming as it did while I was still reeling from the previous strike, it hurt more. The awareness that she'd nailed me again made me even angrier, and that made my head throb worse.

Armoring myself with the remaining shreds of my pride, I inquired, with icy hauteur, "Do you know who I am?"

"A desperate man."

Another hit.

Sometimes the only way to win is to allow your opponent to believe that you've lost. Managing to sound more than a little rattled, I asked, "Who in Nia Diva's name are you?" The woman took the bait. "In Nia Diva's name, a Singer."

My certainty that she was lying wasn't much of a weapon, but it was all I had and I didn't scruple to use it. "Really?" I drawled. "Of what Hall?"

She blushed. To her credit, she didn't resort to bluster. "I hope to be of this Hall."

Neither grin nor words did me any credit. "Not if I can help it."

The color in her cheeks deepened; but she said evenly, "You have a right to be angry with me for criticizing your song, but there's no need to be mean spirited. That's not worthy of a Festival Champion."

She was half right; I was being mean spirited. I wasn't accustomed to accepting blame, but I could think of no one else to blame for my loss of both trophy and purse. By being mean spirited, I could make someone else as miserable as I was. I had been named Festival Champion—a glory all Singers dream of but few achieve—at an age when other Singers are still hoping for their first tour. Now I had nothing to show for my triumph but a fleeting memory of the applause…and a hangover. Worthy or not, I intended to indulge in as much mean spiritedness as I wanted.

Though the woman had condescended to allow that I had a right to be angry, she had been wrong in thinking I was angry because she had criticized my song. Indeed, what she had said had been too kind. The thing (it didn't deserve to be called a song) was worse than bad. The tune had been laughable. The lyric—which lacked meter, rhyme and, most importantly, originality— would have been embarrassing coming from a child of two. No amount of work would have made it anything but garbage. No, I was angry because the criticism had come from a nobody—a contentious, deceitful nobody who lacked respect for her betters.

Not even to myself could I admit that I was angry because that nobody had made me feel utterly, cursedly foolish. I wanted to be able to curse her, long and loudly, and by name. I reminded myself that I didn't know her name. To avoid identifying herself, she'd been willing to lie. To find out her name, I'd have to be as deceitful as she was.

I gave her a pitying look and said, "That last gratuitous comment proves you know even less about Festivals and Champions than you do about songs. It also proves that you were lying not only about who you are, but also about knowing who I am. If you said the sky was blue, I'd look out the window to be sure you weren't lying again."

"It's sunset; the sky isn't blue." She sounded sulky.

"Oh, that put me in my place," I jeered. "If you really want to prove me wrong about your being a liar, you could start by telling me the truth about who you are. I already know you're not a Singer. I assume even nobodies have names. What's yours? Something stupid, I suppose."

"Zhia." Sulkier yet.

My smile was smug. The situation was all but under control. My control. "That's a stupid name, all right. But let's make that 'Zhia sir.'" I couldn't have foreseen that insisting she recognize my rank would be so great a mistake.

With deference so exaggerated it was mocking, she bowed and said, "Pardon me; I have no intention of telling you my surname." She saw me wince, and added, "If I may say so, sir, you deserved that."

In the sizzling silence that followed I heard the supper bell ringing. My stomach growled. I got angry again. Though I had lost the prizes, I was still Festival Champion. Other, older Singers would now defer to me. I didn't have to stand here and swallow insolence from a nobody. I told the woman to take her broom and leave, though my actual suggestion of what she should do with the broom was far more vulgar.

I expected her to be shocked or, better yet, to burst into tears. Instead, she stood there with her lips tight and her face flushed, looking for all the world like she was trying to relieve constipation, with her bloated maggot of a body blocking the doorway and keeping me from my meal.

I said as much, and added, "Why are you staring at me?"

"I'm wondering how such sweet music can come from so foul a mouth." Her scorn was salt on the wounds she had already inflicted on my pride.

"Are you judging me?" I asked, astonished.

"No need. Your own words have revealed the man you truly are." Then her voice, which she had just demonstrated could slash like a knife, became wistful. "It's a pity, really, that your appearance and your voice—both of which are quite pleasing—are so at odds with your personality. With all the adulation you've received from those who've seen only the Singer, I suppose you couldn't help turning into an arrogant, spoiled brat."

That's when I lost it. It's probably just as well that I don't know exactly what I said. I wasn't simply talking crap, as Singers put it, I had a full-blown flux of the mouth, and I couldn't seem to stop. I don't know if the woman eventually tired of my tirade, or if I finally transgressed the bounds of decency. I suspect the former; I had probably left any semblance of decency far behind. Her open hand hit my face with enough force to knock me flat on my back on the bed.

As I sat up again, my astonishment became outrage. I was aware of only two things: the pain in my cheek (the hand print was visible for days), and a fervent hope that she would say something, anything—derisive, condescending, or even kind—so I would have an excuse to kill her.

I don't know if murder showed in my face or if I spoke what I believed I had only thought; but the woman pulled me to my feet, dragged me from my cubicle to the dining hall, pushed me into a chair, snatched a plate of food from a server, slammed it onto the table in front of me, and stalked out of the room, all in frigid silence.

When the plate hit the table, the food bounced and spattered. Much of my meal was now spread across the tabletop, my shirt front, and my lap. I knew the other Singers who were still eating had been watching; I could whispering and muffled laughter.

The woman might have thought she was doing me a favor. Instead, she had made a fool of me again, this time in public.

I had never hated anyone more.

CHAPTER TWO

TOURING SEASON CAME AND went, without me. A Festival Champion isn't expected to face the risks and hardships of a tour. Though I was expected to sing at important events—if these were of a civic nature, I received no recompense—there weren't many important events where my Hall was. I didn't have all that much to do, which was good, because I didn't have the means to do much besides sit around and learn new songs. I began to understand why successful Singers often go to fat.

The wheel of the stars turned. At the next Festival I was again chosen Champion, and again gave a party. Allow me to repeat: a party. Not a bash. Not an orgy. I had learned my lesson.

I used to wonder why Masters did so little to protect Singers from themselves. Now that I'm Master of a Hall, I've realized that Masters can lecture and issue cautions until they're blue in the face, only to see their Singers do precisely what they've been warned against. It's better if Masters follow an unwritten rule I call "let them be stupid and they'll get smart". Put simply, if stupidity is allowed to run its course, astute Singers learn from their own and others' mistakes. Of those unable to learn from experience, some are unsuited to being Singers for other reasons, as well, and are dismissed. Others pay the ultimate price for their obtuseness. Looking back, I can be glad my lesson was not more painful than it was.

Among the women at this second party was Eia. She let me know both that she remembered me and, to my great pleasure, that she was glad to see me. Because I spent the party mostly sober, in the morning I was able to remember the excitement of the night. (Now that I'm older and more experienced—I don't presume to say "wiser"—I have to wonder if anything actually happened with Eia at that first party. If I was too drunk to wake when I got rained on, I may have been too drunk to do anything else.) Memory can be a powerful stimulus. Eia had told me where she lived. With no urgent business planned for the afternoon—I'd better say "Singer-related business"—I was considering paying a call on Eia. An urgent call.

I had just thrown a wet towel onto the bed and was reaching for my second-gaudiest shirt—my most flamboyant one I'd worn the night before—when Dolin appeared in the doorway. Though older than I, Dolin has one of those faces that always looks boyish. When he puts on a much-practiced look of childish innocence, he can tell the most outrageous stories and people will believe him. More often, he looks mischievous, reminding me of the representations of Darl, one of the naughtier daemons.

He started with innocence. "In case I didn't say so yesterday, congratulations."

"You did say that yesterday; but thanks again."

"Got plans for the afternoon?"

"No. I'm still tired from the party. I thought I'd just lie around."

"On whom?"

I grinned at the joke, stale though it was. "That would be telling."

Now his Darl face showed. "You'd better tell me so I can tell the lady, because you won't be seeing her today."

"What's that supposed to mean?"

"You drew short straw."

Impatient to be gone and distracted by Dolin's hints, I tried to put my head through the shirt's sleeve. Dolin laughed until tears were streaming down his cheeks. "Ha, ha," I said as I pulled off the garment and found the right opening. "I don't have time for guessing games, Dolin. If you're not going to tell me what this is about, go away."

"You sure are cranky when you're hor…" He broke off when I glared at him. "You're partnering a first-timer."

"I'm what? No, don't repeat it; I heard you." I continued to dress as I spoke. "There must be some mistake. Champions don't tour. And don't talk any crap about short straws. I know as well as you that partners aren't chosen; they're assigned."

"Usually. The Master let us draw straws this time."

"What 'us'? I wasn't there. I didn't get to take the luck of the draw. I'm not going."

"She said you'd say that," Dolin said. I wanted to smack the smirk off his face.

"'She'? Now I know you're talking crap. The only 'shes' at this Hall are servants, and—here's news for you, friend—they don't tour."

"Shows what you know. While you've been living in the cushy world of a Champion, things in the real world have been changing."

Reluctantly, I said, "You're telling me there are now female Singers at this Hall?" Dolin nodded. "How many?"

"Only two…so far. The one you're partnering says she's met you."

Though I thought I had succeeded in putting that day and, especially, the woman out of my mind, I knew at once to whom he referred. My insides knotted; I bit back a curse. "Don't tell me it's that…that…What was her name?"

"Zhia."

"That was it. Nia Diva!" I slammed my fist into the wall. (The stone was hard. Imagine that.) Wincing, rubbing my hand, I asked, "Is there any way I can get out of this?"

Dolin shrugged. "Next time, slam your head into the wall?" Then the teasing note left his voice. "Come on, Rois, how bad could it be? Even if you hate the woman's guts, which I gather you do, all you have to do is stand up on a stage and sing with her in a few rinky-dink backwaters. It's not like you're being forced to sleep with her."

"I'll have to travel with her."

"So ride in front and let her eat your dust."

"Then she won't be able to sing—assuming she can sing—and the Master will have my hide."

"I'm glad it's your problem, not mine." Dolin grinned and turned to go.

"Some kind of friend you turned out to be," I said. "Wait. How come no one wanted to partner her? What do you know that I don't?"

"Nothing, Rois. She's a 'she' but she's also a Singer, which means you get all of the problems of females and none of the benefits. Who needs it?" He left.

"Who needs it?" I echoed, dully. Clasping the chain with the Champion's trophy around my neck, I went to the Master's office for formal notification of the coming ordeal.

As any Master would be quick to agree, rank has its privileges. The furnishings in Singers' cubicles are so austerely utilitarian that one wonders how much extra effort had to be expended to find so many items utterly devoid of beauty.

By contrast, the Master's office, which was also his living quarters, was opulently furnished. The shutter curtains, fluttering in a breeze that made the room a bit chilly, were lavishly embroidered. The Champion's purse would not have sufficed to purchase the pierced metal lamp on the costly wood of the cluttered table at which the Master sat. Since it was still daylight, the lamp was not lighted; even so, I could smell the fragrant oil that filled it, fine oil pressed from the timi fruit. (For their lamps, Singers are given oil derived from riku seeds, oil so impure it's gritty. When burning, it can smoke abominably.) The storage cubes lining the wall behind the Master's table were adorned with fretwork...

Rank should not have so many privileges.

The Master glanced up as I approached. "Ah, Rois, I was about to send for..." He grimaced. The long ends of his graying mustache, waxed until they were as stiff and pointed as his small grizzled beard, emphasized the expression. "Who told you?"

"Dolin."

The Master shook his head. "You—I use it in the plural—gossip like a bunch of old ladies. I suppose if he hadn't blabbed, someone else would have. I take it there's a problem."

"Yes, sir. What happened to 'Champions don't tour'?"

"Did I ever make that statement to you, Rois?"

I had to think about it. Apparently I took too long; to the accompaniment of tuneless humming, the Master began to brush from the richly textured black of his robe something that was invisible to me. The green stone in a large, beautiful ring on his left forefinger glinted as it caught the light. I quickly abandoned my reflection and gave him the answer he wanted. "No, sir, I don't recall your saying that." Offended by his blatant unconcern, I added, a bit sharply, "Others have, though."

His look quelled me. "Are any of those 'others' Master of this Hall?" I shook my head. "Very well. Here…" After a brief search, he found the paper he wanted and handed it to me. "Here is the schedule. You leave at daybreak. You may pay the usual visits to your families." When I didn't leave, he looked up again. "Is there still a problem?"

"No, s…Yes, sir. Isn't there someone else—anyone else—I could partner? I'm not objecting to a tour, I just…"

"Object to the company you'll be keeping? Zhia said there had been unpleasantness between you. She said it was over. It is over, isn't it, Rois?" I didn't want to tell a lie to the Master, so I nodded. "Good. Look at it this way: if you don't linger between engagements, this tour should be over in no time."

Let's hope so, I thought, wondering why the Master thought I would "linger"—become involved—with a woman I despised. "Who else is going, sir?" He recited names. "All first-timers, sir?" I asked, surprised.

"Yes." He sounded curiously defensive. "What better way to find out what being a Singer is about than by touring with a two-time Champion?" I could think of any number of ways, but knew the question was not meant to be answered. The Master added, "I have every confidence in you, Rois."

"Thank you, sir." My mood as I left his office was even glummer than it had been. Neither my being a two-time Champion nor the fact that I had toured before meant that I knew a single thing about being in charge of a tour. I could expect no help from the other Singers; without exception, they were not only first-timers, but also so new to the Hall that I had recognized none of the names but Zhia's. Inexperienced Singers partnered on tour with an equally inexperienced leader added up to an infinite number of ways to make hash of things. Failure was practically a given.

A Singer's success both reflects on and is shared by his or her Hall and its Master. There is only one Festival Champion. Other Singers win what fame and glory they can on tour, so tours are planned well. "As hard as getting a tour on the road" is a saying among Singers precisely because it is hard. Overlooked details, especially ones that seem minor, have been known to break otherwise well-planned tours.

Tours are also planned well in advance. Never before had a lead Singer received his assignment and schedule the afternoon before the tour was to leave. While every Singer knows a basic body of music and, because of his or her training, can perform with any other Singer on short notice, no other tour had set out without its members practicing together even once.

When a Master says "daybreak", he means dawn. Singers understand "day-break" to mean any time between dawn and dark. Even if the tour didn't leave until the following evening it would still be all but impossible to get every-thing organized, since starting the already-overdue preparations would be have to be further delayed so I could take Zhia to pay the customary visits to our parents. Those would use most of the rest of the day.

Reading the list of engagements only increased my anxiety. Tours that involve first-timers go no farther than the towns a few days' ride any direc-tion from the Hall of origin. From my own first tour, I knew the names of most of the towns in the immediate vicinity of this Hall. Subsequent tours had supplied the names of more distant destinations. In conversation with Singers who had ventured even farther afield, I had learned the names of still other places. I recognized the names of only two of the towns on the schedule. Neither town was close to the Hall. I could only assume the others were equally, if not more, distant. There had to be a mistake.

I returned to the Master's office. His cold "Yes?" wasn't encouraging, but I said, "I'm wondering if you gave me the right schedule, sir."

He took it from me, glanced at it, and handed it back. "Yes, this is your schedule."

I thanked him and left. In my cubicle, I flopped on my bed and buried my face in my hands. Before the next day was over, I would be on tour with Singers I had never met who would be trusting me to bring them on schedule to places I had never been.

The Master had expressed his confidence in me. I began to wonder if he had meant his confidence that I would fail. But why would any Master put responsibility for a tour in the hands of someone he believed incapable of carrying out such an assignment? Could any Master want a tour to fail?

Not even a two-time Champion would dare ask a Master that question.

Chapter Three

"What am I doing here?" Zhia asked, panting a little as she tried to keep up with me. She's not much over average height. I'm quite a bit taller than average, at least a head taller than Zhia. My legs are considerably longer than Zhia's. I had no intention of taking shorter steps for her.

I didn't answer at once, not because I didn't know the answer but because I didn't want to answer until I could do so without snapping at her.

Since it's impossible to prepare for everything that can happen during a performance, Singers have to be able both to adjust and to improvise, and to do so quickly. I didn't lack quickness; at the moment, I lacked inclination. Though I was professional enough to know that the sooner I accepted the situation and adjusted to it, the better it would be for me and the others on the tour, that didn't stop me from resenting the situation, the manner in which it been thrust upon me, and the woman who was the cause of it all. That she probably liked it no better than I was little comfort.

Regardless of what I'd told the Master, whatever happened the day I met Zhia still lay between us. Though my memory held few, if any, details of our meeting, my vague impression that it had been less than amicable had been confirmed by the Master.

No Singer can afford to harbor or indulge grievances on tour, both because aggravations are the one thing of which every tour has a surplus, and because a Singer who has a reputation for being a wretched traveling companion is all too likely to be repaid in kind. After a few days on tour, handling annoyances about which I could do something, likely I'd be better able to deal with Zhia, an annoyance about which I could do nothing. For now, I'd be doing well simply to keep my temper in check.

I said, "It's a custom that Singers who tour visit their families before they leave. You know, one of those 'just in case' sorts of things, so bereaved parents don't spend the rest of their lives saying, 'Oh, if I'd only had the chance to hug my child once more!'"

Zhia grinned, probably because I'd spoken the quote in falsetto, and said, "I know that. So why am I here?"

"Because I'm partnering you. Those who tour together visit as…as partners." I swallowed, wondering how long it would be before the word stopped sticking in my craw. "When we finish with my parents, we'll visit your family."

She looked at me in what I took to be confusion or disbelief. I wondered how just how dim she was. "No, we won't," she said.

"Yes, we will. It's the custom."

"No, we won't," she repeated, more firmly.

Already I was in danger of breaking my resolve not to lose my temper. Taking a deep breath, I said, "I'm in charge of the tour. I say we're going to visit your family."

"You can visit them if you want," she flared. "I won't go with you."

My temper flared, too. "You will if I say you will."

"No. Not to that house."

I remember interpreting that statement to mean that my being a Champion had made her ashamed to reveal how modest were her circumstances. I remember thinking that, now she had finally understood the difference in our rank, I could be gracious. I curbed my anger and asked, mildly, "Is something wrong with their house?"

Her eyes and her expression were frosty. Her voice was colder. "You might put it that way, considering that no one can just visit it and the living can't go there at all."

I had never before blushed. The feeling that I had just made an utter fool of myself was, for some reason, uncomfortably familiar. I knew there was no way to make amends for the blunder. After some moments I said, sincerely, "I'm sorry. I am so very sorry."

"Thank you." There was silence, then she added, "I need to apologize, too."

"For what?"

"For not speaking plainly. I should have realized you hadn't just…" With something that she probably meant to be a smile, she said, "So, now you know all about my family. Tell me about yours."

At that moment I knew the relief a drowning man must feel if he can suddenly raise his head above water. I had been drowning in embarrassment. Rather than saying I was pardoned, which I would have resented, Zhia had smoothed over my misstep with a graceful change of subject. Her tactful invitation to talk about my family might have been nothing but simple courtesy; but talking about something familiar would put me at ease and give me a chance to pull myself together. It was an unexpected and undeserved respite. At that moment I began to realize that, while she might not yet be an ally, Zhia wasn't an adversary.

As if a hex had been lifted, I felt tension leave my shoulders and back. My insides unknotted. Without anger tightening my throat, my voice sounded better when I said, "There's not much to tell, really. I'm an only child, though Mother was fond of saying that she and Father had two children. She'd pause and then say that instead of having them stair step like others do, they'd had them one atop the other." Zhia looked up at me and laughed; I grinned. "Though after hearing that quip you might find it hard to believe, Mother's always been reclusive. Lately, she's gotten worse." I felt my grin fade. "In fact, you likely won't get to meet her. She won't even leave the house anymore."

"That's a shame. Missing being outside on a nice day like this would be awful."

I'd been absorbed in worrying about the tour; I wouldn't have noticed if I'd been standing in a downpour. I looked up and around. "It is a nice day. I'm glad I didn't miss seeing it. Now, my father was a Singer." The statement was too mild. "My father was a Singer's Singer." Frowning, I asked, "I'm not saying this very well, am I?"

"I get the idea. Go on."

"Well, he's also old-fashioned. He's been opposed to women being Singers since the first woman set foot inside a Hall. He'll probably say outrageous things to you."

"That wouldn't be the first time that's happened."

Nothing suggested that she was harking back to our first meeting, but suddenly I had to know what I'd done and, more importantly, said that day. When I asked Zhia to tell me, she paled and refused. When I asked her why, she said, "Because we're starting to be civil to each other and I don't want to lose that. You won't like what you hear. You'll lose your temper and then…" She broke off, her mouth hard.

"I promise I won't lose my temper." At the assurance, the tight line of her lips trembled. I said, "Zhia, please. You said you like that we're starting to be civil; so do I. You don't want to lose what appears to be the beginnings of accord; neither do I. But how am I going to avoid making the same stupid mistakes if I don't know what the stupid mistakes were?"

She relented. I asked her to include every detail she could remember, a request I quickly regretted. (Happily, she couldn't remember exactly what I'd said before she slapped my face.) I was glad I had to devote some attention to my footing on the rutted lane we were following; seeing the whole play of expressions on her face while she relived that day would have been unbearable. As she spoke, my hazy memories were doing what little they could to flesh out the account; imagination allowed me to fill in what I couldn't remember and she, perhaps, chose not to reveal, even if she did remember. During the recital, I managed to hold onto my temper, though doing so was the hardest thing I've ever done. When she finished talking, I could find no words. Had I looked in a mirror just then, I would have expected to see a monster leering back.

At last I said, "And after all that, you were willing to go on tour with me?"

She had been clasping and unclasping her hands throughout the recital.

Now she spread them in a little gesture of appeal. "The wheel of the stars has turned since then; we've both changed. By the way, did the food stains ever wash out of those clothes?"

"Not entirely. Though, remembering what that shirt looked like, I'm not sure anyone could tell the difference." Then I realized she hadn't answered my question. "Don't change the subject. At least, not yet."

"Okay, but I don't think you'll like this, either. What does every Singer want? A tour. Only a handful are like you, worthy of being named Champion, not once, but twice. But every Singer who works hard and proves reliable can tour. I want to tour. After standing there today and listening to Dolin and Chaz and Rork and the others—all Singers I thought were friends...well, maybe not friends, but certainly not detractors—saying how awful it would be to draw short straw and have to partner me, I realized it would be better to tour with you, because you hadn't pretended you liked me. I can handle honesty, even if it hurts. I knew I could trust you; you spoke your mind. After today, I can't trust Dolin or Chaz or Rork or the others."

I wasn't sure whether I'd been complimented or insulted. I could imagine the scene; it must have been mortifying. Then, remembering Dolin's saying that the Master had allowed them to draw straws—a way of choosing a tour partner as unwise as it was unprecedented—I wondered whether the Master had been present at Zhia's humiliation. I had been considering having a chat with Dolin. If, as now seemed likely, the blame lay with the Master, I could do nothing that would not make the situation worse.

Once again I was struck by the oddness of the preparations for this tour.

"A bad attitude makes a bad beginning" was one of the aphorisms my father had beaten into me. "There's no point in expecting the worst; the worst can happen even if you don't expect it" was another one. I put aside my misgivings and returned to a more immediate problem. "If my father says something awful, will you be able to control your temper?"

She stopped and stared at me. "That's the second time you've brought that up. If this visit is going to be torture for all concerned, why don't we go back to the Hall now and save everyone the anguish?"

"Trust me: no matter how cranky Father is when we do visit, he'd be immeasurably worse if we didn't. We'd have failed to observe the custom. I guess I implied but didn't say in so many words that Father is a stickler for custom." I heard Zhia muttering. "I didn't catch that. What did you say?"

"I said, 'If it were the custom to jump off a cliff...'"

"My father would. He'd lead the way and sneer at anyone who balked."

She shook her head. "Then why don't just I go back to the Hall, since we know my presence will only provoke him?"

"You can't go back."

"Why not? I know the way. I follow this lane."

"Because we're here." I gestured at a tall stone house within a stone's throw of where we were standing. Lofty though it was, the placement of the windows suggested it had only two stories. Flowers softened the lowest tiers of stones; clumps of trees dotted the area behind the structure. In the afternoon sunlight, it looked serene and gracious.

I knew that what awaited us was about as serene and gracious as a hail storm during haying. I didn't want to take those last few steps up to the house. Zhia was even more reluctant. Fearing she might try to bolt, I took her arm.

She stiffened as though I'd struck her. I could almost feel the heat as her indignant gaze traveled from my hand to my face. Through clenched teeth, she asked, "Is dragging your partner somewhere you know she doesn't want to go also some custom?"

Startled, I apologized and released her arm.

When I knocked on the door it opened, though no person was visible. Ducking so I wouldn't bump my head on the lintel, I stepped inside and beckoned Zhia to follow.

"Hiding again, Father?" I asked, peering behind the door. "That trick doesn't fool me, you know. I'm not a boy any more."

From covert came the muffled words, "You're not a man, either; you still don't have a beard. Were you gelded to keep you singing tenor?"

Having removed any doubts Zhia might have had about his capacity for making outrageous statements, my father stood up. I saw Zhia's astonishment as his full height was revealed. He'd had to crouch to conceal himself behind the door, for he was taller than it was, which made him half a head taller than I am. (Though he professed not to like being as tall as he was, I think he really did.) His luxuriant beard, once golden brown but now fading to dun, was carefully arranged with its ends fanning out, an outdated style which didn't suit Father. I think he insisted on it to draw eyes away from the top of his head, which had less hair every time I saw him.

I heard him draw breath to speak again. He had already demolished me; there was no question who would be his next target. I said, quickly, "I'm starting a tour at daybreak, Father, so I came to pay my respects."

"Who's the woman?" He didn't say "woman". His broken, rasping whisper—all that remained of a once-fine voice—made the vulgarity sound like an obscenity.

I bit my tongue; it wasn't for me to chide my father. "She's the first-timer I've been assigned to partner. Come out and meet her. I assure you her bark is worse than her bite." That was a poor choice of words, I thought. I was right.

Father said, "Are you suggesting she's a bitch, or that I'm afraid of her?"

Father probably thought he was being witty. "Uncouth" would be closer, though entirely too kind. Whatever his intention, I never knew quite how to respond to his more unexpected utterances.

Zhia's voice broke the awkward silence. "I'm the one who's afraid, sir, or, more accurately, intimidated. Accounts of your career are inspiring, especially to a new Singer like me. It's an honor to meet you." She bowed.

Father walked away. He returned with a wooden chair, on which he stood. Now his head touched the ceiling. Seeing my puzzled look, he explained, "It's getting deep in here." To Zhia he said, "I believe you can sing no more than a fish can walk, but there's no question that you can talk crap. If 'Ugly and Stupid' is already taken, 'Crap Mouth' would be a good stage name for you. What partners you and my son will be, Crap Mouth and Golden Throat, though only you deserve your stage name." Blows would have been kinder; bruises fade.

"You know why you've been partnered with my son, don't you?" he went on. "It's a bait and switch. No one wants to hear you, so you let the nobodies think they're going to hear Golden Throat. Once they've made the trip, to avoid wasting the effort they'll listen to anything, even a squeaky wheel. They'd probably enjoy the squeaky wheel more."

Zhia's back was to the open door. Against the light I couldn't see her face; her voice was steadier than mine would have been in similar circumstances. "You may be right, sir. I won't intrude any longer. I must say this has been an occasion I'll never forget."

Father chuckled. "Think I'm so old I don't know when I'm being insulted, Crap Mouth? I hope the raiders get you!"

Zhia turned and went out the door.

Mother—soft, demure, reclusive Mother—burst in, bristling with fury and shouting recriminations. Probably because he was as surprised as I, Father endured it longer than I expected he would. When Mother paused for breath, he stepped off the chair, told Mother to be quiet—in much harsher words— and remarked, "You're making a mistake, Son. She'll never make it as a Singer. How will she stand up to a crowd of heckling nobodies if she can't even take teasing from a few friends?"

Though I doubted that the term "friend" applied to anyone still in the room, my father's question was valid. I would have to consider it later. As calmly as possible, I said, "Father, you've faced more crowds of heckling nobodies than I have. Did anyone ever say to you, 'I hope the raiders get you'? That's just plain cruel. And bear in mind that if the raiders get her, they get me, too."

Father folded his arms across his chest. "I was never heckled," he said, flatly.

For all I knew, the statement was true. Some Singers have voices and personalities so compelling that the nobodies are virtually spellbound. Father might have been one of them, once. But Father had missed the point I was trying to make.

While I was pondering some other way to make him understand, Mother said, "What is your young lady's name, Son?"

"Her name is Zhia, Mother; but she's not my young lady. I've been assigned to partner her on her first tour, that's all. I'm not asking her to be my wife!"

"That's a mercy," Father drawled. "With Crap Mouth for a wife, you'd beget fools, and ugly ones, at that." He proceeded to elaborate on the theme.

I could only stare in appalled disbelief. It didn't make me feel better to know that, though my father was being undeniably and needlessly offensive, he was being less crudely vicious than I'd been when I first met Zhia. Zhia had left the house; she couldn't hear the filth Father was spewing. The day I met her, though she could have escaped my poisonous tongue, she hadn't. She must have realized that running away would have made me think even more poorly of her. Knowing that she'd had to listen to the vile, unwarranted abuse I'd heaped on her that day shamed me. Knowing that today, at my request, she'd had to remember and repeat every unpardonable word filled me with remorse.

That I'd thoughtlessly been echoing sentiments I'd so often heard from Father while growing up—the same kind of nastiness of which I was even now getting another earful—didn't excuse me. No matter what Father thought, it took more than a beard to make a male a man. I was a man; I was responsible for my own choices. That I'd never thought twice about some of those choices was even more damning.

I felt a surge of disgust, loathing both for myself and for this man who, in so many ways, towered above me. I had always been in awe of him. He awed me no longer.

"Father, stop!" I shouted. To my surprise and relief, the spate of smut ceased. "You've been ranting about ugly people. Have you considered what kind of man you've become? Zhia showed you the respect and courtesy due you as a Singer. You don't have to like the fact that she's a woman; but she is a Singer. As such, she deserves better of you than to be treated like something you scraped off the bottom of your shoe. For the first time in my life, I'm ashamed to say that you're my father."

I said goodbye to Mother, kissed her cheek, and left.

I didn't slam the door behind me.

Father did.

Chapter Four

Remorse and repentance aren't the same thing.

Though I had awakened to the fact that Father's behavior was deplorable and my mirroring of it reprehensible, naming the evil was not the same as taming it. I still had to excise deeply rooted, malignant patterns of behavior, and nurture new habits, a process that wasn't going to happen just because Rois—Singer and Champion, accustomed to having his own way—wanted it to. It would take vigilance. It would take work. It wouldn't be easy.

Just how deeply rooted the malignancy was, I was yet to learn.

When I left the house, Zhia was nowhere in sight. The lane that leads to my parents' house is fairly straight, flat, and open; short people can see long distances down it. Even with the advantage of my height I could see no other people. I didn't want to try shouting Zhia's name until all other options had been exhausted.

I started back toward the Hall, walking quietly so I listen. I heard labored breathing before I heard footsteps, and knew someone was following me. I turned, wondering if Mother had found the courage to leave the house.

She hadn't. The person behind me was Zhia.

"Where have you been?" I asked with unnecessary sharpness.

She pointed. "In that clump of trees behind your house."

I knew the trees well. They stood outside the kitchen window. Mother used to let me climb them to get me out of the house while keeping me in sight. (Of course, I would have climbed them even had she said I shouldn't.) Then I realized that Zhia might have heard what had been said after she left. "What were you doing there? Eavesdropping?"

"Eavesdropping? With that many Singers shouting, anyone within a stone's throw of the place could have heard what was going on, whether they wanted to or not. I am one of the latter, by the way."

Since I had no reason to believe otherwise, I accepted the truth of her last statement. The one before it I could and did challenge. "What's with this 'that many'? Can't you count to two?"

She gave me a strange look. "Have you never actually listened to your mother's voice? Had it been allowed in her day, I'm sure she would have been a Singer."

In all honesty, I had never paid my mother any more attention than was absolutely necessary. To avoid getting in trouble with my father I'd had to make sure I heard her when she spoke. When Father was at home, I usually obeyed. When he wasn't, Mother seemed to be satisfied with no more than an outward show of compliance.

Now that I thought about it, I realized Zhia was right. "Even had it been allowed, Father would never have agreed," I said, and was surprised at the regret I felt.

Zhia started kicking a stone down the rutted surface of the lane. She looked at me and said, "I didn't know you were a tenor."

"I'm not. I sing baritone, like my father did."

"That's what I thought. Pardon me if I'm being impertinent, but what's wrong with his voice? Listening to him, I kept wanting to clear my throat."

"That's how it affects me, too. And no, you're not impertinent. Remember two…no, three cold spells ago, when everyone was sick? Wait, you weren't at the Hall yet."

"Not only Singers got sick. I never heard so much coughing."

"Me, either. Well, Father took it worse than most. For a while, we weren't sure he'd even survive. I'm not sure he doesn't regret that he did, because he coughed so much and so hard that something in his throat was damaged. You heard him; he can hardly talk. He shouldn't talk. And he can't sing a note."

"Poor man. How awful for him."

I stared at her. "Poor man? You feel sorry for him, after he was so insufferable?"

She hesitated before asking, "Has he always been that, um, candid?"

"Say 'rude'; it's shorter. No, I'm told he used to be charming, quite the smooth talker. He didn't waste charm on me, of course; but he didn't treat Mother like he did today. That's right, you didn't see that little scene." I shook my head. "I don't remember exactly when he changed."

"Do you remember if it was before or after he lost his voice?"

"Definitely before. Quite some time before. Why?"

A pair of creases formed between her eyebrows. "Maybe not next tour season, but likely the one after that, when you go to pay your respects, he won't know who you are. He won't know who your mother is. He won't even know his own name."

"What makes you think that?"

"I saw it happen to my grandmother, the one who raised me after my parents' death." She cleared her throat and went on. "She had always been the sweetest person. Then she started acting just like your father is now, and then one day she…" Again she cleared her throat. "It's hard when the only person in your life who cares about you no longer recognizes you."

"Is she still alive?" I asked, quietly.

"No. She had become increasingly confused. One cold night, when I thought she was safely tucked into bed, she left the house and, apparently, was unable to find her way back in. It wasn't until morning, when it was too late to help her, that I discovered she was missing."

"I'm sorry."

"Thank you." She kept the stone skittering down the lane. Raising her voice above the annoying rattle, she asked, "Do they really geld Singers to keep their voices high?"

"Not since women started being Singers."

Shocked, Zhia let the stone roll to a stop. Seeing her look, I said, "I was joking. Frankly, I've never heard of the practice."

"Then why would your father say something like that?"

"It's sensational. It's outrageous. It's Father." Then I thought of what Zhia had said. Though I was annoyed at and often embarrassed by the man my father had become, he still knew who I was. I would do well to appreciate that situation while I could.

I didn't need to entertain another gloomy thought; that the tour was imminent was depressing enough. I said, "You never said what you were doing in the clump of trees."

The look she gave me would have cowed a lesser man. "I'd been nervous about meeting your family. When I get nervous, I have to...But now that the subject has come up, this would be a good time to mention that on tour I would appreciate if I...if you...You know." Color flooded her cheeks.

"Yes, I do know. I don't know why you're having such a hard time talking about it. It's one of the more basic bodily functions."

"For a man it's basic. For a woman it's complicated."

Though much about a woman's body is complicated—I would go so far as to say "mysterious"—its excretory process is not. However, the observation has been made that the most insurmountable obstacles are in the mind.

Zhia was watching me. "You'd better not be thinking of laughing," she warned.

I wasn't. I was thinking of something Dolin had said and was beginning to wonder if my father's objection to female Singers was more practical than I first believed.

In a tone of utter indifference, I remarked, "If you're going to make that big a deal out of something that little, do everyone, including yourself, a favor and back out while you can, because accommodations on a tour are minimal."

"Minimal like primitive?"

"Minimal like non-existent. There can be long stretches—some days-long—of empty road between engagements. The various Halls have put up little way stations known as Quarter Rests, but they're usually just rough shelters in defensible places, always near water but not always near a source of firewood."

"Defensible places? Then is a tour really dangerous?"

"Yes and no. Yes, because raiders are real. You were aware of that, weren't you?" She nodded. "And no; but I say that only because no tour I've been on has had any mishaps." Maybe because I wasn't leading any of them, I thought. "I don't know of anyone from our Hall who died or was killed or even seriously injured on tour. Everyone's heard the horror stories; you can never find anyone who actually knows the people the awful things happened to. So I guess what I'm saying is that a tour is like life: there are no guarantees. You make the preparations and take the precautions you can, but at some point you have to leave what is safe and familiar and take a chance."

I spoke confidently, but I was thinking, What chance? I was no more optimistic about the success of the tour now than I had been when I'd left the Master's office. No matter who was to blame when the all-too-likely disaster occurred, in the final analysis, I would be at fault; I was leading the tour. Zhia and the other new Singers (I was ashamed that I could remember none of their names) could and often did rise above a bad start and eventually succeed. There wasn't enough honor in being a two-time Champion to cover the disgrace of a failed tour. A Champion had nowhere to go but down.

Zhia had been following her previous train of thought. "Since your phrase was 'a source of firewood', I take it we cut our own; so we'll need to bring an ax. We'll need water jugs, food, blankets, and..."

"And everything. That being said, I also need to tell you that we travel light."

With a humorless smile, she said, "That's not much of a challenge. Take everything as long as you take nothing."

"Take only what you'll need," I amended.

"How am I supposed to know what I'll need when I've never toured before?" she demanded. "How come this kind of information isn't part of a Singer's preparation? When was I going to be told?"

In fact, that kind of information was part of a Singer's preparation. I wondered if she'd missed class the day it was discussed, or if she hadn't been paying attention. I raised my hands in the gesture that, on stage, means "stop", and said, "I'm telling you now, if you'll calm down and listen. You probably haven't done much traveling, but try to imagine what you'd take along if you were traveling somewhere. For a tour, you'll need a few other things, like something to wear on stage. If you're fussy about things like dirt and odors, you might want a change of clothes for traveling. I usually don't change clothes until I'm ready to put on stage garb, but that doesn't mean you can't." She mumbled something that had the word "clothespin" in it. Grinning, I said, "Of course you'll need a comb and…whatever."

"I can figure out the details of 'whatever', thank you."

"We'll need our instruments, of course, and, as you said, ax and water jugs, blankets and food. We won't have to carry food for our mounts; tebecs can live off the land." A thought struck me. "You do ride, don't you?"

"I have ridden."

The evasive answer prompted me to ask, "Have you ridden a tebec?"

She didn't answer, which I took as a "no". I wasn't surprised. Nobodies use a variety of riding and pack animals, including tebecs, if nothing better can be found. There are a number of good, practical reasons Singers use only tebecs when touring. There are no aesthetic reasons. Even a rider on a desdal, the least impressive of the hoofed animals, can make an entrance much grander than can someone astride one of the oversize, unattractive birds. But the creatures' long legs and unexpected strength allow them to carry people or goods rapidly and long, the latter in the sense both of distance and of duration.

As I told Zhia, tebecs forage for their food, meaning less to carry on tour. Tebecs don't require the care other mounts do. They don't have to be groomed or have their feet tended; attempting to raise a tebec's clawed foot is asking to be kicked, which can be fatal. As the birds are flightless, all that is needed to settle them for any long stop is to hobble them and put them near water and something to eat (though they don't eat everything, they aren't fussy).

They have their drawbacks, as well. Some Singers—and, apparently, most nobodies—consider the drawbacks to be greater than the advantages. They have necks as long as their tempers are short, so they can and do nip the unwary. Their beaks are sharp; the nips hurt. The best way to ride the fool things is bareback, with one's legs in front of the birds' stubby wings. Enough riders were injured by bites on the legs or even more sensitive areas that the practice was soon abandoned. The basket-like saddles that were developed to protect the riders' legs and lower torso are heavy and unwieldy. The birds don't like them and rarely if ever stand still for being saddled. Two people can saddle a tebec; three are better: one to keep the bird from moving while the other two put the saddle in place. Once a bird is saddled, it remains saddled until the tour reaches its goal. By then, one or more Singers has saddle sores.

No matter how experienced a rider is or how much padding is used, tebec saddles chafe riders. (Or maybe the cause is the tebec's unusual gait. Whichever, riders invariably get saddle sores.) A tour leader will neglect to bring music before he forgets saddle sore ointment.

If Zhia had never ridden a tebec, she would soon need the ointment. Since few can effectively treat the abrasions where they occur, the task usually falls to the tour leader.

I groaned. "Great. Between stopping so you can hide and pee and stopping so I can put ointment on your butt, we'll won't late to our first engagement by more than five or six days." I caught myself. "I'm sorry. I told myself I wouldn't be snide. My resolution is better than my execution."

"I guess that's what people mean when they say 'do or die.'" Zhia went back to kicking the stone. Just before the clatter again became unbearable, she stopped and said, "Okay. When we get back to the Hall, I'll go to the Master and tell him I changed my mind about wanting to tour."

"No, you won't."

"Why not? Wasn't it your suggestion that I do just that?"

"I didn't think you'd take my advice. Besides, you've already told the Master there'd been unpleasantness between us. If you back out now, he'll think I've done something else to annoy you."

"You did, but you apologized." She sighed and squared her shoulders. "Okay. I just won't go back to the Hall."

"Where would you go?"

"What difference would it make to you? I'm not sixteen going on seventeen; you don't have to take care of me."

"That's a mercy." The words were out before I knew they were coming.

The stone got another twenty or so hard kicks and a handful of less forceful ones before she looked at me and asked, quite mildly, "Do you know what's wrong with us?"

Once again, old habits answered for me. "Yes: we can't stand each other." I was aghast. For a moment I did what I'm sure was an amusingly accurate imitation of a fish. Then I said, "Zhia, I…"

She was exasperated. "Don't bother saying you're sorry," she snapped. "The first time, I believed it. You didn't even bother to apologize the second time. If you said it this time, I'd know you were talking crap. I told you I can handle honesty. All things considered, 'we can't stand each other' rings much truer than 'I'm sorry'." She lapsed back into silent kicking. The stone was now leaving the ground, flying in graceful arcs before landing and rolling toward a new resting place.

I remember how glad I was that Zhia wasn't kicking it at me.

I didn't know why we were so annoyed with each other. That we were annoyed was indisputable. That Zhia was handling her aggravation better than I was also quite clear: the stone was taking the brunt of her irritation; Zhia had been taking the brunt of mine. It was equally clear that she was not only able but also quite willing to go on ignoring me; for all I knew, indefinitely.

That bothered me. I didn't know why. What I did know was that if the silence wasn't broken soon, it would soon be unbreakable, and the tour would end here, as would my future as a Singer.

As the stone landed yet again and began to roll, I stopped it with my foot and put myself squarely in Zhia's path. She kept trying to go around me. I kept barring her way. I finally said, "We can keep up this bizarre dance until we're stuck out here in the dark and the rain, or you can stand still and let me say I'm sorry. Thank you," I added when she stopped trying to dodge me. She wouldn't look at me. "I know my credibility is pretty low right now, but

I am truly sorry for the mean, unnecessary things I've said to you, not just today but…before. I wasn't talking crap when I said I didn't want to be snide. Hearing Father today was like looking in a mirror. I despise my father for what he said to you. I'm none too pleased with myself, either. Please accept my apology and give me one more chance. I'll try to be…"

I stopped, stuck. What I wanted to say was either "not my father", which was absurd, because I already wasn't my father; or "someone other than myself", which was crazy.

"A Champion in deed as well as name?" Zhia suggested, now looking at me.

"The impossible dream," I said, bitterly. "I'd prefer a reachable goal, like being half as decent as you are. Did I thank you for being so kind to Father?"

She shook her head. "I don't want your thanks, and I don't want to be anyone's touchstone of anything. You know nothing about me. Setting up some virtue you think I have as a goal is no wiser than starting to climb a rope without finding out whether the rope is sound and anchored to something solid. You think you're getting where you want to go, when—BAM!—the rope snaps and you fall, or—WHAM!—a chunk of rock or tree breaks off and smacks you in the head. Then, assuming you survive, you have to find a new rope and a new anchor, and start all over again. Set yourself a goal that's not just reachable, but worth reaching." She gave me a small, tight smile. "I don't know about you, but I'm hungry. May I suggest that an immediate, reachable goal that's worth reaching would be to get back to the Hall for something to eat?"

Now that she mentioned it, I realized I was hungry, too; I'd eaten nothing that day. "That's certainly preferable to standing here until we're stuck in the dark and the rain."

We went on. The stone Zhia had been kicking remained where I had stopped it.

Chapter Five

The evening rain was a little early. Though we didn't have our oiled cloaks, we weren't very wet when the Hall came into view, nor had we missed supper. Once I got food into me, I realized that the answer to Zhia's earlier question about what was wrong with us had been "hunger".

Since we were so late in returning, we had the dining hall almost to ourselves. After supper, when Singers are either in their cubicles conning music or away from the Hall in pursuit of a different kind of harmony, the corridors also are fairly empty.

"This is eerie," Zhia said, speaking over the echoing of our footsteps.

"After you've been on tour, you'll think even this many people looks like a town square on market day, and your cubicle will look like the height of luxury."

"I'll take your word on that."

I looked at her. "Are you still thinking it would be a good idea to back out?"

"Nothing has happened to make me think otherwise." She added, quickly, "Don't worry; I'll make sure the Master knows this is entirely my decision, that I'm not annoyed with you or anything like that."

"Thank you; but I don't see how you're going to say that you don't want to go on tour with me without its sounding like I'm the reason you don't want to go on tour."

There was a pause before she spoke. "If I say what you just said, the Master won't understand it, either." She smiled, but I thought she looked nervous.

That the Master frowned when we appeared in the doorway of his office did nothing to calm her. In the shadows cast by the lamp, which was now lighted—the scent of the timi oil filled the room—he looked menacing. His first words left me unsettled, as well. "I've been wondering where you two were. Did you forget the way?"

For the second time that day I found myself staring, speechless. Unaware that "forget the way" is Singers' slang for being unable to function in bed, Zhia started to reply. The Master saw me give her the hand signal that means "don't sing" or "be quiet".

He laughed. "Haven't you taught her that phrase, Rois?"

I found my voice. "No, sir. She's not likely to suffer from that particular problem."

"Depending on just who has the problem, she might well suffer from it."

Even though Zhia still didn't understand what we were talking about, she understood the tone of the Master's voice and the expression on his face. She turned away.

"Where do you think you're going?"

Zhia did not make the mistake of thinking that the Master was simply requesting information. She turned back. "I'd like to go to my cubicle, sir." Glancing at me, she added, "To pack." Again looking at the Master, she said, "Please do excuse me, sir. I fear my presence is keeping you from speaking as openly as you'd like." Without waiting for him to give her leave, she left.

I wondered if the Master had been drinking or if he was simply impervious to sarcasm, for he chuckled and said, "I never saw a woman more in need of a good man", though "man" wasn't the word he used. "I suppose she came to say she wanted to back out of the tour?" I nodded. "I can't say I didn't expect it. I'm actually a little surprised she didn't wimp out before now. She might be tougher than I thought. Are you going to be able to handle things?"

As I've said, Singers know each other's voices. The Master wasn't asking about the logistics of the tour. Like his earlier comment, this inquiry was prurient.

I couldn't entirely keep reproach out of my voice when I said, "Sir, she's a Singer."

His careless gesture as he dismissed this objection made his ring flash. "I assure you, Rois, there's no one listening; you don't have to pretend to be shocked. I know you don't want a woman here, not as an equal, at any rate. How is your father, by the way?"

Until that afternoon, I would have thought he was changing the subject. Now I knew the two thoughts followed as naturally as the notes of the scale. Without thinking, I answered, "He's all right, sir." Then I said, "Who am I trying to fool? He's not all right; he's pitiable."

The Master, probably assuming I'd said or meant "pitiful", nodded. "He was the last of the great Singers. He was a true Singer, a purist. He knew how things were done and why they had to be done that way. If he still had a voice, I'd have him teaching here."

"Father would be pleased to know that, sir." I was becoming impatient with the conversation, not only because it was only too reminiscent of what I'd had to listen to that afternoon. Even if I still endorsed my father's views, I needed to be packing.

I was about to excuse myself when the Master asked, "What have you told your first-timers about raiders?"

"Raiders, sir?" While learning new music, many a Singer has had the experience of turning two pages instead of one and being lost. The abrupt change of subject left me feeling lost, though I was fairly certain that it was the Master who had turned more than one page. "I've told them nothing, sir. The only one of the tour group I've even met is Zhia. Why do you ask? Has there been an increase in attacks where we'll be traveling?"

"Not to my knowledge. My concern was that you not frighten them needlessly."

"Needlessly, sir? Is that possible where raiders are concerned? I don't believe all the reports I hear, but most of them indicate that raiders are fearless, striking randomly and entirely without warning—in daylight, no less—snatching up anything that will fetch a price, and massacring everyone. Nothing short of a small army daunts them. Anyone old enough to be at this Hall knows about raiders."

The Master agreed, then remarked, "So you weren't aware that they do not kill everyone."

I knew my mouth fell open. I mastered my dismay. "No, sir."

"Reliable sources tell me they also take people, especially women, to sell in the slave markets. You need to caution your group to stay together at all times and to do nothing that will draw attention to their presence. We'd hate to lose anyone."

"Yes, sir. I'll convey your warning to everyone, especially Zhia. Now, if you don't mind, sir, I haven't packed, either. Daybreak is coming."

"Then you'd better go. Rois," he added, just before I stepped out of his office, "every tour has mishaps. Some can't be helped; some can."

"I'll do my best, sir."

"I knew I'd be able to count on you."

Chapter Six

THAT FIRST TOUR I led holds the unenviable distinction of covering the least distance the first day out of any tour. Ever.

Looking back at that day, I can now laugh. At the time, I was torn between despairing that we'd ever leave the Hall and hoping the saying was true that any tour that started so abysmally could only improve. No one person was to blame for the chaotic prelude to our departure. With so much to do to get ready, I didn't sleep; the dark-circled eyes of the first-timers told me they were as exhausted as I. Tempers were short; squabbles, frequent.

It's been said that looking for the good helps one deal with the bad. One good thing that arose from the pandemonium was that I soon learned the names of the first-timers; I shouted them often enough. Besides Zhia, there were Hink, Norjy, Hadden, Vel, Mariz, Turiz, Taf, and Birl.

Another good result is that I got acquainted with the tour group more quickly than I would have, had conditions been less tense. Under stress, a person is less likely to be able to maintain a "public" personality, especially one that differs considerably from his or her true personality. The Singers on this tour were revealed as the usual mixed bag. Watching the group jostle and joke, annoy and appease, hinder and help, I knew I would be amazed when we finally got on stage and music would blend these individual parts not only into a whole, but also a harmonious one. At the moment, however, the parts just seemed mismatched.

Hink was small and quiet. My first impression was that he was far too reserved to do well as a performer. Since he was at the Hall I knew he could sing and could also play at least one instrument. What or how he sang and what he played, I didn't know.

Norjy already had the nickname "Rangy", because he was the tallest of the first-timers—after me, the tallest Singer at the Hall, in fact—and painfully thin. He seemed reliable and was quick to help out, whatever the chore.

Hadden was as much a shirker as Norjy was a worker. Since I'd already had to say his name so often, I'd quickly learned which one he was. His greatest strength seemed to be offering unsolicited observations and advice, which is hard to take at any time and is even less welcome on tour. I was pretty sure he'd be trouble.

If you ask the average nobody to describe a Singer, he or she will probably refer to talent, and then mention words like "cocky" or "snobbish". Vel fit that description. He was good looking and knew it; before we were underway, we were all tired of hearing of how women pursued him and what happened when he let them catch him. Norjy finally put an end to his boasting by saying, "There are only so many variations on that theme, Vel; I'm a lot more interested in learning if you're any good on stage."

Mariz and Turiz were identical twins. Though I never did learn to tell them apart, they were clearly used to be being called by the wrong name and took no offense at my mistakes. This good nature was evident in almost everything they did and said.

Taf eventually got the stage name "Tebec", both because his angular features gave his face a beaky look and because his father raised the birds. Realizing he had far more experience in that area than I, I put him in charge of the birds.

I had even more doubts about Birl's future as a Singer than I did about Hink's. Seeing Birl's round face and ample girth, one would have expected him to be cheerful and easy going. Instead, he was a malcontent. Nothing pleased him;

if he had a grievance, everyone had to know about it.

The grievances began almost at once. My height required that I ride the tallest bird, a male, which was also the largest one. Norjy was assigned a female which, though slender, was the second-tallest of the tebecs. Because Birl was hefty, Taf paired him with the second-largest bird, another male. The male of many creatures, including tebecs, is more aggressive than the female. It turned out that Birl's tebec wasn't simply aggressive, it was vicious. When Birl bent to fasten his pack to the saddle, which as yet lay on the ground—despite his having been told not to load the saddle until it was on the tebec—the bird nipped him on the back of the thigh. The skin was broken; he bled.

You'd have thought he lost a chunk of flesh. He accused me of negligence for putting Taf in charge of the birds, conveniently forgetting that Taf had warned everyone never to turn their backs on their mount. He accused Taf of malicious intent for pairing him with that particular bird. He said he never wanted to see a tebec again, then belied that assertion by claiming that his future as a Singer had been jeopardized because he was too badly hurt to go on his first tour, a tour he could not go on if he eschewed any further contact with tebecs. Those were the last even slightly reasonable statements he made.

The uproar finally brought Aplin, our resident doctor, to the scene. He cleaned and bandaged the injury, with Birl carrying on like his leg was being amputated. When Aplin told Birl it was not serious and would not prevent his going on tour, Birl's dramatics became even worse. It was probably good that he didn't hear Aplin say to me, "If he starts that crybaby act on tour, give him a good hard kick in the rear."

I managed not to smile…too much. "If you insist."

The others had long since returned to their own preparations. I had quit hovering when Aplin arrived, to give him room to work. When the doctor, the last of his audience, left, Birl fell silent, letting an occasional groan or heartfelt sigh remind us of his ordeal.

By then the sun was at zenith. Since meals on tour are usually meager, I interrupted our preparations so everyone could have a hearty lunch. Tempers improved somewhat after we ate.

As we resumed our ongoing attempt to get on the road, Zhia came up to me and said, "If my tebec can carry Birl, I'll swap birds with him. Mine is more placid."

I called Taf over and had Zhia repeat her suggestion. Taf looked surprised but said, "Any of these birds should be able to lift Birl. If you think you can handle his tebec, it's fine with me."

Zhia said, "The question is, is it fine with you if I handle it effectively?"

Taf grinned.

I learned that day that there is a way temporarily to curb a tebec's aggressiveness. I still don't know exactly what it involves; I'm sure I don't want to know. What I saw was enough. Zhia approached Birl's biter. Circling out of reach of its beak, she stepped up to its rear end and did something. The bird let loose an indignant squawk and gave Zhia a look that, from a person, would have been called a glare. Zhia returned its glare and went off, saying she had to wash her hands. Laughing appreciatively, Taf helped me saddle the bird, which stood still.

Finding Zhia's pack still attached to the saddle of the bird he would now be riding gave Birl a new grievance. To deny him reason to revive his crabbiness, I unfastened Zhia's pack. It was very light, and was one of the smallest bags I'd seen being loaded. When she returned, hands damp, I handed Zhia her baggage, saying, "Where's the rest of your stuff?"

"This is all I have."

Though her mount continued to stand still, it curved its neck and eyed her as she secured her bundle. "I wouldn't advise it, chum," she warned. Then, with ease that spoke of familiarity, she got into the saddle.

Now I was eying her, too. "You told me you hadn't ridden a tebec." She said nothing, but raised her eyebrows slightly in an expression that was partly quizzical and partly a challenge. "Well, you implied…" Her eyebrows rose slightly higher. "Why didn't you tell me you knew how to ride one?"

"I got the impression it would be a waste of breath. The answer I would have given you wasn't the answer you wanted to hear."

"So it was better to let me know today, like this, and make me look a fool in front of everyone?"

The heat in my voice didn't come close to equaling the quiet chill in hers. "Pull yourself together. The only thing any of the others know is what they're seeing and hearing right now. Quit scowling and lower your voice, and they'll have no reason to think anything's wrong."

I did as she advised, but I asked, "Do you think they're stupid?"

"No. I think that, like me, they're hoping they haven't put their safety into the hands of a man who isn't enough of a leader to control his temper."

"You're angry, too."

"I'm not the leader." As I drew breath, she snapped, "Don't say 'there's a mercy'. We're getting a bad enough start as it is."

I hate to be shown up. I already knew Zhia was right about the less than promising outset of the tour. When I went to help Vel saddle his tebec, I found out Zhia was right about the others' perception of what was going on. Vel gave me a knowing leer and asked, "Lovers' quarrel?"

"You think we're lovers? Must I remind you that she's a Singer, Vel?"

"Oh, come on, Rois; she's a female. She's not much to look at; but by the time we've been on the road a few days, I imagine she'll look pretty good."

I shook my head. "One, you address me as "sir". Two, no female looks good enough to risk being kicked out the Hall. In case you didn't know, that's what would happen were you to forget yourself. Be warned: I don't give instructions twice."

He muttered something as I walked away. I hoped I hadn't heard him right.

Birl was the last one who needed help getting on a tebec. It took Taf and me together to put him into his saddle. He fit so tightly I wondered whether we would have to cut him out of it. As I mounted my own bird, I found myself hoping Birl wouldn't get saddle sores. There are some torments even a tour leader shouldn't have to suffer.

I gave those who needed it a little time to get used to controlling their mounts, then called everyone close so I could relay the Master's warning. At the mention of raiders Birl began to howl, but quickly subsided when everyone else, including his tebec, glared at him. I didn't bother to repeat what the Master had said about the raiders taking women captive, because no one looking at our group would have suspected that it included a woman.

Zhia was not wearing a skirt and shirt, she was wearing shirt and trousers. The only difference between her clothing and the men's was hers was not as colorful. As had the men, Zhia had tied her hair, which was an indifferent brown, at the nape. It reached the middle of her back. Most of the men had hair as long as hers, if not longer. Though well-rounded below the waist, Zhia not especially bosomy; the fit of her shirt would not betray her gender. Were raiders to attack us, likely they would take Zhia for another man and kill her. Of course, if we never actually started the tour, raiders wouldn't be a concern.

The sun was three quarters across the sky when we finally left the Hall. Scarcely had we left behind the Hall's town when I noticed we were missing one of our pack birds. There were supposed to be four; Mariz, Turiz, Birl, and Hadden had each been put in charge of leading a bird. Hadden, who was bringing up the rear, was leading nothing. His bird had our instruments. Singers are skilled at improvisation; improvisation is difficult without instruments. I sent Hadden back.

Not even in my thoughts did I censure him for his smirk when I had to return to the Hall for the schedule, which I'd left in the dining hall. Of course, it had been cleared away with the dirty dishes, so I had to wait until it could be found.

The sun had slipped farther westward before I rejoined the group and we started yet again. I knew there wasn't a chance of our reaching the nearest Quarter Rest before both dark and rain fell. We should have returned to the Hall for the night; I decided we would go on. My decision was not based on a wish to spare my little group the derision they would surely face if we returned that night. It wasn't based on my wanting to start toughening them for the longer than usual journey they faced.

We kept going because I knew being on tour was the best chance Zhia had of staying alive.

The Master wanted her dead.

Chapter Seven

Though I knew exactly when and how I'd come to that realization, I was still having trouble believing it.

The Master had been careful to say nothing outright, nothing that might later be used against him; but the wheel of the stars had turned many times since he had last been on stage. He was out of practice controlling his voice.

When he'd mentioned raiders, I'd been confused. When he'd told me they captured and enslaved women, I'd had misgivings. When he'd remarked that every tour had mishaps, I'd begun to harbor suspicions.

It was when, in reference to those same mishaps, he said, "Some can't be helped; some can," that his voice betrayed him. The way he said those six words left me no doubt that, far from urging me to employ greater precautions, he was telling me either to allow or to arrange an accident for Zhia. It had taken every bit of my own stage training to put the right amount of guarded enthusiasm into my reply, and to make that reply safely noncommittal while suggesting compliance.

Did I intend to comply? Never. No matter my personal feelings for Zhia, which were far different than they had been a day or even half a day earlier, she was a Singer; I was partnering her on a tour. If Singers learn nothing else, they learn that the tour comes first. Pettiness, backbiting, antagonism do not go on stage with Singers.

Though I had briefly considered taking my suspicions to a magistrate, I had rejected the idea for three reasons. First, I'd had no time. Second—and most importantly—I had no proof other than what the Master had said and, as I mentioned, it was his tone that had convinced me there was need for concern. No magistrate would consider a charge brought against a Hall Master based on nothing more than a suspicious tone of voice. Third, the Master knew that Zhia and I had once been at odds; for all he knew, we still were. Were I to involve a magistrate, the Master would almost certainly and quite easily shift suspicion to me.

I had also considered the likelihood that I was not the only person the Master had approached. In allowing Dolin and the others to draw straws and in the comments made to me—and, I presumed, to others; Vel's remarks came to mind—the Master had not only been subtly promoting an atmosphere of hostility toward female Singers in general and Zhia in particular, but also fostering the impression that, were something to befall Zhia, he would take no action.

Mishaps do occur on tour, but not necessarily to the right person. If I were hurt or killed without accomplishing the task, the Master would want to have another tool ready. I wouldn't know that man's identity, or if he was at the Hall or in the group that rode with me, until it was too late. At the Hall, with its maze of corridors and cubicles, there would be entirely too many opportunities to find Zhia alone and strike unobserved.

Here on tour, with only eight men to watch and the Master's own instructions to stay together, the opportunities would be far fewer. With us traveling as a group and our route already decided, should something tragic happen, another member of the tour would almost certainly witness it. He would be able to testify that I wasn't guilty. That was important, because it was likely that should Zhia be victim of a mishap, the Master would deny any complicity in the matter. While he would likely not bring in magistrates, neither would he do anything to defend whoever had done his bidding. Someone else would take the Master's guilt and his punishment.

The first cold drops of the evening rain interrupted my musing. My hooded cloak of oiled cloth was fastened to the back of the saddle. I freed it and pulled it around myself. The others also donned cloaks. My plan had been to continue on at least until we reached the closest Quarter Rest. With a different group, that plan would have been sound. With this group, it was doomed even before I thought it.

To be fair, I can't place all the blame on the other Singers. Tebecs aren't especially fond of rain; they kept heading for the shelter of the trees along the road. The little bit of practice controlling the birds the inexperienced riders had had at the Hall had not given them the skill or the courage to compel their mounts to obey. Even without the Master's injunction to stay together, leaving some of the group behind not was an option. I bowed to the inevitable and led the way into a knot of trees where we dismounted, though we didn't release the reins until Taf hobbled the tebecs. We huddled together for a cold, inadequate meal. Since the ground was damp and there would be no time to allow blankets to dry, when I suggested that we do without them that night, the others agreed. Huddled even closer, we tried to sleep. Even Vel was too miserable to comment on the sleeping arrangements.

Hard though it may be to credit, the tour went downhill from there. Since that tour, I have never left the Hall without first making a lavish offering of appeasement to Darl. I'm still not sure even that would have made any difference on that first tour I led; either Darl was giving that tour his full attention, or he had enlisted every lesser daemon available to help make things go wrong.

The mischief began even before we woke. Though I suspect I know who was at fault, it doesn't particularly matter who failed to close the packs with our foodstuffs. What mattered was that during the night, the tebecs found food that they could eat without getting wet, and helped themselves. By morning, little was left for breakfast, let alone for subsequent meals.

All of us were already out of sorts from a less-than-restful night. The bird-pecked remains of our provisions were far from appetizing. None of us was eager for that food; Birl was especially vehement in his objections. I didn't dare say anything because I knew anything I said would be cruel. It was reserved little Hink who observed, quietly, "If you don't want to eat, Birl, there'll be that much more for the rest of us."

Birl quit complaining and choked down his portion.

When Taf and I were helping the group mount, I noticed that our instruments were wet. "Hadden," I said, "didn't I tell you to cover the instruments with an oiled cloak?"

"Yes, sir, you did; and I did so," he replied.

"Then why is everything wet?"

"It started to rain, sir; I needed the cloak."

"Your cloak is fastened to the back of your tebec's saddle," I said as mildly as I could. I was inspecting the damage. I finally said, "The wind instruments and the metal percussion pieces might be all right. Assuming nothing warps from getting wet and then drying, we'll have to replace strings and drum heads before we can play the others, so we can forget about doing any practicing before our first engagement. I'm not sure we'll be able to play at all, since we might not be able to get strings and drum heads where we're going."

Norjy asked, "Could we get them at other Halls, sir?"

I felt foolish for not having thought of that myself, but made myself say, "Yes, we can. Thank you, Rangy."

As we set off, I tried to picture in my mind where the closest Hall was in relation to where our schedule had us going. (I imagine anyone with a scrap of pride understands why I didn't even consider returning to our own Hall, which was actually the closest one.) I was not encouraged to realize that repairing the damage to our instruments would make us more than two days behind on our schedule. Had there been just one more experienced Singer in the group, I would have made him temporary leader and sent the others ahead. Meanwhile, raiders or no raiders, I would have made as much haste as possible to the Hall. A tour without instruments is not much of a tour.

A tour without food is not much of a tour, either. I had already warned the group not to expect a midday meal. By the time the sun was westering, we were riding to the accompaniment of growling stomachs. We could have gone farther that day, but we were nearing a Quarter Rest. The group had no choice about traveling on short rations; I could do something about providing a warm, dry place to sleep.

When the tebecs were settled and the instruments were properly covered—as fine an example of "too little, too late" as ever I've seen—I assigned Vel and Norjy the task of filling the water jugs. I drew the ax from its sling on the back of my saddle and held it up before the others. "Who knows how to use this?"

Hadden, smirking again, said, "There's a pile of wood just outside. Sir."

I hadn't seen it; I hadn't expected to see one. In the past, Quarter Rests had offered, among other amenities, a stack of firewood. Raiders had so often stripped the shelters of every comfort and convenience that the Hall Masters had long since given up on anything but keeping the way stations standing. That there was firewood already cut told me some tour had been this way fairly recently.

I derived some mean satisfaction from putting Hadden in charge of starting the fire. Clearly, he had never before had that chore. He didn't arrange the wood; he dropped an armful into the hearth. When he asked what to do next, I gestured at one of the tebecs, said—impatiently—"Firestone," and went back to sharing out as much food as I dared.

It never occurred to me that a man could reach Hadden's age without ever having used firestone. While a reliable source of fire, the rock must be handled carefully, because it bursts into flame when removed from the riku oil in which it is carried. Hadden didn't know to bring the jug of oil to the fire; he removed one of the rocks and tried to carry it in his bare hand. He dropped the suddenly flaming stone before it did more than redden two fingers; Mariz quickly nudged the rock into the hearth, where a blaze soon lifted our spirits. Without being told, Mariz brought in more wood. Shortly after he did so, the evening rain began to fall.

I tipped some riku oil onto a rag, told Hadden to wrap it around his burned fingers, and went back to handing out the food. I noticed Zhia was missing. I assumed—correctly, as I soon learned—that she had sought privacy for whatever "complicated" procedure she was handling. I didn't consider it wise to call attention to her absence.

The others were already eating when she came in, water streaming from her cloak. She held a large leaf that was filled with berries. "These are uebers," she said as she laid the leaf on the floor. "They're not quite ripe, so they're not as sweet as they should be, but they're food."

"Are you sure that's what they are?" I asked. I had heard tales of Singers eating fruits that looked harmless but were not.

Zhia wiped a trickle of water from her face. "Rangy, didn't you say your parents farm? Are these uebers?"

"They sure look like it," he answered. He bent over and sniffed the fruit. "They smell like it."

As he lifted one to his mouth, I said sharply, "Don't taste it." To Zhia I said, "I take it you ate some?" When she nodded, I went on, "I suggest we set these aside—where the tebecs can't get at them—and if Zhia has shown no ill effects by morning, we'll have the berries for breakfast."

"Nice of you to put my welfare below that of the birds, sir," Zhia said as I handed her the remaining portion of food, but she wasn't frowning.

"I'm tour leader; that's my job." The silence that followed this comment was eloquent with remarks the others left unexpressed. I was grateful, both because no one chose to criticize my admittedly less-than-admirable leadership, and because I had caught myself before saying the words that had been on the tip of my tongue: "We can't ride you." I was sure that Vel, at least, would have enjoyed making me regret a comment like that.

When morning came, we woke dry, warm, and rested. Zhia showed no sign of suffering from the berries she had eaten, so we broke our fast with portions that, while still not sufficient, were more than we had been eating. I began to think that things were looking up.

I should have known Darl wouldn't relent that easily.

Darl is not to blame for the usual, beneficial effect of fresh fruit on the excretory process. That the effect was likely intensified because the fruit wasn't quite ripe and our stomachs had been too long under-filled isn't Darl's fault, either. After the second time we had to stop suddenly so one of the group could run for the trees, I told everyone to dismount. We didn't get underway again until everyone had visited the woods.

While we were waiting, I changed the bandage on Birl's bite. It was healing well; I put a new bandage on only to keep Birl from complaining. The effort was vain; Birl's newest grievance was the berries he had so greedily gobbled. He was convinced he'd been poisoned, though he was experiencing nothing different from what everyone else was.

One of the twins remarked to no one in particular, "I would say Birl is acting like a girl, but I don't see Zhia carrying on like that."

"You're all against me," Birl whined. The ensuing silence was even more eloquent than the one to which I had been treated the night before. Birl kept pouting, but managed to mount his tebec without help. Someone slowly clapped: a sound of derision, not acclaim. I didn't look to see who it was. I resisted the impulse to join in.

I was slow to get back onto my own bird. Perhaps a season without touring wasn't a factor, but I suspected it might be part of the reason I was getting saddle sores. I didn't dare tell any of the others. My hope was that the lesions wouldn't get too much worse.

Before I mounted, I drew the schedule from my pack. Reviewing it as we rode, I confirmed my suspicion that we couldn't make our first engagement on time. It's a truism among Singers that it's better to skip a town than to arrive late; when the road branched, I turned my tebec to the right. Making Torlea, the scheduled second stop, our first stop would do two things: it would take us closer to the Hall where I hoped to get strings and drum heads, and—if I could get what we needed so our instruments would again be playable—it would allow us time after we arrived at Torlea to do some practicing. We wouldn't even have to skip our assigned first engagement; we could stop in Rillford on the way back to our Hall.

That day, as my discomfort steadily increased, we covered almost the expected distance, and met two groups of travelers on the road, which was most unexpected. We passed in mutual silence; raiders' activity had made caution more valued than courtesy. The clouds were beginning to gather when

I spotted a Quarter Rest atop a low, tree-clad hill to our left.

Taf again took charge of the birds; Vel and Norjy had water jug duty. I told Hadden that I would let him try his hand again at the fire…and the firestone. Having made sure there was no wood already cut, I asked the other five who would volunteer to wield the ax. (I need to make clear that, while I was capable of cutting firewood, I didn't intend to make the mistake some tour leaders do of assuming responsibilities I could delegate.) I hadn't expected Zhia, Hink, or Birl to volunteer. Though the twins were good-sized men, they professed to have no experience with an ax.

Finally, Zhia said, "I can cut wood."

Just then Taf came up. "I'll do it," he said, and reached for the ax.

"The birds are in your care. You don't need to take on another chore, especially if you haven't finished the one you have," I said, knowing he couldn't have settled fourteen tebecs that quickly. I handed the ax to Zhia, saying, "Watch out for swarmers."

"Yes, sir; but they aren't active in the rain," she replied.

She was right; the aggressive, stinging insects kept to their large, branch-hung nests in rain. And the rain was beginning, which would make gripping an ax handle that much harder. I thought about warning her to be careful, but said, instead, "If you see any berries, don't pick them." Laughing, Zhia slung on her cloak and went into the woods.

"That's quite a woman," Taf said, admiration plain in his voice.

"Are you joking? She's not very pretty."

"Allow me to disagree, sir. Besides, while you and that Henz person I've heard so much about seem to be content with one night with the prettiest woman at hand, some of us want more than that. When a man is looking for a wife, he looks for things besides beauty; things that don't fade with time."

"Zhia is a Singer," I reminded him, both startled and dismayed at the direction the conversation had taken.

"I've never heard that a Singer can't ask a woman to be his wife, even though she's also a Singer. With Singers for parents, think what the children could be!"

In my mind I could hear my father saying, "Ugly and stupid." I shut out the memory and asked, "But what do you know about her?"

He gave me a measuring look. "What does it matter to you? The only female around is yours, or something? You'd better know that Vel thinks the same thing."

"I'm aware of Vel's designs on Zhia. He's already heard this lecture; you haven't. While we're on tour, Zhia is a Singer, nothing more, nothing less. If you want to pursue her when we get back to our Hall, that's a different matter altogether."

"So you're not jealous."

"No; you have my sympathy. I've already been flayed by Zhia's tongue."

Taf looked amused. "I'll find a better use for it." He went back to settling the tebecs.

I began parceling out food, hoping what remained could be stretched until we found either a village or the closest Hall. I preferred to restock at a Hall; for obvious reasons, Singers on tour don't carry much money. The Hall Master would not ask to be paid for supplies. I hoped.

Not only Birl scowled at the portions I was setting out. Norjy remarked, "I've been the subject of a lot of jokes about making a little food go a long way, but isn't this getting a bit ridiculous, sir?"

"I'm as hungry as the rest of you," I said, not as calmly as I would have liked. I wondered how soon I'd be free to attend to what hurt. "I hope to get additional supplies the day after tomorrow."

"We should live so long," was Hadden's contribution to the general dissatisfaction.

"I'll eat your food if you don't want it," came Zhia's voice from outside the shelter.

She shed her cloak and handed the wood to Hadden, who this time did a better job of arranging it. He managed to get the firestone from the jug into the wood before it ignited. I considered complimenting him, but didn't know whether that would make him think I'd been expecting another failure. I decided the safest comment was, "That's welcome."

Actually, it wasn't. The fire's warmth brought out smells of unwashed bodies.

The food I distributed to the group gathered around the blaze could be held in one hand. When Zhia held out her hand, I stifled an exclamation and kept passing out the evening's ration. I didn't try to sit to eat.

After the unsatisfying meal was over, I took Zhia aside. Reaching for her hands, I turned them over so I could see her blistered palms.

"Refresh my memory," I said. "Why are we out here in the middle of nowhere?"

She pulled her hands away and put them behind her. She wouldn't meet my eyes. "We're on tour."

"And what do we do on tour?"

"We sing."

"And play instruments," I added. "If we were on a stage right now, would you be able to hold an instrument, let alone play one?"

Now she looked at me, her brow furrowed in puzzlement. "I don't play an instrument."

CHAPTER EIGHT

"YOU DON'T PLAY AN instrument," I echoed, dully. If daemons laugh, Darl was rolling.

"No."

"You play no instrument?"

"No."

"Not wind, not string, not percussion?"

She was now staring at me. Finally, she said, "No. You know, you don't do obtuse very well. Better stick with annoyed."

Taf came up. "Is something wrong?"

I caught myself before I snapped at him. "Nothing that concerns you." When he went back to the others, I drew Zhia farther away and said, softly, "Actually, this does concern Taf and everyone else on this tour. How in Nia Diva's name did you get to be a Singer if you don't play any instruments?"

"The Master asked me."

"What were you and the Master doing when he asked you?" I caught her hand before it hit my cheek and held it fast. I didn't apologize for what I'd implied; I had no intention of apologizing for my assumption, even if it was wrong. However, I didn't risk asking the same question again. "What were you doing when the Master asked you?"

"I was sweeping outside his office." She threw the answer at me, one white-hot word at a time.

I saw movement out of the corner of my eye. When I saw who it was, I released Zhia's hand and snapped, "Taf, don't make me tell you again that this doesn't concern you." I reined in my temper and said to Zhia, "And the Master didn't ask what you played or ask to hear you sing, or anything?"

Now realizing that something was wrong besides my temper, Zhia replied quietly, haltingly, "No. I may have been humming while I swept."

"So if you haven't been practicing music, what have you been doing for the last turn of the stars?"

"Sweeping and…well, I suppose I'd have to say I've been eavesdropping. If I could hear what was going on inside the classes, I'd try to listen."

It had to be astonishment that was making me feel light headed. "'If you could hear'?" I echoed. "You never actually went to classes?"

"No."

That explained a lot. It didn't explain why Zhia was given special treatment—or, more accurately, why she wasn't required to have the same treatment—but I was beginning to suspect what the answer might be. "What happened the day you learned you would be touring?"

"I guess I'd gotten careless. I wasn't sweeping; I was standing outside a door where I shouldn't have been, repeating a song I'd just heard so I could remember it, and the Master came around the corner and saw me. I guess he heard me, too, and knew what I'd been doing. He had to know I hadn't been sweeping; there was no dust in the air. He told me to go with him. I followed him to his office. I was sure he was going to tell me to leave the Hall; instead, he asked me if I wanted to tour."

I felt hot; my mind was reeling. Had I been wrong about the Master's wanting Zhia dead? He had sent her on tour, knowing she was utterly untrained. He had sent her with all first-timers and an untried leader. Perhaps my original suspicion had been correct, or at least half right. The Master did want this tour to fail, but not before Zhia had suffered abject, public humiliation. On stage, her unfitness to be a Singer could not be hidden. Thereafter the Master—all Hall Masters—would be justified in refusing to allow women to be Singers. The plot I suspected against Zhia's life might have been nothing more than my imagination.

Or—I could hardly make myself consider the possibility that had just occurred to me—it might have been the Master's intent that Zhia die after her spectacular failure so she couldn't tell anyone else what she had just told me. The Master knew that I was cursed both with pride and with a quick temper. He knew Zhia and I had been at odds. Had he been counting on my taking Zhia's abysmal performance so personally that, to salvage my pride, I would act against her?

Once again, the term "tool" occurred to me. Surely the Master knew that a proud man would not take kindly to knowing that he had been used to further another's ends. There was a possibility—slim, to be sure—that the Master's stooge would escape punishment. If the magistrates failed to remove his agent, the Master would have to have some other means of disposing of someone who knew entirely too much.

I remembered the Master's question about raiders, and felt a chill.

I realized Zhia was saying something. I forced myself to listen. In a whisper, she said, "Taf keeps looking at us. What does he want?"

Without thinking, I said, "He wants you to be his wife."

"What?"

I didn't yet know if Zhia could carry a tune; I now knew her voice had both range and volume. The loud, high pitched exclamation didn't just draw the others' attention, it also unsettled the tebecs. They began to mill around. Had they not been hobbled, likely some would have bolted. Taf spoke to Norjy and went to calm the birds.

The others approached. Norjy spoke. "Sir, I think we have a right to know what's going on."

Before I could even draw breath, Zhia said with a smile that was as blatantly false as the cheerful note in her voice, "I have just been informed that, as tour partner, it is my privilege to tend our leader's saddle sores. I don't suppose I could persuade one of you to do it instead?" The silence was deafening. Zhia's smile wilted. She sighed. "I guess I'll have to force myself not to take liberties."

The others laughed and went back to what they had been doing.

I was impressed by her quick thinking, and said so. "How did you know?" I added.

"From the way you're walking and the way you're not sitting. How bad are they?"

"They're sore, but I don't think they're too bad yet. Really, though, do you mind…" I gestured.

"Actually, yes; but someone has to take care of you so you can take care of us. Let's get it over with. Where's the ointment?"

I told her it was in my pack. When she returned with it, she went to the others and said, tartly, "Since I couldn't persuade you to spare me this, could I at least persuade you to give us some privacy?" They grabbed their cloaks and went out into the rain.

I would have preferred to stay in the shadowed corner where we had been talking. Citing the need for light, a need with which I couldn't argue, Zhia had me lie on the floor on the side of the fire closest to the door. She knelt between me and the door, using her body to shield me from view.

"I'm going to have to wash these before I put ointment on them," she said when the lesions were exposed. She rose, grabbed the cloak she had been wearing for cutting wood, and swirled it over me before fetching a water jug and some rags. "This will hurt," she added when she was again kneeling beside me. She stuffed a rag into my hand. "If you don't want to scream, you might try biting on that."

I bit right through the fabric. If it's true that the pain women experience in childbirth is worse than what I felt that night, I'm thankful I'm a man. Zhia's voice, impersonal and cool, filtered through the haze. "That was the worst part. They'll soon feel better."

Her touch was lighter than the breeze that brushed cold fingers across my exposed skin. The pain did subside. I took the rag out of my mouth and rested my forehead on my crossed arms. The fire flared briefly when Zhia threw the used rags into it. I heard water splashing on the floor; she was washing her hands. I saw her feet next to me. "How are you doing?" she asked.

"I'm all right." My voice sounded slurred.

"Sure you are. Lift your head; I want to feel if you're feverish."

"Why would I be feverish?" All I felt was drowsy.

"Because inside those soiled trousers you had open sores. They hurt as much as they did because they were going bad. Lift your head."

I obeyed. A cool, slightly damp hand rested on my face, then gently pushed my head back down. I felt a blanket settling on me.

The next thing I knew, it was morning. Though I knew I had slept through the night, I felt bone tired. I was chilly. As I snuggled into the blanket, my bare legs scraped on the floor. Lingering sleepiness fled when I realized that my trousers were not simply pulled down, they were gone. Then I saw that the fire was burning. The amount of ash that had accumulated told me it had been burning for some time. The cool morning air wafted to me a residual aroma that smelled like, but couldn't be, cooked meat.

A hand touched my forehead. Zhia's voice said, "The fever's broken. Bring broth."

I raised myself on my elbows and was dismayed to feel my arms trembling. Hands took my shoulders and eased me onto my side. I looked up into Zhia's face, pale and etched with concern. "Are you lying on the lesions?" she asked. I shook my head; I'd forgotten about the saddle sores. "Hink!" she called. "Where is that broth?"

I heard him say, "Here it is, sir," and tried to smile. "He calls you sir?"

"That was just to keep everyone in practice until you were better," she said. "Can you hold this cup? Careful now, it might be a bit hot."

It was hot. It tasted strange but wonderful. "Where did you get meat?"

"Mariz and Turiz have been hunting. And it turns out that Hink is quite a cook."

My mind began to work. Hunting, long-simmered broth, the thick layer of ash…"How long have we been delayed?"

"A couple of days."

"Three days, to be precise." That was Vel's voice.

I saw the look Zhia gave him. I wouldn't have been smiling had she looked that way at me. Quickly, she said, "I don't want to hear anything about the tour.

We'll get where we're going when we get there, and that won't be until you're strong enough to travel. And I'm the one saying when that will be."

"Yes, sir." I could feel sleep reclaiming me. "What is your surname, anyway?"

She must have bent down; I could feel her breath on my ear but was asleep before I heard what she said.

The sun was westering when I next woke. I raised myself on my elbows, pleased to find that my arms were steady. Before I could ask how long I'd slept, Taf's whisper reached me. "Sssh. Since she's quit tossing and turning, I think Zhia's finally asleep."

I looked around. Taf was sitting next to Zhia, who was lying on the floor across the fire from me. She looked even more spent than she had when I first awoke. Taf rose, circled the fire, and crouched by me. He continued to whisper as he said, "She hasn't slept since you…well, for three days. When she wasn't tending you, she was washing clothes and blankets, or cutting wood. I was hoping you'd wake soon so I could ask whether the ointment would be good for blisters."

"Her hands?"

He nodded. "They're raw. I don't know how she's been using the ax."

"The ointment ought to be good for blisters. By the way, have we lost another day?"

"No. It was this morning when you first woke. Are you hungry?"

I was. Taf brought me meat and more of the broth. After I ate, I said, "Zhia told me the twins had been hunting. That meat didn't taste familiar. What did they bag?"

His face split in silent laughter. "They didn't bag anything; but I can understand why she told you that. She didn't want you to worry that one of the pack tebecs broke a leg in the confusion three nights ago. When I told her there was nothing to do for the thing but put it out of its misery, she handed the twins the ax and told them to dispatch the bird and dress it out so we could eat it. She said, 'Alive or dead, we'll get some use out of it.'

"I don't think they'd ever done anything like that before, but they didn't refuse. She's had everyone hauling and heating water practically non-stop. No one's argued with her, not even when she told us she was going to wash everyone's clothes."

"Is that what happened to my trousers?"

"Yes. If it's any comfort, she gave Vel and Norjy the job of…of bringing them to her. You should have seen us all, sitting around wrapped in blankets and practicing songs."

"Wrapped in blankets? Surely all of you brought clean clothes."

"Yes, our stage garb. Zhia wouldn't let us wear it. As I recall, her exact words were, 'If you think I'm going to wash any more clothes than I have, you're out of your minds.'"

"I can imagine her saying that. She would have needed a lot of water to wash clothes and blankets. What did you heat it in?" Taf became absorbed in cleaning his nails. Clutching the blanket, I gingerly sat up. Now able see more both of the shelter and of the surrounding area, I saw familiar shapes over a fire outside. "Not the rimba!"

Taf grimaced. "Even though you'd said the heads were ruined, she thought you'd be upset. She said we were not to run out of hot water. She also said it wasn't for her to decide that you were worth less than a set of metal drums, no matter how costly."

"Since the fire probably ruined them, I hope others will see things in that light." Then I realized there was no one else in sight but Taf and Zhia. "Where is everyone?"

"Zhia sent them to the Hall for strings, drum heads, and food; as she said, one tebec won't last forever. In fact, you just ate the last of it. I couldn't keep an eye on Zhia all the time; but I don't think she ate any of it." He frowned, but went on, "She found out that Birl was somewhat familiar with this region, since he'd traveled with his father, who's a merchant. I must admit she was a bit short with him when that information came out. She asked why he couldn't be bothered to let anyone know that before. I have to give him credit; he didn't blubber or offer excuses. She put him in charge of making sure they found the Hall, and gave Vel the job of getting what supplies we need. When the others asked why they had to go, she gave them a cold look and said, 'One: there's safety in numbers. Two: we're nearly out of food again; at the Hall they'll feed you. Three: the tebecs need exercise. Four: I need a break from all of you.'" He smiled as he again said, "That's quite a woman."

I was surprised at how much I resented hearing him praise Zhia. I said, "I know Vel and Hink were here this morning. When did the group leave?"

"Right after you went back to sleep. If they don't get back before dark, they'll be here first thing in the morning. For Zhia's sake, I'm hoping for the latter."

I looked across the fire at her sleeping form. One hand was outside the tangled blankets, laying palm up on the ground. Taf was right; it was raw. "You weren't going to try treat the blisters right now, were you?"

"No. The only reason I'd wake Zhia would be if raiders attacked."

"That's a cheerful thought, with only three of us here. In fact, there aren't even really three of us: I'm weak and she's exhausted. Are you feeling like a hero?" Suddenly I felt ashamed for taunting him when I should have thanked him. Not only had he seen how badly Zhia needed to sleep, he had overruled her objections—that she had objected I knew as certainly as if I'd been awake to witness the conversation—and remained behind so she could rest. In an attempt to make amends, I said, "Forget raiders. You'd be enough of a hero if you could tell me where my trousers are."

His smile returned; he fetched the garment. I slung the trousers over my shoulder—I needed one hand to keep the blanket around me and the other to hold it high enough so I didn't trip over it—and went out of the shelter. When I returned, trousers on and blanket drawn around me like a cape to keep off the rain which began while I was outside, I had to sit down.

"You're really pale!" Taf exclaimed. "Maybe you should lie down again."

I had to agree. This renewed evidence of the toll the fever had taken was anything but encouraging. When I was again horizontal and the shelter had stopped spinning, I said, "At this rate, we won't get even to our third engagement on schedule."

"Taftan Noniantivem!"

Chapter Nine

Across the fire, Zhia was awake and wrestling with the blankets so she could get to her feet. I remember thinking how glad I was that, for once, I wasn't the focus of her fury. Then I realized she had addressed Taf by his full name, which not even I had known. He had to have told it to her. I could think of only one reason he would have done so. Rage filled me, as well. Though the emotion was sapping what little strength I had, I was upright before Zhia was. I don't know which of us was angrier.

"You asked her to be your wife!" I snapped at Taf.

The look he gave me might have been defiance. "You knew that was my intent."

"And you knew that I told you to wait until we were back at the Hall."

"I had reason to wonder how much longer that order would be in effect," he replied.

When I realized what he meant, I looked at Zhia, who had managed to untangle herself and was now on her feet. "I was that ill?"

She said "yes" to my question, but she was glaring at Taf. Shaking a finger at him in emphasis, she snarled, "When you talked me into resting, I told you to wake me as soon as he woke. You said you would. You also said you would keep him from exerting himself. Now I find he's not only awake, but has also been up and walking around! Is that how you carry out orders?"

My anger didn't daunt Taf; Zhia's did. "They weren't really orders; you aren't the leader," he said: a feeble excuse, indeed.

"If for any reason a tour leader cannot fulfill his responsibilities, the partner is the leader," Zhia lashed back.

Taf looked at me; I nodded. "Don't be too hard on him," I said to Zhia. "I had to pee. You wouldn't have wanted me to go on the floor, would you?"

I should have held my tongue. Zhia turned her wrath on me. "And what do you think you did when you were ill? Did you think we were hauling you outside and propping you against a tree?" She shook her head. She was still weary and anger hadn't made her any less so. The movement made her reel. Taf grabbed her.

"Take your hands off me," she said in a knife-edged whisper. She didn't have to say it twice. She pointed at me. "You lie down." She didn't have to say that twice, either. She returned her glare to Taf. "After what has happened, do you still require an answer?"

He reached toward her. She stepped back. He dropped his hands. "I'm sorry. Could I have another chance?"

Though neither was looking at me, I was wishing myself elsewhere. I suspected that what was coming wouldn't be pretty; I was sure it should have been private.

"Another chance to do what?" she grated. "Risk another life? Maybe a child's?"

Of all the things Taf could have said, he chose the worst. "You're overreacting."

"For three days a man has been so ill that I didn't dare leave him long enough even to sleep, you let him be active the first day he's awake, and I'm overreacting?" The crescendo of indignation ended on a shout. Zhia drew a deep breath and said in a voice which, though quieter, still trembled with outrage. "Had it been your life you risked, or even mine, that would have been one thing. On the strength of your word, I trusted you with someone else's life, and you..." Her voice broke. "How can I be your wife if I can't trust you?" She fled into the rain.

Taf took a step toward the door.

"Don't," I said. "Going after her would be the worst thing you could do right now."

"But she'll get cold and wet."

That was my concern as well. Zhia was so tired and, apparently, short on food that she would be especially susceptible to a chill. I didn't dare express that thought; in light of what I had just witnessed, callous practicality seemed best. "Then she'll cool down. When she's more miserable from being wet than she is from being disappointed with you, she'll return. In the meantime, you might stoke the fire. She'll need the warmth when she comes back."

It was clear that Taf complied only because doing so would benefit Zhia. "You're glad about this, aren't you?" he asked as he added fuel to the blaze.

I was startled and offended. "What makes you think that?"

"Because you didn't want me to ask her to be my wife."

"That is not true. My concern was that your asking her before the tour was over would prove a distraction to her. In case you've forgotten—or, perhaps, never knew—this tour is for Zhia. I've already told you I'm not jealous of your feelings for her. Now if you're jealous because she spent a lot of time tending to me—including cleaning me up after I wet myself; three days of that should have been enough to make her despise the very sight of me—I can't think of any way to reassure you. It's your problem."

After a long silence that was broken only by the hiss and sputter of wet wood catching fire, Taf said, "I'm sorry. Everything's wrong; nothing is right." The line of his shoulders and back was eloquent with discouragement.

I said, "I used to get real annoyed when my father would make me look for the good in situations that were bothering me, so you may not appreciate my saying that there is something good in this situation: the others weren't here. You have my assurance they will hear nothing about it from me."

"Thank you." He lapsed into silence; I lapsed into a half-sleep. Not surprisingly, in view of what we had been discussing, the doze was filled with thoughts of Eia. Taf's voice startled me awake. "What color would you say Zhia's eyes are?"

Had I not been remembering my lady love, the question would have left me utterly bewildered. Since Eia had been on my mind, I asked, "Are you making a song?" At his nod, I smiled and said, "I tried to make a song once, a song about a lady."

"I'll bet it was good."

"No. It was bad, embarrassingly bad. If anyone had heard it…" My voice died away as I remembered that Zhia had heard it.

"I don't think anyone will get to hear this song, either," Taf said. "Not all songs are meant to be shared, are they?"

"No. As for your question, though I am aware that Zhia has eyes, I have no idea what color they are. When her eyes are on me, it's usually because she's angry, and that's when I try to stay as far away from her as I can."

My answer was not calculated to be anything but the truth; but the tense lines in Taf's face relaxed. "I think they're a funny gold-green," he muttered. "What rhymes with that? 'Seen' does. Let's see. Pretty eyes…no, prettiest eyes I've ever seen…"

Hidden by the blanket, I winced. If what I was hearing was Taf's best, his song would be even worse than mine. Before I had to listen to more of his heartfelt but utterly awful songcraft, I fell asleep.

I probably hadn't been asleep long before I was wakened again, this time by Zhia's excited exclamation of "Look what I caught!"

My eyes flew open in time to see her cringe in dismay. "I'm sorry!" she cried, softly.

"A bit late for paying attention to the dynamics," Taf remarked, in unison with my "What have you caught?"

Water streamed off her arms as she held up her prize. "A shellort!"

It was a good-sized specimen of the creature, easily the size of the head of the largest of the rimba. The legs which stuck out of its mismatched pair of shells were flailing vainly in the air; its horny mouth was trying to reach the hands of its captor.

"Very nice," I said, without conviction. "What are you going to do with it?"

"Cook it, of course. Aren't either of you hungry?"

Taf said, "I'm hungry. I'm just not sure I'm hungry for…for that."

"Haven't you ever had shellort stew? It's delicious! Of course, I can't really make stew since all I have is the 'lort; but it ought to be good roasted. Wait, it wouldn't. One this old would probably be real tough. I could stew it, even without the other stuff. See, they're better for roasting when they're bab…" Her face, which had been rosy from cold, was suddenly ashen. I thought I heard a sob before she said, in a strangled voice, "I'm going to let the poor thing go." She went back into the rain. Not much later, I heard the sound of the ax biting into wood.

Taf, who had been staring in the direction Zhia had gone, turned, grabbed his cloak, and glared at me. "I don't care what you say; I'm going after her."

"I was about to suggest that very thing."

While I was concerned that Zhia, who was exhausted to the point of babbling and whose grip was impaired both by blistered hands and by rain, was chopping wood in the dark; I was even more concerned by her alarming pallor and obvious distress when she talked about roasting baby shellorts. From Taf's account of the fate of the injured tebec, I had no reason to believe Zhia was softhearted or squeamish about butchering animals for food. I didn't think Taf's and my less than enthusiastic response to her trophy had offended her; until she had mentioned cooking the young of the creature, she had kept trying to interest us in the prospect of shellort stew for supper. I wished now my wits had been quicker; I should have told her to go ahead and cook the thing, tough or not. All of us had good teeth…and empty stomachs.

Taf appeared just outside the shelter. He propped the ax against a doorpost and said, "Grab your cloak and give me a hand, please."

As I scrambled to my feet, I asked, sharply, "Did you find her? Is she hurt?"

"Yes. And no. She's asleep under a tree, so out of it I could probably play a whole set of rimba next to her head and she'd never stir. I can't wake her; I can't carry her by myself; and I don't want to drag her."

The rain was diminishing as I followed him out of the shelter. Zhia was not far away but, as Taf had said, she was deeply asleep. Neither our moving her inside, our clumsy efforts to wrestle her out of her wet clothes, or our tending her blistered palms disturbed her in the slightest. After she was well wrapped in blankets and Taf once more fed the fire, he again went outside, returning almost at once with something large, roundish, and dark in his hands.

"Zhia's friend hadn't gone very far. What do you say we try shellort stew for supper?"

Shellort stew is delicious. Though I had my doubts that Zhia would have wanted any, she didn't get any; not because Taf and I ate all of it, but because the others of our tour returned shortly after she went to sleep, and ate what was left. They had been able to get everything we needed, including a generous supply of food and another pack tebec, and were understandably but loudly proud of themselves for managing the task.

Taf's and my pleas to keep the noise down were, for the most part, vain; but Zhia slept though the commotion, which included fastening the new heads to the drums and testing them. As I had feared, the rimba were not the same. The patterns the heat had made on the metal of their bodies was not the only change. To my surprise, the drums sounded better: their tone richer, fuller. We got busy trying the new sound with that of other drums and instruments, and agreed that the blend was pleasing.

I was so involved with the music that I forgot I was supposed to be resting. Not until I stood up, promptly fell when my knees buckled, and had to be helped to my blankets did the merriment subside.

The sun was well up when I woke; not until it was at zenith did Zhia open her eyes. Taf and I were able to stop her before she pushed the blankets aside. I put her now-dry clothing next to her before I joined the group that Taf had herded outside. Zhia soon appeared at the door and said, "I need to talk to you," and pointed to me.

· "What'd you do now, sir?" Hadden gibed.

Vel punched his shoulder. "A gentleman doesn't tell, fool. So what did you do, sir?"

I had forgotten how annoying those two could be. I managed to grin. "When Zhia tells me, I'll know."

Hadden had to have the last word. "Must have been some party."

As I approached the shelter, my expression was likely rather sour. "Good morning, or I guess I should say good afternoon," I said to Zhia. "What did you want?"

"My clothes," she said, so softly I could hardly hear her.

"What about them?"

"Who took them off me?"

"Taf and I, who else? No one else was here. Is there a problem?"

"I was wondering…I mean, I was hoping…" She looked away.

I said, "I see you removed the bandages from your hands. May I look at them and see if they need new bandages?"

"No, thank you; they're all right. How are you?"

"I think I'm quite a bit better. Are you rested?"

"Enough for now."

That was more honest than a simple "yes"; the shadows under her eyes were in stark contrast to her pallor. I lifted my hand, paused, and asked, "May I touch you?"

"Why?"

"I want to find out if you have a fever. Last night you got wet and chilled." Her expression showed nothing but bewilderment. "Don't you remember?"

"No. So that's why you took my clothes off."

"Did you suspect some other reason?"

Now color flooded into her face. "I didn't. I mean, there wasn't…I'm not feverish. Excuse me." She edged past me and went into the woods.

Taf came up. "What did she want?"

"She wanted reassurance. She was so tired she doesn't remember any of last night."

He whistled softly. "I take it you weren't able to find out if she got sick."

"No. She says she doesn't have a fever, but she doesn't look well. We'll rest here another day, just to be sure." Taf went away; Hadden came up, plainly brimming with questions. Before he could say anything, I said, "You and the others have my thanks for handling that errand so well and so promptly; but don't presume that I'm so grateful I'll overlook insolence. When there is a matter that needs to be brought to the entire group, I will bring it to all of you without your asking. If I don't bring something to all of you, it's because it doesn't concern all of you, so don't ask. Now, do you have any questions that aren't covered by what I just said?"

Hadden walked away, mumbling under his breath. I don't know what he told the others, but for the rest of the day, everywhere I turned I saw faces that were shuttered and grim. Had I been fully recovered and a little more sure of my leadership, I might have addressed their surliness then and there, before it became rebellion. By the end of the day, when my strength was all but gone, it was rebellion. Members of the group were ignoring my instructions but acting immediately if Zhia told them to do the same thing.

I didn't know what to do; indeed, I had no real authority. I couldn't compel obedience; I could impose no effective penalties for disobedience. There was no one to whom I could go for counsel.

Supper was long over before I discovered what the problem was. I had put on my cloak and gone outside, ostensibly to make sure the tebecs were ready for a morning departure, but actually because the rain was less chill than the atmosphere inside the shelter. I was feeling shaky, so I sat down with my back against the wall. I may have dozed; the sound of voices raised in an argument woke me.

Taf's was the first voice I heard. "How many times do I have to tell you, neither Rois nor I took liberties with Zhia while you were gone." (Some of what I've recorded, such as the phrase "took liberties", is a cleaned-up version of what was actually said, which was often quite crude.) "If you don't believe me, ask her."

Then Vel spoke. "Ask her? That's safe; she's asleep. Besides, we all saw that she had no clothes on this morning."

"And you can think of only one reason anyone would sleep without clothes? The woman was out in the rain without her cloak, chopping wood. She was soaked. I've told you that already, too."

"That's awfully hard to believe." That came from Mariz.

"She's too sensible to do anything like that," Turiz added.

Then Norjy joined in. "And how about that long, private conference she and Rois had this morning, when he was so evasive? Then he talked to you—again, very privately—but wouldn't talk to Hadden. It looked like 'morning after' kind of talk to me."

Sounding beleaguered, Taf said, "All of you saw how weak Rois still is. All of you saw how hard Zhia worked caring for him. What makes you think either that he's had the strength to mess around or that Zhia would have allowed it?"

Hadden chimed in. "Since when does anyone wait for a woman to say 'yes'? I'll grant that Rois looks like he doesn't have the strength to be too frisky, but he could be faking it. Or maybe Zhia has the hots for him and took matters into her own hand, so to speak. The man doesn't always have to be on top, you know. And you haven't been ill. What's to have stopped you from having a little fun on the side?"

"If my word that I have not been with Zhia isn't good enough for you, I can't provide you with any proof that would carry more weight," Taf snapped.

To my surprise, Birl joined in. "Taf, we don't care if you and Rois and Zhia had a jolly little party while we were away. If she can take care of two, she ought to be able to fit in the rest of us. We just want equal time."

"Equal time?" Taf exploded.

I hoped Taf remembered that none of them knew he had asked Zhia to be his wife. They probably interpreted his indignation on behalf of a woman for whom he cared as reluctance to share a woman they believed he had simply used. The reason behind their defiance of me and their fawning obedience to Zhia was now clear; each was hoping to be the next to enjoy her favors.

Their voices had been growing steadily louder. I was wondering when, not if, the disagreement would come to blows and what, if anything, I could do to prevent it when I heard Zhia's voice. I expected her to blast the offenders with the fury that was all too familiar to me. Instead, she spoke with a cold, quiet intensity that was more intimidating than any rage could have been. "You two-faced, foul-mouthed, despicable, lecherous, degenerates! Do you really think I'm here to tear blisters on my hands for you all day and then lie still for you all night?"

Hadden never did learn when to keep his mouth shut. Though I couldn't
see him, I knew he was smirking when he said, "I can't speak for the others,
but I'd prefer you not just lie still."

I heard the unmistakable sound of flesh striking flesh and Hadden's startled
yelp. Not until later did I learn that, to avoid further hurting her palms, rather
than slap Hadden's face, Zhia backhanded him. Ordinarily I would consider
that excessive. Given the nature of the provocation, Hadden got off lightly.

In the same low, controlled voice, Zhia asked, "Does anyone else think I'm
joking? Then pack and get some sleep. We leave at daybreak."

She must have left the group, for after a tense silence Hink said, "What's
with her? Didn't the Master say…"

Vel told him to shut his mouth.

Discretion came too late; I had already learned what I wasn't supposed
to know.

Chapter Ten

WE WERE ON THE road quite a bit before daybreak.

While the burden of the men's complaints upon being unceremoniously wakened while it was still dark was that Zhia was being vindictive—which was likely true and, if so, understandable—I think she was equally impatient to resume the tour. In the long delay while I was ill the men had become, among other things, bored and restive. Getting back on the road would give them renewed and objective purpose.

To judge from the size and color of the shadows under Zhia's eyes, she hadn't slept. There wasn't time even for a token breakfast before she told us to mount. Though I had seen her moving among the birds while the men prepared to leave, she again checked the pack tebecs' baggage just before we left the Quarter Rest. Not until she saw the last pack bird being led away did she give her mount the signal to go.

One of the few good things about the design of a tebec's saddle is that one can sleep in it without fear of falling out. Though I had done little real work the day before, I was still weak and the day's emotional stresses had been wearing. Both since I was already tired and since I'm accustomed to thinking I should be sleeping if it's dark, I was soon dozing. When the sun finally lifted itself above the trees and its light fell full on my face, I opened my eyes and saw that only Zhia and I were awake.

I edged my bird closer to hers. "When do we eat?"

"When the others wake."

Then I realized what she'd done. "You deliberately left that early so everyone would sleep, didn't you?"

She nodded, swallowed, and grimaced.

"Is your throat sore?" I asked. She hesitated, then nodded again. "I was afraid that would happen when you got so wet and cold night before last."

"I'm sorry."

"Don't apologize to me; I'm not the one who won't be able to sing."

"Should we go back to the Hall?"

My first impulse was to say "yes". Then I remembered Hink's reference to the Master, a reference which not only confirmed but also increased my already-existing concerns for Zhia's welfare. I knew the Hall was the last place she needed to be, but I couldn't tell her that or she'd ask why. I had no proofs to offer, only suspicions. I thought fast and replied, "No. Even if your throat is so sore you can't sing, the others deserve their first tour. Speaking of which…" I twisted in the saddle and reached into my pack, a feat which sounds harder than it is. After a few tours, most Singers with any flexibility learn how to get things out of their packs without having to dismount. "Where did I…? Don't tell me I lost it."

"What are you looking for?"

"The schedule. I'd already decided we'd skip Rillford and go straight to Torlea. I need to see if we would do better now to skip Torlea and go to our third assignment." I turned back around, extended my open hand, and said, "Here. This will help your throat."

She took the pale yellow, thumbnail-sized ball and asked, "What's in it?"

"I don't know; I just know it works. Of course, it doesn't work in your hand."

Zhia made a face when she put the lozenge in her mouth, which reminded me that I had neglected to warn her about its rather unpleasant flavor. I was turning back to continue searching my pack when Zhia said, "I have the schedule."

I straightened so fast I heard my spine crack. "Why?"

"So I could give Birl an idea of where the Quarter Rest was before he went looking for the Hall where we replaced our supplies." Her attempt to reach her pack ended in a soft moan. "I'm stiff. It's been a while since I've cut wood or done that much laundry. You have long arms; can you get it? I put it on top so I could give it to you when we stopped."

I drew it out; something else came with it. "What's this?" I said, surprised that Zhia owned anything as beautiful as a mirror framed with delicate metal filigree.

She snatched it out of my hand. "I assume you aren't asking the identity of the object. I thought someone might want to shave before we reach our first engagement."

"Are you saying we men look scruffy?" I felt the stubble on my face and neck. "This is nothing."

"Your father might say that, too," she teased, "but I've no right to criticize. It will feel so good to wash my hair properly."

I acted surprised. "What? Standing in cold rain doesn't get your hair clean?" Actually, I was a little surprised. So far, Zhia had shown only minimal concern for her appearance. I remembered how frequently Eia tidied her hair or fussed with her clothes, and tried to imagine what it would be like to tour with her. I had to conclude that, unless Eia was made of much tougher stuff than she appeared to be, she wouldn't last one day. She would certainly never have caught a shellort, much less have been happy about it.

Zhia reached back to return the mirror to her pack, and was again unable to turn that far. With a sound of disgust, she held the mirror out to me and asked, "Do you mind stowing this for me?"

"Someone should probably give you a back rub this evening," I said. "Riding a tebec all day isn't going to loosen those muscles any." I turned my attention to the schedule. After studying it a while, I shook my head. "Unless we can teach the tebecs to fly, we can't get to Torlea on time; but there's a good chance we can make Hollan's Town on schedule. That's a few days away; you just might be able to sing if you rest your voice."

And she did…for about a heartbeat. "Rois?"

"If I ask 'what' you'll talk, so I'm not going to ask."

"I'm going to tell you anyway. That isn't our schedule."

I remember thinking she was starting to take her role as substitute leader a little too much to heart, so I made no effort to conceal my irritation when I said, "Oh, yes, it is. I thought it wasn't the right one, too; so I went back and asked the Master in so many words. It's the strangest schedule I've ever seen for a first tour; but it's our schedule."

"What I should have said is, 'That isn't our only schedule.'"

"Why would there be more than one?"

Before she replied, she looked to be sure that the others still slept. Though snores were plainly audible, she lowered her voice. "That's what I can't figure out. You know that I've been sweeping instead of learning to be a real Singer. The Master's office is one of the places I clean. He always leaves his office when I sweep; to get away from the dust, I suppose. Please don't think I snoop, because I don't; but one day I saw laying on his desk a piece of paper that had my name on it. Now you may not do this, but when I see something with my name on it, I have to look at it. It was a tour schedule. It looked like the one you're holding, but it had all different place names on it, names I recognized, names of places a lot closer to the Hall than Rillford and Torlea and Hollan's Town, and…and wherever. I didn't think much about it at the time; but now that I've seen both schedules, it strikes me as rather odd." In a lighter tone, she added, "Of course, there may be no mystery at all. Perhaps after the Master wrote the one I saw, he decided to try something different, and made the schedule you have."

"Then why wouldn't he throw away the first one?"

"Paper is expensive. Maybe he saves it so he can write on the other side. I would."

Remembering the opulent furnishings of the Master's office, I doubted he was likely to care about the cost of paper. It was more likely that Zhia's sense of something's not being right was sound. The existence of two markedly different schedules fit only too well into the pattern of irregularities that marked this tour.

Whatever catastrophe the Master had in mind for us, he had to be able to prove he had no part in it. My best surmise was that the disaster—whatever it was going to be—would happen some ridiculous distance from our Hall. Since no one can be two places at once, no suspicion would fall on the Master. He would look still more innocent when he produced the schedule Zhia had seen, undeniable proof that he and the Hall had suffered a double tragedy. It would be obvious to everyone that a tour had become thoroughly and inexplicably lost and, while lost, had also...What?

It was that gap in my guesswork that most concerned me, because without some idea of where, when, and how the calamity was coming, there was nothing I could do to thwart the Master's plan.

Since Zhia had suspicions, I decided I would share mine. She was silent while I rehearsed the plot that I had built from the bits and pieces I knew, then she said, "While I hope you're not right, what you've said explains a lot, especially how I ended up being part of this. However, considering how long it's been since women were first admitted as Singers and how many there must be by now, is there still enough sentiment against them that a plot like the one you've described would have such far-reaching effects?"

"You remember how my father talked to you. The Master wasn't exactly a model of decency the night before we left, either."

"That's true. But they're only two people. How much influence does your father have? How much authority does the Master of our Hall have over any of the others? Even should a tour with a female Singer fail, I don't see how that would besmirch every other woman who already is a Singer—and, one assumes, has already successfully toured—or who aspires to be a Singer. While you've made a good case for the plot you've postulated, my own opinion is that it's more localized than you fear.

"As you noted, the Master of our Hall doesn't like me any more than your father does. You said it was the tone of his voice that convinced you. I'll accept your word on that, because I don't know his voice well enough to catch the nuances. My question is, does the Master object to me, or to female Singers in general? Remember, Noia is still at the Hall. Even should I provide the probable failure on stage, what does he do about Noia? She is being trained; she could tour tomorrow and probably do very well.

"As for your concern about a mishap, should both the female Singers at the same Hall meet untimely and tragic ends, or even suffer serious mishaps, there would be questions. No matter how badly the Master may want to purge our Hall of female Singers, unless he's completely lost his mind—and there would probably be other evidence were that the case—he dare not strike only at them. He would have to be willing to sacrifice male Singers, as well. And that would be just plain stupid."

I stared. "I expected you to say it was wrong. Why do you say it would be stupid?"

"It's most certainly wrong; I didn't say it because it's self-evident. Look at it this way. What is the purpose of a Singer?" When I frowned, she said, "It might help to ask instead 'What is the purpose of a lamp'? So you can learn how to mine and shape metal, grow timi trees or riku grass and press out the oil, twist wicks, and study where firestone is found? No. You have a lamp for light. Similarly, the purpose of a Singer is not to sit in a Hall and study music. Granted, just as a lamp won't give light unless someone has gone to the trouble of mining and shaping metal, pressing oil, making wicks, and digging firestone, a Singer needs preparation. But once that's done, once the lamp is filled, it needs to be set alight."

"I know about lamps," I said. "What are you getting at?"

Laughing, she exclaimed, "The only real purpose of Singers is to tour! Who benefits from Singers' tours? The Halls do, of course, from the tour fees. The more Singers there are, the more fees there are, which is why it would be stupid to decrease the number of Singers. But the ordinary people also benefit, and benefit more. The more Singers there are, the better it is for the ordinary people. Most of the people in the audience aren't musicians; they don't know or care how long the performers have studied as long as they can sing and play well enough so the music is pleasing. And they certainly don't care if the people on stage are men or women. They just want a break from their chores. They want to be entertained, to forget if only for a while about the crops that failed; or whether the shop will turn a profit; or Grandmother's aches and pains that get worse every night when it rains; or the roof that keeps leaking, no matter how often it's patched. They want to lose themselves in music.

"Music is a gift Nia Diva gives us. Why? Not so we can decide who is the best and give ourselves prizes—no offense, Rois!" she added quickly when my hand went to the gold cup on its chain—"but so we can give to others the gift of music—the gift of joy!—which is a gift worth far more than the largest fees."

We were both startled when applause burst out behind us. The rest of the group were awake. While I knew they were cheering what Zhia said, I wondered what else they had heard. I tried to remember when the snoring had stopped, but couldn't.

Zhia looked back. "You didn't know you'd have to listen to lectures on tour, did you?" The others laughed. She went on, "Keep your eyes open for water. When we find some, we'll stop and eat a hot meal."

The cheering began again. Swallowing painfully, she waved in acknowledgment.

I gave her another lozenge. I should have cautioned her to rest her voice; but her pallor and her over-exuberant chattiness were the same signs of exhaustion she had shown the evening she found the shellort, when she had sunk into so deep a sleep she couldn't be roused. If I could keep her awake until we had eaten—allowing her to talk seemed as good a way as any—then when we got back on the road, I would resume my duties as leader so she could sleep.

Norjy said, "Zhia, why in your lecture, as you called it, did you keep saying 'ordinary people' instead of 'nobodies'? It's twice as many syllables."

"And at least twice as rude," she replied, reining in her bird so she was riding among the others. "Think Rangy: you, I—all of us—were what Singers call nobodies before we were Singers. Were you really nobody then? Of course not. You had a name, you had a family, you had plans for your life. That Nia Diva had other plans for you didn't make you better than anyone else; in fact, one would expect becoming a Singer to be humbling."

"So you really believe there is a Nia Diva?" Vel asked. "I'm sure most of the teachers at the Hall pay only lip service, if that."

"That's sad, because Singers have all been given a wonderful gift. Gifts come from someone. Some gifts we get from our parents, like Taf's ability with tebecs. Except for Rois, how many of you have a parent who is or was a Singer?" No one spoke. "My parents weren't Singers, either. So where does the gift come from?" Again no one spoke. There was a note of disappointment in Zhia's voice when she said, "I hope I never become so conceited that I no longer acknowledge Nia Diva."

"I take it you're saying our teachers are conceited. It's one thing to talk like that when we're out here in the middle of nowhere. Would you say that to a teacher's face, when that teacher had the power to have you ousted from the Hall?" Birl asked.

"If fear of consequences keeps a person from speaking the truth, he or she doesn't really believe it's the truth," Zhia said.

Of course Hadden had to have his say. "How about cutting out the crap and just answering the question? Would you tell—who's a good one?—would you tell Instructor Neron he was conceited?"

I don't know whether Hadden and the others knew that Zhia hadn't attended classes. I'm not sure that Zhia knew the teachers' names, let alone their personalities. I had studied with Instructor Neron. Even though I was a two-time Champion and likely in no danger of being ousted from the Hall, I would have thought twice before telling the man something he didn't want to hear, no matter how true it was.

Zhia cleared her throat, likely as much to gain time as because she was becoming increasingly hoarse. Turiz's shout spared her having to answer. "Water! I see water!"

In the ensuing, expectant silence, we could all hear the water, too. Since we left the low hill on which the last Quarter Rest had been situated, we had been crossing fairly level, forested land. Now rocky hills were beginning to swell on either side of us. The trees no longer shadowed the road. Instead, they clustered thickly in the shallow dales between the barren hilltops. Sunlight-spangled water sprang from the tallest of these peaks and pooled in a low hollow before becoming a stream that cut across both the mouth of the hollow and the road beyond, where I could see the narrow arch of a bridge.

I frowned. Tebecs handle all kinds of terrain fairly well, but they don't like bridges. If the span is wide enough that the bird can't see it's above the ground, it can be made to cross. With a bridge as narrow as the one ahead, it would be a losing battle. We would have to ford the stream, an expedient which the tebecs would also resist, though not as strenuously as they balked at bridges.

Though we couldn't yet smell the water, the tebecs could, and were eager to get to it. I had to caution everyone to rein them in, because the closer we got to the hollow, the more rocks there were in the roadway. Most were fairly small; some were as big as skulls. A misstep on even some of the smaller ones could cost us another bird, a loss we couldn't afford.

I'm always amazed that, once the destination has been sighted, the remaining distance seems the longest. That we were all more than ready to break our fast likely contributed to our impatience with every finger length we still had to cover. In fact, the sun was only halfway to its zenith when we dismounted. Since the hollow was fenced with a fairly sheer rise, a pool, and rapidly running water, Taf decided not to hobble the tebecs.

Groaning, the men stretched. Zhia took her cloak from her saddle, the ax from mine.

"Why do you need your cloak?" I asked.

"To carry a lot of wood in one trip." She said "Make a hearth" to no one in particular, and went up the slope opposite the pool and into the woods.

There were plenty of rocks in the hollow with which to ring a fire. We gathered fallen twigs and set them ablaze, then unpacked the food. The fire wasn't hot enough for cooking meat, but we warmed slightly stale bread and ate it while we waited. We sat or lay on the scrubby growth that grew between the rocks, enjoying sunshine and a teasing breeze. The water of the pool was clear and crisply refreshing; the warmed bread was enough to satisfy until the promised hot meal was ready.

One thing kept me from being completely content: regret that I hadn't reminded Zhia to watch for swarmers. The sunshine and breeze that enticed people to rest made the insects more active. Their nests were most often found in dense woods, like those in which Zhia was chopping wood…with blistered hands.

I cursed silently. How could I have forgotten about her hands? Knowing that I was resting again when she hadn't slept at all, and knowing also that I should be the one cutting wood dispelled the last of my calm. Perhaps I would never be the Champion in deed that Zhia had challenged me to be, but I could at least be a man and do the right thing. I stood.

"Where are you going, Rois?" Taf inquired. "Or shouldn't I ask?"

"I've got to find Zhia. I forgot again about her hands. She shouldn't be cutting wood."

Taf also rose. "I'll help you look. She went up that way, didn't she?"

"Yes." To the others, sprawled in various posture of relaxation, I said, "If Zhia shows up and we're not with her, whistle or yell or something."

"Can do," Norjy said, lazily, leaning back on his elbows and chewing a stem.

Taf and I had started up the slope when the air was suddenly filled with small, speeding shapes, raining down from the hill behind the pool. At first, I thought they were swarmers. Then I saw that they glinted like metal. I cursed again, this time aloud. They were metal. They were darts: raiders' darts.

Even had stunned disbelief not rooted Taf and me where we stood, there was nothing we could do but watch as, one by one, the resting men went to their final rest. Norjy was the last to topple. Even before his body hit the ground, a mass of dark-clad men poured over the hill and into the hollow. Some clustered around the bodies, rapidly searching for valuables. More went to where the tebecs stood. The attack on their riders had made the birds uneasy; their wicked beaks were snapping at anything that moved, including each other. Avoiding the beaks, the raiders grabbed the birds' reins and, beginning with the pack birds, started to lead them away. A handful of attackers headed for the hill where Taf and I stood.

Taf quickly turned and disappeared into the woods. Neither my wits nor my legs moved as quickly; before I could follow Taf's example, the raiders were upon me. One snagged the tail of my hair and jumped onto my back. We fell and rolled down the hill, coming to a bruising stop against the rocks around the dying fire. I grabbed a handful of hot ash and threw it in the raider's face. With a cry, he fell back. Another took his place. This man was much bigger, and he held a knife. I dodged the blade as well as I could, but I was bleeding from a number of shallow cuts before I managed to catch the man's knife hand and slam the back of it against a rock. He cried out and dropped the knife, but his unhurt hand closed around my throat. As I struggled to free myself from the brutal grip, I could see other raiders coming in for the kill.

Then I saw Zhia hurtling down the hill, the ax in one hand and a wadded cloak in the other. At the bottom of the hill, she kicked a skull-sized rock, sending it flying. At the same time, she screamed and threw the cloak, which arced into the middle of the hollow. Hearing the scream, the man who was strangling me turned. The rock struck him full in the chest, toppling him. The sudden noise also panicked the remaining tebecs, which became even more aggressive. Some raiders were crushed by the heavy, saddle-laden bodies of the milling birds; others who got in the way of birds trying to flee were kicked to death. When the cloak landed, it fell open. Inside it was a swarmer's nest, which burst as it hit the ground, releasing a cloud of stinging fury. Raiders, both those who had been robbing the corpses and others who were nearby, fled, with the swarmers in agitated, vengeful pursuit.

Then Zhia and her ax entered the battle.

With the dispassionate precision of a reaper, she mowed down six or seven men, including the one the rock had already hurt. Then one of the raiders dived at her legs and brought her down. When he wasn't able simply to wrest the ax from her, he choked her until it fell from her hand. He stood and snatched up the tool. As he raised it to strike, Zhia's heel slammed into the side of his knee. He dropped the ax and fell, clutching the injured joint. As Zhia struggled to rise, he managed to trip her. She landed on top of him, the full force of her not-inconsiderable weight leaving him winded. He began striking her with his fists. Most of the blows hit her face. She groped for and found a large stone, and began striking back. Even when his hands fell limply to his sides, she kept raining blows on him.

Except for that first scream she had fought in silence. Now she was again screaming, not in pain but apparently in anguish, for what she screamed was a name.

When all that was left of the man's head was a pulverized mass of blood, bone, and brain, she stood, panting. Then she picked up the ax and took a step toward the few remaining raiders.

They fled, leaving the hollow empty of all but Zhia, me, and the dead.

Chapter Eleven

"I'll never again wonder why the daemon of war is female," Taf said as Zhia, he, and I carried Birl's body and laid it next to the corpses of the other Singers. "Which reminds me: did you intend to panic the tebecs, Zhia?"

Taf had showed up as Zhia and I began dealing with the carnage. He had feared we would think less of him for watching the fracas from high in a tree near the waterfall, and had been pleasantly surprised when our only reaction was relief at seeing him not only alive but also unharmed.

"No, panicking the tebecs was nothing I meant to do," she replied. Her throat bore dark marks from the hands that had been crushing it. Her voice was now as harsh and rasping as my father's. "In fact, it would have been better for us had they not all run away or been stolen. I screamed because when I kicked the rock, I"—she coughed and winced—"I hurt my toe. The stone was hard. Imagine that."

"That's why you're limping," Taf said. "Sit down. I'll look at it."

"Not now. We still have to haul enough rocks to cover"—she gestured—"them."

The sun was past zenith and we were caked with sweat, dirt, and blood before the cairn was completed. We stood by the improvised tomb, looking helplessly at one another. We all knew something ought to be said; we were all at a loss for words.

Finally, Zhia spread her hands, bowed, and grated, "Nia Diva, they were your servants. Speak for them. Even so." If the petition sounded like an order, the daemon would surely understand and pardon.

I wasn't as sure that Nia Diva would extend the same pardon to me. As Zhia spoke, in counterpoint I could hear her saying—had it been only last night?— "You two-faced, foul-mouthed, despicable, lecherous, degenerates." I had no doubt that the merciless dressing down and the graceful committal were both honest expressions of Zhia's real concern for the Singers she had known so briefly; the Singers she had so decisively avenged, at no small cost to herself.

"Now may I look at your toe?" Taf said to Zhia, as we walked away from the cairn.

"No. Now we have to do something with the raiders' bodies."

"Why?" Taf and I asked in unison. "Why not just take what we can use from them and leave them for their friends the carrion eaters?" I added.

Zhia's face, badly bruised and bleeding from several cuts, was so swollen I couldn't read her expression, but repugnance was plain in her voice when she said, "Despoil the bodies?" She shuddered. "If you two want to lower yourselves to that, go ahead. I won't help; I don't even want to watch."

When she put it like that, there was no way I could insist on what seemed to me a sensible course of action. "Then what plan did you have for their bodies?" I asked.

My voice didn't sound very good, either, but it was nowhere near as bad as Zhia's. The rock that had hurt her toe had stopped my attacker before he'd been able to do much damage to my throat. I would probably be able to sing again. Zhia might not.

"Since I've cut firewood we won't need, I was thinking we could perhaps burn the bodies; but I don't think we have any firestone."

"The raiders might have been carrying some," I said. "Would you object if we search their bodies for firestone?"

While she admitted that it would be stupid to pile wood and haul more bodies without knowing whether we could set the pyre alight, her agreement was clearly grudging.

Taf said, "How about you bring the firewood and we'll take care of the bodies?"

She said, "All right," and tried to smile. The raider's blows had split her lip; it began to bleed again. She raised one of her grimy hands to blot the blood.

"Don't!" I exclaimed.

She looked at her hands. "You're right." She was trying to clean the backs of them on her trouser legs—ineffectually, I must say—as she went into the middle of the hollow. "Get ready to duck," she called over her shoulder. Cautiously she picked up her cloak and gave it a little shake, then a harder one.

"I don't suppose it even occurred to you to ask one of us to do that?" Taf said, sourly.

There was an undertone of laughter in Zhia's voice when she said, "I'm only risking finding a lingering swarmer. You two risk finding a raider who isn't quite dead. I suggest you keep the ax close at hand." She bundled the cloak under her arm and again went up the hill.

I saw dismay on Taf's face and knew the same expression was on mine. That we might have to finish off a badly wounded man hadn't occurred to either of us.

Taf finally said, "I'll get the ax."

We didn't find any raiders who had to be put out of their misery. On a couple of bodies we did find the small jugs that are the most common way of carrying firestone. Several of the raiders also carried coins, which Taf wanted to keep. I forbade it.

"Why?" he asked. "We sure could use the money."

"I know that; but we told Zhia we would take only firestone. You shouldn't give her any more reasons to distrust you if you still have any intention of making her your wife." Taf laughed, a sound devoid of amusement. "Having just seen her kill eight men—one by beating his head to a pulp, mind you—I'm having second thoughts about that idea. I still think she's quite a woman; she's quite a dangerous woman. I'm a lot more concerned whether I can trust her than whether she can trust me." He added, "And if you tell me you didn't find that scene a little distressing, I'll know you're talking crap."

"It wasn't a little distressing; I found it very distressing." I had probably been more disturbed than Taf; as far as he had been from the hollow and as close as he had been to the sound of the waterfall, he couldn't have heard that Zhia had been screaming, let alone what she had been screaming. I turned to look up the hill, saying, "I wonder if she needs a hand."

"Last I saw, she needs two hands; you're the one who needs only one. How is the burn?"

I looked at my right hand. I had held the handful of hot ash for a mere heartbeat. While palm and fingers were reddened, my desperate measure had left me with only a couple of small blisters. Carrying rocks had opened these; they stung. I could only imagine how Zhia's hands felt. While her blisters weren't from burns, they had been open for several days. It was a wonder they hadn't gone bad.

"I'll take a minor hurt like this over what Norjy and the others suffered," I said. Yes, it was bravado; any man who has been attacked by raiders and lives to tell about it should be allowed to swagger a little. Following that line of thought, I asked, "When we're asked how we survived a raider attack—and I think it's safe to say 'when', not 'if'—what do we tell people? You had a better perspective on the events than I did. Did you see anything that might have contributed to so unheard-of an outcome?"

"I take it you don't intend to admit that Zhia saved us?"

I didn't like the tone in his voice. Somewhat sharply, I replied, "I intend to give Zhia all the credit she's due. However, I was considering glossing over the fact that the three of us weren't in the hollow when the attack began."

"That's fair." Taf thought for a while. "It's well known that raiders successfully attack even armed parties, which means raiders expect armed resistance. I think what made the difference today was not that there was resistance, but that the nature of the resistance was different, unexpected. From what I saw, it was pretty clear that raiders know attacking like Singers know songs. They've done it so often it's become rote; they don't have to think about what they're doing. As Singers know, when you stop paying attention—when you can practically do a song in your sleep—that's when you fail to notice that something has changed. That's when the really big mistakes happen.

"I've heard talk among the Hall instructors that Singers should be issued weapons and trained in their use. I suppose that lets the teachers think they're doing something useful. Had they been armed, Norjy and Hink and the others would be just as dead. There's no defending against a sudden hail of darts, just like there's no defending against panicked tebecs or angry swarmers." He didn't say, "Or an enraged woman with an ax", but we were both thinking it.

"You're right; but no one will listen to all that. Can you condense it?" I asked.

"I'll try." He thought again. "The reason we're here right now talking about surviving a raider attack is because the raiders' own tactics were used against them." After a pause, he added, "Sad to say, now that they've been defeated that way, it won't work again."

Though this last point hadn't occurred to me, it made sense. Discouraging sense. "But," I argued, "We now know at least one of the raiders' tactics. Those darts have a limited range, and are probably most effective loosed from above, which means raiders are more likely to use that form of attack in places where there are heights on either side of the road. Right?"

"Right," Taf said, "provided all of the guesses on which you've based that assumption are also right. For the sake of argument, let's say this truly is information that could help stop raider attacks. Then two more questions arise: what places match that description, and have raider attacks occurred at those places? Do you know if any kind of record has been kept that might help answer those questions?"

"That would be the job of magistrates. I try to avoid them, if I can."

"Don't we all!" Taf laughed. "Even so, if—I guess I should say 'when'—we get back to the Hall, it wouldn't hurt to ask. If magistrates are at all concerned to do their job, they've got to be interested in anything that might make travel safer."

"Stay home; never leave." That was Zhia's contribution. As heavily as she was breathing, we should have heard her approach. She lowered her bulging cloak to the ground with a sigh and stretched to ease her back. I reminded myself that she needed a back rub. She coughed, winced, and added, "I truly hope you found firestone, because if you didn't and neither of you spared me toting the wood down here, I might be just a bit annoyed."

"That's why we kept the ax with us," Taf said, with a grin.

"That's not funny," Zhia and I said together. I said to Zhia, "Yes, we found firestone. Let's get this done."

It was Zhia's suggestion that we build the pyre where the last man she killed lay. It was a welcome suggestion, not only because she limping worse than before; none of us had been looking forward to handling that corpse. When the last body had been placed on the wood—flung, actually; we went to no effort to be gentle with dead raiders—Taf started to open one of the jugs that had the firestone.

"Wait," Zhia said.

"Now what?" he asked. "Do you want to commend the raiders to Henia before we burn their bodies?"

"I very much doubt that the raiders themselves claim to be serving the daemon of war," Zhia retorted. "I want us to wash before we light the pyre, because we won't want to linger once the bodies start burning."

"Why not just light it and leave?" I asked.

"Because you and I have open wounds that need to be washed and, in case you hadn't noticed, our clothes reek."

"But we've nothing clean to put on," Taf reminded her.

"I know. That's why we're going to get into the pool, clothes and all, and wash everything at once. Granted, our clothes won't get very clean, but they'll be cleaner. That will also save us the time we'd need for taking turns bathing."

Taf frowned. "What's the rush? The raiders are either dead or fled. Oh, that sounds like it would be a good song," he added, to himself.

Zhia and I looked at each other. I was grimacing; Zhia was trying to. "Taf," she said, as gently as her hurt throat would allow, "the raiders will regroup and return. They may not return today, but they will be back. Now if you want to be here to welcome them…"

He held up his hands. "All right, all right, you don't have to beat me over the head with it. Let's take a bath."

At the pool's edge, he and I removed our shoes; Zhia kept hers on, explaining that she was concerned about sharp rocks, which seemed reasonable. As we sank up to our shoulders in the colder-than-cool water, Taf remarked, "I always imagined taking a bath with a woman would be more exciting than this… and a lot more comfortable."

He and I laughed. I thought Zhia was laughing, too, then I saw her face was turned away. I listened and realized she was sobbing. "Zhia?" I said softly, and touched her shoulder.

"I'm sorry," she wept. "It's all my fault. I should never have gone on tour."

In those few, strangled words, Zhia revealed more worries and misconceptions than I could address at all, let alone quickly. I suspected what lay behind the outburst was delayed reaction to what she had suffered and done. There were a number of things I could now do, one of which was to hold her. With Taf watching and likely ready to take exception to that most obvious of comforts, I resorted to saying, gently but urgently, "You've held up this far, Zhia; don't fall apart now. As you said, we can't stay here much longer. Let's finish washing and get on the road."

Though she nodded, her shoulders still shook. When she said, "First one done gets to wrap up in the cloak," I knew the trembling was more from cold than from emotion. Taf and I looked at each other in silent agreement. No matter how long Zhia's bath took, she would finish first.

In fact, she did. Like Taf and me she was dirty, bloody, and sweaty; unlike us she was also liberally spattered with bits and pieces of now-dead men, mementos of her work with ax and stone. It took all three of us to get her even a little cleaner. While she scrubbed her clothing and skin, Taf and I worked on her hair. Then she sat by the pool while Taf wrung as much water as he could from her hair—this at his insistence, to spare her hands.

By then Zhia's battered lips were blue. I told her to get the cloak and find a sunny spot where she could rest until Taf and I finished. The pool had been in the sun when we began to bathe; now the height behind was shadowing it.

Watching her slowly limp to where she had left the cloak, Taf said, "I still have to look at that toe."

"And I have to give her a back rub. She's stiff from cutting wood," I explained in answer to Taf's surprised look. "But both will have to wait until we're away from here."

The sun was so close to setting when we finally lit the pyre that I said, "I really think we ought to stay here for the night. Soon it'll be raining; we've only the one cloak, and you need it."

"I'll share it," she said, stubbornly. "There's no shelter here. Besides, as I mentioned, the smell from the pyre won't exactly be pleasant."

Indeed, at that moment a breeze brought acrid smoke to our nostrils. We collected the ax and the jugs with firestone, and hastily retreated. "How can roasting flesh stink so?" I asked, my nose still wrinkled.

"That's the smell of evil being purged," Zhia said austerely.

"Pardon me, Zhia, but no," Taf said. "What makes the smoke smell so bad is the raiders' hair and the badly tanned hides quite a few of them wore. It's a good thing there weren't any dead tebecs. Burning feathers smell even worse, as I well know."

"I'm willing to take your word on that," I said. To Zhia, I said, "So, having made that place unfit for further use, where did you think we should spend the night?"

"If there's not a Quarter Rest just beyond here—and I assume there isn't, or this morning you would have said we should keep going until we got that far—since we have to go back to the Hall, I think we ought to head back to the previous one. Unless I'm wrong in thinking that the tour is over," she added, looking at me with one puffy eye. The other was now swollen shut.

"Why should the tour be over? Just because we have no instruments and only three Singers, two of whom probably shouldn't try to sing any time soon? You sure give up easily."

Zhia was trying not to smile. She didn't succeed; her lip split again. She licked the blood from it. "Yuck." In a rather macabre change of subject, she added, "I'm hungry."

"Nobody else is," Taf said. "Sorry," he added, when I elbowed him, "but let's not talk about food until we can get some."

"And then we won't have to talk about it," Zhia said. She coughed.

Wishing I still had the lozenges, I said, "You need to stop talking."

"A raider tried to help me out with that," was her saucy reply.

"Are you trying to prove you were around Hadden too long? Be quiet!"

In silence, in the last glimmers of daylight, we headed back the way we had come. The chill water of the pool had banished some of our weariness, so we started out at a rather good pace. Zhia soon shed the cloak. Between brisk walking—in Zhia's case, brisk limping—and the breeze that would bring in the evening rain, our hair and clothes were soon mostly dry. Zhia's shoes, however, squelched with each step.

As dusk pooled in shadows on the road, avoiding ruts and rocks became trickier. Zhia, already half-blind, slowed down; even so, a rock turned under her right foot. She went to one knee.

"I'm all right," she said as we helped her up. We went on, though we had to move even more slowly as she favored her right foot. When she began to shiver, Taf put the cloak around her. Her limp worsened. Soon Taf was helping her walk. Not much later, I was supporting her from the other side. When our support was no longer enough to keep her from gasping in pain when she put her foot down, I told Taf to stop. I let go of Zhia, left the road, and walked to a tree-sheltered rocky outcrop I had noticed more than stone's throw distant. There was a deep depression in the rock, not quite a cave but enough to provide shelter from the rain.

When I called, Taf helped Zhia to where I was. I had already set a large, flattened rock inside the depression. I pointed to it and said, "Zhia, sit down. We're going to look at that foot. Besides what you already did to your toe, you probably twisted your ankle."

She started to protest but closed her mouth and sat, shivering inside the cloak.

Taf said, "Give me the ax. I'll get wood and start a fire."

I nodded. It was now dark enough that we'd need the light as much as the heat. The rain was late; I was glad.

When the fire was going well I knelt in front of Zhia to remove her shoe. I couldn't do it, not just because the leather was still wet, but also because the shoe was far tighter than any shoe should be. Zhia had gone so ashen she looked about to faint.

Taf had also noticed her pallor. The rock was large enough for two; Taf sat next to Zhia and drew her against his side. She was breathing roughly, shallowly.

"Lend me your knife." I said to Taf. I knew he now had one; when we were looking for firestone, he'd taken the one I'd knocked out of the one raider's hand.

The blade was sharp; the wet leather was resistant. Zhia was dead white before the shoe was off. Her foot was discolored and badly swollen.

In a voice tight with pent anger, Taf said, "That's not from a twisted ankle or a toe that's just a little hurt. Even if that foot isn't broken, Zhia, the toe certainly is, and you knew it! You kept finding excuses for me not to look at it! You lectured me about trust, and now I find out you've been lying to me all day."

I was nearly as angry. "Had we known your foot was that badly injured, we would never have left the hollow."

"Precisely," Zhia breathed.

Then I understood. "So after doing all that heavy work you shouldn't have been doing, you decided to be the hero and walk who knows how far, and justify the stupidity by suggesting it was to save Taf and me from another raider attack? I have news for you: you're not walking any farther. Raiders or no raiders, we're staying here until we can find someone with a cart, a desdal—something—to get you to a doctor, if it's not too late. Suppose that, thanks to your obstinance, you end up crippled?"

"Save your breath," Taf said. "She's out cold."

Cold was now my main concern. We eased Zhia onto the ground, pulled the cloak closer around her, and got the rock out of the way. Taf went for more firewood. The extra warmth from the enlarged fire felt good and did reach Zhia, but it wouldn't last long. Though Taf had laid the fire close to the depression, the rain, when it came, would extinguish it.

While we had firelight, I had Taf cut the sleeves from my shirt. They were already slashed from the raider's knife. I further slashed them, reducing the cloth to strips so I could bind the knife cuts on my arms, some of which were still bleeding. There was cloth left after I was done. Taf used it to bandage Zhia's hands.

"Should I do anything with her foot?" he asked.

"Yes, if you know what to do with a broken foot. I sure don't."

Taf confessed he was just as ignorant. We agreed the best course was to leave well enough alone. Sitting by Zhia, he looked up at me and asked, "Think she'll be all right?"

"I can pray so, but I can't say so. I'm guessing what's wrong with her right now is reaction, hunger, cold, and pain. There's not much we can do about the reaction and the hunger. We're doing all we can to get her warm. Had she not been so stubborn, she could have spared herself some of the pain. At the risk of sounding callous, if she's not all right, it's her own fault." Something cold struck me, slid down my neck. "Here comes the rain." I ducked under cover.

The depression was not really big enough for three, especially when one of the three was supine. The drops that hit the fire hissed and danced until the rain came with enough force to quench it. Darkness enveloped us.

"Isn't this cozy?" Taf drawled. "We won't have to worry about Zhia being cold."

In fact, she felt too warm. I cut cloth from the bottom of my shirt, let the rain wet it, and sponged her forehead and cheeks. "I wish I could give her a drink, but I've nothing that holds water."

"How about your prize cup?" Taf asked. "Or did the raiders get it?"

"No, they didn't." I unclasped the chain, slid the cup off, collected rain, and held it to Zhia's lips. I was pretty sure as much went on her shirt as into her mouth. I kept refilling the cup and trying to get water into her. "I don't think this is helping," I finally said. "It's too little and too slow."

"Weren't you Champion twice?" Taf asked. "Where's the other cup? I could be filling one while you get her to drink from the other."

"I no longer have the other cup. Please don't ask why not." My tone was harsh.

I heard surprise in Taf's voice. "Whatever you say, Rois. I was just hoping you weren't going to say you didn't want both of your Singer's trophies used for someone who isn't really a Singer."

Chapter Twelve

There was no point in denying the truth.

"How long have you known?" I asked, holding the piece of my shirt in the rain. I had decided that sponging would do more to check the fever than the two sips of water my prize cup would hold, and had again hung the trophy around my neck.

"I began to suspect the day she decided to use the rimba as kettles. While I can't say Instructor Combro ever threatened anyone, he made it pretty clear that if anything happened to the rimba we'd better hope it happened to us, too; because no matter how bad the circumstances under which the drums got damaged or destroyed, they'd be nothing compared to what would happen to us when he got hold of us."

"He didn't threaten you? He told my class he'd skin us alive and make drum heads out of our hide!"

"You have to wonder whether he really would... or did," Taf said. "Anyway, though I knew Zhia looked familiar, I didn't remember seeing her in any of my classes. That could have been because her schedule was different; but it couldn't have been that different.

"But I wasn't certain about her not being a Singer until this morning. I'd be the first to admit that Zhia has courage; but when Hadden mentioned Instructor Neron, even you flinched. I saw you. She didn't even blink. The only people who aren't intimidated by Neron are people who don't know him. And since he teaches Theory and Composition, which is a required class… we both know where the argument goes from there. So she's been lying about that, too," he finished, in disgust. "Who is she really?"

I chose my words carefully. "Since only Singers tour and the Master did send her on tour, she is really a Singer."

Taf muttered something that sounded like "talking crap". That's when I decided he also needed to know what Zhia and I suspected. I said, a bit heatedly, "I'm not going to be able to explain this if you aren't willing to listen with something resembling an open mind, Taf. You're right in thinking that, though Zhia wants to be a Singer and has been at the Hall for at least two turns of the wheel of stars, she's never attended classes. The reason she looks familiar is because you've probably seen her sweeping. She was completely taken aback when the Master offered her a tour, but since touring was something she dearly wanted, she didn't ask too many questions before agreeing."

"Nia Diva!" Taf exclaimed. "If the raiders hadn't attacked, she would have stood up on stage somewhere and made a complete fool of herself and the rest of us!"

"You, Zhia, and I all agree on that. And I have to believe that the Master not only knew that was a likelihood but, in fact, may have been counting on its happening. Ask yourself why the Master would send someone with no training, a bunch of first-timers, and an inexperienced leader on tour."

In the dark I heard Taf's sharp, indrawn breath. "Either he's out of his mind, or he wanted the tour to fail. But why?"

"That's the question Zhia and I have discussed interminably but haven't been able to answer. Why? Why go to such lengths to humiliate a Singer? A person who isn't up to the challenge of being a Singer is simply dismissed from the Hall, without the cruelty of public humiliation."

"Unless the point of the exercise wasn't to get rid of a person—in this case, Zhia—but a group: females."

"Zhia and I have considered that possibility," I said. "But both Zhia and Dolin, a friend of mine, say there's another woman at our Hall."

"Yes: Noia. She's really good. In fact, when I first heard I would be touring with a woman, I was excited because I thought Noia was getting her chance." After a silence broken only by the sounds of diminishing rain and of breathing, Taf said, "If you're right and the Master is behind this, then Noia might not be safe, either. Let me guess: you and Zhia have discussed that, too."

"Yes, we have. I'm telling you our suspicions because you might be able to think of something we've overlooked. Everything we've just been discussing Zhia and I have already gnawed to the bone."

"Please don't talk about eating!" he said.

"Sorry. This morning, Zhia told me something that was really strange. But before I say more, let me ask if you knew that anything about our tour was unusual."

"From comments other Singers made, it's my understanding that everything about our tour was unusual, beginning with how little time we had to get ready."

"That about says it all. Our schedule is unusual, too. Most tours for first-timers stay quite close to the Hall. The schedule the Master gave me for this tour, a schedule we no longer have, had us going places I'd never heard of. Zhia's news was that before we left, she saw a schedule on the Master's desk, a schedule supposedly for this tour, that had us going only to the usual first-timer engagements."

Taf sounded thoughtful when he said, "Should something happen to the tour—which it did—the Master could blame the tour leader for making some terrible mistake... as you and Zhia doubtless already discussed."

Even though Taf couldn't see me, I nodded. A memory woke. "This morning, Zhia also said that if the Master of our Hall was intent on getting rid of female Singers, he would have to be willing to sacrifice some male Singers, as well, or people would soon become suspicious."

"Seven male Singers died today," Taf said. "There's no question the rest of us were supposed to die, too. But I'm not ready to believe the Master told raiders to attack Singers, not when a Festival Champion—the first Champion from our

Hall—was one of them! And why would raiders take orders from a Master?"

"That's another of the questions I can't answer. What the...?" I suddenly exclaimed.

"What's wrong?"

"Something's pulling my hair. Now it's got my ear."

Taf laughed a bit wildly. "That has to be my tebec. It was one of the ones that got away. Biting ears and pulling hair were its favorite ways of being annoying. It must have been wandering around and heard my voice. Can you grab it?"

"Grab it? I'd like to strangle it; my ear is bleeding." I got one hand around the beak that was again tugging at my hair and rose slowly, running my other hand down the long neck until I located the riding gear. "I've got its reins."

Taf stood, also. He felt for the reins and took them from me. I heard him fumbling with the saddle, then he said, "My pack is gone. So are the hobbles."

"You'll just have to tie it to a tree."

"It'd like that; it'd be out of the rain and could eat its fill of leaves, too." The creak of the wicker saddle diminished as Taf led the bird out to be tethered. When he returned, he said, "This is a break! When it's light I can go in search of transport for Zhia."

"Good; but wouldn't it be quicker just to take her with you?"

"Sure it would. Do you think either that she could mount a tebec right now, or that you could lift her up to me once I'm mounted? She's hardly a featherweight."

"Which is one reason we're here insulting her instead of back in the hollow, full of raider darts, with carrion eaters picking at our bodies."

"You don't have to sound so offended, Rois. If I didn't like her, I wouldn't have asked her to be my wife."

"I thought you'd changed your mind at least twice since then, not to mention the little matter you seem to be forgetting: she said 'no.'"

"Only once."

"How many times do you want to be rejected? And what was that tirade about trust I heard from you earlier? I think that makes it Taf rejecting Zhia, three; Zhia rejecting Taf, one. Make up your mind."

"My mind was made up before today. Right now, when she's so bruised..."

I allowed myself to sound derisive. "This from the man who lectured me about what's important in a wife?"

"I never said beauty wasn't important; I said it's not the only thing. You're the one who thinks only a pretty woman is worth having."

"I'll thank you not to put words in my mouth, Taf."

"Those are other people's words. In case you didn't know, sir, even among Singers—who, as a whole, aren't the most fastidious of people—you have an unsavory reputation where women are concerned. I'll admit it's not as bad as that Henz person's, but it's not one I'd want."

"You're not likely to get one, unsavory or otherwise!"

"And what's that supposed to mean?"

From somewhere near our feet came sounds of movement, then suppressed groans. I couldn't see, but I felt someone other than Taf near me. It had to be Zhia. I heard her move haltingly away, toward the rainy darkness.

"Zhia, where are you going?" I asked. No sooner had I spoken than I realized she probably needed to pee. I hoped she wouldn't have to ask for help. I got ready to apologize for asking a question I already knew she didn't want to hear.

"I was going to find somewhere else to sleep so you two won't have to worry about keeping your voices down." Her voice was now barely a thread of a whisper.

I had heard that kind of sarcasm before; Taf hadn't. After an awkward silence he asked, "How do you feel?"

"Tired. I'm sure you're tired, also. And I can tell you're both hungry. Here's an idea. Come sit by me, one on either side." We did so. "That's right, real close; I'm cold. I'll tell you a story to help you sleep. Please don't interrupt, because I can't shout over you. You get only one story tonight. It's nice and dark, so close your eyes, relax, and listen.

"Once there were two very nice boys whose names were Rois and Taf. I said don't interrupt," she admonished, as Taf and I drew breath at the same time. We obeyed, though I think we already suspected we would regret humoring Zhia.

"Now, Rois and Taf lived in a nice house—indeed, it was a very, very, very fine house—with everything they wanted, including a room full every kind of toy imaginable. For a long time they played well together. Then one day, they started tugging on the same toy, a plain, ordinary toy. They got angrier and angrier, and the angrier they got, they harder they pulled, until the toy was about to break. The toy was sad, because there were so many other, wonderful toys the boys could choose from; and because the pulling hurt.

"Then someone who cared very much for both boys"—she had to pause to get her voice under control—"fearing they might hurt each other, made them stop fighting and asked what the problem was. What a surprise to discover that neither Rois nor Taf really wanted to have that toy, but neither had been willing to let go of it for fear that the other would get it. Then the boys were glad that they hadn't let a silly thing like an old, worn-out toy ruin their friendship. And the toy was glad, because toys were never meant to be fought over. The end. Now go to sleep."

She leaned her head against me, probably because I was on her right and that side of her face was less bruised, and was asleep at once. The cheek that rested on my bare arm was hot and damp. She was feverish; she had been weeping.

Taf said quietly, "If she'd shouted at us, I'd feel better."

Just as quietly, I replied, "I don't think we're supposed to feel better. At least, not yet." Silence followed, not the tense silence of a string that's stretched so tightly it will snap if touched, but a chastened and—in my case, at least—reflective one.

The story had been anything but soothing. Since meeting Zhia I had become more accustomed to looking at myself honestly, but lying to oneself is a habit that's hard to break. Even if tonight I arrived at no answers to the questions the fable had raised, I owed it to myself and Taf, but most of all to Zhia, at least to consider them.

Foremost was the question of my feelings for Zhia. While I thought I felt mostly generalized annoyance, it was obvious that both Taf and Zhia saw something else. (Vel had, as well; but Vel had been all but unaware of interaction between a man and a woman that wasn't horizontal.) I imagined myself asking Zhia to be my wife, and further imagined her saying "yes". I felt nothing. Next, I imagined asking Eia the same thing and receiving the same answer. My reaction was immediately and intensely physical, but the image that filled my mind was not Eia's beauty but Zhia's battle-scarred face. I told myself that proved nothing except that I'd seen Zhia more recently.

For all that he and I had almost come to blows, Taf was a good man and, more, a friend. I didn't know if he was a good Singer. Nia Diva forbid I should ever again face the kind of perils I'd encountered on this tour! Should such trials come again, I'd rather face them with a man who had proven himself courageous and reliable, even if he couldn't sing or play a note. Zhia had been right in reminding Taf and me that we had been and should be friends.

Though I knew that the details in fables were there to make them interesting and that each one didn't necessarily have a special meaning, it concerned me that Zhia—both the toy and the peacemaker in the tale—described herself as plain, ordinary, old, and worn out. While she admitted that she cared for both Taf and me, it seemed that she was trying to convince us that she wasn't worthy of our attention. Even when it's clear that people aren't being honest about themselves, it's easier for others to accept a person's self-valuation, even if it's wrong.

I thought Zhia's was wrong.

She hadn't been wrong that we were all tired. She was, of course, asleep. I had heard nothing more from Taf but quiet breathing. My eyelids were drooping when Taf whispered, "I can't sleep sitting up. Can you?"

I thought it would undo whatever good Zhia's fable had done to mention that not only could I sleep sitting up, but I had, indeed, almost been asleep, so I said, "Only if I'm listening to an instructor or riding a tebec."

He laughed softly. "Though I'll be riding a tebec tomorrow, I won't dare sleep. I'll have to be watching if I'm to find someone to give us a ride back to the Hall. Do you think it will wake Zhia if I lie down?"

"It doesn't seem likely. But since she's leaning on me, why don't you hold her up and peel the cloak off her while I lie down next to the inside wall. You can have the cloak and be on the outside so in the morning you can leave without waking anyone, assuming we're not awake when you leave."

"I was thinking pretty much the same thing, though I hadn't thought about getting the cloak. Do you think Zhia will be warm enough?"

"Lying between us, probably. And since the rain's almost over, you should be fairly comfortable; but we can exchange places if you find it too wet or cold."

We got situated as I had suggested without disturbing Zhia's sleep. Taf kept saying he was fine, even though I could tell from the sound of drops hitting the cloak that he wasn't entirely under the overhang. I didn't insist he and I trade places; had the situation been reversed, I would also have claimed the manly right to be more miserable than anyone else. Then Zhia murmured and turned on her side, and Taf was able to move the necessary few hand's breadth farther in.

The sound of rain dripping from the overhang to the ground lulled me to sleep.

I dreamed again of Eia. She and I were naked and playing in the pool in the hollow, the sun-spangled water warm and caressing. We were laughing and splashing each other, and kissing the water from each other's faces and bodies. Gradually there was more kissing than splashing, and our play became passion so intense that the water seemed cool.

Suddenly, a cloud of swarmers settled on Eia's head, stinging her until her face was an unrecognizable mass. Calling her name, I tried to pull her from the pool; but my wet hand kept losing its grip.

She sank slowly under the water.

Chapter Thirteen

The nightmare didn't end when I woke. The first thing I saw when I opened my eyes was Zhia. Bad as she looked—with her bruises even darker, the flesh around the cuts even more swollen, and one champion of a black eye—she looked better than my last glimpse of Eia in my dream.

I was still trying to shake off the night-borne horror when Zhia's good eye opened as far as it could, which wasn't very far. I said, "Good morning."

"Nightmare?" she responded, her voice stronger than it had been the night before, but still gravelly.

"What?"

"Did you have a nightmare? You were tossing and calling a name. It woke me."

"Sorry." I drew a few deep breaths, trying to get my composure. Thinking talking commonplaces would help, I said, "How are you today?"

"I've been better. And you?"

The burn blisters and the knife cuts were stinging, and my throat was still sore from being crushed. "What you said goes for me."

"No one should have this much fun on tour," she remarked, dryly.

I laughed, and the lingering shreds of nightmare fled. Becoming aware of a need, I said, "Since I'm going out anyway, can I help you get anywhere?"

"Thank you, no. Taf helped me before he left. He found a stream. I had a good, long drink, so I'll probably have to ask you to help me later, if you don't mind." She sat up so she could look across the sun-washed expanse outside the shelter. After a moment she said, "I'm sorry, even though I was there, I can't tell you where it was."

"That's all right. Even if I can't find the stream, I'm sure I can find something." I did find the stream by listening for the sound of its water. When I returned, I asked, "When did Taf leave?"

"Not very long ago, I think. It seemed like I'd just drifted off again when you... take it 'Eia' is someone special?"

"I'd like to think so." I didn't want to talk about my lady love to another woman, so I said, "It's too nice a day to huddle in this hole. Let's find a place to sit under a tree."

"Suits me. You choose the tree."

When I saw Zhia had to hop, probably jarring her hurt foot, I steered her to a tree closer than the one I had originally chosen. The second time she had to grab my arm after failing to avoid landing on a rock I said, "You can't see at all, can you?"

She sighed in exasperation. "I can see, just not much. It'll get better, but not today."

"Not for a number of 'todays', as I'm sure you know." When she was sitting against the tree I went back to the depression for the ax, which was where Taf had left it. I also brought the rock which had been Zhia's chair the night before. I leaned the ax against the tree, then padded the rock with leaves and placed it under Zhia's right foot. As I was settling myself next to Zhia, she asked me what the rock was for. "I remember hearing that raising an injured foot is good for it," I explained.

"Oh? I suppose it can't hurt." She was quiet for a while. She was probably thinking, as I was, about food. "Dare I inquire further about Eia?"

I was about to say "no" when I remembered something that had sparked my curiosity. "If I tell you about Eia, will you tell me something I want to know?"

"That's fair," she said, but her tone was cautious.

"I met Eia at a party the day I was first named Festival Champion. She's…
she's… I suppose 'someone special' says everything anyone with imagination
needs to know."

"And she's beautiful, of course. Hair of gold, eyes like the sky, maybe?"

I rounded on her. "How long were you eavesdropping that day?"

"I wasn't eavesdropping," was her mild reply. "You're a Singer; I could have
heard what you were saying from a lot farther down the corridor than I was.
And I was only guessing that you'd been singing about Eia. Losing your temper
just served to confirm what you apparently didn't want me to know."

Without saying so aloud, I admitted she was right. "Now that you've dug
into my personal life, it's my turn. Who's Pandy?"

"Pandy? I don't know any… Oh!" The syllable was a sob. She bowed her head.

I was alarmed. "If it upsets you that much, you don't have to tell me."

She raised her head and wiped her nose on her sleeve. "It's all right. It just
took me by surprise. I'm curious: when did you hear that name?"

"When you were…" I decided a gentler answer was needed. "Yesterday."

She nodded. "The name you heard wasn't 'Pandy', it was 'Pandizh'. Pandizh
was my son." At my startled, half-muffled exclamation, she gave me a wry
smile. "Yes, I had a son. I even had a husband, hard though that may be to
believe. I met Pandir while I was caring for my grandmother. You remember
I told you about her?" I nodded, and she continued, "After Grandmother's
death, Pandir asked me to be his wife. He was a merchant's son, but he was
willing to quit traveling and live with me in my grandmother's house. In due
time we had a son. Pandizh hadn't even seen two turns of the star wheel when
his father died of the same illness that ruined your father's voice. My grandmother was dead; the wheel of the stars had turned six times since raiders
killed my father, mother, and older brother; so I had nowhere to live except
with Pandir's parents. They had come to Tarnsedge to lay their son to rest, so
when they were ready to go home, Pandizh and I went with them. We were a
large group, a heavily-guarded merchant train. You'll never guess what happened," she added, bitterly.

"Raiders?" I was fervently wishing I'd never made that cursed bargain.

"Raiders. You've seen what they do, but you haven't seen it all. Of course they killed Pandir's parents and the other merchants, despoiled the bodies, and stole the pack animals along with the goods they carried. They didn't kill Pandizh or me. They took us to their camp. And there"—she stopped and drew a shuddering breath—"there they spitted and roasted my baby, and ate him. I was tied to a tree; they made me watch. Then they made me eat some. It didn't stay down, of course. They thought that was terribly funny." After another sobbing breath, she said, "Having dined so well, they were ready for a different kind of entertainment."

I knew what was coming. "You don't have to tell me, if you don't want to."

"If you don't mind, I'd like to tell you. I've never told anyone else. Do you mind?"

I did mind, but thinking of the unpleasant things Zhia had been willing to do for me, I said, "I'll listen."

"Thank you. Whenever Pandir had been satisfied in bed, he would fall into a deep sleep. I hoped raiders had that much in common with other men, so after I allowed them to think they had overcome my reluctance—don't men think all women want to be raped?—I started begging for more. Since they thought I was cooperating, they untied me. They weren't too brutal. One good thing is that part of their plunder was a large amount of wine. The raiders didn't stint themselves, so some weren't able to join in at all and others couldn't last very long. I kept pretending I was as excited as they, all the while imagining how I would be revenged, if I got a chance. It helped to know that I was using them just as much as they were using me.

"When they were all drunk, asleep, or too spent to do anything, I got away. Another good thing is, I didn't quicken."

To my horror, I found myself saying, "So yesterday…"

She turned to face me. "Yesterday I was settling many scores—a score of scores—though until you asked, I didn't know that's what I was doing."

I was silent, remembering some of the things Zhia had told me I said to her when she and I first met. In light of the ghastly account I had just heard, I was even more ashamed of some of those remarks, which I now knew had been cruel beyond imagining. I also remembered Zhia's vehement rejection of my comment about her decency, and her telling me I knew nothing about her. Then I remembered the crude discussion I had overheard among my first-timers, and knew Zhia had heard at least some of it, as well.

It was far too late for the other Singers from the tour to apologize to Zhia or anyone else for anything. It was probably too late for me to apologize for what had happened on our first encounter—I didn't recall having done so when I asked Zhia to rehearse the event for me—but I could resolve to change my ways. Taf's reference to my unsavory reputation had rattled me; as Taf had mentioned, Singers aren't noted for being all that fastidious. If Singers objected to my actions, they must have been quite objectionable.

I thought again about Zhia's question "Don't men think all women want to be raped?"

When she had asked it, I been about to blurt "no", but had realized I was fooling myself. Since I became a Singer, my dealings with women had had only one goal. Some women took longer to seduce than others; some met me quite a bit more than halfway.

Did I rape women? No. Did I use women? Yes. Emphatically yes. At that moment I realized that, often as not, the women were using me, as well. Some accommodated me for money, others for the prestige of associating with a Singer, especially a Champion. Suddenly I wondered whether Eia was one of the latter.

I decided a change of subject was called for. The question I asked, "How did you survive when your father, mother, and brother were killed?", hardly qualified as a change of subject. My thoughtlessness staggered me. I could only say, "I'm sorry. Please don't tell me you..." I couldn't speak the ugly words.

Gently, she said, "No, the raiders didn't use me that way twice. I wasn't there when my family was massacred. I was ill and was staying with my grandmother."

Fixing upon a safer topic, I asked, "So how did you come to be at the Hall?"

"Pandir knew quite a bit about Singers because his brother is one. I used to sing Pandizh to sleep, and Pandir would tell me I should be a Singer. Then he died. That's when I learned that Grandmother had borrowed money against the house so she and I could live, and that Pandir had assumed the debt. I had no way to pay it off. So, finding myself with neither home nor family, I thought I would see if Pandir had been right. I had no money and since I had nowhere to live, I could depend on no town to sponsor me; but the Master agreed to let me stay and pay for training by working. Somehow, the work was never quite enough. When the Master asked if I wanted to tour, I thought my debt was finally paid. I thought I would, at last, become a Singer, and something of Pandir would live; but now that's gone, too. He's dead. Our baby's dead. Everything's dead, and the Master gets the failed tour and the disgraced female Singer—who isn't a Singer—he wanted!" Suddenly tears poured down her battered face and she was shaking uncontrollably. Even had Taf been there and protesting, I would have gathered Zhia into my arms.

As I held her, feeling her tears burn on the not-yet-closed cuts the knife had inflicted on me, I reflected that, in its own way, this second tale was as harrowing as the first one. Apparently, the "quite a bit" Pandir had known about Singers didn't include the knowledge that Singers who neither came from well-to-do families nor were sponsored by their hometown paid for their training after the fact, in touring fees.

Far from making Zhia a Singer, the Master had made her a slave.

A Master is in charge of every aspect of a Hall's operation, including employment of staff and servants. Thinking of the scant number of females being trained as Singers at my Hall but the large number of them working there, women I had always assumed were employed, I began to wonder if any of them had also been taken in by the kind of promise Zhia had been given and, if so, how many.

I thought again of the opulence of the Master's office. If, as I now suspected, the Hall wasn't paying wages to all the people who worked there, the Master could certainly maintain the level of luxury he enjoyed. The Master also enjoyed the luxury of being answerable to no one. If women who thought they were going to be trained as Singers were, instead, being enslaved, they could complain to no one but the Master who had enslaved them. He would placate them with smooth promises, glib assurances. "Soon," he would say; only "soon" would never come.

The Master was supposed to keep a record of each Singer, a record which included such things as when his or her training began, how he or she was paying, and how much, if any, each owed. Singers who came from less-than-wealthy families or who weren't sponsored were, in a sense, slaves—or, more accurately, indentured servants—because they remained at one Hall until the cost of training was paid. The difference between their situation and Zhia's was twofold: they knew what the arrangement was when they were admitted to the Hall, and if they were talented and worked hard, they would be touring and could be fairly certain of quickly discharging their debt.

I thought of my first-timers, and wondered how many of them still owed the Hall for their training. Taf had been right; even if the Master could, the Master wouldn't order raiders to attack his Singers. That would be taking money out of his own pockets.

Even so, I would have given a lot to see the records of my Hall.

Chapter Fourteen

Zhia's sobs finally abated. She slumped in my arms a little longer, then pushed herself away. "I'm sorry," she said, scrubbing tears from her face with her sleeve and tearing open cuts on her cheeks. "That wasn't good," she added, when she saw blood on her shirt. "Maybe you could help me to the stream. I need to… to wash my face."

While she was occupied, I went a short distance away and looked around to see if Taf was in sight. I saw no sign of him or the tebec, but I did spot a nest in a tree. When I investigated, I found eggs. My stomach growled. Had I been certain the eggs were not close to hatching, I would have collected and shared them. After what Zhia had told me, I strongly suspected she would think ill of eating unhatched birds. I now understood her reaction to the idea of roasting baby shellort.

A detail from her nightmare narrative returned. She had said the raiders had spitted and roasted her son. She had not said they first killed the child. Somehow, I knew she hadn't simply forgotten to mention it. Suddenly, I was no longer very hungry.

When I was certain Zhia had had enough time for whatever she needed to do besides wash her face, I went back to the stream. She was sitting against a tree that overhung it, dangling her injured foot in the water. I noticed the bandages were again off her hands. Realizing both that the cloth had become wet when she washed her face and that no bandage was better than a wet one, I said nothing.

"Do you think Taf will be able to find us if we stay here?" she asked. "I'd like to stay here. The cool water feels good on my foot, and being here already will save you having to help me next time."

"If Taf doesn't find us where he left us, he'll call or look or both. I'll get the stuff we left, so he'll know we weren't just carried off." When I returned with the ax and firestone I said, "I saw a nest full of eggs. I wondered..."

"Where is it?" She tried to twist to see where I pointed. Moaning, she stopped.

"You're still stiff, aren't you?"

"A stiff back is the least of my worries."

"But it's one I can do something about. I can't do a thing for your foot or your throat or your hands or your bruises and cuts and black eye, but I can rub your back."

"Not with blistered hands, you can't."

"Both hands aren't blistered."

She tilted her head back so she could see me with her half-swollen eye. "Why are you so insistent?"

"Until we get back to the Hall, I'm tour leader and you're tour partner. My job is to take care of you. I haven't done a very good job so far."

"I would argue with that, if for no other reason than because I haven't made it very easy for you to do a good job."

"So quit making my job so hard."

She said, "Yes, sir," and stretched out on the grass.

I soon realized that I was rubbing her shirt, not her back. I told her this, and added, "Do you mind if I...?"

"You may touch me," she said, irritably. "Wouldn't you agree that the likelihood of your forgetting yourself while doing so is less than none at all?" Immediately, she added, "I'm sorry. You're trying to be respectful and I'm not making that easy, am I?"

As I adjusted her shirt so her back was exposed, I said, "Just be quiet. I won't be able to do this properly if you're taking the kind of breaths you need for talking."

I should explain that one thing Singers do to prepare for being on stage is to stand in a circle, with each rubbing the back—the neck and shoulders, especially—of the person in front of him or her. Offering this service to Zhia was neither improper nor unusual. It wasn't even unusual that I was rubbing bare skin; I had previously toured only with men and, as I'd been reminded when I began to work on Zhia, a back rub isn't as effective through clothing.

It should be no surprise when I say that I was accustomed to the feel of a woman's bare back, as well. Eia's back was soft, supple as a sapling. Zhia's was as muscular as many a man's. At the moment, it was about as supple as a tree trunk. By using my fingertips, I was able to employ both hands on the knots in her muscles.

I soon realized that, rather than becoming looser, the muscles in her back had become tighter. Zhia wasn't breathing; from the feel of her ribs, I knew she was holding her breath. Angry for Zhia rather than with her, I lifted my hands and, careful to touch only cloth, pulled down her shirt. I stood and said, "I'm going to look at that nest."

Zhia nodded as she sat up. I saw blood on the back of her right hand; she had been biting her knuckle, probably to keep from weeping or even screaming. I said, "You'd better wash that hand," and went to the tree where I'd seen the nest.

I knew Zhia hadn't been reacting to what I'd been doing. Though I have used a back rub as an introduction to other things, I'd had no intention of violating Zhia's trust—"confirming her distrust" might be more accurate—and so had consciously and carefully avoided any touch that Zhia might have construed as overly familiar.

I had erred in insisting on any contact. I suspected that on some other day she would have welcomed and, perhaps, even enjoyed the massage. With the memory of a devastating experience newly wakened, she hadn't been able to tolerate my touch.

Some memories should not live again.

While I debated telling Taf what I had learned, I took two of the five eggs from the nest and ate them raw, an indication of how hungry I was. I eyed the remaining eggs and decided to leave them for Zhia, if she wanted them. If she didn't, perhaps Taf would.

Zhia politely but firmly declined the food. She was again sitting with her foot in the water. Objects seen through water appear to be larger. Though underwater, Zhia's foot looked like it was somewhat less swollen. The discoloration was more dramatic.

"I once had a shirt with those colors," I remarked, pointing at the submerged foot. I sat next to Zhia and leaned against the tree.

"I'm sorry," she said, the humor back in her voice. "What is it with you Singers and your—what's a polite word?—showy clothing?"

"It's just part of our exuberant approach to life," I said breezily, talking crap as fast as I could. I had never considered the question and certainly didn't know the answer.

"I'm pleased you didn't say 'tasteful'. I had been wondering if it was a way of keeping the audience from listening too closely to your music."

I grinned at her. "Then you don't intend to wear bright colors when you're on stage?"

"On stage doing what? Sweeping?" Now the bitterness was back. "I'm not a Singer."

"Singers tour. You've been on tour. You're a Singer."

"You're talking crap. This wasn't a tour; it was a disaster, as it was meant to be."

"So you're just going to give up and let the Master win?" I challenged.

"What other choice do I have? I have no money, no home, no family, no training, and no desire to become a...a woman of pleasure."

"Suppose I train you to be a Singer?"

"Why would you do that? Because you feel sorry for me?"

Since "yes" would clearly be the wrong answer, even if it was the truth—or, at least, part of the truth—I said, "If you don't want to be a Singer, I with-draw the offer."

She fell silent. Finally, she said, "If you were to train me, would I really be a Singer?"

"To be honest, Zhia, I don't know. I can think of no reason that the training you'd get filtered through me would be less acceptable than the training you'd get directly from the instructors. Though you're justified in wondering whether this fiasco counts as a tour, the fact remains that others at the Hall know you went on tour. They believe you're a Singer.

"The question that needs to be answered first is, will you be able to sing again? I can't answer that question. Listening to you right now—listening to myself, for that matter!—I'd say 'no'; but I'm no doctor. Aplin knows throats. We'll have him look at you when we get back. Until we know whether your throat's been damaged and, if it has, the extent of the damage, we can't make any firm plans."

"I understand. Forgive my asking, but what would you want in return for training me?"

"I don't blame you for asking," I said. "What would I want? I'd want the chance to restore your trust in Singers in general and those at our Hall in particular. I'd want to deny the Master the satisfaction of having all his plots succeed. I suppose I should say all the plots we suspect him of having.

"And I'd want Pandir's wish to be realized: I want you to become a Singer."

Her "thank you" made me feel like I'd again been named Festival Champion.

Before I could get too self-satisfied, she asked, "But you weren't planning to train me at the Hall, were you?"

Because the idea of my training Zhia had been purely spur of the moment, I couldn't truthfully claim to have planned anything. After thinking about the question, I replied, "No, that would make it too easy for the Master to put a broom back into your hands. I wonder if Father and Mother would be willing to…"

"No," she said, firmly. "I was hardly able to hold my tongue for a short time the day I met your Father. I very much doubt I could be civil to him for a day or longer."

"So don't be civil. Tell him off. He's no right to talk to anyone the way he talked to you, no matter how famous he used to be or who he used to hobnob with."

"He knew lots of important people?"

"To hear him talk, he knew everyone worth knowing. Of course, the star wheel has turned at least twelve times since then."

"Twelve?" The upturn of her mouth wasn't a smile. "We'll go visit your parents."

Chapter Fifteen

Three days later, the tour that would soon become known among Singers as "The Tour That Wasn't" (or "TTTW", for short) was over.

Even after the covered, chero-drawn cart Taf had been able to borrow creaked to a stop in front of my parents' home, Taf continued his three-day attempt to persuade Zhia and me to return to the Hall.

"No," she and I said in unison.

"Don't make me go through it again," I added. "Just remember two things…"

"I know, I know," Taf said, holding up his hands. "One: ask Aplin to come here; and two: try to find out whether there are other women at the Hall who thought they were going to be Singers but aren't."

I had, of course, shared with Taf my latest suspicions of the Master. I had decided to tell him nothing of the other things Zhia had told me. If Taf ever decided he wanted Zhia to be his wife, she could tell him herself.

"One more thing," Zhia said, "be sure the others' families are notified."

"As if I need to be reminded of that," Taf said, glumly. "But don't look for anything to happen for at least five days, because first I have to return the chero and the cart to the farmer, get my tebec back, and get back to the Hall. I never thought I'd see a draft animal that would make me prefer a tebec. This chero is pathetic."

It was a sorry example of its kind, sway-backed and poor-spirited, with lackluster hide and a plodding gait. (The chero is another of the hoofed animals. When well cared for, a chero is usually more impressive than its kin, the desdal; and is superior in nearly every way to a tebec.) I had to admit that compared to how the three of us looked, the beast Taf held in such contempt looked good.

The three-day journey had made for some improvement in our appearance. The wife of the farmer who had loaned Taf the conveyance had provided a few days' worth of food, so we were no longer famished. By taking turns driving, Taf and I had both been able to sleep, while Zhia had done little except sleep the first day and a half, so we were all better rested. Zhia was no longer feverish. Her face was less swollen; she could again open both eyes. The blisters on her and my hands had firm, dry skin and would soon be fully healed. All the knife cuts, my mementos of the raiders, were scabbed, so I had removed the bandages. The bruises on my throat were turning greenish-yellow and my voice was almost normal. Though Zhia couldn't put much weight on her hurt foot, she could go short distances without help.

But we were three days dirtier and our hair three days greasier. The stubble on Taf's and my faces was three days heavier. My shirt had been a wreck since the day of the raider attack. That both it and the rest of our clothes had been lived in three days longer would have been unpleasantly apparent to anyone within a stone's throw of us. I think even the chero, which had a definite reek of its own, was glad to be rid of us.

"On second thought," Taf added, as if reading my mind, "it may be at least six days before I get anything in the works. Once I get back to the Hall, I may do nothing until I've spent about a day soaking in a tub."

We wished him well, then moved out of the way as he turned the cart and tried to urge the chero into something better than a plod. The heat of the zenith sun didn't inspire the beast to make haste.

"Do you think Taf'll ever want to tour again?" Zhia asked as the cart lumbered away.

"Sure. After a few days of being warm and dry and having a soft bed, regular meals, and clean clothes, he'll think the Hall is pretty tame."

Zhia grinned. "Let's see if your parents are home."

Both grin and words worried me. When I hadn't been explaining to Taf why Zhia and I weren't returning at once to the Hall, I'd been trying to get Zhia to tell me what she planned to do when she saw Father again. She had good-naturedly but steadfastly refused. I thought I would die of curiosity, especially considering how reluctant she had been to visit my parents before "TTTW" began.

Now I was the reluctant one. I told myself that the sooner I knocked on the door, the sooner I would know; so I knocked. I had seen Father watching from the window, probably drawn by the sound of a cart on the usually quiet lane. He must have known I saw him, for he didn't resort to his tired trick of hiding behind the door.

"What happened to you?" he demanded as he flung the door open.

"Just what you asked for, Father; the raiders got us."

Yes, that was cruel. It actually kept Father quiet for a moment. Then I saw a familiar look in his eyes, and he said, "I'm glad to see you, Son. I can't say I'm surprised the raiders wouldn't take Crap Mouth. I didn't think she could get any uglier. I was wrong."

Zhia put her hand on my arm and hobbled into the house. She gave Father a wry smile. "I must confess, sir, that you were right. When we first met, I was talking crap; I'd never heard of you. I must confess also that I was remiss in not introducing myself. I'm Zhia. Zhia Vediandruzhin."

Father paled. I was fairly certain it was not because she had told him her surname, even though that information was usually reserved for the most formal or solemn of occasions. Father must have recognized her surname. It meant nothing to me.

"Druzhin?" he echoed. "Your father was Ambassador Druzhin?" I couldn't see Zhia's face; Father could. He paled further.

"You don't look well, sir," Zhia said. "Rois, please bring your father a chair."

I did so. I didn't feel well, either. Zhia had never done or said anything to suggest that her father had been at the top of the religious hierarchy, a position that had both spiritual and political clout.

Even if she wasn't a Singer, Zhia was anything but a nobody.

Father sat down, which made his head slightly lower than Zhia's. He was all but stammering when he said, "It would seem I owe you an apology." I was behind the chair and could now see Zhia. She was giving Father the half-quizzical, half-challenging look she'd once given me. "I do owe you an apology," Father amended.

Zhia looked at me and, with a dismissive gesture, said, "Do you mind?"

I was already starting toward the kitchen. Once there, I reluctantly closed the door.

Mother was in the kitchen. I hushed her anxious questions, trying to hear what was being said in the entrance hall. When I realized I wasn't going to be able to overhear the conversation, I turned back to her.

"Son, what's going on?" she asked, twisting her apron into a knot.

"Father is making his apologies to Ambassador Druzhin's daughter."

Mother's hands flew to her mouth. "How did he offend the Ambassador's daughter? Who is she?"

"Answering the second question will answer the first. She was my tour partner."

"Do you mean Zhia?" I nodded. "Oh, my. Should I serve food, or something?"

I laughed. "Mother, you're wonderful. You always know what's important. We'll probably want something to eat later. It won't have to be anything fancy. Right now, we're both in need of a bath and clean clothes, which is why I haven't hugged you."

"Thank you. I'm aware of that need." She studied me, a furrow between her eyebrows deepening by the moment. "What happened to you, Son? You're all cut, and bruised, and …" Her eyes became wide. "Raiders?" she whispered.

"Yes. Zhia saved my life. Only she, one of the eight others, and I survived."

"Oh, my," Mother said again. She drew a breath and became practical. "Ladies first in the tub, I'd say. If you'll start drawing water, I'll stoke the fire."

The tub in the washing room, just past the larders in the corridor behind the kitchen, was nearly full when Zhia limped into the kitchen. She took the chair Mother offered and allowed Mother to exclaim over her injuries and her ordeal, then expressed sincere appreciation for Mother's hospitality.

"It's the least we could do to thank you for saving our son's life."

When Mother bustled away to pour a final bucket of hot water into the tub and lay out towels, soap, and hairbrush, Zhia lifted her eyes to me. "What else did you tell her?"

"That's all. Is there some reason Mother shouldn't know the truth?"

"If she's going to treat me like someone special, yes."

"If you didn't want to be treated like someone special, why did you slam Father with the fact that you're Ambassador Druzhin's daughter?"

"Because as I understand your father, knowing that my father was important is more likely to encourage him to be decent to me—as decent as his condition allows—than anything else." She smiled. "By the way, he agreed to help you train me."

"Good," I said, though I was thinking that "agreed" was probably less than accurate. The words "duress" and "blackmail" more readily came to mind.

That was between Zhia and my father.

While Zhia bathed, Mother kept me busy heating water for my own bath. She busied herself preparing my former room for use. When Zhia announced she was leaving the washing room, presumably clad in nothing but a towel, Mother sent me into the front of the house, where Father pounced on me.

"Why didn't you tell me who she was?" he demanded.

"Because I found out at the same time you did. I can assure you there's been no reason for her to tell me her full name," I replied. I saw disbelief on his face.

"She never once made reference to her rank?"

"I did notice she was a bit more aware of the daemons than the rest of us; beyond that, which hardly screams 'Ambassador's daughter', no."

"Did she tell you I'm going to help train her?"

"Yes, she did; and I must thank you, Father. Everyone knows you're a Singer's Singer. Your help will be priceless."

I thought he looked pleased, though all he said was, "Strange, isn't it, that 'priceless' and 'worthless' sound like they should be the same but are opposite."

I was wondering what prompted that comment when Mother called that my bath was ready. I would have liked to do as Taf had said he intended and spend a day soaking. I did take a good, long time bathing to the accompaniment of rattling in the kitchen. From the sound of it, Mother was preparing a feast.

When I was clean and shaved, I went back into the kitchen, clutching a towel around my middle. "There are clothes in your room, Son," Mother said, busy with her cooking.

"Where's Zhia?"

"She's dressing in the other bedchamber. That is, if she was able to find something to wear."

The stairway to the second level opened off the kitchen. From old habit, I counted the steps as I climbed; though I didn't, as was my old habit, count aloud. There were nineteen steps, quite a few more and quite a bit steeper than was usual between levels in houses. I wondered how Zhia had managed them.

The door to my parents' bedchamber was closed. On my bed lay shirt and trousers that were, of course, Father's. I had to turn back the ends of the sleeves and the pant legs to make them shorter.

As I left my room, Zhia came out of the other one. Her feet were bare. She was clad in what had to be one my father's shirts that she had lengthened by sewing on part of one of Mother's skirts. Both garments were patterned; though the colors were similar, the designs clashed loudly.

"You decided to dress like a Singer," I teased.

"Very funny," she said, without appreciation. "I hope your mother won't mind. She did tell me to take whatever I could use. She didn't tell me I could help myself to her sewing basket; but only your father's shirts were big enough, and I couldn't wear just a shirt. As you can tell, it barely covered my knees."

"I don't think she'll mind. She's always wanted a girl to dress."

Along with the sounds of cooking, aromas were wafting up the stairs. Ignoring my last comment, Zhia leaned on the railing, sniffed, and said, "Whatever your mother is cooking smells wonderful."

I also leaned and sniffed. "It does. Mother's been at it the practically whole time we were bathing. I think it's going to be a banquet."

"Then I'll insist that she allow me to do the dishes. I'll also wash our clothes. In fact, I'll do that now while she's too busy to notice. Laundry is done in the washing room?"

I nodded. "The water from my bath is probably still there and still warm enough."

"Good. If you could haul rinse water for me, I'll get to that chore. By the way, what should I call your mother? If I'm going to be here a while, I can hardly point and say 'you', and 'Mother' just wouldn't be right."

"I doubt she'd object if you called her 'Mother'. Her name is Isia. Father's is Robil."

"So you're Rois Isianrobil." Dismay covered her face. "I am so sorry. I was thinking aloud. I don't expect you to ask me to be your wife just because I know your full name."

"Since I didn't actually tell you my full name, I wasn't planning to ask you. In fact, I hardly recognize my own name. Growing up I was usually known as 'High Note's son.'"

She laughed and winced. "'High Note' was your father's stage name? That's clever, and certainly appropriate." She eyed me. "With your bruises as yellow as they are, 'Golden Throat' is just right for you. Of course, once I hear you sing, I'll know the real reason that's your stage name."

That comment could have been either complimentary or critical. Though I hoped it was the former, I decided not to ask. I did ask, "Does Taf know your full name?"

She bristled. "Certainly not! Do you think I'm the kind of woman who goes around telling men my full name just because they've told me theirs?" Then, more mildly, she said, "I know, you're thinking that I told your father. I did that because if he had, indeed, known my father, he would then have the option of reconsidering how he treated me. If he and my father never met, it was nothing more than a formal introduction. Considering that our first meeting was anything but friendly, a formal introduction was appropriate."

"It was almost the last introduction he ever heard. I thought he was going to die of astonishment."

"I'm sorry. I certainly never expected so strong a reaction." She sounded truly contrite. "He's all right, isn't he?"

"Yes, once he got over suspecting me of knowing who you were and not telling him."

"So I got you in trouble with your father."

"It doesn't take much." The words were full of bitter resignation.

She laid her hand on mine and said, again, "I'm sorry." Then, as quickly as if my hand was hot, she removed hers. She leaned farther over the railing. "Call me a coward, but I don't especially want to go down those stairs. Going up wasn't easy."

"Oh, yes, I think you're a coward," I said, with undisguised sarcasm. In normal tones, I asked, "Why don't you do it sitting down rather than standing up? That would spare your foot, at least a little."

"I guess that'd be best." She made a sound of derision. "What a spectacle that'll be! I just hope your parents don't see me. You don't need to watch, either."

"I'll start drawing rinse water," I said, and went downstairs.

Mother was entirely involved with her cooking. Both Zhia and I were able to return to the washing room without her seeing us. As Zhia rather half-heartedly scrubbed the clothes, she said, "I'm glad your mother doesn't have to do this. These are vile."

"Why bother washing them, then? We can get different ones."

"You might be comfortable with the idea of going to a market dressed in borrowed clothes; I'm not. Besides, how would I pay for anything?"

Before I could answer, I heard Mother calling my name. "Coming!" I replied, and went to the kitchen. "Yes, Mother?"

"Would you see if Zhia is ready to eat? I'm about to put the food on the table."

She went into the dining room. I slipped quickly back into the washing room. "Come on. Food's ready."

"All right. A good soak won't hurt those clothes at all."

"You gave yourself a good soak, too, I see," I said.

Mother frowned when she saw Zhia. Whether it was because her clothes were wet or because of what she had chosen, I didn't know.

Quickly, Zhia said, "Please pardon me if I was presumptuous in taking these clothes. I know you said I could use what I needed, but I'm sure you were expecting to have anything I borrowed back in one piece. The only thing I could find that fit was one of your husband's shirts, and I didn't dare be seen in just a shirt; but that meal smells so wonderful I had to figure out some way to be able to come downstairs and eat."

Looking a little bemused at the torrent of words, Mother said, "That's quite all right."

"Thank you. You're very gracious. And though I already know you're Rois' mother and we've chatted and I'm wearing your clothes and am about to eat your food, we haven't really been introduced. I'm Zhia."

"I'm Isia. But surely I'm not to address you simply as 'Zhia.'"

"I wish you would. Even when my parents were alive, they didn't encourage me to stand on formality or insist on titles. As the wheel of the stars has turned many times since they died, I'm even less accustomed to deference. And, since Rois has indicated that I will possibly be staying with you and your husband for some time—if that is acceptable to you, of course—I would appreciate not being treated like a guest."

"But you are our guest."

"Perhaps today. But that makes you and your husband my hosts. Since I brought no gift to thank you for your hospitality, I insist on washing the dishes."

Mother looked even more confused. With consummate courtesy, Zhia had put Mother in the position of being unable to refuse her offer of cleaning up after the meal.

Mother wasn't that easily cornered. "But you must allow someone to help you. With your hurt foot, you shouldn't be drawing water."

Zhia smiled warmly. "Thank you for thinking of that. Rois will help me. After working so hard, first to provide baths for us—that was the most welcome bath I've had in a long time!—and then to prepare this lovely meal, you've earned the right to sit and relax."

Beaming, Mother collected a platter of food and hurried into the dining room.

"Thanks for volunteering me," I said, quietly. "I think Mother was looking for another chance to chat with you."

"Very likely," Zhia replied, also quietly. "But am I not right in thinking that the water is outside? Your mother won't be able to draw it."

"That's true. Why don't I just do the dishes and you can also sit and relax?"

Mother returned for yet more food. When she left the kitchen, Zhia answered, "Because talking is still hard on my voice, and trying to carry on polite conversation with people I don't know is tiring. Your mother is a lovely person. I want to get to know both her and your father better; but I'm not up to it yet."

"I'd noticed your voice is raspy again. I'll handle conversation at the table."

"All right." Raising her voice, Zhia said, "If you and I help your mother, we can eat that much sooner."

CHAPTER SIXTEEN

MOTHER TRULY HAD SPREAD a feast. As we seated ourselves, I said, "Mother, didn't I say the meal didn't have to be fancy? This would be enough for the whole tour. In fact, I doubt even those we lost are eating this well where they now dwell."

Mother smiled. Father said, "Would Ambassador Druzhin's daughter ask a blessing?"

I think I hid surprise better than Mother did. Though the ritual is sometimes observed at the Hall, I couldn't remember its ever being part of a meal at my parents' home.

Zhia smiled and said, "I'm honored, sir; but not even an Ambassador's daughter would think of depriving her host of that privilege."

Father had no choice but to bow his head and mumble something. He was probably cursing Zhia's quickness.

As he raised his head, Zhia murmured, "Even so," the ritual close which Father had forgotten to say.

Father was a proud man. He had agreed to train Zhia, but he wasn't going to tolerate being made to look a fool at his own table. It didn't matter to him that he had more or less asked to be shamed. Though I knew he would retaliate,

I didn't know when or how.

Father wasn't a patient man. His next attempt to discomfit Zhia was immediate and no more successful than the first one. As he served himself from the heaping platters and passed one platter to me, he said to Zhia, "That is a very ugly shirt."

Gravely, she replied, "I'm glad to hear you say that, sir. I was worried you would miss it when I won't be able to return it to you."

Father looked across the table at Mother, who nodded. Tacitly admitting defeat, at least for the moment, Father turned to me and said, "So tell me about your tour, Son. How did it go before the raiders ended it?"

To give myself time to think, I took another platter from Father and piled yet more food on my plate. If I glossed over too much, I would look remiss, because the reason why the tour was where it was when the raiders struck wouldn't be clear. If I gave all the details, I would look incompetent. I glanced at Zhia, who was across the table from me. She was complimenting Mother on the meal and didn't see my unspoken plea. I was on my own.

"The tour was an unmitigated disaster, Father. With less than a day's preparation, I was supposed to lead nine first-timers, most of whom had never even sat on a tebec, to a series of engagements in towns I'd never heard of. The whiner got bitten, the shirker had to go back for the instruments he'd left behind and then let them get rained on, and the tebecs got into our food. And that was just the first day." I paused to eat a few bites, bracing myself for contempt or ridicule, at the least.

All Father said was, "You had less than a day to prepare?"

"Yes. The day the Master told me I was going and gave me a schedule—a very unusual schedule—is the day Zhia and I first came here. After we left here, we went back to the Hall to pack. After the midday meal the next day, we were all on the road."

"Not quite daybreak," was Father's wry comment.

"No, but that meal probably kept the tour from being even worse."

"What else went wrong?"

"Someone got saddle sores. They went bad, and we were delayed at a Quarter

Rest for several days."

"Someone?" Father asked, looking at Zhia with disdain.

With an exasperated sigh, I said, "No, Father; I got them. Zhia cared for me and kept the others busy until we could get back on the road. One of the things she did was send some of the group to another Hall for new strings and drum heads, and food."

For the first time, Father regarded Zhia with something like respect before returning his attention to me. "So did you ever get to any of your engagements?"

"Not a one. We would have been late to the first two, so I was going to have us begin at the third place, Hollan's Town…"

"'Hollan's Town'?" Father echoed in his gravelly whisper. "Gadig had first-timers going that far from the Hall?"

"Gadig is the Master's name?" I asked.

"Yes, and don't let me catch you using it."

"No, sir. And yes, our first three engagements were Rillford, Torlea, and Hollan's Town." Father was shaking his head and muttering under his breath as I listed the names. "As I said, since we wouldn't have made either of the first two places on schedule, I decided we'd start at Hollan's Town. We had stopped along the road for a meal when the raiders attacked. Zhia, a man named Taf, and I survived."

"Your mother says you told her Zhia saved your life."

"Zhia may deny it, but yes. I was grappling with a raider who had a knife. I got him to drop it, but he started to choke me. Zhia kicked a stone that hit him, let loose a scream that panicked the tebecs, and threw a swarmer's nest among the other raiders. The tebecs and the swarmers took care of some of the raiders. Zhia had an ax. She took care of more of them. The rest ran away."

There was a long silence, then Father said, "No one defeats raiders." He looked at Zhia, who was picking at her food. "You killed raiders with an ax." By making it a statement rather than a question, he emphasized the disbelief his tone made all too apparent.

Zhia met his eyes. Though she was flushed with anger or embarrassment (possibly both), she replied, smoothly, "Actually, when they saw me, they laughed themselves to death." She stood and looked at Mother. "Isia, the meal is wonderful. Pardon my not being able to do it justice. Please excuse me." She went into the kitchen.

Mother started to rise. I said, "Please sit down, Mother. I'll speak to Zhia myself when she's... I'll talk to her later." I turned to Father. "Yes, Father, Zhia killed seven raiders with an ax. She killed an eighth man by beating his head in with a stone. Are there any other gory details you would like while we're eating?"

After another and considerably more tense silence, Father said, "Considering raiders have attacked and defeated armed parties, one woman with an ax is not going to be able to beat them off. I'll give Zhia whatever credit you think she's due, but I still want to know how you survived."

Realizing that was as much of an apology as I'd get from Father—and knowing that Zhia wouldn't get even that much—I said, "Taf had managed to get into a tree. He had a good view of the skirmish. He said..."

"'Skirmish'?" Father echoed, a smile tugging at the corners of his mouth.

"That might not be the right word; I'm a Singer, not a soldier," I said. "Anyway, Taf said it looked to him like the raiders were working by rote, so when the unexpected happened—a cloud of stinging insects, milling tebecs, and a furious female in a killing rage—they couldn't change their routine. Their victims had the advantage of surprise."

"The raiders weren't ready to improvise," Father said.

"Precisely. Judging from what happened to us, Taf and I speculated that the raiders prefer to attack from heights. What did the damage to my tour was darts, possibly poisoned, which suddenly rained down on us from above. We thought that if places with heights on either side of the road were identified and there were records of where raider attacks had happened, we might be able to see a pattern that would give travelers an idea of places to avoid. If the travelers had armed escorts, perhaps the guards could scout ahead when potentially dangerous areas were near."

Father was nodding. "That makes sense. But you still haven't told me how three of you survived. Now that you've mentioned a rain of possibly poisoned darts, I'm even more curious."

I had hoped he hadn't noticed the omission. "I told you we'd stopped for a meal. Zhia had gone to cut firewood—other than me, she was apparently the only one on the tour who knew how to use an ax—and the rest of us were just lazing around. I became concerned with how long she was gone, and decided to look for her. Taf offered to help, so the three of us weren't with the others when the attack began."

"Now that I believe. I can't believe that, once you knew your tour was being attacked—which I assume you did—you didn't run as fast as you could the opposite direction."

"Taf did run. Seeing my group being massacred stunned me. I may not have been a good tour leader, but I was that much of a tour leader. By the time I knew I'd better run, too, it was too late. Had Zhia not acted, it would have been irrevocably too late."

"Why haven't you asked her to be your wife?" Mother asked. She had been silent so long the question startled both Father and me.

I stared at her. "Why should I do that? Because she saved my life?"

"Because you care for her. Don't look at me like that, Son. I may not know your voice as well as I know your father's, but I know it well enough. You may have succeeded in lying to yourself; you don't fool me. It's just as clear that this Taf person did ask her."

"How is it clear?" I asked.

Mother gave me a pitying look. "Because you say his name with the same intonation you use when you say 'raiders'. And because two people don't have to look for someone who's chopping wood. One need only follow the sound of the ax. However, if Zhia is more to the two of you than just another tour member, neither of you would be willing to allow the other to search for her alone."

"Assuming all those things are right, Mother—and I'm not saying they are— that still doesn't mean I'd ask her to be my wife."

"Then you deserve whatever merely pretty, empty-headed toy you end up with." With an air of finality, Mother rose and began to clear the table.

I turned to Father, who was trying not to look amused. When Mother had gone into the kitchen, he said, "Your mother's right about how you sound when you say Zhia's name, Son. You're right not to mistake gratitude for anything else. Were Ambassador Druzhin still alive, I would probably encourage you to cultivate Zhia's friendship… if nothing else. It's good to have friends in high places; relatives in high places are even better. Since Zhia's an orphan and isn't very pretty—your mother doesn't understand what that means to a man—and her escapade with the raiders is likely to leave lasting marks…Well, I disagree with your mother. I think you can do better than Zhia."

I stood and began grabbing things from the table. "Thank you for your advice. I need to say that what you and Mother have interpreted as a distinctive and, apparently, even betraying tone in my voice is only the result of my having been throttled by a raider. I have no intention of asking Zhia to be my wife."

"Even so," Father said as I carried a stack of dishes to the kitchen.

I walked into the middle of a polite argument. Zhia, whose hands were already in the dishwater, was reminding Mother that she—Zhia—was assuming the chore as a gift to Mother, as hostess. Mother was insisting that Zhia shouldn't be standing on her hurt foot. Obviously, both were right. It was also obvious that the argument wouldn't stay polite much longer.

"Ladies," I said in a lull, setting the dishes on a table, "you already came to an agreement about this chore. Mother, if you'll put the leftovers away, I'll finish clearing the table and then help Zhia with the dishes."

When Mother had stored the uneaten food, I poured wine and, a goblet in each hand, shooed her into the front room, where she sat on the divan next to Father. With my foot I nudged a hassock in front of her, then handed wine to her and to Father, said, "Thank you for a great meal, Mother," and bent to kiss her cheek.

"You're welcome, Son. I'm so glad you're still here to eat a meal in this house," was her tearful reply.

I returned to the kitchen. There was very little left for me to do except to dry the dishes and put them away. When that was done, I asked, "Have the clothes soaked long enough?"

"Yes. They're already hanging to dry."

"Then it's time for you to make Mother happy and get off your foot. Shall we join my parents in the front room?"

"No, thank you. I don't think I can avoid any more verbal traps today. Besides, with all the cooking, it's hot in here."

It was. "Then let's sit outside the back door until the rain comes." When she nodded, I added, "You go ahead. I'll see if my parents need a refill."

Father had his arm around Mother. Both were asleep. Quietly, I collected their empty goblets and took them to the kitchen. Taking the wine jug and two more goblets, I joined Zhia outside. I filled the cups and handed one to Zhia.

"The old folks are asleep. Now we can have a party," I said, with false heartiness.

Zhia stared at me. "What?"

"It's a joke. Didn't you ever pretend to be asleep and get up after your parents were really asleep and do things you knew they wouldn't approve of?"

"No." Zhia drank deeply.

Alarmed, I said, "Better slow down. You didn't eat much supper."

"How could I, with you and your father rehashing the tour and him baiting me with every other word?" She sipped, then said, slowly, "I know you meant well when you proposed training me to be a Singer. I'm grateful. I was surprised and pleased when your father agreed to help; but I'm not going to be able to do this. I can't be on guard all the time. I can't be clever all the time. I don't care if I have to spend the rest of my life sweeping, tomorrow I'm going back to the Hall."

I couldn't assure her that Father wouldn't bait her; most likely he would. In fact, if Zhia was right, his condition (as she had termed it) would compel him to be increasingly cruel in his speech. However, I doubted Father would harm her with more than words. The vigilance Zhia dreaded needing around Father was nothing compared to what I knew she'd need at the Hall. I hadn't told her of the danger I feared for her at the Hall, or of my suspicion that the Master was behind it.

Remembering that the Master's name was Gadig made me remember my relief when Father had also shown dismay at the tour arrangements. Reason had already told me I wasn't to blame for the tour's failure; pride doesn't always listen to reason.

I hoped Zhia's pride would listen to reason. "I'm not trying to make you change your mind. However, I'm suggesting you not make a final decision until morning."

"That's fair; but I don't expect anything to be different in the morning." She drained her cup and held it out to be refilled. With what was obviously a deliberate change of subject, she said, "I'm glad you suggested coming outside. The air out here feels like it did in the hollow before…" She had some wine to clear her throat. "Had things turned out differently, would the tour have been to Hollan's Town by now?"

I counted back. "Actually, we would have been on our way to our fourth engagement. I don't remember the name. Cliff something? It doesn't matter now."

Another sip, then she asked, "Ought we to get a message to the Hall sooner than five or six days from now so families will know their sons aren't coming home?"

"That would be a decent thing to do. Drinking to those we lost would also be decent." I stood, faced the sunset, and raised my goblet. "To Norjy. To Vel. To Hink. To Birl. To Hadden. To Mariz. To Turiz." I paused after each name for a sip of wine.

"Wait," Zhia said. "I'm still on the fourth name." She lowered her goblet and asked, "Who did you say after Nirl? Birl, I mean?" Her voice was slurred. Her goblet was empty.

I picked up the wine jug. It had been more than half full; it was now nearly empty. "Zhia, were you drinking an entire cup of wine for each name? The ritual is a sip." I took the goblet from her and set it aside. "You're going to feel terrible in the morning."

"I feel fine now. My foot doesn't hurt."

"I don't doubt that." It would surprise me to learn she could feel her feet at all. I sat down. She leaned against me. I'm fairly certain that, had I not been sitting beside her, she would have fallen over.

"We didn't drink to Taf's tebec. It helped us a lot," she managed to say.

I poured enough wine for one swallow into each goblet. "To Taf's tebec."

The eyes that regarded me over the newly-emptied cup were already blood-shot. "Could we drink to Pandir?"

Again, I doled out a scant mouthful. "Let's make this one to Pandir and your family and Pandir's family. And that's all we're going to drink to."

When that wine was gone, Zhia sat looking mournfully into her goblet. "I'll never be a Singer."

"Yes, you will, "I said gently. "It'll take work, but I know you're willing to work. You can do it. Pandir knew that, too."

"No. I failed him. When he was sick, I couldn't help him. And then I couldn't keep Grandmother's house. And then the tour was a disaster. It's all my fault." Her voice was grating worse with every word, whether from overuse or emotion, I didn't know.

I knew part of her discouragement was from the amount of wine she'd had. Though I doubted it would do much good, I thought I should try to counter her misconceptions. "The illness that took Pandir was beyond the remedying of doctors. You aren't a doctor; but you did save me. Since you were just a child and didn't know what arrangements your grandmother had made, of course you weren't ready or able to assume a large debt. And if I have to say it every day the rest of my life before you believe it, I will: it's thanks to you that the tour wasn't more of a disaster than it was. None of us was supposed to return. Three of us did."

"But Pandir's parents and the rest of the merchants didn't. My baby didn't." Her eyes brimmed; she sniffed. "Why did they do that to Pandizh?" She looked at me. "Do you know what baby tastes like? It tastes like what your mother cooked today."

Her face suddenly ashen, she rose and hobbled quickly into the clump of trees. When I reached her, she had already emptied herself of the wine and the little bit of supper she'd eaten. She was sitting back on her heels, clutching her middle and wincing as her weight crushed her foot. "I can't do this," she repeated.

"I don't know what 'this' you mean, but if you ever drink that much wine again, I'll…"

"You'll do what?" Bitter amusement colored the question. "Kill me? Please?"

"No, I'll think of something you wouldn't want me to do." The wind was freshening; the rain was closing in. "Let's get back to the house before we get wet. You'll want to wash your face and rinse the taste out of your mouth."

She nodded. "And I want to lie down, but if I tell your mother I can't manage the steps she'll say I shouldn't have done the dishes, and your father will think…"

I interrupted her. "Father will think that neither of us has sense enough to come in out of the rain." It was much closer; I could smell the moisture in the air. "Grab my hand; I'll help you up. Do you want to lean on me, or can you walk that far?"

"I think I can walk." She raised bleary eyes to me. "I love you."

Knowing she had drunk enough wine to make her feel affection for a raider, all I did was smile and say, "Hurry. Here comes the rain."

CHAPTER SEVENTEEN

W HETHER OR NOT ZHIA remembered her resolve to return to the Hall, Father gave her no chance to act on her decision.

The merest sliver of sun was visible when he pulled the covers off me and almost literally dragged me out of bed, saying, "Come on. We have work to do."

I struggled into my—his—clothes and followed him down the steep stairs, stumbling occasionally because he hadn't given me time to re-roll the trouser legs. I was hoping either that he hadn't already been downstairs or that he hadn't wakened Zhia so rudely.

When we had come inside the previous night, we had found that Father and Mother had vacated the divan. I had gathered blankets, settled Zhia there, and told her to give me what she was wearing, because it had been fouled when she was sick. I had washed the garment and hung it with our other clothes. If Father had pulled the covers off Zhia, who was sleeping naked…

I told myself that had Zhia been awakened so unceremoniously, I would have heard her reaction. In fact, it would likely have been audible at the Hall. My fears were allayed when we reached the kitchen and Father said, "Where's Zhia? I thought she wanted to be trained as a Singer. She can't sleep all day if she's going to learn what she needs to know."

I regarded Father with pleased surprise. Save for his damaged voice, he
looked and acted like the enthusiastic, vigorous Singer I remembered. I
remembered his comment about worthless and priceless, and realized he
had been talking about himself.

"Shouldn't we break our fast before we start work?" I asked. "Maybe you
aren't hungry, but I am, and Zhia didn't have much supper. I know she'd be
pleased if there was food ready when she got up." Realizing Father would
probably bring out supper leftovers and fearing what seeing that food again
might do to Zhia, I added, "What would be best, just bread and something to
drink, like before a performance?" Father nodded. "All right. I'll wake Zhia."

I went into the washing room. The last-laundered garment was still damp;
Zhia's shirt and trousers were dry. I took them with me into the front room.
When I shook Zhia's shoulder, she groaned and opened her eyes just a slit.
"Go away."

"Sorry, but no. Instructor Robil says it's time to start training."

She turned her head so she could see out the window. "It's not even daybreak."

"I know; but Father is all eager. Here, I brought your clothes."

Clutching the blanket to herself, she sat up and groaned again. "Your father
was right; I'm stupid."

"Some food will help your headache," I said. "Father's fixing it now."

"Not…"

"Not what you had last night. Bread and fruit juice or water or something."

"Does your father know I intend to return to the Hall today?" When I said
nothing, she asked, sharply, "Didn't you tell him? I told you I wouldn't change
my mind. And you told me you wouldn't try to make me do so."

"I said that, and I meant it; but I didn't know this meant so much to Father."
I was so intent on pleading Father's case that I sank to my knees in front of
the divan and put my hands over Zhia's. "You should see him this morning.
He's excited. He's purposeful. He knows he's again needed for something he
thought he'd lost, something that used to be everything to him. He feels valued
again. You've given him back himself.

"I'm not asking you to change your mind, just change your schedule. Can't

you give Father one day to enjoy again having a reason to get out of bed, even
if it's before daybreak?"

Tears sparkled in Zhia's eyes and made her nose red. Those, along with a
brusque, "Get out of here so I can get dressed," were the only answer she gave
me, but I knew she would stay at least the one day I had requested.

Father was all but dancing with impatience. He kept urging us to eat quickly
until I said, "Father, how often when I was younger did you tell me Singers
don't gulp their food? Do you want to start by giving Zhia something to
unlearn?"

When Father finally ushered us into the front room, I was amused to see
that Zhia had taken time to fold the blankets and stack them neatly on the
divan. The message was clear: she was complying, not capitulating.

"Don't sit," Father said as Zhia and I headed for the divan. "We're going to
start at the beginning. Today you learn to breathe."

"With all respect, sir, I've been breathing all my life," Zhia said.

"But not properly. Breath is the basis for all sung music and all music from
wind instruments." He went on, making the lecture quite a bit more interesting than the one I'd heard from my instructor at the Hall. "You're standing
because that's the way a Singer breathes best," he finished. "Now, I want to see a
good, deep breath. No, no!" he exclaimed when Zhia obeyed. "You lifted your
shoulders. A Singer's shoulders do not move when he breathes. He breathes
from here." He pulled off his shirt, placed his hands just below his rib cage,
and drew several breaths, his hands moving outward a considerable distance
with each inhalation.

"Now try it again," he told Zhia. "Do as I did; put your hands on your belly
and make them move." He watched critically. "No, still not right. You stopped
lifting your shoulders, but you're not breathing any deeper than your chest.
Son, take off your shirt and show her how it's done."

"Good morning," came Mother's voice from the doorway. She sounded surprised, as well she might, seeing two of us half-dressed and all of us doing
nothing but breathing. "Has anyone eaten?"

"Yes, thank you," I replied. "But we didn't wash the dishes."

"I can see you're all far too busy for that," was her parting comment. The breathing lesson was interrupted by laughter.

As a good teacher will, Father made the interruption part of the lesson. "When you were laughing, Zhia, the breath was going where it was supposed to go. Say 'ha, ha, ha' with your hands in place. Do you feel that? That's where you breathe from. Try another deep breath." Obviously dissatisfied with the effort and just as obviously trying to be patient, Father said, "Though you say you've been breathing all your life, if you ate as ineffectively as you breathe, you'd have starved to death long ago." He stepped up to Zhia, put his hands around her body with his thumbs just below her rib cage and, saying "Breathe from here," pushed hard.

Zhia didn't breathe; she gasped. She became so pale that Father grabbed her upper arms and tried to steer her toward the divan.

She resisted, saying, "Thank you. I'm all right," but one hand cradled her left ribs. Suddenly, I guessed what was wrong. "Zhia, lift your shirt."

"Son," Father began.

"Father, this isn't what you think. Zhia, lift your shirt or I'll lift it for you."

When she gave me an all-too-familiar cold glare, I knew my guess was right. She stepped away from Father, raised the left side of her shirt to just under her breast, and briefly exposed a livid bruise so big some of it was still hidden by her clothes.

Over Father's shocked exclamation, I snapped, "Zhia..."

"Scolding her won't do anything for cracked or broken ribs," Father said. "Who is the doctor at the Hall?"

"Aplin."

"I'll fetch him." As Father pulled on his shirt, he nodded at the divan and said to Zhia, "Sit there and don't go anywhere." Zhia obeyed; Father left the house.

As I put my own shirt on, I said, "You may think you're being heroic walking around hurt and in pain. I call it stupid. That happened when the raider tripped you, didn't it?" She nodded. "So when you grabbed the rock to bash in his head, you already knew it was there, because that's what hurt you." She nodded again. "When I was trying to rub your back, was I hurting your ribs, or was I making you remember… that other day?"

"Both, but mostly the second."

"That's a mercy, I guess. But that bathing with your clothes on, you did that to hide that injury, too, didn't you?" Another nod. "How did you manage to carry a cloakful of firewood, or all those bodies? Did it occur to you that that kind of exertion might make the injury worse? Did it occur to you that that one injury was probably the worst one you suffered, and that it probably slowed your recovering from the others? Don't you want to get better?"

"I didn't want to be a problem." She spoke so softly I could hardly hear her.

"Well, you are a problem! To yourself. You can forget your plan to return to the Hall. I'll be surprised if Aplin doesn't tell you to go to bed and stay there for a good five days."

"But I can't stay in this room."

"You let us worry about that." Mother came in, looking nearly as angry as she had the day before the tour began. "Son, I know very well you were not raised to think it's all right to shout at a woman. I'm ashamed of you. And where is your father?"

"He's gone to fetch the Hall doctor to look at Zhia."

"Is she ill?" Mother asked, then turned to Zhia. "Are you ill?"

"No," Zhia and I answered together. I added, "The doctor is going to look at Zhia's injuries." I hoped Mother hadn't noticed the pause when I caught myself before saying "ribs".

"First intelligent thing anyone has done since the two of you arrived," was Mother's scathing remark. Then she looked at Zhia and said, more gently, "You'll want to tidy yourself before the doctor looks at you. Robil was so eager to begin he must have had you at lessons before you could even smooth your hair. Come with me. You'll have time to freshen up."

"Only if your husband won't be angry," Zhia said. "He told me to sit here and not go anywhere."

Mother made a dismissive gesture. "He's being overruled. Come along."

I smiled as they left the front room. Rarely had I seen Mother so decisive. I wondered whether that was because such resoluteness was new for Mother, or because she had been deferring to Father ever since he asked her to be his wife and hadn't needed to show her ability to be firm.

When Father returned with Aplin, I decided it was the latter. Mother sent Father and me out of the front room while she remained to help Aplin. At least, that's why she said she remained. I suspected the real reason was two-fold: she considered it improper for Aplin to see Zhia without someone else present, and she thought Zhia would likely be more at ease if the "someone else" were a woman.

Father and I waited in the dining room. I brought in bread, a jug of wine, and goblets. While we nibbled, Father said, "I saw the Master when I was at the Hall. He hadn't yet heard about the fate of your tour, and was quite upset when I told him. He couldn't tell me often enough how glad he was that you survived. When I asked him about your schedule, he again became distressed and showed me a schedule that listed none of the places you mentioned. He said he couldn't imagine how you'd gotten your hands on the wrong schedule." He paused to drink.

"And?" I prompted, fearing Father no longer believed me.

"Even when he was just a Singer and not a Master Gadig couldn't control his voice," Father said, contempt evident despite his rasping voice. "He was lying with every word."

"Does he know you didn't believe him?"

With a pitying look, Father said, "Son, I am not a fool. The man is hiding something, but I won't be able to find out what it is if I put him on his guard. I don't know exactly what he's doing; but it almost cost me my son, and I'm going to find out. It was curious that he didn't inquire about Zhia."

"Does he know she survived?"

"Yes. Since I was there to fetch the doctor, I had to tell him she was injured. If he understood what I said to mean that she's badly injured, that's his problem." With a satisfied smile, he drained his goblet.

Never had I admired Father more. Still… "But Aplin will tell him the truth," I said.

"No matter. Until then, Gadig can worry."

"If he's worrying, Father, I doubt it's about whether Zhia will recover, but about what she can say when she does." Then I told him what Zhia had said about her arrangement with the Master, and how the debt—a debt she had not yet incurred—had never been paid off.

"By Darl!" Father said, his expression hard. "I noticed there seemed to be an unusual number of women employed at that Hall. If wonder if any of them fell into the same trap."

Pleased that he was reasoning as I had, I started to tell him that Taf was supposed to make just that inquiry. Then I hesitated, struck by the oddness of Father's seeming sympathy for the plight of would-be female Singers. Some of my strongest memories were of this man's railing against women at the Hall. Surely meeting Zhia hadn't wrought such a fundamental change in his attitude!

Cautiously, I said, "It's a rather clever way of keeping women from being Singers. I always thought you and the Master saw eye to eye on that matter."

"We do; but I don't approve of the use of deceit to accomplish that or any end. If Gadig simply told women who wanted to be admitted to his Hall they weren't welcome, that would be one thing. Leading them to believe that they were getting what they wanted and then using them as slaves is quite another, and quite unacceptable."

Though encouraged, I wanted to be sure of Father's allegiance before my plans went further. "If it could be proved that Zhia wasn't the only woman who had been given a false promise, where would you stand?"

"I'm a Singer. I claim to serve Nia Diva, so I stand for truth. I'm not so old and stuck in my ways that I think women can be prevented from being Singers. The wheel of the stars has turned fourteen times since I realized that was a hopeless cause! I didn't like it then. I don't like it now; but there is no one so foolish as the one who refuses to change when the change has already happened." He poured himself more wine, sipped, and added, "And yes, Son, Zhia is one reason I'm not as opposed to women Singers as I was before, even if right now she's only a Singer by virtue of having been on a tour."

"That's fair," I said. I raised my goblet. "To finding out what's going on at the Hall."

"To truth," Father said by way of agreement. We drank.

Aplin came in. I fetched another goblet and poured wine. After he thanked me, he said, "Zhia has broken ribs. Breathing lessons, any singing, or even much talking will be things she shouldn't do until the ribs mend."

"Did I…" Father began.

"They were broken before today. Your pressing on them didn't help; but you didn't break them." Father looked relieved. "Her foot is also broken. I set it as well as I could; but it will never be right. She used it too much. I think the broken edges of the bones have been somewhat crushed. Her throat doesn't appear to have any lasting damage. Refraining from singing and doing little speaking will help it as well as her ribs." He refreshed himself, then said to me, "I understand you were also injured."

"Besides my throat, just some cuts on my arms."

"Shirt off. Let me see." As he examined me, Aplin added, "From what your mother told me, Zhia isn't one to spare herself unnecessary exertion."

Mother wouldn't have said that simply because Zhia insisted on washing the dishes. She must have overheard what I'd said to Zhia after Father left. I had probably been shouting. Being around Zhia often makes me want to shout.

I said, "I've noticed that, too. Worse, she doesn't tell anyone when she's hurt."

"What is it with these women?" Aplin mused. "I ran into the same thing with Noia."

"What happened to Noia?" I asked, sharply.

"She fell down stairs and tried to go to class with a sprained ankle and a cracked skull. No one knew she'd been hurt until she passed out."

Chapter Eighteen

"Noia's been hurt?" Taf echoed.

It was four days later. Taf was on his way back to the Hall. He had stopped at my parents' house to find out how Zhia was. The explanation he offered was that, if she was no better or if she had become worse, he would send Aplin before he had his day-long soak. He needed the bath worse than ever, but that's not why I was speaking with him outside. My going out to meet him spared him having to dismount and remount the tebec the farmer had been keeping as surety against the return of the cart and chero. It was only natural that in telling him what the doctor had said about Zhia I would share news of Noia's mishap, also.

"Aplin says Noia will be all right," I assured Taf, who didn't look convinced.

"What does he know?" Taf exclaimed. "I'll bet anything someone pushed her down those stairs. Now that she's got a sprained ankle, she'll be that much more vulnerable. I've got to get back." His tone suggested he'd finally come to a decision about making Zhia his wife.

"Taf, as a friend, let me suggest you have a bath before you see Noia."

He grinned. "That bad, huh?"

"Maybe it's the tebec, but I think it's you. And Taf, try to remember to ask the female servants how they happen to be working there."

"I will. I've already been working out clever ways of introducing both myself and the subject. Don't worry. Tell Zhia I sent greetings."

"I'll do that." When tebec and rider were out of sight I returned to the front room. Zhia sat on the divan, her injured foot propped on a hassock, just as she'd done the last four days, listening to Father explain music theory, just as he'd done the last four days.

"If I may interrupt," I began.

"Please do," Zhia said, on a note of desperation. "I'm still not getting this."

"All the more reason not to interrupt," I said, sympathetically. Music theory had never been my best class. When Father had announced music theory lessons would substitute for the banned breathing lessons, I had thought with dread that I'd have to listen, too. As it turned out, with Father teaching and unavailable to run errands for Mother, that job became mine. I had spent the last four days making trips to market.

I went on, "However, I told Taf I'd convey his greetings. Zhia, greetings from Taf."

Zhia smiled. "Thank you." Her smile drooped. "I still say that this might be easier if there were something to look at while you're talking, Instructor Robil, something that showed what you're trying to teach me." Father agreed. He and I had thought long and hard about the problem, but had arrived at no answer. Father had proposed writing on the wall, but Mother had immediately and indignantly rejected the idea. Paper would have been ideal had it been larger and not so expensive.

"Even if I didn't understand, I'd be better able to ask stupid questions," Zhia finished.

Father tried to hide a smile. Though it pleased him when she called him "Instructor Robil", he sounded stern when he said, "Lacking that, you'll simply have to pay closer attention. But you're asking plenty of stupid questions already."

Mother came in with a tray of food. "I can tell it's time for everyone to stop and eat. No wonder the child can't understand what you're trying to say, Robil, she's hungry!"

Father struggled visibly to keep back another snide comment. When he succeeded, he apologized for his comment about stupid questions.

"Don't apologize for truth," Zhia said as she began to eat. "I never imagined music was so complicated! This is a lot different from…from what I thought it would be."

"You thought all there was to being a Singer was singing?" Father asked. "I think that's why the Theory and Composition class is required; it helps weed out those who aren't willing to work at the craft." Then he added, "Of course, I still don't know if you can sing. Son, did you ever hear her?"

"No." I was wondering whether what Zhia had stopped herself from saying had been a reference to singing lullabies to Pandizh.

"Frankly, sir, I'm not sure of that myself," Zhia said. "Someone whose brother is a Singer told me I should be a Singer. I may actually sound like the squeaky wheel you once likened me to."

"I apologize for that," Father said.

"It's in the past." A smile lit her face. "What do you think? Would 'Squeaky Wheel' be a good stage name for me?"

"Right now, yes," I said. "Aplin did tell you not to talk very much, didn't he? Besides, you don't choose your own stage name."

"Really? So if you had a choice, Rois—sorry about that," she said, grimacing. "If the choice were yours, Rois, what would your stage name be?"

I had never considered the question, and admitted as much.

Mother spoke up. "I never thought 'Golden Throat' was good, because it suggests a more metallic quality than your voice has. Your voice sounds more like twilight would sound, if it could be heard."

"That's a bit long for a name; but the idea is beautiful," Father said.

"'Eventide'," Zhia murmured.

The silence that ensued was clearly approving. Reluctantly, I said, "I hate to be the one who has to say it, but no matter how wonderful a stage name 'Eventide' might be for me, I already have one and don't get to have another. But thanks for thinking of it, Zhia."

"Back to music theory," Father said, setting aside his dishes.

Mother collected the uneaten food; I carried the plates back to the kitchen. When I set them down, I saw something written in a dusting of flour where Mother had been kneading bread dough. "What's this, Mother?" I asked, pointing.

"Oh, that's just things I need to remember to have you pick up at market tomorrow."

I know I was grinning as I cleared the remains of the meal from the wooden tray. I took flour from the crock and sprinkled it on the tray until a thin layer covered it.

Mother had been watching me. Now she voiced the thought her face clearly showed. "Son, have you lost your mind?"

"No, Mother, I think I've found an answer." I carried the tray into the front room and set it on the divan. With my finger, I drew musical notation in the flour and looked at Zhia. "Would this be helpful?"

I would like to be able to say that Zhia made rapid progress after that, but she didn't. However, she made steady progress. Even Father seemed pleased. Zhia was also pleased, less because she was finally starting to understand music theory than because Father had decided to teach Theory and Composition only until the midday meal. After that meal, Father began teaching her various rhythms. There were no drums in the house, but as mothers of small children know, just about anything can be drummed on.

Mother endured this addition to Zhia's lessons for three or four days before she decreed that rhythm would be taught outside. I was usually back from market by then, and joined these lessons. Rhythm is one of my stronger skills. It was soon clear that Zhia would never be a drummer.

"Just count," Father would say, with greater or lesser amounts of exasperation. "You can count, can't you? One, two, three. Sometimes it's one, two, three, four. Or one and two and... Just count!"

One day, he lost his patience completely and growled, "You'd better be able to sing, woman, or I've been wasting a lot of time!"

Zhia had been on the verge of tears for most of the lesson, probably for the reason that women often are on the verge of tears. This comment broke her control. With a sobbing breath, she disappeared into the clump of trees.

Father stared after her. His shoulders sagged. "I'm sorry, Son. Sometimes the harsh words just slip out."

"I know that, Father. Zhia does, too. Surely you've noticed that usually she takes them in stride, and sometimes even agrees with you. But today I think you touched on what's probably her biggest fear: finding out that she really can't sing.

"For at least four turns of the star wheel she's dreamed of being a Singer, and she still doesn't know whether she can achieve it. Theory still confuses her, rhythm... well, I've heard it said that either you have it or you don't, and she doesn't; so drums—one instrument she could be learning while she recovers—are out. What does that leave her? Even were there any instruments here for her to practice with, she won't be able to play a wind instrument until her ribs are whole.

"Now that she knows that being able to sing isn't enough, and not knowing whether she even can sing, she's probably convinced herself that besides wasting your time—which her sense of courtesy would find intolerable— she's wasting her own, as well."

"What do you suggest?" Father asked.

I laughed, humorlessly. "Had I known I had to propose a solution, I would have kept my mouth shut. I would say give her a few days off, but I don't think she's accustomed to being idle. The lessons at least give her something to fill the time while she isn't supposed to walk or talk or work or sing or..."

"Or live," Father finished. "I wonder if she could learn some of the basic songs simply by listening rather than singing along."

"It wouldn't hurt to try. She might regard it as more hopeful than spending afternoons beating on things with sticks." I stood. "I'll find her so you can tell her the good news."

Zhia wasn't in the clump of trees. Mother said she hadn't come in the back door, nor was she in any of the rooms Mother couldn't see from the kitchen. However, from one of the upstairs windows I saw two shapes moving on the lane. One limped.

I went out the back door, said to Father, "I think I've found her," and went down the lane—surprisingly far down, actually—to meet the people I'd seen approaching.

One was Zhia; the other, Taf. From the way he was holding Zhia's arm I guessed he was not so much supporting her as restraining her.

Taf said, "This seems to be my day for running into lost things. Zhia wouldn't tell me where she was going. Maybe she'll tell you." He glared at Zhia; she glared back.

"Let me guess," I said. "You were going back to the Hall."

Now she glared at me. "At least I know I can sweep."

"When you're hurt? I don't think so."

"Why not? I've done it before," she snapped.

"When?" Taf and I asked together, in a very different tone of voice.

Now looking concerned rather than defensive, Zhia answered, "Once when I fell down the stairs. When it was clear that I wasn't badly hurt, I was sent back to work."

Taf and I exchanged a grim look. "Who sent you back to work?" Taf asked.

"The Master."

I asked, "How badly hurt were you?"

"I had a headache for a couple of days. I was bruised. Nothing serious." She misinterpreted the expression on Taf's and my faces and said, "So I was clumsy. That wasn't the first time I got hurt working at the Hall."

Taf groaned. "Did you fall down stairs more than once?"

"Yes, actually, a couple of times. Maybe three times."

"Didn't you think that was rather strange?" he persisted.

"No. Once there was oil spilled that I slipped on. For all I know, I spilled it. Another time, a lot of Singers were going down the same stairs and someone jostled me. The time I got hurt, I don't know how I fell. Why?"

Taf glanced at me. I gave him the "you take it" signal. He said, "Noia fell down stairs at the Hall recently. She cracked her skull and sprained an ankle. She doesn't know how it happened, either."

Zhia may have no sense of rhythm, but she has plenty of common sense. "That doesn't sound like a coincidence to me."

"To me, either. And Rois, though I've not spoken to all of the females working at the Hall, of the nine I have spoken with, six think they're going to be trained as Singers as soon as they work off the cost of the training."

"That's also more than coincidence," I said.

"You haven't heard the best part," Taf said. "Our rimba are back at the Hall."

Chapter Nineteen

"Are you certain these are the same ones?" Father whispered as he, Taf, and I huddled by the light of a single lamp in the instrument storage room at the Hall.

"Positive," I said. "You can see the discoloration on the metal from the fire. It looks like someone tried to polish it off; but it's apparently a change in the metal itself."

"And here," Taf pointed, "these are the marks Zhia put on them, so we wouldn't use laundry water for cooking."

"And listen to them, Father." Lightly, I tapped the head of each. "Did you ever hear rimba that sounded like that?"

Wonder and appreciation on his face, Father said, "No. Well, I hope Gadig doesn't have a good explanation for this, because calling in a magistrate falsely is actionable."

I hadn't known that. Apparently Taf hadn't, either; dismay was on both our faces. Taf said, "But after I came back here today, sir, I talked to more of the women. I found four more out of eight or nine who think they're working to pay for training as Singers. That makes ten out of at least seventeen, which is more than half. That's not coincidence."

"No," Father agreed. "Did you happen to get the women's names?"

"Their first names, yes."

"That's what I meant," Father said, irritably. "I've seen enough, Son. In the morning we'll summon a magistrate and see if we can get some answers."

"Be sure to bring Zhia," Taf said.

"No, I think one of the three people who can positively say these are the rimba the raiders stole ought to stay home," I drawled. "Your job is to be sure the women are where they can be found if summoned. Is there any indication that the Master has noticed what you've been doing?"

Taf said "no" and blew out the lamp. We left the storage room on tiptoe. We saw no one as we threaded the dark corridors. Taf left us before we left the Hall; neither Father nor I needed a guide to get out of the building and locate our muddy shoes.

We had waited until the rain was over before going into town to see the drums and either verify or disprove Taf's discovery. Father had been the one to point out that we couldn't afford to leave a muddy trail. When we showed up in the Master's office with a magistrate, we wanted the Master taken completely by surprise. We hoped to keep him so off guard that he might tell the truth.

Despite my certainty that something was seriously wrong at the Hall, too much of the suspicion Father and I were directing at the Master was based on his tone of voice, which couldn't be proven to the satisfaction of a magistrate. That Zhia and Noia had suffered the same mishap seemed more than coincidence, but was it malicious? I couldn't bring that charge against the Master or anyone else. Without knowing how Taf had gone about eliciting information from the seventeen women he had questioned, I had to consider the possibility that he could be shown to have asked questions in such a way that the women were led to give one answer rather than another.

Father, Taf, and I were convinced of the Master's guilt. Convincing a magistrate was quite another matter, and a far more serious one.

In the dark, wrestling with my doubts, the lane to my parents' home seemed twice as long. Morning would come all too soon, and we'd be traveling this path again, this time with Zhia…Zhia with the broken foot.

I wondered if I could get to town at daybreak, hire a cart, and get back quickly enough so she wouldn't even think of trying to walk to the Hall. What if she'd reinjured herself with her foolishness this afternoon? What if Taf hadn't been coming from town just as she had been going to the Hall?

Frustration knotted my stomach. "What ifs" seemed to be all I had. I was nervous about bringing charges against a Hall Master. Knowing that Father, Taf, Zhia, and I might be punished if we couldn't present our suspicions well enough did nothing to increase my confidence.

Father didn't help, either, when he asked, "Is there any chance Gadig will move the rimba before morning?"

I cursed. "Maybe we should have taken them to Taf's cubicle."

"That wouldn't have been a good idea," Father said, thoughtfully. "If they're moved from where Gadig knows they were, he can claim they're different ones, or he can accuse Taf of having done something to them. If they disappear between now and morning, we'll have to hope we have enough evidence from Zhia and the other women to convince a magistrate. I just hope Gadig wasn't clever enough to falsify the Hall records. If the magistrate asks him to produce them, he'll have to, you know."

Suddenly I remembered the second tour schedule, and reminded Father of it. "How hard would it be for the Master to keep two sets of Hall records?"

"I wouldn't expect to learn that he'd done so," was Father's considered reply. "No one except the Master is supposed to see the Hall records. If there were two sets of Hall records and we could prove it, it would pretty much condemn Gadig without the need of further evidence. But we'll know in the morning." I know I cringed at the thought. I must have also made some sound, for Father added, "Scared, Son?"

"Yes, sir, I am; though apprehensive might be a better word. No, I'm scared. I was a lot less scared before I knew this could turn out badly for us."

"Scared enough to change your mind about going through with this?"

"I don't think so. I hope not, anyway."

"I hope not, too. If fear of consequences keeps a person from speaking the truth, he or she doesn't really believe it's the truth."

Though Father couldn't see me in the dark, I stared at him. "Zhia said those exact words the day the raiders attacked."

"And you're wondering how I could say the same thing? Her father said that the day he was named Ambassador. I sang at the ceremony. She must have been there, too."

We went on in silence. As I opened the front door, I asked, "Father, are you scared?"

"What do I have to lose?" The words were intensely bitter, and deeply disturbing.

Even without all the other worries, that question would have kept me awake all night. What did Father have to lose? Reputation? Not really. His days as a Singer were over. Friends? Since Father lost his voice, he didn't seem to have any. Money? He and Mother weren't impoverished; but I didn't know what they owned besides the house.

Remembering the predicament in which Zhia found herself, I realized I would be wise at least to inquire, even if Father wouldn't answer.

What did I have to lose? Reputation? Yes; I was a two-time Champion. Friends? Yes. At least, I thought I had friends. Adversity is said to be a touchstone for friendship; maybe I would discover that I had as few friends as Father did. Money? The purse from my second Championship hadn't made me wealthy. I had earned no fees from TTTW. Were the magistrate to impose a fine, I wouldn't be able to pay it. I would go to prison.

Not surprisingly, I had no trouble being up before daybreak. I filled the vats so Mother wouldn't have to go outside for water, then hired a cart for taking Zhia into town. Father and Zhia were up when I returned. Though Father commended my foresight, he was plainly thinking of other things. None of us ate much.

"We might as well go," Father finally said. When we stood by the cart, he said, "Remember, a bad attitude makes a bad beginning."

"And there's no point in expecting the worst; the worst will happen even if you don't expect it," I added, and felt strangely cheered.

Zhia, however, turned toward the rising sun, bowed, spread her hands, and said, "O you whom we call Unknown, you are Truth. Guide us this day as we seek the truth of matters that tear at our hearts. If you can use us to free those in slavery, we are your willing slaves. May every thing we do this day be to your glory. Even so."

"Even so," Father and I echoed. "Thank you," Father added. He was smiling.

As the desdal-drawn cart trundled toward town we didn't speak, perhaps fearing that speech would somehow alert the Master to our plans. When I drew the desdal to a stop at the magistrate's chambers, Father jumped out of the cart. He took a step toward the building, then turned and said, "You may greet the magistrate. The proper form of address is 'Your Honor'. Beyond that, make no reference to why we need him until we are in the Master's presence. Got that?" He went inside.

"A magistrate keeps more state than my father ever did," Zhia remarked.

"Are you going to tell the magistrate who your father was?" I asked. It had just occurred to me that that piece of information might work in our favor.

"If I am required to give my full name, I will. If the magistrate doesn't know who 'Druzhin' was, it's probably better. I want this matter decided on the basis of truth."

"That's easy for you to say; what do you have to lose?"

She gave me a measuring look. "I was upset when I heard your father say what he did last night when you got back from the Hall. I suppose you agonized over it all night."

"Yes, I did. What did you do, wait up for us?" I asked.

"No; but I was a mother. Mothers learn to wake when they hear things in the night. How do you think we get dark circles under our eyes?"

"Being pounded by a raider."

"Thank you for the reminder. Truly, are the bruises still real dark?"

I studied her face. "They're not dark, but they're still visible, especially around your left eye and wherever you were cut."

"Great. Wearing these scruffy clothes from tour and being all bruised won't do much to inspire confidence in my credibility. I must look like a raider, myself."

I was still wearing borrowed clothes, but Mother had altered them. Suddenly, I was glad. The door of the building started to open. "Here comes Father. No more discussion until we see the Master."

The magistrate was the same one who had taken the remainder of my purse and my trophy after my first Champion's party. He gave no indication he remembered me. I hoped he would have no reason to be reminded of that day. Zhia and I greeted him as Father had instructed. He and Father climbed into the cart, which was now somewhat crowded. Glad that the pair of lesser functionaries who accompanied him were riding behind the cart on cheros, I steered the desdal for the Hall.

Taf was waiting for us in the courtyard. Someone took the desdal's reins so we could climb out of the cart. The cheros were hitched to posts provided for that purpose. As the seven of us—the magistrate, the functionaries, Taf, Zhia, Father, and I—neared the Hall itself, people melted away, likely because they didn't know for whom the magistrate had been summoned. It's been said that everyone is guilty of something; that day I saw proof of the saying.

Were I not committed to Nia Diva, I might consider being a magistrate. A magistrate has power. We went directly to the Master's office and walked right in. The functionaries took positions just outside, one on either side of the door.

The Master was startled; I saw it. He quickly had his face under control, but didn't do as well with his voice. There was a nervous tremor in it when he said, "Good morning, Your Honor. May I ask whether this is a social call?"

"It is not." The magistrate's voice was cold, hard. It matched the somber gray and blue of his robes.

"May I offer you a chair?"

"No. But you may stand."

The Master did so, hastily.

The magistrate turned to Father. "What are the charges you bring against this man?"

"Enslaving this woman and other women who had come here to be trained as Singers, and receiving stolen property," Father answered.

"What evidence have you for these charges?"

"This woman will provide some of the evidence, Your Honor. If you will permit this young man to leave, he will produce other witnesses."

"He is excused." Taf left. The magistrate said to Zhia, "What is your full name?"

"Zhia Vediandruzhin, Your Honor."

"Your father was Ambassador Druzhin?"

"Yes, Your Honor."

"Please explain the circumstances that led to a charge of slavery against this man."

Zhia did so. While she was speaking, Taf returned with twenty-three other women. The magistrate's eyes widened slightly when he saw them standing in the corridor, but he showed no other sign of surprise. To the Master, he said, "May I see the Hall records?"

The Master produced them. After asking when Zhia first came to the Hall, the magistrate found the appropriate place in the book. Running his forefinger down the lines of writing, he finally straightened and said to Zhia, "I find no record that you belong to this Hall, either as Singer or servant. Step aside. I wish to speak to the other women."

The inquiry took a long time, but seemed to go well. Each woman told the same story: arriving full of hope, being assured of training, becoming a drudge, a slave for durations of as much as six turns of the star wheel. None was listed in the records.

When the last woman had answered his questions, the magistrate asked, "And when did any of you become aware that you were not the only one who had been given such promises?" He pointed to one woman. "When did you learn?"

She flinched but said, "Just this morning, Your Honor."

"And you?"

"This morning, Your Honor."

So it went, twenty-three questions and twenty-three identical answers. It took a long time. Then the magistrate turned to Zhia. "When did you learn?"

"If you would indulge me, Your Honor, may I be permitted to sit in your presence?" She was very white; her voice was tight with pain.

I don't think he'd noticed her foot before then. With an exclamation, he pulled the Master's chair from behind the desk and held it for her. "Why didn't you say something before now?"

"You are a magistrate, sir. I don't sit in the Master's presence, either."

"Not even the Master would keep an injured woman standing."

"Certainly not," was the Master's hearty comment. Falseness poured from the words.

"Now this other charge, what evidence is there for it?" Apparently, the magistrate had forgotten that Zhia hadn't answered his question.

"May I have leave to fetch it, Your Honor?" Taf asked. When the magistrate said "yes", he added, "Shall I dismiss the other women, Your Honor?"

"No. I may have more questions for them. They may sit while they wait, if they wish."

I noticed that most decided not to sit. I heard Taf returning quite a while before I saw him. He had enlisted five other Singers to bring not only our set of rimba, but another set, as well. Their knees boomed hollowly against the bodies of the drums as they carried them. The difference in sound between the two sets was readily apparent…to a Singer, at least.

Our set of rimba was placed in the Master's office. One of the women in the corridor gave a cry. "Please, Your Honor, it's not my fault. I tried to get the discoloration off them. Don't beat me, sir!" she added, turning tear-filled eyes on the Master.

"What is this?" the magistrate asked. "What are you talking about?"

"The drums, Your Honor. They came yesterday. The Master told me to polish them so they looked right, like those ones"—she pointed—"but I couldn't. I tried and tried."

"Did the Master beat you?"

"Not yesterday, Your Honor."

The magistrate said to Father, "I thought you said the charge was receiving stolen property. There seems to be more going on than you told me."

"Your Honor, this is the first I've heard anything about beatings," he replied. "The charge of receiving stolen property arises from the fact that this particular set of drums was stolen by raiders when they attacked a tour my son was leading."

"This precise set of drums," the magistrate said, sounding dubious. "How do you know that?"

"Your Honor, if you will look at the set in the corridor—and I could have several more sets brought if you need additional evidence that the set in question is distinctive—you will see no discoloration on the bodies. If you will tap the drum heads on both sets, you may hear a distinct difference in their sound. Again, if you require, additional sets of rimba could be brought for you to test."

The magistrate did as Father suggested. "How were these drums discolored?" he asked him.

"May I answer, Your Honor?" Zhia said. "Our tour leader became desperately ill. To tend him properly, I required large amounts of hot water. We had nothing else in which to heat it. These drums are costly, Your Honor—any Singer can tell you that—but I thought their worth less than a man's life. The fire produced the discoloration the lady in the corridor was not able to polish away. I ask her pardon that my action caused her to fear being punished. Your Honor, it was the fire that changed the tone of the drums, as well. I believe I can safely say there isn't another set of rimba like this anywhere.

"When our tour was attacked by raiders, all but one of our tebecs were stolen. The rimba were on one of the birds. Now, Your Honor, we find the drums here."

The magistrate had been eying Zhia as she spoke. "Do I assume the many injuries I can see you've suffered are the result of the raider attack?"

"Yes, Your Honor. I know it's unusual for anyone to survive a raider attack. Seven of our tour did not. By the mercy of Nia Diva, Rois, Taf, and I did."

"The daemon is merciful," he responded, as was proper. "But that has no bearing on whether the Master has been receiving stolen property. This is not an easy question because, as I understand it, the drums originally belonged to this Hall."

"Yes, Your Honor," the Master said, with an oily smile.

"How did you recover them?"

For the second time that morning, the Master was disconcerted. "Through my usual sources, Your Honor." His voice was smooth; his face, red.

"'Usual sources'? Does that mean you paid for them again, or someone happened to see them somewhere and knew they belonged to you? Please explain in detail."

The Master was looking distinctly uncomfortable. "Once I knew the tour had been attacked, Your Honor, I knew I had to replace the instruments. I have agents who purchase instruments for me."

"And these agents either weren't able to tell that there was a difference between these drums and others, or thought that you might want drums that are noticeably different in sound from others of their type?"

"New sounds are always being experimented with at the Hall, Your Honor."

"Did you purchase these drums from your agent?" the magistrate asked.

"Yes, Your Honor."

"Do you agree with the testimony that they are costly? Yes? Then I assume you kept a record of the purchase. May I see the receipt?"

The Master fumbled with papers on his desk. His ring caught the light. Finally, he straightened. His smile was crooked. "I don't seem to be able to find it at this moment, Your Honor. Bookkeeping can get away from one, you know."

"So it would seem, considering you have twenty-four women working here for whom you have kept no records of employment and compensation."

"A mere oversight, Your Honor."

"An oversight that continues for more than a day or two starts to look deliberate."

"If Your Honor will give me that day or two, I assure you I will be able to provide proper records." Against the black of his robes, his face now looked very pale.

"Are you telling me you have kept pay records for all these women in your mind for five and six turns of the star wheel? I trust people until I have reason to do otherwise. At the moment, I'm more inclined to believe the witness of twenty-four women who claim to have been enslaved than your claim of sloppy bookkeeping."

"But the drums do belong to this Hall, Your Honor," the Master pleaded. "I may have erred in dealing with the women; but I do not receive stolen property."

"There is no such plea as 'half guilty,'" the magistrate said, coldly.

After a long and uncomfortable silence, Zhia said, "If I may beg your indulgence again, Your Honor, might I inquire whether there is an inscription inside the ring the Master wears on his left forefinger?"

At the magistrate's gesture, the Master tugged the ring from his finger and placed it on the desk. The magistrate picked it up, turned it into the light, and said, "Yes."

"Your Honor, does the inscription read 'To Druzhin, love always, Vedia'?"

"Yes." The magistrate looked at the Master. "Is your name Druzhin?"

"No, Your Honor." The Master glared at Zhia when the magistrate wasn't looking.

The magistrate said to Zhia, "You seem to recognize this piece of jewelry."

"Yes, Your Honor. My mother, Vedia Birianvuram, gave that ring to my father on the occasion of his being named Ambassador. From that day, he never took it off. It was taken from his body when he, my mother, and their son were killed by raiders. How it came to be in the Master's possession, I don't know. But as the only surviving member of the Ambassador's family, I believe—and please correct me if I'm wrong, Your Honor—I believe that ring belongs to me."

The magistrate handed it to her. "How did you acquire the ring?" he asked the Master.

"I bought it. Your Honor," he added, hastily.

"It must have been costly. Have you a receipt?"

"I'm sure it's around here somewhere." The Master's search was visibly haphazard, agitated. He even picked up the lamp and looked under it.

I could feel my eyes widen. "Your Honor, may I look at that object under the lamp?"

"This mirror?" The magistrate picked it up. "Why?"

"My mirror!" Zhia exclaimed, then clapped a hand to her mouth. "Your pardon, Your Honor. I didn't mean to forget myself like that."

"Can you prove this is yours?" the magistrate asked.

"Yes, Your Honor. The design is fifteen timi blossoms. Worked into the design are a zha, a vee, and a dee, which are my initials, Your Honor. The mirror was a...a gift from my husband the day he made me his wife." She cleared her throat. "That mirror was in my pack on my tebec when the tour was attacked by raiders and, as I said earlier, all but one of the tebecs stolen."

The magistrate turned to Taf. "Have you ever seen this object?"

"No, Your Honor."

The magistrate turned to me. "How did you happen to recognize it?"

"The day the raiders attacked, Zhia asked me to get our tour schedule from her pack. The schedule was on top of the mirror. When I reached for the schedule—not an easy feat when riding a moving tebec, Your Honor—the mirror came with it."

"And the raider attack in which your tebecs were stolen occurred when?"

Zhia, Taf, and looked at one another. I finally said, "Fifteen, sixteen days ago?"

"Are you asking me or telling me?"

Firmly, I said, "It was less than twenty days ago, Your Honor. Pardon my not being able to give you an exact number."

The magistrate again turned to the Master. "Did you purchase this mirror?"

"Yes, Your Honor."

"Since it was stolen by raiders less than twenty days ago, dare I assume you have a receipt for it?"

The Master wet his lips. "Not one I can find, Your Honor."

"Is anyone else in charge of keeping records at this Hall?"

"No, Your Honor."

"Your inability to provide me with proof that you purchased valuable items which are known to have been stolen by raiders neither proves nor disproves the charge that you have been receiving stolen property. Because you are so bad at keeping records, there is no proof that the women I have questioned today—women who include Ambassador Druzhin's daughter—were employed rather than enslaved." Shaking his head, he looked at the Master, then at Father. "What am I to do with you?"

The tension in the office and in the corridor outside was thick.

A sob broke the silence. It came from Zhia. "If I may presume on your forbearance one more time, Your Honor, may I implore you to forget who I am? The wheel of the stars has turned many times since I was orphaned. I came here because I had nowhere else to go. It is these other women who need justice from you. Surely some of them still have families: mothers and fathers who sent them to the Hall, watching them leave with hearts full of pride and hope; families who perhaps have heard nothing from their daughters for turns and turns of the stars. My family is dead; my husband is dead; my future has already died many times. These other women still have a chance to achieve their dream to serve Nia Diva as Singers. As you serve the truth, Your Honor, give them justice." She had extended her hands to the magistrate in a gesture of appeal. Now she covered her face and wept. With a strangled, "Please excuse me," she rose and hobbled out of the office.

When her weeping could no longer be heard, the magistrate said to the Master,

"What is your full name?"

"Gadig Melangarig."

"Gadig Melangarig, you are removed as Master of this Hall. You will remain in prison until such time as you or your agent can provide me with records of the purchase of the items which are known to have been stolen, and also with records of employment and compensation for the women you are accused of enslaving." He motioned. The two gray-uniformed functionaries entered, took the Master's arms, and escorted him out.

The magistrate turned to Father. "Though I no longer recognize your voice, sir—and allow me to express my regret that you were robbed of it—your stature is unmistakable. You are the Singer who was known as High Note, aren't you?"

"Yes, Your Honor."

"I don't know the process of selecting a Hall Master, but I do know that the Hall shouldn't be left without one. Would you consider serving in that capacity for the interim?"

"It would be my pleasure, Your Honor," Father said. "Do I begin at once?"

"If that's convenient for you, sir." The magistrate said to me, "May I request a ride back to my chambers?"

"Certainly, Your Honor."

The magistrate seemed disinclined to talk as the cart rattled and creaked its way from the Hall to the magistrate's chambers, which was fine with me. I had to think.

The Master of a Hall lives at the Hall. Either Mother moved into the Hall, as well—which, considering her aversion to going outside the house, could present a problem—or she made do without Father's company, which neither of them would like. There had to be a way to get Mother to the Hall without frightening her out of her wits. Father would need her help as well as her company. There was a lot to do.

Once all remaining servants at the Hall were questioned, which would have to be a high priority, it was entirely possible that places for even more than twenty-four women would have to be found. A large-scale reassigning of cubicles might be needed. Records would have to be reviewed, updated, corrected. The value of work done by women who had been enslaved would have to be calculated and credited to them. Class sizes would have to be evaluated. More instructors might need to be added. The kitchen staff would have to be advised of the increased numbers. Servants, in the kitchen and elsewhere, would have to be employed to do the work of those who would now be doing what they had come to the Hall to do. Likely some of Gadig's treasures would have to be sold so the Hall could be run the way a Hall was supposed to run. It was going to be daunting.

I never doubted that Father would rise to and enjoy every moment of it.

After I returned the magistrate to his chambers, I went back to the Hall. Father was already perusing the Hall records. I knocked on his door. "Congratulations, Master."

"Thank you, Son. There's a lot to do."

"Yes. Shall we see if we were thinking of the same things?" At his invitation, I reviewed the list which is noted above. Father nodded at some of the items and made notes of others. I finished, "And Father, I now know what Zhia plays."

"Good. I've started a record for her, but it has only her name. What does she play?"

"She plays people."

Chapter Twenty

FATHER LAUGHED AND PUSHED the records away. "That she does, consummately! I just hope the magistrate never realizes she was manipulating him the whole time."

"That's a hope I share. But is 'manipulating' the right word, Father?"

Now he frowned. "You're the one who said Zhia plays people. Used that way, 'plays' usually means 'manipulates.'"

"I'll grant that. But it sounds so...so calculated. I'm sure her emotion, especially in that last speech, was real."

"Of course it was real. While the magistrate can't read voices as well as we do, he would have known if Zhia wasn't being honest. But it was calculated honesty. And Son, let me tell you that calculated honesty is more dangerous than random evil."

I frowned. "Taf also thinks Zhia is dangerous."

"And you don't?" Amazement was evident both in voice and expression. "After seeing her repel raiders, you don't think she's dangerous? After watching her oust the Master of your Hall, you don't think she's dangerous?"

"But she didn't..."

"Yes, she did!" The gravelly rasp somehow added emphasis. "She most certainly did, Son. We were losing. Gadig was right; though he couldn't explain how he got the drums back from the raiders, they belong to the Hall. Since the magistrate wasn't familiar with the Hall's methods, Gadig might have been allowed to get by with no more than a promise to reform his dealings with the would-be female Singers. The magistrate was wavering; what did you think he meant by 'What am I to do with you'? Even though Zhia identified that mirror and her father's ring, it was her last speech that sealed Gadig's fate. Without that, he'd still be sitting here; and you, Zhia, and I would be in prison."

Suddenly, I felt ill. "Oh."

"That's putting it mildly."

Looking for a different subject, I said, "While we were waiting for you to come out of the magistrate's chambers, Zhia said she didn't want to use her father's name as an advantage."

"That's noble, I suppose, but foolish. It betrays how young she is. She must have known she would be testifying, which means she must have known she would be asked to give her full name. Since her brother is dead, there's only one 'Vediandruzhin'; and Druzhin is not a common name. In fact, the only person I've ever known with that name was her father."

Remembering both how Zhia had introduced herself to Father and her comments during the inquiry, I began to suspect that she actually relished the effect her father's name had on people. Maybe her noble plea for today's matter to be decided on the basis of truth had been an attempt to keep me and everyone else from noticing that it had, in fact, been decided on the basis of who her father was. Maybe "manipulating" was the right word, after all.

Even her recognizing her father's ring now rang false. If sweeping the Master's office had been among her chores, she must have seen the ring before today. I remembered her saying the Master always left when she came in to sweep. Zhia's explanation, that he left to avoid dust, suddenly seemed inadequate. Perhaps he had been avoiding Zhia.

"Is the full name of each Singer entered into the Hall records?" I asked Father.

"Of course."

"Would it be safe to assume that even though the former Master—may I now call him Gadig, Father?" Father assented. "Thank you. Can we assume that, though Gadig didn't enter Zhia's name into the Hall records, he knew her full name?"

"That would seem reasonable. So what?"

"I'm thinking about that business with her father's ring. She's only been here for two or three turns of the star wheel. The Master has had that ring for as long as I've been here. At some point he must have seen and read the inscription inside. When Zhia showed up and gave him her full name, he realized not only that the ring was hers, but also that she might notice and recognize it. She might even ask questions he didn't want to answer.

"Until now, I haven't been able to explain to my own or anyone else's satisfaction why Zhia was sent on a tour. Gadig had ensured that Zhia didn't get trained, but by sending her on a tour, by definition he made her a Singer. I speculated that, since he knew she had no training, his intent was for her to be publicly humiliated. But what good would that do? That wouldn't affect even the other Singers on her tour. I had wondered if it might be an attempt to discredit female Singers in general, but it wouldn't have that effect. Public humiliation would affect only Zhia.

"If Gadig feared that Zhia could interfere with an arrangement from which he was profiting, and if he had good enough connections with raiders to be receiving stolen items—I assume there are items besides the rimba, the mirror, and the ring—then maybe he also had good enough connections with them to arrange for a tour to be attacked. He could count on no one's surviving."

"I might be able to believe that, were it not for the fact that you were on that tour," Father said.

"That's the very fact that makes me believe it. Had only Zhia died, there might have been questions. Had the tour been massacred and it was found to be only first-timers, there might have been questions. I was the diversion. If a Champion died on tour, the focus would be on that loss. The raiders would be blamed. No one would look further. Zhia would never identify her father's ring. Gadig could keep feathering his nest, both directly, receiving stolen valuables, and indirectly, by using slave rather than paid labor."

"That's all very interesting, and is possibly true, as well. But since Gadig is in prison, it has no bearing on what I need to be doing." He pulled the records back to easy reach. (Well, close enough so he could write in them. Father could have reached them anywhere on the desk without standing or raising himself even slightly from his chair.) "Does Zhia have a cubicle here?"

"I have no idea. Why?"

"You know why; I have to find cubicles for all the women who are no longer slaves. I think it would good to put them all in the same area, for their comfort if not their safety."

The last word reminded me of what Zhia had said the previous afternoon. "Father, do you recall Aplin's saying that Noia fell down stairs and was injured?" Only half-listening, he nodded. "Well, yesterday I learned that Zhia also has fallen down stairs here, not once but at least three times. She was able to explain away two of the incidents, but has no idea how she fell the third time. If those incidents weren't simply accidents, then someone caused them. Gadig was unfeeling enough to make Zhia keep working after the third mishap, even though she was hurt; but he isn't likely to be the one who pushed or tripped either Zhia or Noia. Someone, maybe even more than one person, was working with him. Until we know who that is, I'd rather Zhia not be here."

Almost sharply, Father asked, "Then how will she be trained? Because I will be here. And so will you." Something must have shown on my face, for he added, gently, "Don't think I'm dismissing your concern, Son. I'm also concerned, not just because I'm now Master. But with Gadig gone, how likely is it that his tool—whoever it was—will continue to act? One assumes the confederate was lured by a promise of some kind of reward. While I'm here, no one will be rewarded for pushing Singers down stairs or in any other way jeopardizing anyone for whom I am now answerable. The only reason Zhia might not remain here today is that I'm not sure the cubicle assignments can be worked out that quickly." He grimaced. "I need your mother here; she's good at organizing."

I accepted the change of subject. "What is it that bothers Mother, just being outside the house, or being able to see that she's outside? I mean, could she travel at night?"

"Good thought, Son; but no, she can't travel at night. Not having the walls is what upsets your mother."

"A closed cart isn't enough walls?" Father shook his head. "Might Aplin have something that we could give her to make her sleep so we could get her here?"

"We could ask. I certainly wouldn't do that without your mother's permission."

"Of course not. I wasn't suggesting that you kidnap your wife."

Father smiled. I think he muttered, "She might like that," but at that moment Taf appeared outside the office, all but bursting with excitement.

"Congratulations, sir!" he exclaimed to Father. "Everyone's celebrating in the dining hall. They want you to come. If that's agreeable with you, sir," he added, quickly.

Father's smile broadened. He unfolded himself from the chair and said, "I can spare some time for a celebration. I appreciate being invited."

Taf and I followed Father down the corridor. Taf whispered to me, "Things sure are going to be different. Can you imagine the other Master saying anything like that?"

I couldn't, nor could I imagine Gadig's even considering attending a party that was by and for his inferiors. Father not only stayed quite a while, he clearly enjoyed himself. The younger Singers enjoyed him. Though an occasional unkind comment slipped out, everyone was in a forgiving mood...not to mention in varying stages of inebriation.

Not until Father proposed drinking a remembrance to the seven from my tour who had died, did I realize that I hadn't seen Zhia since she left the Master's office in tears. When the memorial was done, I found Taf.

"Where's Zhia?"

"How should I know? Maybe she's taking a pee."

"Have you seen her at all since this morning?"

"No. I'm trying to keep an eye on Noia."

I didn't know whether the answer angered or pleased me. "I'm going to look around the Hall. If you see Zhia, ask her to stay here, in the dining hall, I mean."

The search took a while. The Hall was obviously not built all at one time;

at least four different kinds of stone were used and as many different styles of masonry. It's just as obvious that no one made any effort to build additions so they made sense. Corridors tangled like string that has slipped off a spool. While some of the areas were clearly intended for use as Singers' quarters, clusters of cubicles cropped up in odd places like the often-poisonous woodland growth known as ushro. (The most metallic-sounding of the percussion instruments takes its name from that growth, for its shape resembles the round, peaked caps that perch on stems of varying thicknesses.)

If Zhia was still at the Hall, I expected to find her sweeping or employed in some other needless and forbidden drudgery. I looked everywhere. Instructors don't live at the Hall; but they have offices there. I didn't presume to search the offices, but whenever I saw an instructor, I informed him of the change of Mastership and invited him to the party. Though I doubt any of them deigned to hobnob with the students, it gave me an excuse at least to look into each office.

All the Singers' cubicles were deserted. I made a quick circuit of the courtyard, then returned to the dining hall.

"No Zhia?" Taf asked, coming over after spotting me.

I shook my head. "By the way, if any instructors show up, I'm to blame. I had to have an excuse to look in their offices."

This didn't seem to be of concern to Taf. "If any show up, they won't stay long." He saw the look on my face and added, "Don't worry about her. She probably went to your parents' house."

"That's what I'm afraid of. Your concern for Noia—which I'm not criticizing—has apparently made you forget that Zhia is also hurt."

"Oh, yes, she is. Well, do you still have the cart?"

"Yes, but so what? By now she'll be there. She'll have reinjured her foot. Again. This is really getting old."

Taf looked at me far too long for my comfort, then said, "I hate to be the one to tell you, Rois, but you're not much fun. Either forget about the woman and enjoy the party, or forget about the party and go after the woman. If it were me, I'd forget about the woman. She won't thank you for going after her.

Get some food and more wine and enjoy yourself."

Knowing he was right in saying that Zhia wouldn't appreciate any effort on her behalf, I tried to take his advice, but I got tired of pretending to enjoy myself. I noticed Father had left. Though the neglected Hall records needed his immediate attention, he had remained longer than I expected. I thought I could also excuse myself, perhaps with the reason—which, now that I thought about it, was true—that Father's things would have to be fetched to the Hall.

I had just started looking for Taf when he found me. "You can stop worrying about Zhia," he said. "She was here; the party was her idea. Right before you and your father joined us, she left to go to your folks' house. Chaz and Rork went with her."

"That's good. But listen, I have to leave anyway. Father's going to need his things, so I'll go home and bring them back."

"Scold Zhia for me, too," Taf said, with a grin.

I laughed. "Count on it." I went to the Master's office to ask Father if there was anything he needed right away besides his clothing and other personal items. He asked for some books, the titles of which I wrote on a scrap of paper. "I'll be back later."

"No hurry, Son. I expect these records will keep me busy the rest of the… the turn of the star wheel."

I was disgusted to see that curiosity about the magistrate's errand had lured even the stable hands from their work. No one had unhitched the desdal from the cart, or so much as hitched the reins to a post. Dragging the cart, the loose, unattended animal had gone toward the stables, where it had been able to reach a water trough outside them. As the cart was too big to get through the door, the desdal had been reduced to chewing on what it could reach, which was stray straw.

I really don't like putting my fingers in desdal's mouths. Their bite is almost as painful as a tebec's. Because I felt guilty that the animal had been neglected, and because I feared its owner might demand additional compensation if the neglect was obvious, I made myself do the right thing.

"It's a good thing you're strong," I told it as it cleaned the inedible stalks from its mouth and bit, "because when it comes to smarts or looks, you're a loser." At that, it opened its mouth, apparently thinking to grab a mouthful of my shirt. Along its teeth I saw a fragment of straw I'd missed. I removed it as held it for the animal to see. "What did I tell you? You're a loser. Look, you got the short straw."

I was turning the animal and the cart around when I remembered Dolin's telling me that, though I hadn't been there, I had drawn short straw and had to partner Zhia. Then I remembered that in speaking of that humiliating event, Zhia had said that besides Dolin, Chaz and Rork had been there. Chaz and Rork had left with Zhia.

The sudden churning in my middle had nothing to do with the wine I had drunk. I took a deep breath to calm myself and returned to the dining room. Raising my voice above the merriment, I asked, "Is Dolin here?"

Someone called back, "He left a while ago."

I waved a hand in acknowledgment. Something prompted me to go to the Master's office. "Father, I think you'd better come with me."

Immediately, he was on his feet. "Where? What's happened, Son?"

"I'm not sure anything's happened yet; but we need to go home."

The desdal, resenting its poor treatment—or maybe because of it; it might have been hungry—refused to do more than shamble. Scarcely had we left town when I turned it and the cart to the side of the road and hitched the reins to a tree. "We'll make better time on foot," I said, more anxious than disgusted.

As we walked, I told Father that Gadig had allowed Singers to draw straws to choose Zhia's partner. I told him of the conversation with Gadig in which I was given permission to allow or arrange for Zhia's being harmed, and of my suspicion at the time that I was not the only one the former Master had approached. I told Father that Chaz, Rork, and Dolin were three who had been allowed to draw straws. Then I said that Chaz and Rork were known to have left with Zhia, and that Dolin had also left the party.

Father stopped walking. "We already discussed this, Son. Gadig is in prison; he can't reward anyone for harming Zhia. She's in no danger. And though I regret having to say so, even were Zhia in danger, Gadig stays in prison. He is a disgrace to the name of Singer. I will not drop the charges against him." His regard was daunting. "If you're done jumping at shadows, I'm going back to the Hall. I have work to do. You go back for the cart and bring my things. Ask your mother to start packing hers, as well. I'll talk to Aplin about something to make her sleep." Then he chuckled. "Kidnap my wife, indeed!"

Then I understood what dread had been gnawing at me. Slowly, I said, "Father, would you drop the charges against Gadig if Mother were in danger?"

He paled, but all he said was, "Hurry."

We covered much of the remaining distance at a run. When the house was in sight, Father put his hand on my arm and panted, "Wait. Everything looks all right from here. If nothing's wrong, we don't want to burst in all a-lather. If something's wrong, we'll need our breath, so let's stop and catch it."

I don't know how Father managed to look so composed when he opened the front door. I felt like I was going to crawl out of my skin. The entryway was deserted. The front room was in disarray, with a tray, food, and an assortment of dishes—some broken—laying on the floor in a puddle of wine. A dusting of flour lay on the divan and everything near it.

Father and I looked at each other. Neither of us spoke.

Though there were floury footprints on the dining room floor, that room was otherwise untouched. But there was a body on the kitchen floor, face down in a puddle of water. A large, empty pot lay near the body. I knelt and lifted the head by the hair. The face was blistered, but recognizable. It was Dolin.

Another body lay near the staircase. I didn't even try to identify it: its head had been burned; the face was charred beyond recognition. It required only a glance to tell me no one was in the larders or the washing room. Nothing unusual was to be seen outside the back door.

We had trouble going upstairs, not only because the steps were slick with oil. The staircase was blocked with bedding, clothing, pieces of furniture, and another body. This one had a knife buried in its middle. I recognized Chaz. Flour made his clothing as white as his face.

I hoped the badly burned body was Rork's, because if it wasn't, some of Gadig's stooges were still somewhere about. I was more than ready for the grim succession of bodies to cease. We hadn't yet found Mother or Zhia, though what I had seen led me to hope they were alive.

Sounding quite unlike himself, Father voiced just that thought. I didn't trust my voice; I simply nodded.

Despite what I had seen on the stairs, I wasn't prepared for the appearance of my bedchamber. I have seen similar damage after strong windstorms. Only a few pieces of furniture remained, and those weren't in their usual places. The bed frame was partly dismantled; I thought I had seen pieces of it blocking the stairs. From where the clothes chests rested, I guessed they also would have gone down the stairs, if needed.

There was blood on the floor near them. A smear of blood led from them to my parents' bedchamber. It, too, was seemingly wind-tossed. Headboard first, the bed was blocking the doorway. The only coverings on the bed were my parents' clothes chests, which were empty. The trail of blood went under the bed, though no one was there.

"Isia?" Father called, softly.

"Robil?" Mother's voice was tremulous.

"Where are you? Are you hurt?"

"We're behind the door. I'm only frightened. Zhia is hurt."

Father shoved the bed out of the way and jerked back the door. On the floor in the little alcove where Mother's dressing table usually stood sat Mother. She was pale, shaken, and disheveled, but apparently unharmed. Zhia lay in front of her, even paler, even more disheveled, but not shaken. In fact, Zhia wasn't moving at all. With the fingers of both hands, Mother was pressing a wad of already blood-soaked cloth to Zhia's left arm.

I don't remember moving, I just know that I found myself kneeling beside Mother. "How bad is it?"

"I don't know. I can't get it to stop bleeding."

I peeled off my shirt. "Let me try." I put my shirt on top of the cloth Mother had been pressing onto the wound. As soon as she lifted her hands, I put mine in their place.

"Use your palm, Son," Father said as he gathered Mother into his arms.

I nodded and obeyed.

Still holding Mother, Father sat on the edge of the denuded bed. "Can you tell me what happened?"

Mother nodded. "They seemed like such nice young men, I invited them in. Since they came all this way to make sure Zhia got back all right I thought I should give them refreshments, so I put water on to heat for washing up and then prepared food. When I got back to the front room, one of the men was holding a knife at Zhia's throat and the other two were walking toward me. They said something about taking me outside, and I panicked. I threw the tray at them. They stumbled back and jostled the man who was threatening Zhia. She shouted 'Run!' and threw the tray of flour in his face.

"We were in the kitchen when the men caught us again. Zhia had already told me to run upstairs and start throwing things down the stairs, it didn't matter what, as long as it blocked the stairs. But one of the men grabbed my arm. Zhia took the pot off the fire and threw boiling water in the man's face and then smashed his head with the pot."

With my free hand, I picked up Zhia's left hand. The palm was badly blistered. The right hand was no better.

Mother was saying, "I got upstairs. Zhia started up the stairs. The man with the knife did, too. Zhia couldn't go fast because of her foot and because I was doing what she'd told me to do. When she slowed to dodge something that was falling, the man with the knife slashed her. I screamed. Zhia screamed also, telling me to keep doing what I was doing. She and the man with the knife kept climbing up the stairs and I kept throwing things down them. Some of them hit the man. My dressing table knocked him a little way down the stairs.

"Just as Zhia reached the landing, I threw a lamp. When Zhia saw the oil spilling over the steps, she took the jug with the firestone from my other hand, leaned over the railing and dropped it on the head of the man who didn't have the knife. He hadn't started climbing the stairs. The jug broke, and the firestone ignited the oil. I think the man with the knife got scared then. It looked like he was trying to get away when he slipped on the lamp oil and fell on his knife. The man who was burning was probably dead, but we weren't sure about the others. Zhia started to move the chests from Rois' room. Then she collapsed. I got her in here and blocked the door with the bed and chests. And then you came and rescued us."

I was about to express my admiration for Mother's calm when it shattered. As she trembled and wept Father held her closer and rocked her, stroking her hair and kissing the top of her head. Father was also weeping.

I kept pressing my palm against the wound in Zhia's arm, aware of growing warmth under my hand as her blood saturated my shirt and wishing I could be sure that Zhia's part of the story also had a happy ending.

"How is Zhia, Son?" Father asked when Mother's sobs began to lessen.

"The bleeding doesn't seem to be slowing any."

"Raise her arm while you press on the wound."

I did so.

After accepting Mother's assurance that she was calmer, Father stood and said, "I'm going to clear the stairway so we can get Zhia out of here and to a doctor."

"Be careful of the oil," Mother said.

"It's a wonder the whole thing didn't go up in flames," he replied.

I heard the thud and clatter of the furniture he tossed over the railings, and the softer whooshes of the bedding being moved. There was a pause in the sounds, and Father came back into the room with a blanket. He stooped and covered Zhia. His fingers rested for a moment on the inside of her right wrist. When he rose to resume clearing the stairs, he wouldn't look at me.

He did look at me when a voice coming from downstairs startled us.

"Rois? Zhia? Are you all right?"

"Taf?" I called. "What are you doing here? Don't answer that now. Did you walk?"

"No, I rode my tebec. What happened?"

"Zhia's arm has been slashed by a knife and I can't stop the bleeding. Get back to the Hall as fast as that tebec can run and tell Aplin we need him." I looked over at the bed. "Mother, Aplin will need hot water. Is enough left of the kitchen for you to take care of that?"

"Yes, Son." She kissed my forehead before she left the room.

Looking back, I know that it was not long between then and when Aplin arrived. It seemed interminable, probably because I was alone and, for all I knew, Zhia was dying.

Chapter Twenty-One

To this day, Aplin insists he doesn't know how Zhia survived.

To this day, I insist it was thanks to the intervention of Nia Diva, if not the Unknown. When I tell Singers that, many give me a rather patronizing look. They may sneer if they wish. Father—whose experience with injuries in general is minimal and who had no experience at all with the kind of injury inflicted on Zhia—couldn't explain how he knew what measures to use to stop her from bleeding to death, measures of which Aplin himself approved. If more evidence is needed, Father said that Mother wasn't capable of moving the big bed she and Father shared, nor could she move their clothes chests, even when empty; but she did. As has been mentioned, it takes two men to carry Zhia when she can't move by herself. Mother alone moved Zhia from my chamber to hers.

Then there's the matter of Taf's timely arrival at the scene. He later explained that he'd come out to the house only because, on being told what I had been discussing with him, Noia had scolded him for not making sure that Zhia was all right. Taf had taken a tebec because he'd wanted to get back to the Hall (and the party) quickly. He claims no tebec ever moved as fast as his did when he returned to fetch Aplin.

Again, as in the hollow, Taf's thinking had been quicker than mine. Rather than take time to saddle another tebec, Taf had gotten Aplin mounted on the one he'd been riding and sent him off. Then Taf had returned to my parent's home, traveling on foot only until he reached the cart and desdal. Perhaps because the animal had been grazing, perhaps because Taf is just better with creatures than I am, or—most likely, in my opinion—because Nia Diva was acting to save Zhia, the desdal moved at a reasonable pace.

By the time Taf arrived at my parents' home, Aplin had sewn both a torn blood vessel and the gash, had dressed Zhia's raw, blistered hands, and had her ready to be moved to the Hall. Father had cleared the staircase and buried the corpses. Mother had cleaned oil off the steps and was busy restoring order to her home.

To this day, I shudder when I remember how Zhia looked as Father and I carried her to the cart. She was wrapped in a white blanket. It wasn't easy to tell where blanket ended and flesh began.

Aplin and I rode in the cart. Taf drove it. Once Zhia was delivered to the Hall's clinic, Taf would return yet again with the cart so Father and Mother could move to the Hall. I was upstairs with Zhia when Father told Mother of his appointment and their imminent relocation. He said that after she congratulated him, she looked at the shambles of their tidy, cozy home and remarked, "At least there won't be much to pack."

Aplin had left something to make Mother sleep. Once their remaining possessions were loaded and Mother was protected from her fear of being outdoors, Father would drive the cart to the Hall. Taf would ride the tebec, which deserved a better reward for its work that day than the unsaddling and turning out to pasture it would receive. Taf would return to the party (which, if I knew Singers' parties, would still be going strong).

I knew Father wouldn't need help carrying Mother from the cart into their new rooms at the Hall. I hoped he wouldn't need me to help him carry in his and Mother's things, because I also wanted to return to the party. I wanted to get roaring drunk.

When he reached the Hall, Father did request my help carrying things in. The next day he had me helping Mother arrange their quarters. The day after that, I helped Mother furnish an adjoining room as a nursery.

Why a nursery?

Father had been speaking at length with the women Gadig had enslaved, and had discovered four Taf had missed. One of them, strikingly pretty but so shy she blushed whenever anyone spoke to her, refused to speak to Father but had confided to Mother that Gadig had required her to make herself available to him, Dolin, Chaz, Rork, and two other men whose names I was unable to learn. Father did tell me they were sent to another Hall. The woman didn't know which man fathered the daughter she had borne, and didn't feel any particular affection for the child, which was almost of an age to start crawling. Mother persuaded Father to allow her to care for the baby, which as yet had no name. Mother named the child Lisia and thereafter helped Father with a baby comfortably perched on her left hip and a satisfied smile on her face.

On the fourth day after Father became Master of the Hall, he called me into his office. "Yes, Father?" I said when I stood in front of his desk.

The first two days of Father's Mastership I hadn't always remembered to call him "sir", and the other Singers had taken to calling him "Father". Mother might have been partly to blame for this; from the first day, she had told the Singers to call her "Mother".

Father looked up from the Hall records. "Son, you've shown you can organize a tour in one day. I need as many tours as possible on the road within the next three days, and I need you to lead one."

I flinched at those last words; I hoped Father hadn't noticed. "Certainly, Father. But may I ask why?"

He sighed deeply, a sound of intense frustration. "For one thing, the Hall needs the money. Unless along with his other bookkeeping failures, Gadig failed to record tours, there haven't been anywhere near enough tours from this Hall for the past several turns of the star wheel. Singers who were to pay for their training by touring haven't been touring. The Hall is on the verge of being unable to pay the instructors.

"Secondly, putting as many experienced Singers on the road as possible will give me time to work out the housing situation. Asking Singers to return from tour to different quarters isn't how I'd like to handle this; but the only way I can see to effect a large-scale reassigning of cubicles is to have many of them vacated for a time. That will also solve the problem of the cubicles left empty by the deaths both of the Singers from your tour and the three more recent ones, which should improve morale.

"And I'm asking you to lead a tour because with Chaz, Dolin, and Rork dead and the two others sent away, I'm short of experienced leaders."

"But Zhia needs…" I began. I'd been so busy I hadn't had time to look in on her. Aplin was very strict about when those under his care could have visitors, and it was always at those times that I was in the middle of something that couldn't be interrupted.

Heavily, Father said, "What Zhia needs right now you can't give her. Aplin says she is recovering, but not quickly. Your moping around here won't speed her healing. You can't help Zhia; you can help the Hall. You can help me. And you can help yourself. I saw your reaction when I mentioned your leading a tour. Even if I had more tour leaders than I could use, I would have you lead a tour—a successful tour—so you can regain your confidence."

"The success isn't guaranteed, though, is it, Father? What if…"

"No 'what ifs', Son. A bad attitude makes a bad beginning. We can only hope that the havoc Zhia wreaked on the raiders will keep them inactive for a while."

While I was personally of the opinion that the raiders would more likely be thirsting for revenge, nothing would be gained by mentioning it to Father. "With the instruments and tebecs on hand, how many tours can we fit out?" I asked.

"Possibly as many as six. I'd settle for five, but they need to go as soon as possible."

Though Nia Diva was watching over Zhia, she must have found time to help me, as well. Before the midday meal three days later, five tours were ready to leave the Hall. Father put me in charge of a tour of first-timers, including Noia. Our schedule was the usual one for green Singers. Taf was on a different tour, one scheduled to visit the same towns my first tour had failed to reach.

Father came to the courtyard to send off the tours. Father invoked Nia Diva for protection for the Singers. I had already made my private petitions and offerings of appeasement to Darl. I had been working hard to get everything ready and expected to be groggy the first day; but I found myself tense and overly-watchful, an annoyance both to the first-timers and to myself.

By the start of the second day I was more relaxed. The first-timers also relaxed, and the tour proceeded nicely. We reached each engagement on schedule and without mishap. Several of the first-timers, especially Noia, showed such talent as Singers that they could be expected to prosper. Without going into lengthy detail—which even Singers find tedious—I can say that the second tour I led was predictable to the point of being boring: uneventful, unmemorable and, therefore, thoroughly enjoyable.

The night we returned, my first-timers were too happy and too tired to care about more than a bath and sleeping in a real bed, so there was no complaint when said bed was in a new cubicle. By the time another tour returned, two days later, the paperwork from my tour had been completed and the Hall's equipment stored. The Singers from the second tour also accepted their new quarters without question.

And so it continued, with a tour returning every few days and the necessary work being done when it was supposed to be done, as it was supposed to be done. Since I had been in charge of arranging all the tours, Father put me in charge of supervising the routine of return, as well, which kept me so busy that I could think of nothing else.

The last tour, Taf's tour, returned eighteen days after it had left the Hall. While Gadig was Master, returning tours were pretty much ignored. Father had me arrange a party in the evening of the day the last tour returned, a gathering which all the Singers attended. Mother wasn't there; it was past Lisia's bedtime.

Spirits were high, even without wine, though there was no lack of either wine or food. While the tours were gone, Father had been able to sell some of Gadig's loot. Between the money those sales brought in and the tour fees, Father was able not only to throw the party but also to pay the instructors (no, those are not in reverse order; Singers have their own priorities). Some of the instructors actually attended the event.

Things were starting to get a little rowdy when Taf climbed onto a table and called for silence. I can't say everyone heeded the request, but the noise dropped dramatically.

Taf also dropped, to his knees. Holding out his hand to Noia, who stood in front of the table, he said, "Taftan Noniantivem asks you to be his wife."

Noia smiled—she has a delightful smile—put her hand in his, and said, "Noia Dimianbazel is honored, and pleased to accept."

There was a stunned silence, then the revelers had recovered from their surprise and surged forward to congratulate Taf and Noia and to refill wine cups. The noise and festivity reached new heights.

Then Father, impressive in new black robes, called for silence. I looked at him apprehensively, wondering what he intended to say. Surely he remembered that he had already called for the memorial cup for those lost from my first tour. I hoped he was aware that Taf had ensured that everyone knew what had happened in the hollow.

What had happened at my parents' house was no secret, either. My first-timers had talked of little else the first night out, which might have contributed to my being tense. Along with everyone else who had heard of the events, they held Chaz, Rork, and Dolin in utter contempt. Probably because the Singers had become as fond of Mother as she was of them, sentiment ran so strongly against the three who had threatened her that anyone who had been friends with any of them—like me—didn't mention the fact.

Zhia's name was often spoken, both with respect and with fear. Many Singers had already come to regard Zhia almost as a legend; some wondered whether she was real. After all, they'd never seen her in classes. Of those who had seen her on tour, only Taf and I remained. Since that tour ended, she'd been at my parents' home. It was known she'd been at the Hall the day Gadig ceased to be Master, but she had been inside the Master's office where only a few had been able to see her. Those who had prepared the party had seen her. Since then she'd been in the clinic.

I suppose I shouldn't have been surprised that some Singers sounded frightened when they referred to her. Stories running unchecked in the Hall didn't exaggerate her exploits; they didn't need to be exaggerated to be incredible.

She had routed raiders—raiders!—with insect, stone, and ax; she had rescued Mother with water, oil, and fire. I would guess that two out of three Singers thought she was a hero. Most of the others shared Taf's and Father's opinion: Zhia was dangerous. While only a few thought she was a threat, they weren't reluctant to voice that judgment.

So there was silence broken only by the sound of the evening rain when Father said, "Tonight we give thanks to Nia Diva. We are rejoicing in the safe return of many touring Singers. We are rejoicing as well in the prospect of new Singers to come from the union we have been privileged to witness." Cheers and a few ribald comments followed this remark. Father waited until it was again quiet before he went on, "But I would ask you to remember with me tonight three men who are no longer with us. Though, sadly, they fell away, for a time they did serve Nia Diva. May she speak for them. I ask you to drink with me. To Dolin. To Chaz. To Rork."

Everyone drank. The usual silence which followed the memorial was prolonged and, I think, healing; then Father said, "Taf, while I wish you and Noia the best, why couldn't you have asked her to be your wife before I reassigned all the cubicles?"

Everyone laughed, and the party got noisy again. It didn't break up until Mother came in to say that the uproar had already wakened the baby three times and could we hold it down? There was more laughter and a friendly confusion of people saying good night and leaving the dining hall or grabbing a last bite to eat or a final swallow of wine.

Not until I was in my cubicle, a place I'd spent hardly any time in the last twenty days, did I realize that, though I'd seen Aplin at the party, I hadn't seen Zhia. Surely by now Aplin had released her from his care. If he hadn't, how much longer would it be until she recovered? Though she'd missed this tour season, the Singers' Festival would soon be here. With the other inexperienced Singers, she should attend so she could see what being a Singer was about. Besides touring, I reminded myself, remembering the lecture Zhia had given the day her tour ended so disastrously.

I didn't want to think about that day. I went to bed and had no trouble sleeping.

Early the next morning, before Father could find some chore for me, I went to the clinic. It was deserted; not even Aplin was there. Satisfied that Zhia was recovered and thinking that Aplin might be recovering from the party, I went to the dining hall to break my fast.

There weren't many Singers there. The kitchen workers were indulging in the usual chaff, pretending to be surprised that anyone was already hungry after eating so much at the party, and asking whether I knew how late they'd been up washing the dishes. Joining in the fun, I said no, I didn't know; how late had they been up, and had they really been washing dishes the whole time? Things got somewhat risque after that. The silliness ended with a long, hearty laugh.

It was good to see the cheer with which people were going about their tasks. Under Gadig's Mastership, smiles and joking among the servants had been rare. This light-heartedness was because of Father, the man who, not so long ago, I had been thinking I despised.

As I left the dining hall, heading for Father's office to learn what he needed me to do next, I wondered how much of the change in Father was due to his new duties. Had the verbal ugliness which had made him so pitiable been caused as much by frustration as by what Zhia believed to be some degenerative condition? It may have been that he had simply quit trying to control his outbursts, even though they sometimes hurt Mother.

Had I ever questioned my Father's feelings for Mother, the events of the day Father became Master had allayed my doubts. Father's voice was no longer eloquent; better than any words, that day his face had expressed his true concern for Mother. I was glad I could again respect my father. I was even more glad that, thanks to Zhia, I still had a mother.

Mother and Lisia were in Father's office when I knocked on the door. Mother broke off in mid-sentence, turned troubled eyes on me, and left.

"Your pardon, Father," I said, distressed by the way Mother had looked at me. "Did I come at a bad time? I just wanted to know what you need me to do today."

The look he gave me was even more distressing. "I need you and Taf to come with me to the magistrate's chambers. Zhia is in prison."

Chapter Twenty-Two

"Tell me I didn't hear you correctly," I said. My throat felt very tight. I saw pity in Father's eyes and knew my ears hadn't deceived me. "Why?"

"I don't know, Son. The day after your tour left, two soldiers and a functionary came to the Hall. The soldiers took Zhia away, very much over Aplin's protests. The functionary left a formal summons for you and Taf. I told him you were both on tour and wouldn't be back for several days, and asked whether Zhia could remain here until you returned. I was told charges had been brought against her and she would remain in prison until they could be answered.

"Aplin has been going to the prison every day to check on her. She's not doing well, which is hardly surprising." The last words were so soft I could hardly hear them.

I felt like I'd taken a blow in my middle. "So Zhia has been in prison for a good—let's make that 'a bad'—nineteen days?" Father nodded. "This will be a nice wake-up for Taf the morning after he took a wife."

"I know. Had I known last night what he planned, I would have tried to dissuade him."

"Where is Taf?" I asked, sharply.

"I'm here," Taf said, coming into the office. It was obvious he'd dressed in a hurry. "This had better be important. If it's just a joke played on a man with a new wife, it's in very bad taste."

Father handed the summons to Taf. Father had no trouble finding it, and not only because, over the last double handful of days, he had probably read and re-read it. The table—the only item in the office which had outlasted Gadig—was now tidy, with its ever-present paperwork in organized stacks. Presumably, the other, opulent furnishings had been sold. Those that replaced them were both simpler and more functional.

When Taf finished reading the document, he looked up at Father, his face quizzical. "The magistrate doesn't know I'm back yet, right? Can I go back to bed now and we'll take care of this in a couple of days?"

"Sure," I said, unable to keep sarcasm from my voice. "Zhia's only been in prison since we left on tour. She won't mind being there a couple more days so you can enjoy your wife."

"Son," Father chided. I confess my choice of words was cruder than what I've written.

I never saw anyone go as white as Taf did without fainting. "But Zhia is hurt," he whispered.

"Yes, and she won't recover in prison," Father added.

Taf and I wanted to leave at once, but Father said, "We'll need our wits about us today," and took Taf to the dining hall. While he ate, Father sent a stable hand to the magistrate with the message that those from the Hall who had been summoned had returned, and inquiring whether we should be at his chambers that morning. "I'd hate to waste a whole day waiting for Zhia's accuser," Father remarked.

The stable hand returned with word that the magistrate would see us as soon as we arrived. Father thanked him, asked him to ready a cart and desdal, and sent him away before loosing a gusty sigh. "That doesn't sound good. Someone really has it in for Zhia." I started to ask a question, but Father held up a hand. "Speculating will do no good, Son. Let's save our breath and get to the magistrate's chambers."

I've mentioned that much of the Hall is built of rough brown stone. The magistrate's chambers were constructed of some black stone, highly polished. Aside from necessary furnishings, the area was bare, even bleak. It was cold, unwelcoming, intimidating.

The magistrate's eyes were, if possible, even colder, less welcoming, and more intimidating. The well-dressed man who was with him was scowling, but next to the magistrate he looked like a songbird trying to out-glare a tebec.

The magistrate seated himself. Taf, Father, the other man, and I remained standing.

After a few moments, the door opened and two functionaries dragged in Zhia by the arms. She had been wrapped in a filthy blanket. When the functionaries released her and she fell heavily to the floor, the blanket shifted. Under it, Zhia was naked. Not even her injured arm and hands or her broken foot were covered. As she lay senseless, blood began to pool under her arm.

Father held my arm in a bruising grip. I held Taf's. None of us dared speak.

"Cover her," the magistrate said to the functionaries. They did so, carelessly. To the richly-attired man, he said, "What is your full name?"

"Mirlov Tariantirlov, Your Honor."

"And what is the charge you bring?"

"Your Honor, the accused is responsible for the death of my son."

"What was your son's full name?"

"Birlov Ogianmirlov, Your Honor."

Taf and I sneaked a glance at each other. The man was Birl's father! Zhia had said Birl's father was a merchant; a wealthy one, to judge from the clothing he wore.

"What were the circumstances of your son's death?"

"He was a Singer, Your Honor. He was sent on a tour. The accused was on the tour. I don't know any of those men, but I assume the younger ones were the other two who survived when everyone else died. The Hall Master told me the accused was a servant who had been sent to…to provide pleasure for the men. He told me that when my son and the others were killed, no one was standing guard because the accused was…was with the tour leader and the other man who survived, even though it was morning. No one was standing guard! Raiders attacked, and my son was killed!"

The magistrate spoke to the functionaries. "Is the accused able to speak?"

One of them nudged the unresponsive shape with his toe. "No, Your Honor."

The magistrate looked at us. "Who will answer these charges?"

Father stepped forward. "Your Honor, as acting Master of the Hall, I request the opportunity to answer those charges that I can."

"What is your full name?"

"Robil Liulanrobig, Your Honor."

"Proceed."

"Your Honor, it is not now, nor has it ever been, the practice among Singers to send servants on tour. Singers tour. And while you are aware that the name of the accused was not entered in the Hall records as a Singer, you have already heard her testimony that she was working at the Hall on the strength of the promise that the work was in exchange for training as a Singer. That the former Master broke his promise to her doesn't change the fact that she was there to become a Singer.

"I must also emphatically reject the assertion that any female Singer is sent on tour to provide intimate services to the male Singers. Were that to happen on tour, Your Honor, I can assure you and the accuser that none of those men would continue to be Singers.

"If the accuser would like additional information about the practices at the Hall, I will gladly provide them in whatever detail he deems needful. But as the accused, a Singer from my Hall, was taken from my Hall clinic over the protests of the doctor tending her, may I ask that we speed these proceedings, or the accuser may find himself seeking redress from a corpse."

The magistrate said, "I will caution you only once to moderate your tone."

"Your pardon, Your Honor. Might these Singers be permitted to tell the accuser what actually happened on the day the accuser's son and six other Singers died?"

"Which was the tour leader?"

"I was, Your Honor," I said.

"What is your full name?"

"Rois Isianrobil, Your Honor."

Birl's father gave a strangled cry. "Your Honor, I protest! The tour leader is the son of the acting Hall Master! He can hardly be expected to give impartial testimony!"

The magistrate gave Birl's father a stern look, but turned to Taf. "What is your full name?"

"Taftan Noniantivem, Your Honor."

The magistrate looked at Birl's father. "Does this witness suit you?"

"Yes, Your Honor."

"Taftan Noniantivem, were you on the tour on which the accuser's son died?"

"Yes, Your Honor."

"Where were you when the accuser's son died?"

"I was climbing a hill, Your Honor. I was helping the tour leader look for the accused, who was cutting wood so we could cook a meal. You see, Your Honor, the accused, the tour leader, and I were the only ones on the tour who knew how to use an ax. I was in charge of taking care of the tebecs, and the tour leader isn't supposed to do that kind of work, so Zh...the accused got stuck with the chore."

"So you weren't receiving intimate services from the accused at the time the accuser's son died."

"No, Your Honor. Just the night before I saw the accused backhand one of our tour who suggested she...she entertain him." He glanced at Zhia's motionless form and grimaced. "Your Honor, please pardon if it's improper for me to say so, but I share the Master's concern about the accused. May I just tell you what happened?"

For the briefest moment, I saw the magistrate's face soften. "Proceed. Begin with why you and the tour leader were looking for the accused, when you knew she was cutting wood."

"Because she had already blistered her hands chopping wood, Your Honor. They were raw. The tour leader and I agreed that the longer she used the ax, the greater the chance that it would slip from her grip and she'd get hurt.

Whichever one of us found her was going to take over the chore and let her rest.

"The tour leader and I were climbing a hill out of the hollow where the others were resting. At the back of the hollow was a pretty good cliff with water pouring over it into a pool. The hollow had water, it had wood, and it looked restful. That's why we stopped there. We'd started a fire with small stuff that was on the ground, but it wasn't enough for cooking, which is why the accused was cutting wood.

"The tour leader and I hadn't gone very far up the hill when a hail of darts poured into the hollow from the top of the cliff. The ones resting in the hollow were massacred. Raiders came down from the height. Some started to loot the bodies. Some went after our pack and riding tebecs. The raiders took the pack ones first. There were four of them; fourteen birds in all. I hadn't hobbled them because tebecs don't like to cross running water, and a little stream made a barrier across the opening of the hollow.

"A few raiders came up the hill toward the tour leader and me. I ran and climbed a tree. One raider grabbed the tour leader by the hair. They fell, rolled down the hill, and fetched up against the stones that ringed the little fire. The tour leader grabbed a handful of hot ash and threw it in the raider's face. That raider let go, but another one, armed with a knife, grabbed him. The tour leader got him to let go of the knife, but then the raider went for his throat.

"That's when the accused came down the hill. She had the ax in one hand. She had an oiled cloth cloak bundled in the other. As she ran, she kicked a big rock, she screamed, and she threw the cloak. The scream made the raider who was strangling the tour leader turn. The rock hit him in the chest. The scream also made the tebecs that hadn't been stolen get skittish. If you don't know, Your Honor, tebecs kick. Their kick can kill. Some of the raiders died that way. Some were crushed by the tebec's bodies, which are heavy even without their saddles. These were saddled. A few birds ran away.

"What was in the cloak was a swarmer's nest. When the cloak landed in the midst of the raiders, it fell open and the nest split. Swarmers routed some of the raiders. The accused was using the ax. She killed the raider who had been hit by the rock, and six others. Then one raider dived at her legs and made her fall. He choked her until she dropped the ax. He picked it up and was ready to kill her when she kicked the side of his knee. He fell. The accused was trying to get up when the raider tripped her. She fell on top of him and used a rock to smash in his head. Then she stood up, picked up the ax, and took a step toward the remaining raiders. They ran.

"Then we carried the Singers' bodies and laid them together in a cairn. The accused commended them to Nia Diva. Then she made us burn the raiders' bodies. Then one tebec found us and, riding it, I found a farmer who loaned us a cart and chero, because the accused had broken her foot and couldn't walk."

The silence that followed Taf's narrative was the same as one sometimes hears on tour when an audience is especially moved and there is a hush before the applause begins. This time, there was no applause.

"I don't believe it," Birl's father said. "No one defeats raiders. Your Honor, I say the woman used the ax on the other Singers."

"The charge against the accused is not murder," the magistrate said.

"Well, I said she was responsible for the death of my son. If she hacked him with an ax, she would be responsible for his death, wouldn't she, Your Honor?"

The magistrate turned to Taf. "Can you answer this allegation?"

"Your Honor, what I've told you is what I saw happen. The seven Singers who died were killed by raiders. They were dead before the accused returned to the hollow. The only ones who felt the bite of her ax were raiders."

"That tale is so preposterous it has to be false," Birl's father spat. "This is a Singer, Your Honor. What do Singers do? Make things up! Create entertaining stories and put them to music! Can you believe a word he says?"

"Your Honor," Father said, "may I ask the accuser if his attitude toward Singers would be the same if his son were the one giving testimony? May I remind Your Honor that the accuser's son was on tour because he was a Singer?"

"That is an interesting point, but it has no bearing on the charge," the magistrate said. He spoke again to Taf. "The bodies of the Singers were placed in a cairn, you said?"

"Yes, Your Honor."

"Could you find the place where the accuser's son died?"

"I think so, Your Honor. If I can't find it, my tebec can."

The magistrate gestured to the functionaries. "Return the accused to prison." This time, their handling of Zhia was gentler. They managed to keep the blanket around her. "In the morning, the accuser, these two survivors of the tour, the Hall Master, and I will travel to where the cairn is," the magistrate added. "The bodies will be uncovered, and we will see whether the cause of death can be determined."

I said, "May I suggest, Your Honor, that a doctor—preferably one of the accuser's choosing—accompany us to examine the bodies?"

The magistrate said to Birl's father, "You will arrange for a doctor and transport for our party."

"Yes, Your Honor."

"May I also suggest, Your Honor, that we bring cloths to cover our noses and mouths?" I continued. "Those Singers died some forty days ago." I looked at Birl's father when I said, "Their bodies will be rotting."

He paled. He wasn't as rotund as Birl had been, but he looked soft. He probably hadn't stopped to consider where his charges might lead.

The magistrate didn't look too pleased at the idea of rotting corpses, either. "That is a good suggestion. We will leave from here at daybreak tomorrow."

"One last thing, Your Honor," Father said. "May I send the Hall doctor to tend the accused? He was here this morning; since then, the injury the accused incurred while saving my wife's life has apparently torn open. It may need new stitches."

Whatever the magistrate had been expecting, it wasn't that. The play of emotions on his face would have been amusing had something other than Zhia's life rested on his answer. "You may."

"Thank you, Your Honor."

On his return from the prison, Aplin reported that the situation was as Father had feared. Further blood loss had done Zhia no good. "How long will it take you to find the bodies and come back?" he asked me.

"Possibly six days. Maybe longer."

"Rois, if Zhia stays in that prison, I don't think she'll live another six days."

I cleared my throat. "You know we can't break her out of prison. If Nia Diva wants her as a Singer, she'll live. If she dies, I'll know you did all you could."

"Don't get your hopes up, Rois," was his parting comment.

I didn't sleep that night. Father looked like he hadn't slept, either. We had to pound on Taf's door to wake him. We heard a groggy, "I'm coming," the sound of a soggy kiss, a muffled giggle, and then assorted bumps and groans as Taf struggled into his clothes.

I had spent my night imagining both what we would find in the cairn at the hollow and, worse, what we might find when we got back to the Hall. Father had clearly spent his night productively: before we headed for the magistrate's chambers, we stopped in the dining hall to collect a large amount of food and other supplies that were prepared as for a tour. Beside those provisions sat three portions ready for us to eat on our way to the magistrate's chambers.

The cart and desdal were in the courtyard. We loaded the supplies into the bed of the cart. Taf climbed in with the supplies and was soon snoring. Father and I climbed onto the seat. Father told me to drive.

Father turned, looked at Taf, and smiled. "Tough night."

I tried to make some joking reply, but couldn't. I resented Taf's needing to sleep during the day because having a wife kept him from sleeping at night. At least, that's what I told myself, though I knew what was really wrong was that I was anxious for Zhia.

I hated the casual way the functionaries had handled her the day before, and their carelessness even though she was obviously injured. I hated their lack of regard for her modesty. I could only assume she had been transported to prison wearing only that blanket. I hated how the one man had nudged her with his toe as though she were something disgusting. What I hated, resented, and abhorred most was everyone's referring to her as "the accused". I'd lost count of how many times I'd bitten my tongue to keep from shouting, "She has a name!" That would have done no one any good.

I knew the only way to get her out of that cursed prison was to go on this cursed trip to that cursed hollow and prove to Birl's cursed father that his cursed son had, indeed, died from cursed raiders' cursed darts…

"Son, you're hurting the desdal," Father said, taking the whip from my hand. "Perhaps I should drive."

I was appalled to see welts on the animal's hide. I had been striking it without being aware of doing so.

"Aplin says he doesn't think she'll live another six days," I said. I couldn't keep my voice steady.

"Hitting the desdal won't change that. Or was it Mirlov you thought you were hitting?"

"Mirlov? Oh, Birl's father. No, I don't want to hit him, Father. I suppose it's because he has money that the magistrate didn't just laugh at him and tell him to come back when he had a real grievance. Birl was like that, too, always whining about something. He's the one the tebec bit before we even left the courtyard. He carried on like he'd lost a leg. After Aplin bandaged him, he told me to give Birl a swift kick in the rear if he started acting that way on tour."

Father chuckled. "Did you get to follow the doctor's orders?"

"No. The others stomped him pretty well. With words, that is. I think it was one of the twins (I never did learn to tell them apart) who said, 'I would say Birl is acting like a girl, but I don't see Zhia carrying on like that.'" This time I was able to laugh with Father. "And I think we were starting to get him straightened out. Zhia found out he'd traveled with his father, who is a merchant—you may have guessed that—and so knew some of the territory where we were delayed while I was ill. She put Birl in charge of leading the group to the Hall in that area, and he handled that responsibility just fine."

"Do you wonder why only Birl's father brought charges against Zhia?" Father asked. "I'm curious whether Gadig told the same lie to all the bereaved parents."

A memory stirred. "I don't know about that, but I'm almost certain Gadig told the Singers who toured with Zhia that she was there for their enjoyment. I never told you about that part of the tour, did I, Father? When the seven went to the other Hall, Taf remained at the Quarter Rest where I'd fallen ill because Zhia was exhausted from caring for me, and I was too weak to do much.

"In the evening, Zhia got upset and went out in the rain to cut wood without her cloak. Taf went out to look for her and found her asleep under a tree. We brought her in and took the wet clothes off her before we put her by the fire to sleep. The others returned from their errand while she was sleeping. In the morning—actually, it was midmorning—she woke, and the seven saw that she'd been sleeping undressed. They got the idea that Taf, Zhia, and I had been carrying on while they were gone.

"That night, which was the night before they died, when Zhia was asleep and I was outside the Quarter Rest making sure the tebecs were ready for a morning departure, they confronted Taf. The gist of their complaint was not that Taf and I presumably had been having fun, but that they wanted what one of them called 'equal time'. They were all angry, and kept getting louder. They woke Zhia, who heard some of the discussion. I heard most of what was said, and I can tell you, Father, it was crude.

"Zhia didn't shout at them. She got quiet and icy angry, and asked them if they really thought she was on tour to blister her hands chopping wood for them all day and then lie still for them all night."

"That was blunt," Father remarked. "Did they have sense enough to apologize?"

"No. One, who'd been making smart remarks the whole tour, said he would prefer that she do more than lie still."

Father stared at me. "And he lived long enough for raiders to kill him?"

I smiled grimly. "Yes. He's the one Zhia backhanded. Then she said, 'Does anyone else think I'm joking?'; and told them all to get ready to leave in the morning."

"I take it at the time she was still acting as tour leader."

"Yes. Anyway, after she left them, one of them said, 'What's with her? Didn't the Master say...' and then another told him to be quiet. And Father, the evening before the tour began Gadig had been making comments to me that suggested I had permission to use Zhia for my pleasure."

"Need I ask whether you did so?"

"I'm not likely to get excited about a woman who's had to tend my saddle sores."

"That doesn't answer the question."

"No, Father. There has been no impropriety of any kind between Zhia and me."

"But Gadig didn't know that. He did know you had a reputation for being a ladies' man. By the way, I don't think your mother knows about your reputation, Son; I know it would distress her to learn that not everyone regards you as highly as she does. No matter how low Gadig thought you would stoop, I can hardly believe he would stoop so low as to defame Singers from his own Hall."

"But he didn't regard Zhia as a Singer," I said, trying to avoid further discussion of my reputation. I don't know why it had never occurred to me that my antics might cause my parents grief.

Father said, patiently, "He wasn't defaming Zhia; he was defaming you. What we learned from Lisia's mother tells me that Gadig didn't consider anything done with a slave improper. He didn't spread a lie about you and Taf being involved with Zhia to hurt Zhia. He had to discredit you so no matter what the actual cause, you would take the blame for the tour's failure."

I didn't want to think about that, but it was hard to avoid the subject. "Do you suppose the magistrate believed what Birl's father says Gadig told him?"

"Right now, I suspect the magistrate doesn't believe or even like any of us. He doesn't like Mirlov because the man is wasting his time with a charge that just misses being frivolous enough to dismiss. I think he'd love to throw Mirlov in prison. He doesn't like Zhia because he apparently was aware that she was manipulating him. He's getting even by doing exactly as she asked; he's not treating her like anyone special. She's languishing in prison, injured. The magistrate doesn't like Taf because, like Mirlov, he doesn't want to believe what he heard, but what he heard compelled belief. Taf told the story well. Despite what Mirlov said, no Singer would make up a story like that; it's not believable. The magistrate doesn't like you because now he knows what he's going to have to face in a few days. And yes, I brought good, thick cloths. And he doesn't like me because I forced him to recognize the injustice of the way he's treating Zhia."

"That sounds like he's anything but impartial," I said, feeling like I'd swallowed a rock.

"No one is ever entirely impartial, Son. But I'm glad you thought to ask for a doctor to accompany us. If the bodies are badly decomposed—no 'if' about it, actually—the question of Zhia's guilt or innocence will rest on a doctor's opinion. Mirlov may be wealthy enough to buy a doctor's opinion. But there's no point in worrying about that.

"What I'm worried about is how we're going to manage a six-day or longer trip with a man who is so mad with grief he would do anything, including deny the evidence of his own reason and senses, to hurt the one he blames for his loss: Zhia.

"I'm afraid that no matter what the doctor finds when we uncover the bodies, the verdict will be the same: guilty. Given that probability, it may be somewhat comforting to know that Zhia isn't likely to languish in prison much longer."

Chapter Twenty-Three

Is there anyone who has never said, "I see it, but I don't believe it"?

As Birl's father had said, Singers are known for their imagination. Imagination helps improvisation, another skill Singers exhibit. That said, before going farther with this story I must assert that the events recorded in the following pages aren't—are not—imagined. There were numerous witnesses, most of them neutral, if not hostile. Many are still alive.

There is no official record of what I am about to relate. No magistrate would admit the truth of what happened, let alone enter it into the archives. Even now, so many turns of the star wheel later, I would still be willing to give one of my Champion's cups—what can one do with five, anyway?—to know how the magistrate explained his decision in the case.

But I'm getting ahead of myself.

Father, Taf (still sleeping), and I reached the magistrate's chambers a bit before daybreak. The magistrate and his usual functionaries soon emerged from the building. They were joined by a small troop of chero-mounted soldiers, which emerged from somewhere behind the building. Birl's father and a stranger whom I took to be the doctor arrived in a desdal-drawn cart just as the first bit of the sun was visible.

Father muttered, "Why soldiers, I wonder?" I had no answer, so I said nothing. "That cart isn't big enough for everyone," was Father's next aside.

"Then I guess we drive our cart, too," I replied. Like Father, I kept my voice low.

"I don't see any supplies in their cart."

Neither did I. "Did we bring enough for that many?"

"It looks like the soldiers have their own supplies; but we certainly don't have enough for the rest of the group, even if no one ate much and half of us were willing to sleep in the rain."

The magistrate had been frowning at Father and me. Finally noticing what we were talking about, he turned the frown on Birl's father.

We heard Mirlov stammer an explanation, something to the effect that he had done just as he had been requested. We also heard the magistrate's question: "So you are willing to do without food or shelter for the duration of this undertaking?"

There was more stammering, more explaining, more evasion. If I closed my eyes, I could imagine Birl was speaking. Finally, the magistrate told the functionaries to fetch the necessary provisions from the soldiers' stores, and informed Mirlov that he would be paying for the use and replacement of said provisions.

Surprisingly, the sun wasn't yet very high when we finally left. Taf wakened and joined Father and me on the cart seat, leaving room for the functionaries to load the additional supplies in our cart, which was larger. The magistrate decreed that he and the doctor would ride on the seat of the other cart. Birl's father and the functionaries crowded into the back. Mirlov looked very sour. Remembering how rocky some of the roads were, I was sure he would look even more sour before we reached the hollow.

"I wish I were riding a tebec," Taf said.

I had been thinking the same thing. Every moment that was wasted lessened the chance that Zhia would still be alive when we returned.

It wasn't a comfortable trip, and not just because a cart is misery on wheels. The sole advantage a cart has over a tebec is that I've never heard of anyone getting sores on the rear from riding in a cart. Riding a tebec, one can ride side by side and converse. Talking from one cart to another is much more difficult. The first day, the magistrate had little to say to anyone. Birl's father sulked (there's no other word for it) and the doctor, whose name was Capis, looked like he would regret the day he agreed to accompany this strange venture until the day he died.

Before the first day was over, Birl's father looked like that inevitable day couldn't be soon enough. One would expect a merchant to be accustomed to the hardships of travel. Not Mirlov. When we stopped that first night, he recoiled at the sight of the soldiers' tents and sneered at ones Father had brought for our use. (Tents aren't used on tours, but are sometimes needed when Festival attendees overfill lodgings in town and stay at the Hall.) When he learned that the magistrate would not allow him to seek more comfortable accommodations in the nearest town, which was probably the one we had left that morning, he finally deigned to use one of our tents, which were marginally better than the soldiers' shelters.

Since the soldiers didn't offer their extra tent for our use, it looked like Taf and I would have to share one. Father had brought four because, at his height, he needed two. It turned out I could have used two, as well. Taf offered to sleep under our cart, but I told him he didn't want to risk falling ill so soon after taking a wife. With ill-disguised relief, he agreed. The cart's bed didn't leak much. After I spread an oiled cloth cloak in it, I stayed fairly dry. However, in the morning I was so cold and stiff I could hardly move.

The magistrate watched me making my not-yet-limber way toward the fire Taf had kindled. "Is this what being a Singer is about?" he asked me, not quite managing to keep mockery out of his voice.

"Not entirely, Your Honor," I said. "Being a Singer is about touring. Accommodations on tours aren't plush. I will admit they're usually somewhat nicer than we had last night."

"Do you enjoy touring?"

Thinking of the applause and the smiles on the faces of the nobodies, I remembered what Zhia had said the day her tour came to so inglorious an end. "Yes, Your Honor, I enjoy it. I like to sing. People like to hear me. 'Fun' isn't the right word for what it feels like when the music is coming together like it should, but I can't think of a better word right now. The best times on tour are when the Singers feel each other's excitement, and the audience feels the Singers' excitement, and it just gets bigger and bigger. There's nothing that compares with that thrill."

"Nothing?" the magistrate echoed, with a meaningful smile.

"Taf!" I called. When he looked over, I asked, "You have a new wife. Tell the magistrate if anything compares with the thrill of making music when everything is right."

Without hesitation, Taf replied, "Not a thing. And, Your Honor, my wife, who's just had both her first tour and her first nights with me, would agree."

"Then allow me to congratulate both of you on being able to do what you love. Not everyone has that pleasure. And congratulations to you, Taf, on your wife."

"Thank you, Your Honor. It's very much my pleasure."

Our laughter apparently woke Birl's father. As he came out of the tent, he grumbled at how early it was. As he ate, he grumbled at how ordinary the food was. As we prepared to get back on the road, he grumbled because Osrum—as Taf, Father, and I had been invited to call the magistrate—refused to change the seating arrangements. He grumbled because it was hot, but refused to shed any of his weighty clothing. He grumbled because it was dusty. (It wasn't; the evening rains keep the roads remarkably dust-free.) He grumbled at insects. He grumbled because the cart jostled him.

Not until mid-afternoon did Osrum turn and say, "One more word and I'll ask you to get out of the cart and walk so I won't have to listen to you any longer. Your complaining is prejudicing me against your case."

It was all Father, Taf, and I could do to act like we hadn't heard. Happily, Osrum's warning was effective, though the silence from the smaller cart was decidedly chilly. The soldiers, of course, carried on their own low-voiced conversations. I think Osrum would have been willing to talk with Capis, but before the second day was done, the doctor was a queasy shade of green. It was probably just as well he didn't try to speak. Mirlov would, of course, regard the functionaries as below his status. The latter rarely spoke and, except for when sleeping, never relaxed. Thinking back, I now realize that they never slept at the same time. Watching their ever-alert eyes and posture, I began to suspect that they were Osrum's personal guards. I wondered if Osrum really thought they could keep him safe from a hail of raiders' darts.

As the sun approached zenith the third day, I began to recognize the terrain, and informed Osrum that we were close to the hollow. He asked that the carts stop, and sent the soldiers to scout ahead, telling them to pay special attention to the height behind the pool. They rattled up the road almost as though attempting to make as much noise as possible. Perhaps they hoped to frighten away any raiders who might be lurking.

It wasn't long before they returned with word that there was no sign of danger, but that there was an abandoned camp at the top of the falls. I couldn't help wondering if it were the same camp where Zhia and Pandizh had been so abused.

From then until we reached the hollow, the carts were surrounded by soldiers, who apparently believed they were protecting us. After looking around at the troop, Taf looked at the wide-open space above us and then at me. We both shook our heads.

Osrum's cart was behind ours. He must have seen Taf's and my reaction, for he said, "I take it you don't consider these measures adequate for our defense."

Taf climbed into the bed of the cart and sat facing backwards so he could more easily converse. "Your Honor, I don't know if we're the only people to have survived a raider attack. I do know that the measures you've implemented wouldn't have prevented any deaths on the tour I was on with Birl, Zhia, Rois, and the others. We're completely unprotected from above. Above is where the attack that killed my friends came from."

"This is the first time you've referred to them as friends," Osrum said.

"With all respect, Your Honor—your pardon; I can't call you 'Osrum' to your face—that's because in your chambers I was intimidated. I was afraid if I said something wrong, I'd end up where Zhia is.

"But yes, they were my friends. Most of them started at the Hall the same time I did. We went to the same classes, and had the same gripes about our instructors. We had the same hopes, we had the same goals. We had our differences, both at the Hall and on tour, but I would never have wished on any of them the death they suffered.

"When someone my age thinks about death, which isn't often, it's in some heroic context. One dies saving someone else's life, or in battle for a noble cause. There was nothing heroic or noble in the way my friends died. Birl, Vel, Hink, Norjy, Hadden, Mariz, and Turiz were slaughtered. I was going to say 'slaughtered like animals', but they weren't. I've slaughtered animals, Your Honor. When I kill an animal, I know I'm killing a living thing, so I try not to frighten the creature, or hurt it any more than is required. I understand there's a basic but necessary injustice when I take an animal's life to sustain my own. I respect the animal because, without it, I can't live.

"The raiders acted like what they were doing wasn't killing. To them, those seven Singers weren't even people; they were just another raid, just another source of loot. The raiders didn't just take my friends' lives, they took their worth as persons. But Zhia, in showing their bodies the respect she did, returned that worth to them."

There was a long pause, then Osrum said, "Do I recall that in your testimony you said Zhia had you burn the raiders' bodies?"

"Yes. Rois and I were against it, and not just because we all knew the raiders could regroup and return. He and I thought we should take what we could use from the bodies and leave them to the carrion eaters."

"As raiders do."

"I guess so. Zhia said pretty much that same thing. How did she put it, Rois?" Taf asked, twisting so I could hear him better (I could hear him quite well).

I said, "She said something like 'If you two want to lower yourselves to that, go ahead. I won't help; I don't even want to watch.'"

"Did she help carry bodies?" Osrum asked.

"Of course she did." Taf replied. "Never let it be said that blistered hands and a broken foot stop Zhia from being stupid."

"You forgot the broken ribs," said Father, who had been surprisingly quiet.

"I wish you could, too," I said to him so only he could hear. "You know you didn't hurt her deliberately."

"I don't recall any mention of broken ribs." Osrum looked concerned.

I said, "In your chambers, Taf mentioned the raider who grabbed Zhia's legs and made her fall. When she fell, she landed on a large rock and broke ribs. That was the same rock that not much later she used so devastatingly on that raider."

Mirlov, who at first had made a show of paying no attention to the conversation, had abandoned the pretense. Now he exclaimed, "May I ask the acting Hall Master what a dangerous woman like the accused was doing among decent people like my son?"

Father didn't deign to turn to look at Mirlov. Even so, his raspy answer was easily heard. "May I remind the accuser that it is because Zhia is what he calls 'dangerous' that his son was buried? Had Zhia not been willing to face danger—a phrase I prefer to the term 'dangerous'—there would be no decomposing bodies to find, and maybe not even scattered bones."

Capis gagged and covered his mouth. "Are you really a doctor?" Osrum asked him. He nodded weakly.

Father continued, "The accuser may also wish to consider that because Zhia is compassionate—let him call her dangerous if he wishes—he may yet see her spend her remaining days in prison. And because she didn't face that or later danger unscathed, those days may not be many."

Birl's father wisely said nothing.

Osrum rubbed the rust-colored stubble on his chin. "Why could Zhia defeat raiders?"

I gave Taf the signal to answer. "Let me answer with an illustration from my own profession, Your Honor. Singers know some songs so well they can sing them half asleep."

Father muttered something uncomplimentary with the words "present company" in it. I grinned.

Ignoring or, perhaps, not hearing us, Taf went on, "Of course, if someone decides to modulate, or change the tempo, those who are half-asleep aren't ready to do something different.

"That was the raiders' mistake; they were complacent. They're used to success. They've fallen into a routine, a mindless one. They attack without warning, from above, so defense isn't possible. When everyone's dead, they despoil the bodies and steal anything else that's worth taking. But when they encountered panicked tebecs, angry swarmers, and Zhia's ax, they weren't ready to do anything different. Their victims are supposed to die, not fight back. Zhia didn't play by their rules."

"How unfair of her," Osrum remarked, with a broad smile.

"Your Honor, it seems to me that the tour leader and this witness are attempting to prejudice you toward the accused," Mirlov said.

Turning to him with no trace of a smile, Osrum said, "We are not in my chambers. The accused has a name, which you may use."

"I choose not to speak her name, Your Honor. I don't wish to curse in your presence."

"'Don't confuse me with facts; my mind is made up,'" Father whispered to me.

Osrum's voice became hard. "What I am doing is gathering additional information relative to the events surrounding your son's death. The more details I have, the better I am able to make the right decision. Or don't you care whether I render a fair judgment?"

Realizing the question was of the "Do you still beat your wife?" variety, Mirlov quickly said, "Of course I care, Your Honor. All I want is justice for my son."

"Are you certain that's all you want?" Osrum asked.

Birl's father didn't answer, because just then we reached the hollow. Once again, the soldiers fanned out and searched the surrounding area. When their leader gave an "all clear" signal—I was a little surprised that soldiers and Singers use some of the same ones—we got out of the carts.

While Father located the cloths for our noses and mouths I reminded everyone we'd want, I drew Taf aside. "I have to apologize. I don't know why it didn't occur to me that those men were your friends. I never expressed any concern to you for their deaths."

"That's all right, Rois," he said. "You had something more important to think about right then: staying alive." With a rather crooked smile, he added, "When I was growing up—feeding tebecs, shoveling tebec manure, keeping predators from tebec eggs, making sure tebec chicks didn't get trampled by the adult birds—I used to imagine going on adventures. Now I've been on an adventure. If I have a long, uneventful 'ever after' with Noia, I'll be perfectly happy."

"If you and Noia are planning to have children, it won't exactly be uneventful," Father said, coming up to give us the cloths for masking our faces.

Taf laughed. "I suppose the secret is sharing your adventures with someone you care about."

Father agreed. I was again thinking of Eia, and wondering how she would fare in the kinds of situations Zhia had encountered in the past forty-plus days. The thought of bruises and cuts on her flawless face made me shudder. It would be like desecrating the symbol of Nia Diva.

"Let's get this over with," Father said when we were protected from the reek to come.

As we walked toward the others, I saw that none of them had covered their noses and mouths. Osrum was looking coldly at Birl's father who, it seemed, had forgotten to bring protective cloths, as well. I untied the cloth from my face and handed it to Osrum. Taf gave his to Capis. I was pretty sure that, unless forced to, Mirlov wouldn't get anywhere near the stench and ugliness of the long-dead bodies.

Osrum had soldiers move the upper layer of rock from the cairn. Taf and I took deep breaths to prepare for not breathing as soon as the first whiff of decay reached us. Capis was reluctantly moving closer. Osrum stood near the head of the cairn, arms folded across his chest.

The first exclamation came from him. Capis' came a beat later. Father wasn't standing close, but his height enabled him to see without being close. He didn't exclaim, but I saw his frame jerk with surprise. A moment later, he, Osrum, and Capis were helping the soldiers remove the stones.

Taf and I exchanged a puzzled look and also edged forward, cautiously sniffing and ready to cover our faces. No stench reached us. We moved closer, then stopped short and stared, speechless.

The seven bodies were just as they had been when we placed them in the cairn. They had not decayed.

Chapter Twenty-Four

"Nia Diva!" Taf breathed, reverently.

Birl's father rounded on me. "Explain this!"

Echoing Taf's tone, I said, "I believe Taf just did, sir."

Osrum uncovered his mouth. When he spoke to Mirlov I could tell he was making an effort to keep his voice steady. "Is your son's body here?"

"Yes, Your Honor."

"Which is his?"

Mirlov pointed.

Capis pulled off his mask and stepped in among the bodies. After a cursory examination, he looked up at me. "How long ago did these men die?"

"More than forty days."

"Impossible."

Osrum said, "We are here for the purpose of determining how these men died. Can you make that determination?"

Capis looked at each body. "Your Honor, I find nothing that might have caused their deaths but these darts." He held one up.

"Might the darts be poisoned?" Taf asked. "They killed fairly quickly."

Immediately, the doctor dropped the dart and went to the pool to wash his hands. When he came back, he said, "I saw no evidence that the number of darts that struck each man was enough to cause death, or that darts struck vital areas, so poison is certainly a possibility."

Almost eagerly, Birl's father asked, "Is there any sign that the bodies were hewn by an ax?"

Giving him a strange look, Capis replied, "No. There is no damage to the bodies save for the darts."

Osrum said to Mirlov, "Do you wish to take your son's body back with you, or do you want it to remain here?"

He hesitated. Father said, "Your Honor, regardless of what the accuser decides, the families of the other victims will likely want their sons' bodies returned. Since we now have fewer supplies, if the smaller cart carries all the remaining supplies, the bodies can be transported in our cart."

"Thank you," Osrum said, and instructed the soldiers to make the arrangements Father suggested. Then he said to me, quietly, "Can you explain this?"

"I don't presume to explain miracles, Your Honor."

With a set to his mouth that suggested he found the answer not at all to his taste, Osrum walked away.

When Birl's body was the only one left in the opened cairn, Mirlov was able to decide that he wanted it brought back for burial. His attempt to appear overcome with grief was quite unconvincing. When he asked, "May I ask what your decision is, Your Honor?" it was even more evident that his sole interest was in seeing Zhia sentenced to prison.

Plainly, Osrum also realized this. He said, stiffly, "You will be advised of my decision when we return to my chambers."

The bodies were covered with oiled cloth cloaks, the soldiers mounted their cheros, and the rest of us took the places in the carts we'd occupied on the trip out.

As he flicked our desdal with the whip, Father said, "Let's hope the bodies don't start to decay until we return."

"That would be a trick worthy of Darl, Father. I think Taf is right about which daemon we have to thank for Capis being able to tell how those Singers died. Nia Diva has taken care of things thus far. She won't abandon us now."

"While I hope you're right, Son, I'm keeping the cloths for our faces at hand."

Osrum's thoughts were apparently the same as Father's; the smaller cart now led the way. The troop of soldiers still brought up the rear. More than once, when lifting a corner of the cloak to check on the condition of the bodies, I saw soldiers cast doubtful looks at our cart. Soldiers deal in the solid, the practical, the familiar. What they had seen was unknown territory for them.

That might explain why they seemed more tense on the return trip. They rode in all-but-unbroken silence. What little talking there was, was hushed. Like them, we also traveled wrapped in our own thoughts. Only Mirlov seemed unaffected by what had happened; but he had never impressed me as someone with the imagination or the devotion to appreciate a wonder. His petty, peevish complaints seemed to grate in the silence, rasping nerves and eroding patience.

Though the return trip took only slightly longer than the outbound one, it seemed much longer. The sun was not yet at zenith when we reached Osrum's chambers on the third day after our departure from the hollow.

Since no further testimony was needed from Capis, he was dismissed. His expression made clear his relief to be rid of us.

A pair of soldiers was detailed to drive our cart and its sad burden to the Hall; others were sent to return their own provisions to their stores. While this took place, Osrum led Mirlov, Taf, Father, and me into his chambers. The functionaries followed.

Osrum took his seat and said, "Mirlov Tiriantirlov, the charge that the accused was responsible for the death of your son, Birlov Ogianmirlov, has not been proven. I could have you committed to prison for bringing a false charge; but because you have a son to bury, I will spare you that.

"Instead, you will be fined. In addition to paying for the use and replacement of the supplies which had to be taken from the soldiers' stores, you will give the acting Hall Master the full amount required for the falsely-accused to be trained as a Singer. You will pay both these penalties before you are dismissed from these chambers."

Mirlov's smile was sickly. "Your Honor, I'm not carrying a large amount of money. I'll need to go to my office for the remainder."

"No. You may send a message to your office by one of my men—I will furnish you with writing materials—but you will remain here."

When Birl's father found out how much money he was going to need, he looked even more ill. When he finished writing the message, Osrum asked to read it. When he saw that Mirlov had asked for a lesser amount, he told him the penalty had doubled. Mirlov paled, clutched his chest, and moaned. Osrum grudgingly sent a functionary for wine, which restored the stricken merchant to the point that he was able to write a new message, this time for the correct amount.

When the functionary returned with the money, Osrum counted out what was needed for the soldiers' stores and handed the remainder to Father. "Do you want to count it?" he asked.

"No, Your Honor. This is already as much a miracle as what I saw three days ago. I thank you for your wise decision. My only request is that Zhia be returned to the Hall."

At Osrum's gesture, the functionaries left. Before I saw Zhia, I heard her voice, weakly warning, "I said, don't touch me." Then there was a sound of scuffling, and a yelp from a man. (I later learned that when one of the functionaries had attempted to help Zhia, who was none too steady, she accidentally trod on his foot.)

Soon Zhia limped into Osrum's chambers, still wrapped in the now far filthier blanket. Her hair was lank and dull; her face, ashen and haggard; her eyes, sunken and darkly shadowed. The parts of her skin that showed were marked both by the knife wound and by bites from the vermin that infest all prisons. She looked like she should have been in the back of the Hall's cart with the corpses.

I smelled her almost as soon as she entered the room, and tried not to react. Taf gagged and turned away, his hands over his nose and mouth. Father did nothing more than frown. Perhaps the odor hadn't yet reached his nose. I remember thinking that if just one person from the prison smelled that bad, the cumulative stench must have been intolerable.

The functionaries stopped Zhia quite a bit before she reached Osrum's chair. Breathing through their mouths, they flanked her.

Osrum said, "Zhia Vediandruzhin, the charge against you was not proven. You may leave. The accuser will drive you to the Hall."

Zhia looked at Birl's father, then at Osrum. I hoped she wouldn't say anything that would make the magistrate decide to punish her for the tone she had taken with his functionaries. Finally, she said, "Thank you, Your Honor."

She turned and headed for the door, and her freedom. Even had she not been limping, she too weak to move quickly. I took a step toward her, intending to offer assistance, but she wrinkled her nose and shied away.

Then I understood. "Father, where are those cloths?"

He produced them from somewhere inside his robe. I tied one over my nose and mouth and said to Zhia, "Now may I help you?"

The smile that bloomed on her face made her look even worse. "Do you have one for me?" she asked.

Birl's father, Taf, Father, and I wore masks on the short trip to the Hall. Zhia had given the one I handed her to Mirlov, saying he would need it worse than she did, a courtesy that even he understood. He thanked Zhia as she got out of the back of the cart in the Hall courtyard.

Pity and disgust mingled in the look she gave him as she said, "Since it's due to you that I stink like this, I can't say 'you're welcome'. I will say I'm sorry Birl is dead. I'll also say that I hope never to see you again."

I assume Mirlov collected Birl's body. I paid no attention to what he did once we got the Hall's supplies out of the cart. Taf said he would take care of them. I think he wanted both an excuse to be away from Zhia—heavy as the cloths were, they weren't heavy enough—and a task he could finish quickly so he could clean up and return to Noia.

Father went to greet Mother and Lisia, wash and change, and then send messages to the other bereaved families that their sons' bodies had been returned to the Hall.

Mother prepared a bath for Zhia. She offered to stay to help, but Zhia spared Mother that. Or perhaps Zhia was sparing herself Mother's reaction to how she looked and smelled.

It had been all I could do to keep from recoiling visibly at the sight of Zhia. I suppose at some other time I would have found it ironic that I had found the dead more bearable than the living. The image of Zhia's gaunt face kept drifting through my mind while I bathed. I knew I had to put some other image there, so when I was washed, shaved, combed, and in clean clothes I went into town and visited Eia.

That was a good decision. As the last glimmers of sunset set fire to the edges of the gathering clouds, I returned to the Hall relaxed and satisfied, with my nostrils full of the fragrance of Eia's perfume and my eyes rejoicing in the memory of her beauty.

From his clinic windows, Aplin saw me crossing the courtyard and came out to ask whether Zhia was back. When I said "yes", he asked that I have Zhia come to the clinic right away. I told him I would do so. With my mind on other, far more pleasant, things, I promptly forgot.

Not until I was going to supper did I remember his request. I went to where I knew Zhia had been bathing. She wasn't there, so I stopped at the clinic to tell Aplin that I hadn't been able to deliver his message.

That was a bad decision. Apparently when Zhia failed to show up as requested, Aplin, who hadn't been allowed into the prison to see her after Osrum left with us to go to the hollow, grew impatient and went to find her. She was asleep in a tub full of water that, by then, was quite cold. He'd almost literally snatched her from the tub, wrapped her in a towel, and hauled her to the clinic, where he'd taken a long, shocked look at her. In addition to the hurts he'd already known about, some of her vermin bites were festering and needed immediate treatment.

Though I admit I erred in not delivering Aplin's message as requested, I didn't think I deserved the scolding he gave me. I was no longer Zhia's tour partner; her welfare was no longer my responsibility. Aplin scolded me again when I told him that, and unwisely mentioned that I owed Zhia my life.

I remember shouting, "Just because I didn't have sense enough to run when

Taf did doesn't mean I'm going to be responsible for Zhia the rest of my life!"

Then Aplin got angry and told me to get out of the clinic, which I was only too happy to do. I confess my supper was mostly liquid. I was annoyed that the encounter with Aplin had again fixed the picture of Zhia's ill-used countenance in my mind. I wondered what Eia would think if I visited her again. I decided to find out.

Eia wasn't as pleased to see me as she had been earlier in the day, perhaps because I was quite wet. I had been in such turmoil when I left the Hall that I'd forgotten to take a cloak with me. I think she forgave me; this time I didn't get back to the Hall until morning.

I can't say I didn't think at all about Zhia after that delightful night, but I managed to maintain my resolve not to be her nursemaid. It helped that the Singers' Festival was approaching. For a number of reasons already noted I hadn't been practicing as often as is my wont. In fact, once I realized that I was so out of practice that I didn't have a chance at the Championship, I decided simply to attend the Festival. Though I wasn't entering the competition, there was still music to learn. One highlight of the event comes just before the Champion is named, when all Singers attending gather on stage and perform a song. It's usually a new composition, and always extremely challenging.

I hadn't been able to work on the song as diligently as I'd have liked, because the seven Singers from TTTW were all laid to rest in the first five or six days after I returned to the Hall, and I'd felt obliged to be present. Eight days after my return I was in my cubicle, working on the song in something of a panic— the Festival was three days away and, by custom, the song is always done from memory—when a servant delivered a message that Father wanted to see me in his office. Thinking "Now what?", I went there.

After greeting me, Father asked, "Are you entering the Festival, Son?"

"Not this time, Father. I'd be the first to admit I'm out of practice."

I thought he looked disappointed, but he said, "No one else can make that decision for you. I wish someone from our Hall was entering."

"How about Noia, Father? She's toured; she's eligible. She's good."

"I confess I hadn't thought of her. I'll ask her. It will be some time before I remember that there are also women Singers from whom to choose. Which reminds me, Son," he added, as I turned to leave, "how is Zhia doing?"

I don't think I was able to hide that the question took me by surprise. Then I decided that it wouldn't hurt Father to know that I was no longer going to be answerable for Zhia. Deliberately unconcerned, I replied, "I really can't say, Father. I haven't seen her since we got back."

Now I was certain he looked disappointed, though "disapproving" might be more accurate. He said, "You found time to pay your respects to the dead but not to the living? We'll remedy that discourtesy right now."

Zhia was still under Aplin's care, though she wasn't in her bed in the clinic. Aplin greeted Father but not me, and directed us to a grassy, shaded area outside the clinic.

"Aplin isn't usually rude. What was that about?" Father asked as we headed for a door that went outside.

"He thinks I'm lacking in gratitude," I replied carelessly, hoping Father wouldn't press for details.

"To Zhia?" Father guessed. "When two people interpret your actions the same way, isn't it possible that you, and not they, are wrong?"

I managed to keep my voice from being edged when I said, "Father, as far as I'm concerned, whatever it is you and Aplin imagine I owe Zhia was repaid when I went to the hollow again so she could get out of prison. And aren't you the man who, not all that long ago, told me I could do better than Zhia?"

"I can admit when I'm wrong. Why can't you?"

I bit back a sharp retort and followed Father outside. The sun was brilliant; the air, warm and fragrant with the scents of timi blossoms and riku grass. Not for the first time I wondered how something like riku grass that smelled so sweet growing could produce something else—riku seed oil—that had such an offensive smell.

Zhia was lying prone on the grass in a patch of sunlight with her head propped on her folded arms. She was clad in something white; the light reflecting off it was dazzling. Not until we were closer did I see that it was a sheet. In the center of it, a hole had been torn for her head. The overlapped edges of the sheet were more or less secured at the sides by a strip of cloth Zhia had torn from one of its long edges and tied around her waist. The garment, such as it was, covered what was necessary, but bared her arms and also her legs below mid-thigh. I couldn't help but notice that her legs, though strong, weren't especially attractive.

Equally dazzling in the direct sunlight was the flour on a tray that lay on the ground next to her.

When she saw us, Zhia quickly sat up. Her attempt to cover her legs more fully with the sheet was quite futile. She must have been spending quite a bit of time in the sun; her skin, which I had last seen pallid and marked with angry red bites, was now a warm brown. The bites were either gone or healing. Even the knife wound was closed. Her face wasn't as gaunt, nor were her eyes as shadowed.

Father stepped closer, stooped, and examined the notation Zhia had written in the flour. "This isn't right, you know," he said, gently.

"I know," she said, with evident frustration. "That's why I stopped; I didn't want to learn it wrong. Actually, I don't know why I'm bothering to learn it at all."

"You're a Singer."

"With all respect, sir, no, I'm not. I've been pursuing some dream that was my husband's, because it was all I had left of him." Her face twisted. She pulled at the sheet and went on, "But I can't be what he wanted me to be. I'm not sure what I can be; but tomorrow, which is when Aplin has said I can leave the clinic, I'll be leaving the Hall."

"You want to leave before the Festival?" Father asked.

"What have I to do with Festivals, sir? They're for Singers. Give me a broom and let me stay here and work, but don't pretend that you think I can be a Singer. You never did. As we've seen again, theory eludes me. I have no sense of rhythm. Perhaps I can sing. Birds can, too, but they don't presume to be anything more than what the Unknown made them to be."

"Then what am I to do with the fine Birl's father paid, which the magistrate said was to be used to train you as a Singer?"

"Return it to him, buy something for the Hall, or use it to train someone who really ought to be a Singer but can't afford the training." She cleared her throat. "Call it 'The Seven Singers Memorial Fund' and let people—let women—apply for it. I don't care. Even if I were planning to stay at the Hall, I wouldn't accept anything from Birl's father. I would sell my father's ri…" She paled. "My father's ring. Chaz took it."

"I found it on Chaz when I buried him," Father said. "It's in my office. I'll fetch it now."

When he went back inside, I sat in the shade with my back against the nearest tree. "May I say you're looking better?"

"I couldn't have looked worse. At least I don't stink." She wouldn't meet my eyes, even when she asked, "Are you entering the Festival?"

"No, but I suggested to Father that he encourage Noia to do so."

"Good. The Hall should be represented."

"That's what Father thought."

"How's Taf?" Face, body lines, and tone alike said that she was simply making conversation, and that doing so was an effort.

"He's all right. Did you hear that he asked Noia to be his wife?"

"Aplin made some reference to it. I'm glad for both of them."

"Yes, I can tell that from your enthusiasm," I said, hoping to provoke some response. Even anger would have been preferable to this apathetic monotone. When she didn't respond, I added, "Noia has given Taf a stage name: 'Tebec'. He's given her one: 'Toy'. She thinks it's cute."

At that I saw something flicker in Zhia's eyes, but all she said was, "It is. I'm surprised he was listening."

When she pulled at the sheet again, I realized that what I had taken for indifference was sheer embarrassment at what she was wearing. I tried not to look lower than her face when I asked, "Have you heard what we found at the hollow?"

"At the hollow? What do you mean?"

"We had to go back to the hollow to prove to Birl's father that you didn't take that ax to the Singers from your tour."

"Did he actually believe I might have done that?"

"I think he was ready to believe anything that would keep you in prison."

Indignantly, she said, "Now I'm even more glad I rejected his money. I suppose you had to uncover the cairn." I nodded. She winced. "That must be why you had the cloths along. How bad was it?"

"The bodies hadn't decayed."

Now she looked at me. In fact, she stared. "You're joking."

"No. No stench, no rotting. They were as fresh as they had been the day we put them there."

"Nia Diva," she whispered.

"That's what Taf said, too."

"What did Birl's father say?"

"There wasn't much he could say. We had a doctor along, one Birl's father chose. The only injury he found to our Singers was from the darts."

"Do you know the precise charge Birl's father brought against me?"

"Yes. He said you were responsible for Birl's death."

She buried her face in her hands. The words that emerged were so muffled they were almost unintelligible. "I am."

"How do you figure that?"

"That was my tour, right? If I hadn't been at the Hall, no one would have gone on that tour. They'd all still be alive, as would Chaz, Rork, and Dolin. I should still be in prison."

Forcing a casual tone, I said, "I'm sure the prison is open all night, if you really want to go back there."

She shuddered and looked at me, her eyes haunted. "Never. No one should be kept like that. I wouldn't keep even the raiders who killed Pandizh in conditions like those. It would be more merciful to kill them."

"I can't say I'm sorry I don't have an opinion on that which is based on experience. Of course, Gadig is there. Did you see him?"

"He wasn't in the common prison."

I forgot to be casual. "Osrum put you in the common prison?"

With unfeigned confusion, she asked, "Who's Osrum?"

"The magistrate."

"His name isn't 'Your Honor'? The order must have come from him, but I didn't see him until the day I was released. The only ones I saw were the men in the gray uniforms, who put me there, and the guards. They..." She drew a harsh breath. "They shouldn't be allowed to use prisoners that way." Then, with a travesty of a smile, she said, "They don't bother the insensible ones. Of course, if you're supposed to be insensible, you can't eat or do anything else."

"So you pretended to be insensible for..." I tried to think.

"A good many days," she finished. "Don't look so distressed. Haven't you learned yet that very little can be gained without some kind of risk? To gain the honor of being Festival Champion, you have to risk losing. To gain love, you have to risk rejection. To gain safety, sometimes you have to risk peril. Actually, I probably wasn't pretending to be insensible the whole time. After a few days without eating, I wasn't feeling at all good. Aplin has had me eating about six times a day." She fell silent. After a while, she said, "Just because people are being detained or punished doesn't mean they should be treated worse than animals. A good scrubbing would at least rid the prison of the vermin. When I leave here, I'll go to the magistrate and offer to clean that stinking place."

Father came back then. He showed Zhia her father's ring, then put back it into his pocket and said, "You're not going anywhere except to the Festival and on tour. You declined the money Birl's father gave for your training. Since there's the small matter of the instruments that were stolen from your tour that were not recovered, and the fees the Hall won't get from the Singers who died, you're going to tour as a Singer until those losses are recovered. I'll keep your father's ring so you won't be tempted to sell it. There's not going to be any easy way out for you."

Struck dumb as well as looking stricken at what even I regarded as betrayal, Zhia could only stare at him in disbelief.

Apparently oblivious to her dismay, Father turned and left without another word.

I followed him to his office. "Father, when did you make those rules?"

Now he looked stricken. "They aren't rules, Son; they're emergency measures. One of Osrum's functionaries just brought word that Gadig escaped from prison."

CHAPTER TWENTY-FIVE

I CURSED, SOFTLY. "HOW?"

"Once the guards were killed by darts—in broad daylight, no less—no one was watching the prisoners."

"Raiders! In town!" I exclaimed, and cursed again. "And Osrum thinks that now Gadig's on the loose he'll try to get even with Zhia?"

"It's a possibility we have to consider."

"But why will sending her on tour keep Gadig or his confederates from being able to find her? Touring season is over."

"Not for this Hall, it isn't. Our financial crisis isn't over," Father said, grimly. "If a number of tours leave at the same time, they can't all be watched."

"They won't have to be, Father. As soon as Gadig's men see which one includes a woman, they can ignore the others."

"Then what do you suggest?"

"You might consult the person whose life you're trying to arrange," said Zhia from the doorway. She limped in and stood next to me. (As Aplin had predicted, Zhia's right foot didn't mend properly. It troubled her for the rest of her life.)

Father got up and offered his chair.

"Thank you, sir; I prefer to stand," she said.

Frowning, Father looked at me. Hoping Zhia wouldn't notice, I motioned and mouthed the words "the sheet". Father nodded and again sat.

"Lest you think I was eavesdropping," Zhia said, glancing at me, "I will first say that I was coming here to inquire how I could go anywhere dressed—or, more accurately, underdressed—in this. On the thought that I was now so far in debt to the Hall that owing a little more wouldn't hurt, I was going to beg money to buy clothing or, at least, fabric." The look she gave Father held no warmth. "Pardon my being blunt, sir, but I must say that I resent your attempt to keep information from me. I resent your using that information to try to force me to change my plans. I resent your not even giving me the chance to cooperate with whatever measures you, the acting Hall Master, consider necessary to deal with this development.

"I'm assuming it's because the news took you by surprise that you kept it from me, and not because you believe me incapable of dealing calmly with threat."

Father stood. "I beg your pardon, Zhia. You are quite right in resenting my clumsy effort to coerce you. I must also tell you that you owe the Hall nothing, not because Birl's father was required to pay for your training—twice, in fact!—but because you saved the life of both my son and my wife. In fact, the Hall owes you far more than can be valued in mere money. You need not beg money for purchasing clothing; you may have all you need." He dug in his pocket and brought out the ring. "Much as I regret the other mistakes I've just made, keeping this from you is the one I regret most."

Sounding like her throat was tight, Zhia said, "I'm glad I can like you again, sir."

Father smiled. "I'm glad I again merit your regard. And you should know that it's pretty much become the practice for everyone here to call me 'Father.'"

"Really?" she said. "Then, Father, would you be so good as to continue to safeguard my father's ring until I return from touring?"

"If that is your wish." Father put the jewel into a box which could be locked. Again seated, he asked, "So you consider touring a good idea?"

"Yes, si…Father. As you implied, the Hall needs the tour fees (I won't ask why; the details are Hall business, not mine). Also, if Gadig is, indeed, thirsting for revenge—and may I point out that the former Master may be thirsting for nothing more than freedom—having me on tour lessens the danger to other Singers at this Hall, especially the other women. If you decide to send me on tour, Father, allow me to suggest that the others touring be volunteers who have been fully apprised of the possible danger. I don't want to be part of another disaster like…"

"The Tour That Wasn't," I said. "TTTW: that's what the Singers here are calling it," I explained when she looked confused.

"What else have I missed?" she asked, somewhat acerbically.

"You can call Mother 'Mother'," I said, grinning. "And I now have a…a… What would Lisia be to me, Father? A sister of sorts?"

"I trust you are in no way related to Lisia, Son," was the reproving reply. "However, I'm sure it would please your mother to know that you regard the child as your sister." To Zhia, Father said, "Isia has assumed the care of a baby. The child's antecedents are Hall business and will not be made public."

Zhia's agreement was so bland that I suspected she knew which of the former slaves was Lisia's mother. She went on, "If I may change the subject, si… Father, am I correct that my tour would leave immediately after the Festival?" Father nodded. "So either I use the three days remaining before the Festival to learn enough music to make my being on a tour believable, or you send one extra person on tour so there will be the right number of performers on stage while I stay with the tebecs or mingle with the audience. Because I can tell you, sir, no one will believe I ought to be on that stage."

Her voice became hard. "There is, of course, a third option: you accept that you owe me nothing and therefore don't have to protect me; admit that I'm not a Singer; and allow me to leave the Hall tomorrow. Then if Gadig thinks he has to be revenged on me, it won't hurt any Singers; and if anything happens to me, you won't have to know it.

"Tell me why that isn't the best option, sir," she finished, defiantly.

I noticed she had stopped saying "Father". Father had noticed, also. He didn't look happy about it. When he spoke, it was to me. "It seems I was right from the start, Son. I told you she wouldn't make it as a Singer. You thought I was being unkind."

"You can't shame me into doing this, sir," Zhia flared. "You said the Hall owes me far more than can be valued with money. Let's look a little more closely at what I've brought the Hall: the shame of a failed tour, the theft of valuable instruments, the ruin of even more valuable ones, the loss of twelve or thirteen tebecs, and the deaths of ten—ten!—Singers. Even if no one considers me a threat—which I would find hard to believe; I scare myself—do you think anyone regards me as an asset?

"Do I play an instrument? No. What part do I sing? No one knows. Can I sing? No one knows that, either. Singers are supposed to improvise. That expectation is based on the assumption that everyone knows the same songs. I know nothing. How much more blunt do I need to be, sir?" She almost shouted the last words.

Father stood, reached across the desk, slapped her face, and said, calmly, "I will not tolerate another outburst. If you can't control yourself any better than that, then you don't deserve a chance to be a Singer. You keep saying no one knows whether you can sing. We'll answer that question here and now. Sing."

Her hand pressed to her cheek, Zhia glared at him. "What would like me to sing, sir?"

Still in a mild tone, he replied, "As you so rudely reminded me, you don't know any of the Hall repertoire, so you'll have to sing a song you do know." He turned. On top of the storage cubes behind the desk were a wine jug and cup. Father filled the cup and handed it to Zhia. "Relax. Drink this. I want to hear you at your best."

Staring into the cup, in a small voice Zhia said, "I'm sorry I was rude, sir."

"That's 'Father,'" he said as he returned to his chair. Noticing tears gathering in the corners of Zhia's eyes, he said, "None of that, now. If you try to sing when you're choked up, you'll sound like a squeaky wheel."

Zhia laughed, or tried to. She took a couple of sips of wine and set the cup on Father's desk. Startled, I looked at Father. I wondered whether Zhia knew

what she had just done was the ritual Singers observe before performing.
"Could you maybe not look at me while I sing?" she asked.

"No," Father said. "How am I supposed to know if you're breathing properly
if I'm not looking at you? Are you ready, then?"

I found myself fervently hoping she had at least a passable voice. In seeking
to be a Singer, Zhia had endured enslavement, ridicule, the hardships of the
tour, injury, and imprisonment. If she had no voice to speak of, it would be
worse than embarrassing; it would be tragic.

Her first notes were uncertain and not quite on pitch. I closed my eyes and
hoped I hadn't groaned aloud.

Zhia stopped. "May I start again, si…Father?"

"Go ahead."

She loosened the tie around her waist, sipped a little more wine, and again
set down the cup. The next sound from her throat was sure and true. Her
confidence grew as the music poured from her. Her voice gained strength
and color. I was so lost in amazement that the song was almost over before
I realized it was part of the Hall repertoire, which she claimed not to know.

She should have held the last note a beat or two longer, but she was out of
breath. "I'm sorry," she said. The color which flooded her cheeks hid the mark
left by Father's hand. "I'll go now."

"Please don't," Father said. "Tell me, why did you choose that song?"

"I knew if I tried to sing a lullaby I'd cry, so I had to think of something else."

"Are you aware that song is part of the Hall repertoire?"

Her face lit up. "That's where I heard it!"

"Where?" Father prompted.

"I had the men from my tour practicing songs while Rois was ill. I was
washing their clothes, but I listened."

"You heard that song—in five parts, I imagine—almost sixty days ago and
today were able to sing the melody, note perfect?"

"It wasn't note perfect. I ran out of breath."

"I'll thank you not to contradict me," Father said, sternly. "No, don't apologize. Just listen. Son, sing something."

The first song that came to mind was the one for the Festival, so that's what I sang. When I finished, Father told Zhia to sing it. As I mentioned, it's a challenging piece. Zhia didn't get it note perfect. Neither did I; she sang just what she heard, the baritone part, no less (an octave higher, of course). Next, Father asked me to sing something for which I knew the melody. Zhia echoed it, down to the intonation and phrasing I'd used.

There was a long silence after she finished. Father was looking at Zhia, and she was looking nervous. Finally, he said, "To reply to your challenge, allowing you leave the Hall isn't the best option because you have a rare gift and I want to see what you can do with it. In three days, I'd like you to go to the Festival. The day after that, I am sending you on tour. Even if Gadig were still in prison I'd ask that you accept those engagements. Now you'd better get back to the clinic, or Aplin will wonder what's become of you. Wait," he added as she turned to go. "How much fabric do you need?"

"Twice my height."

Guessing Father's intent, I stepped behind Zhia and noted where the top of her head reached. "Got it. What colors do you want?"

There was laughter in her voice when she replied, "Let's just say I don't want to look like a broken foot." I chuckled.

"Rest well," Father said as Zhia left. Without thinking, he picked up the cup from his desk and drained it. For a time, he sat silent, turning the cup in his hands. Then he looked at me and said, "I've heard of only one other person who can do what Zhia does, and he didn't have a voice anyone would want to listen to."

"I'm curious, Father: why can Zhia do that with songs but not with rhythms?"

"I couldn't say, Son; but I trust you noticed that, after hearing you sing them, she handled the complicated rhythms in the Festival song just fine."

"Yes, I noticed; but I suspect she couldn't beat just the rhythms on a drum. If, as seems to be the case, she can't read music, how is she going to learn songs before the tour? I won't have time to learn her part well enough to sing it for her."

"One of the tenors will know the parts she'll be singing. I believe Taf is a tenor." Father refilled the cup and offered it to me. I declined. He drank. "Sometime I need to hear Zhia sing with Noia, but not before the Festival. Since I haven't yet asked Noia to represent our Hall, she'll need time to prepare."

I hid a smile. Noia was good, but probably not quite good enough to be ready to sing at the Festival in three days.

Father asked, "What did you think of the quality of Zhia's voice, Son?"

"In the lower part of her range, it's resonant, warm. The word 'caressing' comes to mind. On the higher notes, it's brighter. I would suggest she needs to work on making the quality the same throughout her range, which I found fairly wide. I can't say she has the best voice I've ever heard, but it's certainly no hardship to listen to."

Father nodded. "I kept thinking that if she was that good without training, how will she sound when she's trained? Without being trained, her enunciation was good; I heard all the final consonants. She breathed properly, though her breath control could have been better. Her pitch wavered slightly, but no more than might be expected from someone who warmed up with only three notes."

"And who recently had a damaged throat," I added.

Father straightened in his chair. "I'd forgotten about that. On tour, you'll have to be sure you don't let her strain her voice."

The bright day suddenly seemed bleak. "I'm partnering her again, Father?"

"Do you object?"

"I've already been on two tours this season."

"I can count, Son; though Zhia's first tour—what did you say it's called? TTTW?—can hardly be included in the reckoning."

"Are you still planning to send out a number of tours the day after the Festival?"

I'm not sure what showed in my voice—panic, maybe—but Father smiled and said, "Yes, I'd like to send out another four or five. But you won't have to leave until two days after the Festival. I'd forgotten you'll need a day to pack and everything."

"Do you want me to organize Zhia's tour?"

"I hoped you would organize all the tours."

I picked up the cup, drank, and refilled it. "That's what I was afraid you'd say." I drank again. "Could I offer a suggestion, Father? Choose the leaders for the other tours and have them meet with me the day after tomorrow. I'll tell them everything I've learned about organizing a tour. They'll be able to make the changes that are needed to fit their particular group or schedule; I won't be dead in the saddle the first day out; and if I actually turn up dead, there'll still be several people here who know the procedure."

"Why not meet with them tomorrow?"

"I figured you'd need at least a day and a half to choose the tour groups. I need the day and a half more to memorize the Festival song. I don't have Zhia's gift."

"You'll have only one day more, Son; you need to purchase fabric for Zhia."

I raised the cup, intending to drink. Father took it from me. "That won't help anything, you know. From what Zhia said, do you have any idea what fabric she might like?"

I stared. "Are you joking? Right now, I feel like I did when the raider grabbed me and I rolled down the hill. I'm waiting to fetch up hard against a rock so I can stop spinning."

With a brusque, "Go ask your mother what she thinks," Father unlocked the box where he'd put Zhia's ring and handed me money.

Mother's first suggestion was to ask Zhia. I told her what Zhia had said. Mother laughed and kept feeding me ideas which most Singers would have found quite acceptable. I had to reject them because I knew Zhia's views on what she termed "showy" clothing. I explained this to Mother so I wouldn't hurt her feelings. Finally, she said, "Something solid-colored then, Son, maybe with a texture or needlework."

I had no idea what she was talking about. "All right. What color?"

"See if you can find a golden green to match her eyes."

CHAPTER TWENTY-SIX

I WAS SO LOST IN thought as I walked into town that I went to Eia's house instead of the market. Maybe that's an excuse; but I'm not aware of having any goal other than the market in mind when I left the Hall. I knocked without thinking. Eia opened the door. "I'm sorry, Rois, you'll have to come back another day."

Usually when a woman says that, she means she has her woman's time.

"Please," I said as she started to shut the door, "I'm here to...to ask a favor." That wasn't exactly true; but once I'd said it, I realized Eia might be just the person I needed. "It's not what you're thinking, and I'm a little embarrassed even to mention it."

She opened the door again. "Rois, I've never seen you like this. What's the matter?"

She put her hand on my arm. Then I really couldn't think.

I blurted, "Can you help me purchase some fabric?"

Her laughter was music, more intoxicating than... That's a cliche, Nia Diva. She laughed, and said, "Of course I'll help you. Give me a moment."

She slipped her arm through mine as we walked toward the market. Eventually, my senses stopped reeling enough to allow me to explain what I had been told to buy and why. At that, she stopped walking, turned to face me, and said, "Why, Rois, that's so sweet of you! That poor thing. Like every other woman, I've often said I haven't a stitch to wear, but I've never been reduced to wearing nothing but a sheet!" She gave me a coy look before adding, "Except by choice." We shared a knowing laugh. "And you said she plans to sew something before the Festival?"

"That's my understanding."

"I wonder if she would consider sewing something for me. Does she sew well?"

"I couldn't tell you. I only know something isn't sewn well if it falls apart when I put it on. I do know she's going on tour two days after the Festival, so she won't have time to make anything but..." I groaned.

"What?" Eia asked, sounding amused.

"She's going on tour two days after the Festival. When she sews the stuff I buy today, she'll own only one garment. She can't tour like that."

There was a different note in Eia's voice when she asked, "Do you lavish such concern on all the Singers with whom you tour?"

"None of the others need as much attention," I replied, carelessly, fully aware that on TTTW Zhia had been the one tending me, but equally aware that the note I heard in Eia's voice was jealousy.

"She's helpless and clinging?" Eia guessed. "Scared of shadows? Hates to get wet?"

I nodded. "She gives everyone a headache." In my mind I could see Zhia, a blood-dripping ax in her hand and a man with a crushed skull at her feet.

Reassured, Eia again put her arm through mine. "Tell me again what kind of fabric you want."

"Mother's suggestion was a solid color with texture or needlework. Golden green."

"Hmm, that color's not in fashion. Strange choice. Why did she suggest it?"

I almost answered with the truth, but thought quickly and said, "Probably because wearing that, the woman will clash with every piece of clothing I own."

"Poor Rois." Eia rested her head on my arm. (She's short, but long in bed, as Singers say.) I was feeling content when we got to the market.

It was uncommonly crowded. I realized Singers who had to travel some distance were already here for the Festival. Merchants had their better wares on display, and were doing a brisk business. Eia admired some trinket, which I bought for her.

She had to show me where fabric was sold. It's possible I could have made the purchase without Eia's help, but I'm sure it would have taken much longer. Eia knew which merchants carried the best goods. They knew her, and showed her cloth that wasn't on display even for the visiting Singers. Listening to her consider and reject fabrics was illuminating. This cloth was too flimsy, this one, too stiff; this green was yellowish, not golden; the needlework on this one wasn't well done…

Finally, she spied something shimmering in the shadows on a bottom shelf in a far corner. The merchant unrolled the fabric on the counter. It was glorious; I have no other word for it. It looked more green when the light hit it from one direction, but more golden when the light came from the other side. I marveled at it for a while before I realized it had a texture like the robe Gadig had worn the day he told me I would be partnering Zhia on TTTW. That didn't make me like it any less.

"This one," I said.

"I assumed that from the way you stood there with your mouth hanging open, looking like an idiot," Eia said. "How much does she need?"

"From my chin to the ground, twice."

"Is she so tall?" Eia asked. Again, jealousy tinged her voice.

Again, I made a show of nonchalance. "I'm just following instructions. How am I supposed to remember what any other woman looks like when I'm with you?" She thanked me for the compliment by pulling my head down and kissing my cheek.

The merchant measured the amount of cloth and offered thread and needles. "I suppose she can't sew without those," I said. Remembering the hole had Zhia torn in the sheet for her head, I also bought scissors. The cost made me gape again. Eia pushed my mouth shut.

As we left the market Eia said, "Rois, I hate to tell you this, but wearing something made out of that cloth, she won't clash with you, she'll outshine you."

"I'm a Champion; do you think I'm jealous of a beginner?" I shifted the parcel so I could curl my arm around Eia's tiny waist. She again rested her head on my arm.

When we reached Eia's house, I thanked her. She kissed me, this time on the mouth, and said, "I wish I could ask you to stay; but if you linger, before you get to the Hall that costly fabric will be a costly rag."

"Will I see you at the Festival?"

A teasing smile lit her face. "Perhaps." Just before the door was fully closed, I heard her say, "Do ask your friend if she sews for other people."

As I left her house, I looked at the sky. The clouds weren't gathering yet. I returned to the place where I'd bought the fabric and bought a length of inexpensive material and thread in reddish brown so Zhia would be able to make more than one piece of clothing.

I was passing a stall that sold wine by the cup when someone hailed me. I turned and recognized Henz, a Singer from another Hall. He was the man whose reputation Taf found so deplorable. In fact, Henz's stage name was "Love 'Em and Leave 'Em". Rather than cause women to avoid him, the name seemed to make them desire him even more.

"Here for the Festival, I take it?" I said after I returned his greeting.

"Yes." He drained the cup he held, flipped a coin onto the counter, picked up a pack, and said, "Mind if I walk with you?"

I had already been moving on. "Of course not; but I'm going to the Hall."

"That's good, because I was going to beg lodging at your Hall. Every place I've tried to get a room is already full up."

"I'm sure Father will be able to find a place for you, even if it's just a tent."

Henz stopped and stared. "'Father'? As in your father?"

"Yes. The former Hall Master was removed forty or fifty days ago. Father has been acting Hall Master since then. But look, I have to get these parcels to the Hall before they get wet, so can we get moving?"

"I don't need to get wet, either." When we were out of the crush of the market area, he said, "I'm entering the competition. I saw that you aren't."

"No. I had a rather unfortunate experience on a tour and need to save my voice."

"So you'll get out of singing that song they inflicted on us?"

I laughed. "'Inflicted' is a good word. I can't recall seeing another song that's as challenging. I do plan to sing it; but don't have it memorized yet."

"Good. I was afraid I'd be the only one on stage hoping the Singer next to me knew it so I could just mouth the words. I'll try to remember not stand next to you."

It wouldn't have been helpful to point out that, since he and I sang different parts, we wouldn't have stood next to each other even if both of us knew the song. As we made our way through town, we saw and greeted more Singers in town for the Festival. I was no longer surprised at how many female Singers there were. I shouldn't have been surprised that so many women, Singers and nobodies, looked first at me—I don't think I'm being vain if I say their glances were appreciative—and then made eyes at Henz.

He was enjoying himself. He wasn't quite strutting, but was undeniably aware of the women's interest.

Of all the things I don't understand about women, what they find attractive in a man is one of the things I understand least. It's my observation that Singers tend to fall into two types: ones like Vel, handsome, self-absorbed cads; and ones like Taf, homely but lovable. (I suspected that Birl, who was of neither type, had been a Singer because his father bought a place for him at the Hall so he could claim the prestige of having a Singer in the family. Having met Mirlov, I was even more convinced that was the case.) I won't try to deny that my then well-deserved reputation put me with the likes of Vel.

Henz was of the first type, as well, so I was immediately wary when he put on a casual air and asked, "Do you know this Zhia person I've heard so much about lately?"

"She's at my Hall."

"I know that. Would you introduce me to her?"

"No."

He laughed. "Why not? Come on, Rois, you can't believe I have designs on her!"

"Don't you? She's female; she's breathing; she's past the age of consent. If you have other criteria, I haven't noticed."

Henz gave me a curious look. "What's with the frosty tone? Have you gone decent, or something? If I'm not mistaken, those are—or used to be—your criteria, too."

I don't know why the suggestion that I had started acting responsibly bothered me; but I said, "So much has been happening I haven't had time to play. I imagine I'll cut loose at the Champion's party."

"As I'm hoping to be the host of that party let me say, first, that you'd better cut loose; and, second, that my party will be a lot more fun than the last one you threw. If you're not going to have a proper bash, don't invite me."

Laughing, I said, "You weren't invited to the last one!"

"I wasn't, was I? What's the point of a party if you can't just drop in?"

"Which misconception should I demolish first?"

"That sounds more like the Rois I know. You had me worried there." When I didn't comment, he asked, "Are you bringing a girl to the party?"

"Perhaps. I'm not sharing her, if that's what you're asking."

"I won't mess with yours if you don't mess with mine."

Astonished, I exclaimed, "You just arrived. Are you saying you already have a woman here?"

"No, but I expect to remedy that. Any women at your Hall you can recommend?"

Feeling like I was again listening to the TTTW group the last night of their lives, I said, "I told you, I haven't had time to play. But I need to warn you to stay away from one woman, a Singer named Noia. She has a husband who is also a Singer. I don't know if they'll be at the party, but I wouldn't want you to make a fool of yourself."

"If a man can't keep his wife..." Henz began, grinning.

"I'm not joking, Henz. The former Hall Master put up with things my father won't. Even though the party won't be at his Hall, he won't tolerate anything that endangers his Singers, so be warned."

"Now I understand why you've become so proper and boring; your father has you on a short leash." With an offensive smile, he asked, "Does he do a bed check at night?"

I ignored the question. Henz was becoming seriously annoying. I reflected that maybe I had "gone decent"; not that long ago, I would have reveled in this kind of bantering. When had I changed?

Hoping Henz would get the point if I changed the subject, I asked, "Did you tour this season?"

"Yes. I partnered a first-timer."

"How'd it go?"

He shrugged. "If it were up to me, Monen would never tour again."

"Why not?"

"Bad attitude, bad performance. Acted like he was already a Champion and didn't have to listen to instructions."

"One of those," I said, and thought, like Birl. "There's usually one on every tour."

Henz agreed, and asked, "Did you tour?"

"Twice."

It was Henz's turn to be astonished. "Twice this season? Why?"

"That's what Father wanted," I replied, wishing I'd kept my mouth shut. "Just because he's my father doesn't mean I can forget he's the Master."

"That's got to be tough."

The wind was picking up, bringing the smell of moisture. I looked up. "The rain's coming early. We'd better hurry. I'll really be in trouble if these parcels get wet."

We reached the Hall just as the rain began in earnest. I took Henz to the Master's office and introduced him to Father, then went to the clinic to give the fabric to Zhia. She wasn't there; Aplin told me he'd already released her and that he didn't know which cubicle was hers. Something in his voice told me he did know where Zhia could be found, but had no intention of telling me. I wouldn't have expected a doctor to hold a grudge so long.

Because I didn't want to deal with Henz again, I waited a while before returning to the Master's office. When I saw Father was no longer there, I realized he was probably eating. I put the parcels next to the stack of storage cubes and went to the dining hall. Father was there. He and Mother were sitting with Henz.

Father noticed me and waved at me to join them. I could hardly refuse. I got a plate of food and sat next to Mother, across the table from Father and Henz. I noticed that Mother looked very tired, then noticed that Lisia wasn't anywhere in sight.

"Where's the baby?" I asked.

"Zhia offered to watch her while I ate," Mother said. "Lisia liked her right away. Zhia would be a good mother, Son."

Hoping Mother hadn't made that same remark to Zhia, I put on my best Birl pout and quavered, "Are you saying you don't want to be my mother any more?"

The laughter that followed this bit of nonsense drew the attention of the others in the dining hall. Some of the kitchen staff even peered out to see what was going on.

Father and Henz picked up the conversation then, discussing the Festival. I turned my attention to the food.

When Mother sighed deeply, I looked up from my plate to see that her eyes were closed. Her head was sagging to one side as weariness overtook her. Reflecting that caring for a baby Lisia's age would probably tire many a younger woman, I caught Father's eye and pointed at Mother. Father nodded, took a chair next to Mother, and drew her against his side.

He whispered, "Son, get a plate of food to take to Zhia and ask her if she can watch the baby a little longer."

I nodded. As I left the dining hall, plate in hand, Taf and Noia came toward me. They had a satisfied glow that at one time would have prompted me to make some racy and uncalled for comment about afternoon delight. Now

I simply greeted them. I was several steps past them when I remembered an earlier concern.

I turned and caught up to the couple. Putting my free hand on Taf's shoulder, I said, "Do you see the man sitting across the table from Father and Mother? That's Henz."

CHAPTER TWENTY-SEVEN

WHEN I REACHED THE nursery, the first thing I saw was the big, comfortable chair Mother had gone to great pains to find for the room. It was a heavy chair. I'd had quite a struggle to get it through the door. What I saw next made all Mother's and my efforts worthwhile.

Zhia was sitting in the chair, holding Lisia, rocking her, and softly singing to her. The baby's eyes were drooping; her dark curls resting on Zhia's breast sharply contrasted with the white sheet Zhia still wore. The evening was cool; Zhia had covered the child with a blanket that draped over her own legs, which were probably feeling the chill of the evening.

Zhia didn't see me. Pausing in the doorway, I found myself wondering what it would be like to have home and wife and child waiting for me at the end of each day. That the idea appealed to me was strange; that I didn't immediately reject its appeal was even more strange.

There was a tenderness on Zhia's face I'd never before seen. Watching her lull the baby to sleep, I realized this woman, not the ax- and stone-wielding servant of Henia, was the real Zhia. She was nurturer, not a destroyer.

I could barely hear the lullaby, but I could see Lisia's body lift with each of Zhia's breaths. Likely that motion as well as the music served to soothe

the baby. It wasn't long before the child's eyes closed fully. Zhia continued to rock her, her mouth curving in a smile of such sweetness that I felt something catch in my throat.

After a time, I remembered the plate of cooling food in my hand and took a step into the nursery. Zhia saw me, mouthed the words, "Thank you", got up, and put Lisia into her bed. Then she took the plate from me and went into the corridor, standing where she could still see the baby.

"I forgot to bring wine, and the food got cold," I said quietly as Zhia began to eat.

"That's all right," she said, also softly. "Getting the baby to sleep is more important than warm food. Poor little thing. She was at the 'I'm so tired I can't sleep' stage, and your poor mother was frustrated, and Lisia knew it. Babies seem to need the most patience right when you're least able to be patient. I admire your mother so much for even considering caring for a child Lisia's age. She's a wonderful person."

I don't know why I didn't show my pleasure at these words. Instead, I said, "She's an exhausted person; she fell asleep at the table. Father asked if you would mind watching the baby a little longer."

"Not at all. What?" she added, at the look on my face.

"Maybe I shouldn't bring this up. It just strikes me as odd that the idea of caring for a baby doesn't bother you."

"Actually, I thought it might; but it doesn't. Haven't you ever sung a song that just didn't go well at all?" With a grimace, I nodded. "You didn't stop singing because of that. Singing is a good thing. A baby is a good thing. And hope is a good thing. I figure no matter how bad things are, you're never really defeated until you decide there's no hope, no reason to try again. I loved Pandizh. I hated what happened to him; but I can't let that stop me from loving another baby, if I have the opportunity." The last words were somewhat strangled; I could see tears shining in the corners of her eyes. Taf and Mother were right; her eyes were golden green.

She finished the food. I took the plate from her, saying, "I'll take this to the kitchen. I have your fabric. I'll bring it when I return." I reminded myself to bring some wine, also.

She nodded. "Thank you. You know where I'll be."

In the dining hall, Mother was still asleep in the curve of Father's arm. Father was still discussing the Festival with Henz. I managed to get to the kitchen without their seeing me and insisting I join them again. Jug of wine and two cups in hand, I went to Father's office, scooped up the parcels, and returned to the nursery.

Before Zhia could open either of the parcels, Mother bustled in, profusely apologetic for her tardiness. She looked somewhat rested. Seeing Lisia asleep, she relaxed even more. "Thank you," she said fervently to Zhia.

"My pleasure," Zhia said with a smile. She picked up the parcels. "I'll be in my cubicle if she wakes and you need help coaxing her back to sleep. Even if I'm asleep, feel free to wake me."

"Thank you," Mother said again.

"Do you want wine now?" I asked as we left the nursery.

"Yes, but it'll slosh too much if you pour it now. I can wait a little longer. I don't know how long I was singing to Lisia. It seemed like a very long time." The captivating, sweet smile made a brief reappearance. "Until your father was showing me how to breathe, I never gave much thought to how I sing. Tonight I realized it takes as much breath, maybe even more, to sing softly as it does to sing loudly. I suppose on tour or at the Festival Singers hardly ever sing softly."

"Those competing for the Championship often do, because that's one of the skills a Singer is expected to have, and the competitors choose songs that allow them to display as wide a range of skills as possible. By the way, has Taf arranged a time for him to teach you the songs you'll need on tour?"

"No. Why would Taf teach me?"

"He sings tenor; when only men are singing, tenors usually have the melody."

"So am I a soprano?"

It occurred to me that I didn't actually know. "Father didn't say that in so many words. If you were a man, I could tell you what part you sing. I can't do the same with women's voices, at least, not as readily. Your quality isn't the same as Noia's. It's brighter, so I assume she's an alto, which would make you a soprano."

Zhia laughed. "That's the longest 'yes' I ever heard."

"Ask a question I know the answer to, and the answer might be shorter."

"I assume 'Why are there two parcels?' is a question you know the answer to."

"Yes, I do; but I don't want to spoil the surprise."

Zhia gave me an amused look but said nothing. We kept walking. We kept going slower as the exertion began to take its toll on Zhia's bad foot.

When the stone and masonry changed, I knew we had entered one of the later additions to the Hall. Zhia had apparently been assigned one of the outlying cubicles. I assumed Father had done that because, by the time Zhia needed a cubicle, all the quarters along the residential corridors had already been assigned.

When Zhia finally went into a cubicle, I stopped in the corridor, looked around, and said, "Well, this is secluded." My voice echoed in the empty corridor.

"I know." Zhia lit the lamp, adorning the austerely-furnished room with the reek of riku oil. "One good thing: when I snore, I won't disturb anyone." She saw me trying to hide a smile. "Go ahead and agree, or laugh, if you wish. I know I snore; Pandir used to tease me all the time. It's one of the things that makes me such a delicate, attractive woman." She grimaced—whether to emphasize what she'd said or from pain in her foot, I didn't know—and said, rather ungraciously, "Why are you standing out there? Come in."

There was nothing in the cubicle, not even as much as a comb, to indicate that it belonged to Zhia. I reminded myself that Zhia didn't have even as much as a comb. Then I remembered that she did have a mirror. I wasn't sure precisely where it was; probably in Father's office. Before the tour, Zhia would have to go to the market to purchase essential items.

"Homelike, isn't it?" Zhia asked, bleakly, as if she knew what I had been thinking.

"About as homelike as a Quarter Rest," I said.

With a humorless chuckle, she said, "Except there's no water and it's not defensible."

"No need to worry about defense: no one would be able to find you here."

"You can say that again. You may not have noticed, but I had to make marks on the corridor walls so I could find it again. This is only the second time I've been here."

I poured wine and handed her a cup. "Here's to having a place to sleep."

"Be it ever so humble," she said, by way of agreement, I suppose. She drained the cup and set it aside. Turning to the parcels, she asked, "Which one should I open first?"

I had intended to let her make the choice. Seeing her change from the approachable, tender woman who had held Lisia to this isolated, brittle person prompted me to say, "The thicker one."

Zhia sat on the bed and undid the cords that tied the cheap, coarse cloth around the good fabric. As it spilled into the lamplight, Zhia exhaled softly. She shook her head, but said nothing.

"You don't like it," I said, when the silence stretched out.

She raised wondering eyes to mine. "Are you joking? It's...it's glorious. There's no other word for it. It's the most beautiful stuff I've ever seen. Look at what it does in the light. It's..." She shook her head again. "Oh, thank you." She lifted a fold of it and caressed it with her other hand. "The texture is so rich. And the color! It's so unusual." Smiling, she looked up at me. "What made you choose this color? I don't know fashion well, but I do know this color isn't fashionable."

"That's what Eia said," I said, without thinking.

Zhia's smile vanished. "Did Eia choose this fabric?"

Berating myself for being a fool, I stammered, "No, but I've never bought fabric before. I didn't even know where to look for it, so I asked Eia to help me. She rejected a lot of fabrics. When I saw this one, I chose it. And that's the color Mother suggested I look for. She said it would match your eyes."

"Oh. Did you tell Eia that?"

"No." Remembering what I had said to Eia, I added, "When Eia heard that you planned to sew something before the Festival, she asked me to ask you if you would sew something for her."

"Certainly." Zhia's voice was quite cold. "On the next rainless evening we have."

Obviously, that meant "no". "Why won't you?" I asked, feeling a bit annoyed.

"Suppose that before you became a Singer, you had made furniture, and Eia knew it. What would you think if now she asked you to build her a table, for example?"

"I wouldn't. Now, I'm a Singer." Then I understood what Zhia was saying. "Oh," I added, lamely. "That was an insult, wasn't it?"

"Of a sort. I can't really say I blame Eia. No matter what you said when you asked her to help you choose fabric, what she heard was that you wanted her to help you buy something for another woman. It doesn't matter that the woman isn't special to you." She tilted her head to one side and asked, "Have you ever bought anything for Eia?"

"Today I bought her a trinket she admired."

"You bought her a trinket, and you bought me this expensive, unbelievably gorgeous cloth." She caressed it again. "I appreciate your helping me, and even more appreciate your superb taste; but I'm sorry that helping me caused a rift between you and Eia." She folded the cloth and set it aside. "And please don't be angry when I say that I won't be wearing anything made from this to the Festival. I don't want to risk someone spilling wine or food on it. I'll make stage garb from it."

"But if Eia sees you at the Festival and you're not wearing that fabric, she'll think you didn't like it," I objected.

"You know I like it. If she believes I didn't, wouldn't that be all the better for you?"

I had to admit she was right. "You must think I'm an idiot."

"Unless you think you're an idiot, no one here thinks you are. No idiot would have bought thread, needles, and scissors when buying cloth. Though I don't particularly care what Eia thinks, since I'm not going to wear this sheet in public and have nothing else to wear, Eia won't see me at the Festival."

"That's up to you," I said carelessly, but secretly pleased at Zhia's reply. "You have another parcel to open."

When she saw the reddish brown material, Zhia said, "Pardon me if I seem surprised that you thought of getting this other cloth. Now I'll have two things to wear. Thank you. I will be going to the Festival, after all. I must confess my curiosity: you bought one fabric to match my eyes. Did you choose this one to match my hair?"

Even I thought I sounded like an idiot when I asked, "Does it match your hair?"

Zhia grinned and pulled her hair over her shoulder so it lay on the fabric. It was a perfect match. "Since you weren't aware of my hair color, why did you choose this?"

"It was inexpensive," I said, bluntly.

"That's a perfectly fine reason." I was pleased that she sounded sincere. "It won't show dirt much, either. I'll still have to come up with trousers, among other things, before the tour. A skirt just doesn't work in a tebec saddle."

I would have liked to see Eia get into a tebec saddle while wearing a skirt. Like the rest of her, her legs are slim and attractive. Zhia I preferred to see in trousers.

"Well, if you're going to get something sewn in two days, I should leave you to do so." I winced and added, "No pun intended."

"I'm so glad to hear that."

"Don't needle me."

"Then cut out the puns."

I put both hands up. "You win. I don't know enough of the words to keep this up."

"That's more gracious than what is probably more accurate, which is that you're tired of stooping so low," Zhia said, laughing. "Thank you again for my fabric. Expecting you to make that purchase was asking a lot. I truly appreciate your willingness to help." I was in the corridor when she mumbled something in which I caught the word "rude", and added, "If I make it to the Festival and Eia is there, please introduce us. I'd like to thank her, also. Maybe I will sew something for her."

Thinking I would never, ever understand Zhia, I headed for my cubicle.

To get to it, I had to pass the nursery. Mother was still there. She was sewing something. By the size of it, I assumed it was for Lisia.

I went into the room and asked, quietly and gently, "Mother, why are you still up?"

"Because this isn't done yet."

"Is there some reason it has to be done tonight?"

Mother frowned. "Your father asked the same question."

"Which I take to mean that you didn't have a good reason to give him, either."

"I'm all right, Son. That nap helped. Don't fuss so."

"If I fuss it's because I care about you."

Now she smiled. "Your father said the same thing." She took a few more stitches, knotted and cut the thread, and said, "There! All done. What do you think?" She held up for my inspection a tiny dress.

"It's beautiful, Mother; but it won't fit you."

She laughed. "Were you able to get fabric for Zhia?"

"Yes. She really likes it. It does match her eyes. Thank you for your advice." I hesitated, then asked, "Mother, did you happen to make any comment to Zhia about her being a good mother?"

"I don't think so. Why?"

"Because she was a mother. Her child was killed. Horribly." Raising my voice above Mother's exclamation, I went on, "That being said, I need to tell you that she said helping with Lisia doesn't bother her, and I believe her when she says it; but I thought you'd want to avoid making an ill-advised remark."

"I appreciate your telling me, Son. Without prying, I should mention that what I can imagine the word 'horribly' means might be worse than what actually happened."

"Trust me, Mother; you couldn't imagine something more horrible than what really happened. If at some time Zhia wants to tell you the details, that will be her choice. I rather doubt she will; she said I was the only person she'd ever told. I promise you'll be happier not knowing. I would prefer I didn't know."

"Is that why you haven't asked her to be your wife?"

I managed to contain a sigh of exasperation. "Among the reasons I haven't asked Zhia to be my wife—besides the fact that I don't feel that way about her—is that if she were my wife, she couldn't tour. A woman great with child doesn't fit into a tebec's saddle. Her dream is to be a Singer; her dream is to tour. I want her to have her dream."

Mother looked like she was biting her tongue. I suspected she wanted to say that my feeling that way meant that I did care about Zhia. And I did; but not as a man should for a woman he wants as his wife.

"And please tell Father—no, I'll tell him myself."

"Please don't converse in intriguing hints," Mother chided.

I apologized. "Did Henz happen to tell you and Father his stage name?" She shook her head. "It's Love 'Em and Leave 'Em. I've already warned him to stay away from Noia; but Henz seems to think that the faster a woman runs, the more she's asking to be caught. I would hope that the Festival would keep him busy enough that he won't have too much time for conquests; but if he's staying here…"

Mother's face and voice were hard. "I understand."

Again, I hesitated. "And just so you won't hear it from anyone else, Mother, I must tell you that some people consider me as much a cad as Henz. Don't protest," I said quickly, as she opened her mouth. "Their opinion was once justified. But I've changed. For the past two turns of the star wheel I've been seeing only one woman. When Father finishes sending me on tours, I hope to ask her to be my wife."

"As long as she makes you happy, Son."

I stooped and kissed Mother's cheek. "Thank you for not scolding me."

"The only reason I didn't scold you is that I don't want to wake the baby," was the tart reply.

I was wise enough not to laugh. "Is Father in his office?"

"No. He went to bed. You should, too."

"I will if you will."

Mother gave me a fond smile. "Good night, Son." She yawned, went into her and Father's quarters, and closed the door.

Fervently hoping Lisia would sleep through the night, I went down the corridor. Henz popped out of a cubicle near mine and said, "It's too early to sleep. Let's go out."

"Be my guest, Henz. I still have the Festival song to learn. Tomorrow I have to meet with tour leaders to tell them how to get a tour on the road in three days."

"You've put a tour on the road in just three days?" Henz sounded impressed.

"Henz, I've put a tour on the road between one sunset and the next."

"In Nia Diva's name, why?"

"Because that's what the former Master wanted."

"Now I know why he's the former Master."

I didn't bother to tell him otherwise. It was Hall business, after all.

Henz did go out. I woke when he staggered in a bit before daybreak, bumping into things and crooning a bawdy song. I went to the nursery to see if the noise had wakened Lisia. Zhia was again in the big chair. She was asleep with the baby sleeping on her breast. On the floor at her feet lay a garment sewn of reddish brown fabric.

Chapter Twenty-Eight

I saw little of Henz between then and the Festival. I don't know how he used his time. As planned, the next day I met with the others Father had chosen as tour leaders to tell them what I knew about putting a tour together at short notice. With the organizing shared, getting five tours on the road in four days didn't look like much of a challenge.

Forcing my memory to absorb what I didn't yet know of the Festival song was a much greater challenge. I thought about sneaking the music on stage with me, but thought better of it. If I couldn't learn the music, my integrity as a Singer demanded that I simply listen to those who had made the effort.

I suddenly realized I didn't know what any of the music I'd ever sung sounded like. I knew what the baritone parts sounded like; I had heard other parts being practiced alone. It was the blend I'd never heard. How could a tour leader effectively please an audience if he'd never listened to what was being performed?

It was about mid-afternoon when I sought out Father. He was working on tour schedules and didn't appear to be pleased with the interruption.

"I won't keep you, Father," I said. "I just wanted to ask how much trouble I'd be in if I don't sing at the Festival tomorrow."

"That would depend on your reason for not singing. Are you getting a sore throat, or have you just not memorized the music?"

"I've pretty well learned the music; but it occurred to me that I've never heard how any of our songs sound from anywhere except on stage. If no Singer ever listens to what we do, how are we going to improve? I think it's a little arrogant to assume that just because we all know the same songs, we all sound good singing them."

Father nodded slowly, but said, "However, hearing the Festival song won't tell you how your tour songs sound."

"I should have thought of that. Sorry I disturbed you."

"Don't apologize, Son. You have a point; blend is important. The day after the Festival, we'll assemble the tour groups and have each sing at least one song. The other instructors and I will be the ones listening so none of the groups will be missing any parts. By the way," he added as I was in the doorway, "if you're not yet note perfect on the Festival song, do everyone a favor and don't sing." There was a scornful note in his voice that I hadn't heard since my visit home with Zhia before TTTW.

"Yes, sir." I went down the corridor, hoping Father wasn't starting to fall back into his old ways. Though he was officially only the acting Hall Master, I knew of no efforts to find someone to take his place. Of course, that was Hall business; there was no reason for me to know. Maybe someone else had been found. Maybe Father was finding the prospect of giving up the Mastership hard to take.

I found myself dreading the thought of anyone else as Hall Master. Without indulging in undue leniency, Father had brought warmth and approachability to the position. When he was strict, it was to help the Singers for whom he was answerable to be better. Yet I had heard no tales of strictness carried to excess, and Singers would be quick to make any such grievance known to one another.

I knew there was no point in getting upset about "what ifs". I decided to apply myself to learning the Festival song. I told myself I would memorize it even if I had to stay up all night. I didn't want to deserve Father's scorn, nor did I want to admit that a song had defeated me. I was, after all, a Champion.

It had been raining for a while before I realized I was both thirsty and hungry. (Singing—singing properly—is hard work.) I used the time it took to go to the dining hall to rehearse the song in my mind, and was pleased to discover that I had, finally, memorized the music. Too bad the Festival wasn't that evening…

A form approaching from the far end of the dining hall corridor told me someone else was eating late. The lamps that lit the corridors left the areas between them and also the floor in shadow. They didn't shed enough light to allow me to make out the person's face. The person was wearing trousers and shirt, so I knew it was a man. I thought most of the men at the Hall were taller than whoever it was. As he drew nearer, I saw the limp, and knew then that "he" was "she": Zhia.

She was limping worse than I'd seen her do for a while. Realizing that the shoes, the deep green shirt, and the dun trousers she wore all were new, I suspected that she had walked into town and back. When she was even closer and I saw that her hair was wet, I knew I was right.

By way of greeting, I asked, "Did you forget that the Hall owns a cart and a desdal?"

Shaking her head, she replied, "I can't forget what I never knew."

I was about to contradict her when I realized that she wouldn't have known that the cart that brought her to the Hall from the prison belonged to the Hall. She might not even remember how she got from the prison to the Hall. "I see you were shopping for the tour."

"Yes. I'm pretty sure I got everything I need. There were so many parcels I felt like I was outfitting the whole group."

"How many parcels did you have?"

"Ten or twelve, maybe."

"How were you carrying that many?"

"In my cloak."

"I should have known you'd think keeping whatever you bought dry was more important than keeping yourself dry. Suppose you take a chill right before your tour?"

"Someone else will get to be a first-timer."

"No, more likely Father will have your hide."

"When he finds out how much I spent, he'll for sure have my hide," was her gloomy prediction.

Hoping she wasn't right, I asked, "Were you on your way to supper?" At her assent, I said, "Your shopping trip did your bad foot no good. May I offer you my arm?"

"I'd really appreciate it."

We weren't that far from the dining hall, but she couldn't go very fast. I think she was trying not to lean too heavily on me. Every other breath was a hiss; her foot was bothering her a lot. I slowed my steps and said, "Since what you're wearing isn't wet, you obviously didn't wear those clothes into town. Knowing how much you cherished that sheet getup of yours, I'm sure you wouldn't have worn that."

Her sidelong look was amused. "If you're asking whether I went into town naked, the answer is 'no'. I wore what I sewed the other night from the brown cloth you bought me. That garment got very wet, so when I went to my cubicle to drop off my parcels, I changed clothes. I even dried my hair a little."

I glanced at the ends of her nape-gathered tresses. Water was dripping off them, and not onto the floor. "I would say 'very little'. Stop a moment." I wrung quite a nice puddle out of her hair. "I don't think you would have wanted to sit at supper with the back of both your shirt and your trousers damp."

"No, that wouldn't have been good." Another hissing breath was cut off. I saw she was biting her lower lip.

"Any chance you'll let Aplin look at your foot?"

"No. He'll just tell me I walked on it too much when it was broken and it'll give me trouble from now on."

I didn't lose my temper. "He might also be able to give you something to lessen the pain. I suspect you'll have trouble sleeping tonight, otherwise."

"Wine will lessen the pain."

"If you drink enough wine to lessen as much pain as your foot is giving you right now, you won't get up tomorrow or the day after. Father wants to hear each tour group sing at least one song the day after tomorrow. You don't know any of the music yet."

"I know one song," she said, defiantly.

I laughed. "If Father will let you sing that one, then you'll be all right, I guess. But you and Taf still have to find time to go over the other songs you need to learn."

"We can do that while I sew my stage garb." Another hissing inhalation, then she grated, "Just a moment, please."

She sat on the floor and pulled off her shoes. She held them in her left hand and grabbed my forearm with her right hand so I could help her to her feet. When she was again in the lamp light, I saw blood where she'd been biting her lower lip. "Good work on your lip. How are you going to sing with a hole in it?"

"Is there a hole in it?"

"Can't you feel the blood?"

"Actually, no. I'm pretty cold."

The hand I touched was very cold. "A good hot meal will warm you up," I said, trying not sound as concerned as I felt. "And we're practically there."

Just as we reached the dining hall, Henz came out. His glance took in Zhia's bare feet, the blood on her lip, and how close she was standing to me. With an offensive smile, he said, "Rois, you did find time to play." He treated Zhia to a long, scornful gaze. "But I see you're going in for quantity rather than quality."

Even as I began, "Henz," Zhia said, "That comment would hurt only if there were any evidence that you were familiar with the latter concept."

Henz stared. "Pardon me?"

"No, I won't," she snapped. "Obviously, you don't recognize me. When we first met, my clothes were soaked and clinging to me. Your eyes never went as high as my face. Just to refresh your memory, I'm the person who asked you for help as you were leaving town this evening after the rain started. I had that large bundle slung on my back. I was limping. You couldn't be bothered to assist someone you thought was a nobody."

"You're a Singer?" he faltered. "You don't dress like one."

"What difference does that make?" she flared. "I was a person in need.

Common decency is clearly another concept that is quite unknown to you."

"Would it help if I said I'm sorry?"

"Not when you say it in that 'humor her; maybe she'll forget about it' tone of voice." Zhia shook her head. "I have better things to do than waste time on the likes of you." The scorn in her voice would have made anyone capable of feeling shame blush. Henz didn't even blink.

Zhia let go of my arm and limped into the dining hall.

Henz watched her for a moment, then looked at me. "How did she hurt her foot?"

"Saving my life," I said, curtly. "And no, I'm not giving you the details."

"Wait, Rois. That's Zhia, isn't it?"

Without answering, I went into the dining hall. Henz followed me. He sat down across the table from Zhia.

She stood. "I just lost my appetite."

I lost my temper. "Zhia, sit down. Henz, get lost."

"Is there a problem?" Father was suddenly looming over our table. I hadn't noticed that he was in the dining hall.

Henz rose, hastily. "I was just leaving."

"Someone who's competing for the Championship tomorrow should be in his cubicle resting for the remainder of the night," was Father's not-so-subtle comment.

"I agree, sir."

"I expect you to do more than simply agree."

Henz's "yes, sir" was mutinous. He left.

"Thank you," I said to Father, and fetched two plates. I asked a kitchen worker to bring Zhia some warmed wine.

"I thought Henz was your friend," Father said as I set the plates the table. He had taken a chair across the table from Zhia.

I sat next to him and began to eat before I answered. "I thought so, too. I take it Mother didn't tell you what I told her night before last."

"Was your mother supposed to give me a message?"

"No; I told her I'd talk to you, but you'd already gone to bed." A kitchen worker put the wine in front of Zhia. "Thank you," I said to the woman. To Zhia, I said, "Drink it while it's warm." I watched until I saw her lift the cup, then turned back to Father. "Do you know Henz's stage name?" His lifted eyebrows invited me to tell him. "It's Love 'Em and Leave 'Em."

Zhia choked on the wine. "Sorry," she said, her coughing muffled by a napkin. "Who gave him that name?" she asked when she recovered from the fit.

"I'm sorry to say that I did."

"And what you wanted to tell me was that he deserves the name?" Father asked.

I nodded. "I've pointed him out to Taf, who already knew his reputation." Father suddenly became interested in some crumbs on the table. Too sharply, I said, "I know what you're trying not to say. And just in case Mother says anything to you, when I told her about Henz I told her about me, too."

Then Father looked at me. "You did? Maybe you are trying to mend your ways. I'm proud of you."

The confession had been both embarrassing and difficult. I didn't acknowledge Father's praise.

"Pardon me if I'm prying," Zhia said, "but do I understand, Rois, that you and Henz are…"

"Were," I said, emphatically. "Henz and I used to do a lot of the same things. He thinks I'm still interested in his idea of amusements." I was even more embarrassed.

"I'm sure you would rather I'd not heard this conversation," Zhia said, quietly. "Rest assured that these chairs will tell people what you've said before I will. And if I may further intrude in what isn't my business, may I say I've never admired you more, Rois."

I couldn't have spoken even had I been able to think of something to say.

Zhia finished the warmed wine and said to Father, "After walking into town I'm not sure how much farther I can walk, but my foot is really sore. Aplin probably ought to look at it. Could I trouble you to help me to the clinic?"

It was obvious to me that her intent was to give me time and privacy to regain my composure. Father just as obviously didn't understand what she was doing, for he said, "Not until you finish your supper. In fact, I'll go fetch Aplin. If you've overused your bad foot, he won't want you to use it any more than is necessary." He stood and asked, "Would you like more wine? That was warmed, right?"

"Yes, I would; and yes, it was. Thank you."

"Thank you," I said to Zhia after Father had brought the wine and left the dining hall.

"I'm just taking care of my tour partner," she said. "Are you all right?"

"It's not easy for me to admit I'm wrong," I muttered.

She drew a deep breath so she could speak quietly. "I don't think many people find that easy to do. Either they try to pretend they aren't wrong, or they do like Henz did earlier, and say it without really meaning it. You've not only admitted it, it sounds like you've also done things to find a new direction, and you've continued on that course even when someone like Henz is trying to distract you, to lead you astray.

"Obviously, Henz thinks he's some big man because he toys with women. You've shown yourself much more of a man than he will ever be. Don't let him shame you into falling back into ways you no longer want to choose. You're stronger than that."

"If you only knew," I said, my voice not yet steady.

"I know what I've seen. If you don't know the Rois I know, ask me some time and I'll tell you what a fine man he is. But don't ask me unless you have a lot of time, because it'll take a long time for me to tell you everything I know." Her voice wasn't steady, either. She took another deep breath. "We'd better pull ourselves together. Father will wonder what we've been doing if we both sound like this." She drank some warmed wine, then pulled a jug toward her and refilled my cup. "When does the Festival begin?"

"After the midday meal. If you're planning to sing, don't eat much more than bread and water at that meal."

"That's good to know, but I probably won't sing. I don't think anyone wants a woman singing the baritone line an octave higher."

"Especially since you didn't hear it right the first time. I finally finished learning it before supper." I had a swallow of wine and shook my head. "I don't know who wrote that song, but it's pretty clear that it wasn't meant to be heard by anyone but Singers."

"What do you mean by that?" Zhia asked, putting her elbow on the table and resting her chin on her hand.

"It's not very enjoyable to sing, and I doubt it's enjoyable to listen to. I suppose an instructor—Neron, for example—would get all excited about the countermelodies and the difficult harmonies and the challenging rhythms. But a non-Singer isn't going to be impressed by those things. A non-Singer won't hear a melody that can be hummed. A non-Singer won't take anything home from the Festival but the impression that Singers are really getting above themselves."

"It sounds like it's the kind of song my father used to say was written more for the composer's glory than the daemon's. So if you were in charge of the Festival, what would the Singers perform?"

I thought. "I'd choose a song that speaks to the audience as well as challenging the Singers. Knowing how hard it was for me to learn tomorrow's song, I can't expect that we'll perform it very well. I'd rather choose a less difficult piece and do it well than a very difficult piece that we do poorly."

"Even so," Father said, returning with Aplin. "Have you finally learned the song?"

"Yes, Father. I'm ready for the Festival."

While we were speaking, Aplin knelt to examine Zhia's foot. She pulled it away and said, "No one who's still eating wants to see this. Can we find a more suitable place?"

Aplin raised his head and looked around. "No one is watching."

"If I scream, they will be."

He was trying not to smile. "I thought the idea was to keep you from using this foot."

"Is anyone volunteering to carry me?" Zhia asked. "Then I guess I walk. In fact, I had suggested to Father that I come to the clinic. However, my cubicle may be closer."

We could almost have ridden tebecs to Hollan's Town faster than we were able to walk to her cubicle. Zhia was so pale and her foot so swollen when she finally sank onto her bed that Aplin immediately gave her something to make her sleep.

When he finished examining her foot, he looked up at Father. "I suppose she expects to attend the Festival."

"She's a Singer; she's expected to attend the Festival," Father corrected.

"In the morning I'll wrap it. That won't do a lot of good, but it'll help." He looked at me. "She's to go to the Festival and return to the Hall in the cart. Once you get to the Festival, don't let her walk around. Make her stay in the cart."

Father and I exchanged a look. Clearly, Aplin didn't know Zhia very well.

Chapter Twenty-Nine

When I woke the next morning, it was to a pleasant sense of anticipation. As a competitor, I hadn't been able to look forward to the last two Festivals. This Festival, all I had to do was sing with the mass group and then applaud the Champion. I pulled on bright new clothes—after I finished instructing the other tour leaders, I had also done some shopping—and went to break my fast.

Taf and Noia were in the dining hall. I thought Noia looked nervous; first-time competitors often do. I asked if I could sit with them, and Noia's face lit up like I'd told her she'd been reprieved. She spent the meal showering me with questions about the competition. I finally realized she wanted reassurance, not information, and stopped giving her answers that applied to previous Festivals but might not be true for today's.

"You know your song, right?" I asked.

She nodded. Taf said, "She sings it in her sleep."

I didn't laugh. "Probably the most important thing is to relax. If you let your throat get tight, you won't sing well. Taf, you might give her a back rub right before she sings."

He nodded.

"All those people," Noia whispered. "And they'll be mostly Singers."

"You're a Singer, too," I said. "Just imagine all those people have no clothes on and are really hoping you're not going to look at them."

Her face relaxed into her delightful smile. "I'll try to remember that."

"Most importantly, remember that you're singing for Nia Diva, not the judges, not the nobodies, not Father. Sing to the daemon."

After a moment, Noia said, "I've heard no woman has ever won."

"I believe that's true. I also believe it's not because female Singers aren't as good as male ones, but in part because the judges aren't as accustomed to judging women's voices. And it may be that there are still some who wish there weren't female Singers."

"Well, if I can't win, that makes it a little easier."

"Don't you dare sing less than your best," Taf said. "You have a wonderful voice."

Color flooded her cheeks. She thanked Taf and kissed him. "And thank you, too, Rois." She sighed, nervously. "I wish it were right now."

"I know the feeling," I said. I finished eating, wondering how to use the time before the Festival. Then I remembered Aplin's instructions about taking the cart. "Zhia is going to the Festival, but Aplin wants her to ride in the cart. She walked into town and back yesterday."

Taf shook his head. "Nothing stops that woman from being stupid."

"Taf, don't be cruel!" Noia chided.

"I'm not being cruel; I'm being honest," he told her.

Hoping to forestall an argument, I said, "Why I mentioned the cart is to ask if you two would like to ride into town, as well."

"That would be good," Noia said, "but won't Father and Mother want to ride?"

"Mother won't be going. If Father wants to ride, there'll be room enough for him. I'm going now to ask a stable hand to have the cart ready right after the midday meal."

When I got to the stables, I found out that Father had already asked that the cart be readied, which told me he was planning to ride. I went back to my cubicle and again looked at the Festival song. I was glad that I did, because overnight I had forgotten some of it.

This is not that hard, I lied to myself. I went over it again and again until I was certain it was fixed in my memory.

"Are you done yet?" came a weary voice from the corridor. Henz was looking in. He was wearing only trousers and clearly had just risen from his bed. I saw a dark mark on his neck I hadn't seen at supper. I wondered who put it there.

"Were you still asleep?" I asked, all innocence.

"I was still in bed," he replied, crossly.

"Sorry, Henz. But if you want a full meal before this evening, you'd better get to the dining hall." I assume he went back to his cubicle. Realizing I didn't want to know whom he had seduced, I went to Father's office. "Do you have any chores I can do?" I asked.

"Let me make a note of this event in the Hall records," he said with a smile. "What's wrong? Are you anxious for the Festival to begin?"

"Nowhere near as anxious as Noia. I asked her if she and Taf want to ride into town in the cart before I found out you'd asked for the cart to be readied. Was that for Zhia's sake, or did I speak out of turn?"

"I hate to make it sound like I'm criticizing a kind thought, but our instruments need to get to the Festival. Since you're looking for something to do, you can take them to the stage now. You'll probably need someone to help you. And, Son, take both the usual rimba and the ones that Zhia improved."

When I reached the storage area, I saw that a Singer named Egion, who had started at the Hall when I did and was one of the Hall's better drummers, was already getting out the instruments. I told him a cart was waiting and offered to help him load it. He balked when he found out that Father wanted the "improved" rimba brought. He had seen the discoloration on the metal bodies and had assumed they were unplayable. I could see them in a far corner of the storage area. I managed to talk Egion into trying them out and listening to their altered sound.

The expression of his face altered, as well, from grudging cooperation to genuine appreciation. "Do you think Father will let me play these at the Festival?" he asked, as the resonant tones died.

"I think Father will insist that someone play them at the Festival," I answered.

"That must be why he wants them there."

"Let it be me," he implored someone, presumably Nia Diva.

As we set out with the loaded cart, we discovered that the road into town was already crowded with people hoping to arrive early enough to get a good place to stand; only the judges sit at the Festival. I had forgotten that detail, and was grateful that Aplin had said Zhia was to stay in the cart. I didn't for a moment think she would; as Taf had said, nothing stopped Zhia from being stupid.

Somehow, Egion had missed the scene in Gadig's office when the improvement to the rimba was explained, so he was full of questions about know how the drums had been changed. I thought he would fall out of the cart when I told him they had been used for boiling water.

"You're joking, aren't you?" he asked, with a pleading tone in his voice. When he finally accepted the truth of the matter, he said, "Those rimba are the only ones of their kind. They may also be the last of their kind. While I assume it was the combination of heat and water that made the change, I wouldn't want to start experimenting to try to find that combination again. And you said they were used as pots over the course of some days?"

"Something like three days, I think."

Egion groaned. "This Zhia person, was she threatening the other Singers? No experienced Singer would do that to rimba, not even to save his own life."

"You know that; I know that. Except for me, that tour was all new Singers. They may have known better, but Zhia was in charge. She can be very forceful. Had I been in any condition to countermand her instructions, Zhia…" I shook my head. "Zhia would have gone ahead and boiled water in the rimba."

"Good thing for her the rimba sound better, or I might consider strangling her."

"Get in line," I laughed.

"Actually, I wish we could get out of this line," Egion remarked, reining in the desdal as the flow of people slowed yet again.

The closer we came to town, the worse the crush became. I was beginning to worry that we wouldn't be able to unload the instruments and get back to the Hall in time to get back for the Festival. As Egion again curbed our progress, I jumped off the cart and left the road. The ground between where we were and where we wanted to be looked fairly smooth. I climbed back onto the cart. "Do you want to try going around the crowd? It looks like the instruments won't get jostled too badly."

Egion nodded, touched the desdal with the whip, and turned the cart off the road. Soon the huge curve of the Festival stage filled our eyes.

It was built of vidu wood, a pale, fine-grained wood which is beautiful without any kind of finish. To protect it from daily exposure to rain, the wood used for the stage is oiled, which turns it a rich brown. The stage itself, farther off the ground than I am tall, is most of a circle. The back wall is more than a half circle, and is as high as a two-story house. In the center of this wall is set, in gold, the symbol of Nia Diva. Where the wall ends, steps lead from the stage to the ground. A roof shelters the stage. Below and to the sides of the stage are rooms for the performers and their equipment. In front of the stage is a vast open area for the nobodies. For the Festival, a table for the judges is set under a canopy, just far enough from the stage so the judges can clearly see and hear the performers, even those at the back of the stage. Also for the Festival, stalls and booths selling food, wine, and baubles, bangles, and beads circle the open area.

No other town has a stage as large as the one used for the Festival, but stages in every town have most of the same features. Even in the smallest of towns, where one performs on stages that are little more than slightly-raised planks under a leaking roof, one sees the symbol of Nia Diva on the back wall. (Getting wet isn't the only drawback to performing in the smaller towns. Some stages are built of boards so worn they're dangerous. Of course, most of those stages are so low that if one falls through, the greatest hazard is splinters, not sprains or broken bones.)

I had never heard of anyone falling off the Festival stage. In fact, the Festival was likely a magistrate's dream because, by and large, people understood that it was for the daemon and acted as one might wish they always did. If there was unseemliness, it was usually confined to the areas around the stalls, where those who had come for something other than music gathered.

As Egion guided the cart toward the steps, we saw that people had already claimed the spots closest to the stage. Their clothing suggested they were servants holding the choice locations for their masters. Quite a bit of the area farther back was full, as well. I didn't remember ever seeing so many people at the Festival; but that could have been because when I was competing, I had been too nervous to see much of anything (which is one reason Singers memorize their music).

When all the instruments were out of the cart and in place, I said, "Are you going back to the Hall?"

Egion shook his head. "It's best that someone stay with the instruments. Besides, I want to play some more on these rimba." He caressed the head of the nearest drum.

Chuckling, I asked, "What about food?"

"I can visit the stalls."

"All right. We'll see you shortly, I imagine."

Both because I didn't have to worry about damaging delicate instruments and because the stream of people going into town had become a river, I kept the cart to the side of the road and so returned to the Hall fairly quickly. Even so, I was later than I wanted to be; most of the Singers from my Hall had already left for the Festival. I grabbed some bread and a hurried swallow of water and went back to the cart, where the others were ready to leave. Father was in front. Taf, Noia, and Zhia were in the cart's bed, which was padded with oiled cloth cloaks.

I got in front with Father and apologized to everyone for the delay. Then I told them how crowded the road was. "If you don't mind more jostling than usual, I'll take measures to avoid the crush," I finished.

Even Noia, who again looked anxious, agreed that haste was desirable. "I'd rather be there and be nervous than be nervous about whether I'd get there," were her words. She looked a little pale when we reached the Festival grounds, but her voice was steady when she assured Father she was ready to sing. She and Taf headed for the competitors' area.

I settled the desdal for a long wait. At Father's suggestion, I had stopped the cart at the back of and just beyond the open area, a little in front of the stalls and booths. I had managed to position the cart so the its tail faced the stage, which would give Zhia a fairly good view of the Festival.

Citing an uneasy stomach from the cart's motion, Zhia went to the closest public convenience as soon as the cart stopped. When she returned, Father gave her Aplin's instructions. "I'm not going to ask whether you understand what Aplin expects of you. I'm telling you that I expect you to obey Aplin's instructions, both the letter and the spirit." He couldn't quite hide his surprise when she said only, "Yes, sir." There was surprise in his voice, also, when he looked at her and said, "Did you know that color matches your hair?" Without waiting for her to answer, he went toward the stage, his long legs covering the distance in a very short time.

Though I was still working with the desdal, I was looking at Zhia. This was the first I'd seen what she'd done with the reddish brown fabric. My interest in women's clothes had been more or less limited to how fast I could get women out of them, but I was able to tell if a woman looked good in what she was wearing.

Zhia looked good. There may be a name for the style of garment she had sewn; if there was, I didn't know it. I did know it wasn't skirt and shirt or shirt and trousers. It was very simple. As far as I could tell, it was similar to the garment Zhia had improvised from the sheet: a large rectangle folded in half with a hole for the head. The reddish brown garment covered much more than the sheet had, everything from Zhia's neck to her feet, in fact. The side edges weren't lapped, they were sewn most of the way up, leaving openings for the arms a bit more than a hand span long. There was no sash or anything else to give the garment shape save the folds of the fabric as it fell from the shoulders, and Zhia's curves. The fabric was opaque; it revealed nothing. But it gave the impression of concealing little, so it drew the eye. Seeing how it looked dry and imagining how it had looked wet, I understood why Henz had stared.

(Regretfully, it is becoming increasingly common for female Singers to wear on stage garments much more suggestive than what Zhia had on. Some would be indecent in the bedchamber. When Father first saw Singers so attired, his comment was, "Do they dress like that because they can't carry a tune?" When the women proved they were quite capable of not only carrying a tune but also carrying it well, Father said, "If their voices are that good, why are they trying to distract people?" While that may sound like the grumbling of someone who not only is behind the times but also can't be pleased, I have to say that I share Father's dislike of the practice. Again quoting Father: "Intimacy is good; music is good. They don't belong together on stage.")

I heard the instruments being warmed up and quickly finished with the desdal. As Zhia climbed into the back of the cart, I saw that she wore only one shoe. Aplin had wrapped her bad foot in wide strips of cloth. "Does that help?" I asked, pointing to the bound foot.

She shook her head. "It's too tight. I'm going to unwrap it."

"As long as you don't walk around."

With obvious patience, she said, "I've already told your father I'll do what I'm supposed to. I have no intention of giving him something else to worry about. He's nervous enough."

"Father? What does he have to be nervous about?"

"The Festival, I imagine. This is his first Festival as Hall Master, and he has a woman who's just finished her first tour competing for Champion. Today will show not only how well Noia knows songs, but also how well your father knows Singers. Right now, Noia is probably more confident than he is." She hesitated, then added, "And I suspect it isn't easy for your father to listen to others doing what he can no longer do."

As I made my way toward the stage, I was wondering why I hadn't thought of that.

The festival began with the usual invocation of Nia Diva, and the ritual two sips of wine. I've heard that it was once the custom for each Singer observe that ritual at the start of his performance, but that was abandoned when the increasing number of participants first caused the Festival to last well into the evening rain. The present practice is for each Singer to be given a small cup as he or she arrives. (There were very few left by the time I reached the area where the non-competing Singers were gathered.) After the invocation, all drink at the same time. There have been complaints that the change in custom has robbed the ritual of any meaning. Others commend the modification as being respectful both of the daemon and of those who don't have the benefit of a roof over their heads. I happen to like it.

Once the formalities had been observed, the competition began. There were more male competitors than female, but there were a number of women. All competitors were excellent, as always. I thought Noia did especially well. Henz's performance didn't overly impress me; but he proved that he was more than a handsome womanizer.

I found myself wishing I were competing. Then I realized I only wanted to do better than Henz, and was able to put aside my pride and listen, making my own judgments. Before the Festival song was performed, Egion got his wish and played the improved rimba. I heard a ripple of appreciation run through the Singers standing around me.

Then it was time for the mass number. We were crammed onto the stage so tightly it was a wonder anyone could breathe. I saw some on the edge lock arms with those one rank closer to the center. Surprisingly, no one fell off the stage.

If I say only that we got through the song, it's because I don't think I should say much more about the piece. (The composer is still alive.) It was difficult and we didn't sing it very well; but we all ended at the same time. There was little applause, and not simply because so many who had been on the ground were now on the stage. The Singers who were leaving the stage looked dejected. The faces of those on the ground the stage wore expressions of either confusion or disappointment.

I saw that many of the nobodies had turned to look at some commotion at the edge of the open area. I was annoyed that someone had disrupted the Festival—probably someone who needed more than music to get excited—but before I could work myself up to full-blown indignation, the Champion was announced.

It was Henz.

And it was Noia.

In the stunned silence, the main judge explained the panel's decision, namely, that judging a woman's voice against a man's was not fair to either and that henceforth, if there were male and female competitors, there would be a male Champion and a female Champion.

There was, of course, only one Champion's trophy on hand. With the judges' permission, I returned to the stage, unclasped the chain from which hung my own Champion's cup, and clasped it around Noia's neck.

"Congratulations. You earned it," I said, and kissed her cheek.

CHAPTER THIRTY

THE PARTY BEGAN IMMEDIATELY.

The prize purse was divided between Henz and Noia, who channeled it to others. One group went to buy wine and other things to drink; another group went to procure food; while a third group went to rent the largest hall they could find. Since some of the business the first two groups needed to transact could be done without leaving the Festival grounds, those Singers returned before the third group achieved its goal. The move from the Festival grounds to the hall didn't put a damper on the festivity.

I was supposed to be in the third group, but Father snagged me before I could leave with the others and had me help him move the instruments from the stage into one of the equipment rooms, where they would stay dry and safe until being returned to the Hall the next day. Somehow, I knew that chore would be mine, also.

As we stored the improved rimba, Father said, "Perhaps the Festival should be expanded to include a prize for instrumentalists. Of the performances today that deserved a trophy, Egion's certainly did."

"Are you serious?" I asked. "About having more prizes, I mean?"

"Very. If I can find any of the judges, I may speak to them about it tonight."

He looked sidelong at me. "You sound like you don't like the idea."

"It caught me by surprise is all. I think it's something that's long overdue."

"Thank you, Son. Speaking of overdue, see if you can get any of my Singers back before midday tomorrow. I do want to hear each tour group sing."

And Taf still had to teach Zhia the melody lines for the Hall repertoire.

It wasn't hard to find where the Champions' party was; when that many Singers are in one place the sound carries a considerable distance.

The food and drinks were set on long tables at either end of the spacious hall. Most of the lamps were also on those tables, so much of the remainder of the hall was dim or shadowed. Between the tables, couches and benches were scattered.

The party was one of the stranger after-Festival parties I've attended, because by the time I arrived it had already become two parties sharing one hall.

Henz and his crowd stayed fairly close to the wine and stronger drinks. Noia and Taf and their friends ate more food and drank sparingly of the wine. Henz's party got noisier and wilder. Noia's friends became increasingly more subdued as the other group became more unrestrained.

I'm not sure when the women of pleasure arrived. Their presence made the party even stranger, for Noia and the other female Singers obviously didn't appreciate their being there. Their censorious looks didn't daunt the men from Henz's crowd. They soon paired off with the new arrivals. Though they moved the couches and benches into the most shadowy areas of the hall, the darkness was not as deep as they obviously believed it to be, nor did the shadows muffle sounds.

Though Noia wasn't enjoying the party, it was clear she was still dazzled by her victory. Time after time her hand stole to the cup around her neck. I smiled, remembering doing the same thing when I was first named Champion… before I got so drunk I didn't know what I was doing. When Noia wasn't fingering the trophy, Taf was. I got the impression he was growing impatient to leave.

The evening was still young when Noia thanked those who had celebrated with her and expressed her regrets at having to leave her own party. "But don't think you have to leave, too," she added, quickly. "That food is paid for; you might as well eat it."

There was a chorus of congratulations as she and Taf went to the door, which was at the edge of the lamp light. It opened just as they reached it. Zhia stood there, hooded and cloaked against the rain that could be seen and heard through the open door.

"I'm sorry I'm late," she began. Then she saw the cup around Noia's neck. "You're Champion? Congratulations! I'm so proud of you!" She stepped aside and waved them out with an uncharacteristically graceful gesture. "The cart is waiting. On second thought, don't go out yet." She went back out and returned with cloaks, which she handed to Taf. He wrapped Noia in one before putting on his own. "Have a good night."

"It's already been a good night," Noia said.

"The best is yet to come," Taf said. He took her hand and led her into the rain.

I was wondering both why Zhia didn't take off even her hood and why she hadn't known that Noia was a Champion when Henz sauntered toward the door.

"Aren't you going to congratulate me, too?" he asked.

"Why?" Zhia asked, frowning. In reply, he raised his Champion's cup—he was holding it in his hand—so it caught the light. "There are two Champions?"

"Yes. What were you doing during the Festival, and who were you doing it with?"

Zhia ignored the innuendo. Her "Congratulations" was anything but hearty.

"You can do better than that," Henz chided. "How about a kiss?"

"Is that the penalty for arriving late?"

Henz had been drinking deeply; he missed the insult. He'd already forgotten he wanted a kiss. "What did you think of my song?"

"Why ask me? I'm not a Singer; I don't dress like one."

Perhaps Henz wasn't as drunk as I thought. He said, "Zhia, you're a woman who would make a man forget the way."

Zhia still didn't know the meaning of that bit of Singer's slang. Even if she'd forgotten the tone and context in which Gadig had used it, Henz's leering voice and expression told her it was rude. The hood shadowed the upper part of her face, but I could see her false smile when she said, "If I had that effect on any man, I'd hope it was you."

Henz guffawed and called her a coarse name. "I've been asking around since the other night. I've heard a lot about you."

"I can assure you that whatever you've heard is either true or not true."

"I hadn't heard you were so good at talking crap. I did hear you saved Rois' life."

"That is not true. Nia Diva saved him. She acts through whomever she will."

"Clever, if you believe that sort of thing," he sneered. "Wiggle out of this one: I've heard you like to play with axes, and that you killed eight men that way."

"That is not true." The calm with which she had been answering was slipping away.

"Liar. I've heard the same story from several people."

"Please accept that what you heard wasn't true, and drop the subject."

"No. I want to know what isn't true about it."

I noticed that the noise in the hall had diminished considerably. People were trying to listen without seeming to do so.

Her voice low, crisp, and cold, Zhia said, "One, I wasn't playing. Two, I didn't like it. Three, there was only one ax. Four, I killed no men, only raiders. Five, only seven raiders fell by the ax. The eighth one..." Her voice faltered. "The eighth one I killed by beating his head to pulp with a rock." She drew a breath that was more of a sob. "Why couldn't you simply accept that your information was wrong?" She went outside and didn't return.

Thinking I would go after her, I looked for a place to set my cup down. For a moment I forgot to breathe.

Eia had come in while Henz was tormenting Zhia. She outshone every other woman in the place. Even the lamps near her looked dimmer. (I won't apologize for those cliches. It seemed like each time I saw Eia, I fell madly in love with her again.)

She hadn't seen me. It felt almost indecent, reveling in her beauty when she didn't know I was looking. I was about to go to her side when Henz quit staring at the open door and saw her, too. He was next to her with what seemed to be only two strides.

I've seen Henz seduce women. I will admit, without pride, that he and I used to compare and discuss techniques. Henz didn't seduce Eia. He didn't need to. The casual way he fondled her while talking with people nearby told me they already knew each other very well.

I stared in cold dismay, my ears ringing as they sometimes do after one receives a hard blow. I couldn't help but wonder whether Eia had been involved with him when I first met her. When my hearing returned, Henz was laughingly describing how Eia had offered herself to the judges in exchange for their making him, Henz, Champion. Eia looked as pleased with the revelation of this chicanery as Henz did. As she pressed herself closer to him, his hand slid into the low neckline of her shirt.

I can't say Eia no longer looked beautiful. I can't say I no longer desired her. In fact, I had to turn away so I didn't have to see Henz's hand moving intimately on her body. Probably because I still found her beautiful and desired her, her betrayal was that much harder to accept.

In the hollow, I had known how it felt to want to kill someone. But that someone had been a raider, and my life had been in danger. Tonight, I wanted to kill for no better reason than wounded pride. I wasn't sure if I wanted to kill Henz or Eia, or both. I was just drunk enough that I didn't really care.

I was saved from a rash deed by Nia Diva, in the guise of one of the former slaves. She was speaking for twelve or so others when she said, "Sir, pardon our bothering you, but we'd really like to get out of here. Can you take us back to the Hall?"

"Certainly," I said, grateful for a valid excuse—any excuse, actually—to leave. "Do you have cloaks?" When it was determined that they were all as unprepared as I was, I said, "Wait by the door. I'll hire a cart."

I didn't bother to tell Henz we were leaving. After all, he wasn't really Champion.

It took me a while to find a covered cart big enough for that many people. The driver's seat wasn't covered, so I was thoroughly wet by the time by the time we reached the Hall. I took time to change into dry clothes and grab a cloak before I returned the cart to town. I didn't even consider going back to the party. The rain was still heavy when I started walking back to the Hall.

I soon overtook Egion, who had lost interest in the party after hearing Henz admit to bribery. I was glad to have someone to walk with; my thoughts weren't comfortable company. Also, had I been by myself, I might have done something stupid like go back and confront Henz, not about Eia—I didn't want to give her the satisfaction of having two besotted and betrayed lovers quarreling over her—but about his dishonesty. It would have been an empty and possibly dangerous gesture; I knew I could do nothing about what I had learned. Neither, for that matter, could Father. Likely all Father could do would be to notify the Master of Henz's Hall. Whether that Master could or would take action, I didn't know. I doubted there was a procedure for forfeiting a Champion's cup. I wasn't aware of any previous incident of cheating at a Festival.

As we walked with the cloak held over our head and our trouser legs getting soaked from water splashing off the road, Egion said that he'd never heard of judges being bribed, either. We agreed that might mean only that the offenders hadn't been caught, not that it hadn't happened. Egion shared my opinion that Henz would get to keep the trophy he didn't win.

Talking about trophies reminded me of what Father had said, which I related to Egion. He was immediately excited and asked a spate of questions for which I had no answers, except to say, "Father can tell you."

Egion proceeded to make a number of excellent suggestions pertinent to adding a prize category to the Festival. I'm pleased to be able to say both that an instrumentalist competition was added, though not for two turns of the star wheel, and that Egion's ideas were extensively used. He now has his own Hall, as well.

We were almost at the Hall when the rain began to let up. We were glad to let down the cloak. Neither of us was accustomed to holding our arms over our heads that long. As I shook what water I could from the cloak so I could tuck it under my arm, Egion asked, "Have you heard what the commotion was during the Festival song?"

To be honest, I had forgotten there had been commotion. "No. What was it?"

"I don't know, either. I saw Father going that direction—he's easy to spot, even in a crowd, isn't he?—and thought he might have told you."

I remembered Zhia's remarks about the state of Father's nerves before the Festival and said, "He was probably just making sure that whoever disrupted his first Festival as Hall Master gets to sit in prison a long time and regret the impiety."

Egion nodded and added, "Too bad we couldn't arrange for Henz to keep whoever it was company."

In my mind I could see how horrible Zhia had looked the day the charges against her were dropped, and knew it wouldn't bother me if Henz spent a long time in the common prison.

It would bother me even less if Eia languished there, too.

Chapter Thirty-One

I HESITATED IN THE DOORWAY, wondering if I were doing the right thing.

It was late at night. I had tried to sleep. I was tired and should have had no trouble sleeping, but my thoughts—the ones I'd held at bay while walking back to the Hall with Egion—gave me no rest.

I had been lying when I told myself I wanted to see Eia in prison. Though I knew she deserved some punishment for her part in making a mockery of both the Festival and the efforts of the other competitors, I recoiled at the thought of vermin bites on that so-touchable skin, and the possibility that she would be used by the prison guards. The truth was, I wanted Eia in my arms, in my bed, not in prison, and certainly not in Henz's embrace, which was where she probably was.

I knew she wasn't worth my time. I think I would have minded less to discover that she was just a woman of pleasure, because I could have comforted myself with the thought that she had to entertain many men to make a living. But nothing I had seen or heard suggested she was anything but the female equivalent of Henz. She used men as casually and carelessly as he did women. They deserved each other.

"They deserve each other," I said aloud, angrily, as I turned yet again on my bed and again couldn't relax, let alone sleep.

I thought about going to the kitchen and getting a cup of wine, but knew that one cup wouldn't help. If I drank as much as I'd need to put me to sleep, I wouldn't be able to do what needed to be done to get a tour on the road, not the next daybreak, but the one after. At the moment, a tour was the last thing I wanted to face.

Perhaps because the tour came to mind, Zhia did, too. Because I was longing for Eia—lusting like an idiot after a woman who had led me on, belittled me, and played me false—I struggled into the less wet pair of trousers I'd worn that day and made my way through the shadowy corridors. I stopped in the darkness just inside the door of Zhia's cubicle.

She was asleep; I could hear her quiet, even breathing. I stepped close to her bed and reached out my hand, then drew it back. Zhia had endured a lot from me and had forgiven me. Could I expect her to forgive me if I used her tonight only so I could sleep? Could I forgive myself if I betrayed her confidence that I could change? Did I still want to be like Henz?

Again in my mind I saw Henz's hand moving inside Eia's shirt, and could almost feel what he had been caressing. I peeled off my soggy trousers, stretched out next to Zhia, and pulled the bedding down to her waist. There was nothing between the bedclothes and her. My hand found a surprisingly full, soft curve. The flesh under my palm warmed and firmed.

Zhia stirred in her sleep. Her hand covered mine, stroking it. For a moment, she pressed my hand to her body. Then, with a shaken breath, she curled her thumb around mine, moved my hand to her side, and kept it there. She whispered, "Rois, why are you here?"

My voice wouldn't obey me. I managed to say "Eia", but nothing else intelligible came out.

In a tender murmur, Zhia said, "You know that being with me tonight won't satisfy you. You want Eia; I'm not Eia. You can stay here if you want, but only to sleep. If you want to stay, wrap the coverlet around you so you aren't cold. It wouldn't do for you to fall ill right before the tour."

I did as she suggested. She drew my head down so it was cradled on her bosom, and began softly to sing. It wasn't a lullaby, but a mournful, minor melody that somehow expressed what I'd been feeling but had been unable to put into words. The song, the gentle rise and fall of her middle as she breathed, and the comforting softness under my head all lured me into sleep.

When I awoke, the sun was up and Zhia was gone. My wet trousers were nowhere to be seen, but dry clothes lay neatly folded beside the bed. Zhia had thought of everything, including what kind of speculation would have arisen had I been seen coming from the direction of her cubicle only half dressed.

Barefoot—since Zhia hadn't brought my shoes I assumed they weren't yet dry—I went to the dining hall and broke my fast. Father was just leaving. He thanked me for having some of the Singers back reasonably early and, as I had anticipated, asked me to go with Egion to collect our instruments from the Festival stage. I went to my cubicle to fetch my shoes, which were unpleasantly damp, then went to find Egion.

I'm sure Egion found me less than good company on the errand. I was preoccupied, not only because my sodden shoes were impossible to ignore. I was also wondering if I should apologize to Zhia or simply allow the events of the previous night to fade from memory. In the end, I decided to act like nothing had happened, because, after all, nothing had. Besides, that was easier.

Egion and I put away the instruments so that the ones that would be needed for tomorrow's tour were all grouped in the front of the storage area. He stayed behind, as eager for more time with the improved rimba as a lover is for his next encounter with his beloved.

Frowning at the poorly-chosen comparison, I headed back to my cubicle. As I went through the classroom corridor, I heard singing, and knew a moment of panic. Had I missed Father's audition of the tour groups? My breathing steadied when I realized I wasn't hearing a group. As I went toward the sound, I remembered that Zhia had sung to me. I wanted to hear that song again.

When I peeked into the room whence the music came, I saw only Taf and Zhia. Zhia was sitting by the window, sewing and listening to Taf singing the Hall repertoire. The sunlight on the gleaming green fabric in her lap was so dazzling that I couldn't see Zhia's face. I did see that she was wearing the reddish brown garment, which looked rather rumpled. Then she began to sing, and what she wore became unimportant. Though I had already witnessed what Zhia could do, I was again amazed to hear her echo the songs accurately, songs I knew she had heard only once.

I remained in the corridor, listening and marveling. When Taf finally said "That's the lot" and Zhia thanked him for his help, I rapped on the door and went in. I had intended to ask Zhia what she had sung to me, but when she gathered up the cloth and moved into the sunlight, I saw a blood-stained bandage was wrapped around her head.

"What happened to you?" I blurted.

"Gadig is back in prison," she said.

"That's good news, but it doesn't answer my question."

Taf said, "Excuse me," and slipped out the door.

Then it all came together: the commotion during the Festival song, Egion's seeing Father going to investigate a disruption that didn't require his presence, Zhia's late arrival at the party, her refusal to take off her hood…

"Gadig attacked you at the Festival, didn't he?" A look of annoyance answered my question. "How badly are you hurt?"

She gestured at her forehead. "He just threw a rock at me. It made me kind of dizzy for a while."

Considering the rock had hit her with enough force to break the skin, I suspected she had been insensible, likely for quite a while. I asked, "Did a doctor look at the injury?"

"Of course. You don't suppose your father would risk someone with a rare gift like mine, do you?" Sarcasm dripped from the words. "Especially since it seems your father and the magistrate suspected Gadig would be at the Festival and used me as bait to catch him."

"They wouldn't."

She gave me her half-quizzical, half-challenging look, and I knew she was right. Father had insisted Zhia attend the Festival, and had suggested where to put the cart. He must have arranged that detail with Osrum several days before the Festival, so Osrum's men wouldn't have to watch the whole of the vast Festival grounds.

A small group of soldiers—out of uniform, of course—wouldn't have been able to watch even the relatively small area near the cart. Though Osrum had known where Zhia would be, he couldn't have known whence or how Gadig might attack. There must have been many soldiers present. No wonder the Festival crowd had looked so much bigger than usual.

And no wonder Father had been so short with me. He hadn't been nervous; he'd been ashamed of how he planned to use Zhia.

Then I was ashamed. I had planned to use her, too, for a far less justifiable purpose. I stammered, "About last night: I didn't know. I…"

"Precisely; you didn't know. What was I supposed to say, 'Not tonight, I have a headache'?"

Something in her voice told me it would be all right to laugh, but I didn't. I asked, "How badly does your head hurt?"

"It's not too bad today. If it were really hurting, I wouldn't sing."

"That reminds me, what was that song?"

"What song?"

"That you sang to me."

"What song did I sing to you?"

I counted to ten before saying, "I just asked you that."

Bewilderment showed in both her face and her voice when she said, "I don't remember singing to you. It is possible you dreamed it?"

Nothing would be gained by my saying that I never dreamed of her. Searching for a different subject, I said, "It must be time to eat. Would you like me to return your sewing to your cubicle?"

"Please. That's thoughtful of you."

I ran the errand and still caught up with her before she reached the dining hall. Seeing that her limp was not much better, I asked, "How did you get back to the Hall from the party? Please don't tell me you walked."

"You'd rather I lie?" she said, with a teasing smile. "In fact, I didn't walk. I rode in the cart with Taf and Noia. Ask them; they'll tell you so."

"I believe you. But didn't they leave the party quite a bit before you did?"

"They left the building." She blushed. "They hadn't yet left for the Hall."

"Oh." I looked around. Save for us, the corridor was deserted, so I dared to ask, "How did you know who was in your cubicle last night?"

Looking at me with a mischievous expression, she answered, "I almost said 'It wasn't hard'. I think I'll say 'It was no mystery'. Besides me, the only people who know where my cubicle is are you, your father, and Aplin. Your father is taller; Aplin is short and round. It had to be you. Besides…" She looked away and cleared her throat. "I missed hearing the Festival song. How did it go? I asked Taf, and he changed the subject."

Wondering what she had decided not to say, I replied, "Remember your asking me if I'd ever sung a song that just hadn't gone well? Well, if I hadn't had that experience before, I've had it now."

"It was that bad?"

"It certainly wasn't satisfying. It seemed like the group never achieved harmony. I'm not saying anyone was out of tune, mind you."

"They wouldn't have been; you're Singers. I'm really sorry I missed seeing Noia named Champion." She paused, then asked, in obvious embarrassment, "What does 'forget the way' mean? I need to know if I insulted a Festival Champion and, if so, how much trouble I'm in."

"It means a man fails to perform in bed," I said, bluntly. "I doubt anyone at the party, Henz included, will take exception to what you said to him. He asked for it, and you were, frankly, a lot kinder to him than he was to you. Besides, just because Henz has a trophy doesn't mean he's a Champion. After you left, he confessed—bragged, actually—that he'd bribed the judges."

Zhia stared. "No!" I nodded. "That's…that's…"

"Cheating."

"That, of course. I was going to say it's blasphemy."

It was my turn to stare. The term seemed excessive. Then I realized the daughter of an Ambassador could be trusted to know blasphemy when she saw it.

Zhia was pursuing her own thoughts. "That must have taken a lot of money."

Wishing I'd foreseen where the subject would go, I nerved myself and said,

"He didn't use money. He used Eia."

She turned to me in obvious dismay. "Rois, I'm so sorry. No wonder you…" She blushed again. "No wonder you were so desperate."

"I don't think the term 'desperate' is apt." Then, since the opportunity had presented itself, I said, "I appreciate your trying to make an excuse for me, but even had you not been injured, what I tried to do last night was inexcusable. Believe it or not, I did wonder whether I was doing the right thing before I went ahead and tried to do the wrong thing."

"But you did do the right thing. You stopped. You could have had me, you know."

"I've done many things of which I'm ashamed; but no one can accuse me of rape," I said, indignantly.

She started to say something, but at that moment Father appeared in the corridor. Scarcely waiting for our replies, he unloosed a volley of comments and questions. "There you are. Where have you been? Have you eaten yet? No? Then hurry. The instructors are waiting to hear the tour groups sing."

I started to obey. Zhia stayed where she was and said, "Yes, my head is better today, sir. Thank you for asking."

Coldly, Father said, "I don't need you to instruct me in courtesy."

Just as coldly, Zhia replied. "No, you just need me to be the unwitting bait to catch a man who has already shown that he'll use any means, including alliance with raiders, to avoid prison. You know I don't like having my life arranged for me. Did you think having possible death arranged for me would be any more to my liking? Did it even occur to anyone that the magistrate's men might not be able to protect me, or was apprehending Gadig the only concern?"

Then her face crumpled. "I'm sorry, sir, I shouldn't have said that; but didn't I tell you that I was willing to cooperate with whatever you thought had to be done to deal with Gadig's escape? You could have trusted me. And I'm already nervous about the tour—what if it's as bad as my first one?—and now I'll have to go on stage with my head bandaged!" Tears slid down her cheeks.

"You keep apologizing to me, even when I'm in the wrong," Father said, after a long silence. "I can't begin to express how concerned I was when I saw that you were injured. Knowing I'm partly to blame for your being put in danger may be the reason—not an excuse—that I haven't asked after your health. I didn't like the idea of using you as bait when Osrum proposed it. I did believe him when he assured me his men would allow you to come to no harm. But you were harmed; and I have no confidence in that squeamish fool Capis. The doctor who treated you yesterday," he explained, when she looked puzzled.

"That I've been trying to find someone to replace Noia shouldn't have kept me from sending Aplin look at you first thing today. If nothing else, that bandage needs to be changed. Take time to see Aplin before the tour groups sing. But if you don't feel well enough to tour, I'll understand."

She dried her eyes on her garment. "I can tour. But if I'm going on the usual first-timer's tour, my head won't be healed before our first engagement." She touched the bandage. "This is a plea for sympathy, if I ever saw one. If I'm not good, I don't want people listening to me only because they feel sorry for me."

"You are good," Father said, emphatically.

"If I may make a suggestion," I said, cautiously, "if all of us on the tour tied white cloths around our heads, we'd all look the same."

Zhia laughed, somewhat raggedly. "We could start a new fashion!"

The all-but-visible tension, which had been easing, vanished. Father excused himself, but soon joined us in the dining hall. He handed Zhia the mirror which had helped convict Gadig, saying, "This might be useful before you go on stage."

"This will make me a better Singer?" she asked, eyes wide in mock astonishment.

"It will help you reflect on the music," he replied, grinning.

I said, "I'm going to get a plate before the jokes get any worse."

After we got our food, I said, "May I ask why you have to replace Noia, Father?"

"Champions don't tour."

"That's not what Gadig told me."

Clearly disapproving, Father said, "The former Master had many unique

ideas about how to do things at this Hall. If you'll excuse me, I want to let the
instructors and the others in the tour groups know the audition will be delayed."

"I'm sorry," Zhia said at once. "I'll hurry."

"Don't apologize; don't hurry," Father said. "But do see Aplin before you
come to the audition."

When we finished our midday meal, Zhia insisted that I go to the audition
while she went to the clinic. "It's better that they be angry with me for delaying
the audition than with you," she said, by way of explanation.

"And why is that better?"

"Because it's true. You have no need to go to the clinic. If your father hadn't
told me to go, I wouldn't go, either; I can change my own bandage. And actually,
there's no need for the audition to be delayed once you get there. There'll be
another person to sing the melody for our tour. But Rois," she added, quickly,
as I started to leave the dining hall, "where is the audition being held?"

I realized I didn't know, either. I said, slowly, "The only place in the Hall
besides the dining hall or the courtyard that would hold that many people is
the percussion classroom. Obviously, they're not meeting here, and the acoustics in the courtyard would be all wrong."

I confess I was relieved to discover that my reasoning had been sound. I
told Father what Zhia had said about starting the audition without her. He
nodded. The instructors were looking impatient. Neron, especially, seemed
annoyed at the waste of time.

Of the many outstanding events that happened while I was at that Hall,
the three biggest were, first, producing a Champion three Festivals in a row;
second, having Gadig replaced as Master; and third, the start of the practice of auditioning the tour groups. Since I was involved in all three, it may
sound like I'm boasting. I'm not; but I'm especially glad that I was there for
the first tour audition.

While most Singers have strong voices, some are stronger than others.
Whether the stronger voices blend with the others depends on who is on any
particular tour. Since the custom is to send different people on each tour, no
one group gets really good at singing together. This is both a strength and

a drawback. It's a strength, because should the composition of a tour group suddenly change—as did the composition of the tour on which Noia was to have gone—the tour can still go. It's a drawback, because the songs for any given tour are often chosen with a particular Singer in mind, so when that person isn't present, the music doesn't necessarily show the group at its best.

Though Father put my group last, Zhia still hadn't shown up when it was our turn to sing. I had been fretting about her tardiness. When I was told I was overpowering the other Singers, I had something else to worry about. Of the five groups, only mine was asked to sing again. The second time, the blend was better.

People were starting to leave the percussion classroom when Zhia arrived. Aplin was with her. She was glowering; he looked no happier. He asked Father to have my group remain.

When only my group, Father, and Aplin were present, Aplin said, "I need the nine of you to help me." He sent Zhia another angry look, which she returned. "Nine men might just be enough to keep this idiot woman from saddling tebecs, fetching water, cutting or carrying firewood, moving instruments, cooking, or doing anything else strenuous. She has my permission to ride, eat, sleep, and sing." He glared again at Zhia as he said, "Nothing else. Rois, as tour leader, you have my permission to scold her, sit on her, or do whatever else you think is needed to ensure that I don't have to see her in my clinic when you return." Sweeping his gaze across the line of men, he asked, "Are my instructions clear?" We nodded.

He looked at Zhia. "For a change, can you do as you're told?"

"Why ask me now?" she said in an icy calm voice. "You didn't bother to ask me before you decided to arrange my life for me. However, if you don't think it would be too strenuous for me, I would like permission to pee while on tour." Her body rigid with anger, Zhia limped out.

Biting back something that might have been a curse, Aplin also left the classroom. Father went with him. While I stored the instruments, the others filed out.

I heard one Singer say, "Just what we need: extra baggage."

Another answered, "I hope I won't be the one who has to lift her onto a tebec." "One?" chortled a third. "It'd take four of us to lift that much weight!"

There was laughter. Someone else asked, "Does any of our music have a part for someone who plays the broom?"

Yet another Singer remarked, "She's shown she knows what to do with a broom. Does anyone know if she can sing?"

I'd had enough experience as a tour leader by then to realize they were talking crap to hide their nervousness.

But the last comment told me I was possibly dealing with more than simple case of pre-tour nerves: "At least they aren't going to let her use an ax. We might survive this."

Chapter Thirty-Two

I'M PLEASED TO REPORT that Azham, Derol, Fras, Garit, Ingbir, Oluzh, Tej, and Volan survived that tour. Obviously, I also survived. Zhia…

I'm getting ahead of myself.

The audition over, we then had to pack and make other preparations for our departure. For some, this included leaving the Hall to visit their families. For once, I didn't have to leave the Hall. I spent part of the evening with Mother and Lisia in the nursery, which left me time to make gifts of appeasement to Darl when my packing was finished and other details handled. The unpleasant feeling that I'd forgotten to do something I ignored as my own pre-tour nervousness.

Daybreak always seemed to come too soon when there was a tour to get on the road. I saw nothing of Zhia between the end of the audition and when the five groups gathered in the courtyard the next morning.

If Zhia's reply to Aplin hadn't been warning enough, the set of her face when she left the percussion classroom should have told me that she hadn't taken kindly to the way Aplin had arranged her life, as she put it. Evidence to the contrary aside, Zhia can be reasonable. Had Aplin chosen to speak to her privately, tell her what he recommended and why, and request her cooperation, she probably would have complied with his wishes…up to a point, at any rate.

As it was, he had made demands that would have affronted even someone of less wit than Zhia and, more, had made those demands in the presence of the men with whom she would be touring. That he had made me the instrument to enforce his expectations boded ill for my ability to deal with Zhia on tour.

Though Zhia rarely insisted on her rank, she was an Ambassador's daughter; she was accustomed to enjoying the deference that had been shown her father. Moreover, this tour, like TTTW, was her tour. The responsibility laid on me and the other eight men was to help her succeed. Both what Aplin had said and how he had phrased it had diminished her in the eyes of men she hadn't formally and possibly not even casually met, men who were experienced Singers. Men who really were Singers.

When I saw Zhia, I knew my misgivings hadn't come close to anticipating the reality.

She was already on a tebec. I didn't have to ask to know that she had saddled it, likely with a stable hand's help; I doubted even Zhia could manage a tebec saddle by herself. Aplin had forbidden her saddling tebecs. Zhia hadn't saddled "tebecs"; she had saddled only one.

The bird was loaded with baggage. I had to stare; not even the ten or twelve parcels of goods Zhia had bought in town the other day would bulk so large. I had no idea what might be in them or in the additional bundle strapped to her back. I wasn't sure I wanted to find out.

I was even less inclined to inquire why she had cut her hair. She hadn't simply trimmed the ends; it was cropped. It looked like she had carefully cut all the strands to the same length, not even as long as my longest finger. I tried to think where I had seen such a style, and realized it looked like most babies' hair. A light wind ruffled it, lifting a fringe of hair from her forehead and exposing an ugly bruised gash near the hairline.

Even had there been no breeze, I would have seen that her head wasn't bandaged. While it was true that I had forgotten our half-joking plan to have all the tour members wear cloths around their heads, Zhia didn't know I'd forgotten. I wondered if she thought that neglecting her injury would somehow settle her score with Aplin.

She may not have considered that neglecting her injury could fulfil Aplin's wish not to see her in his clinic after the tour...or ever again.

She may have been sulking, for she spoke to no one. But then, no one spoke to her. In fact, there was little talking, even though fifty people and seventy tebecs crowded the courtyard. All of us had work to do; none of us was very awake. She and her tebec kept to one side, out of the way of nervous birds and yawning people. The Singers' bright clothing was at odds with their drowsy faces. Zhia's dark green shirt and the plumage of her tebec, a female, blended into the shadows the sunrise had yet to dispel.

We were getting better at putting tours on the road quickly. When Father came out to commend us to Nia Diva, the sun was just starting to gild the top of the courtyard walls. All five tour groups were in the saddle, pack tebecs were loaded, and we were ready to leave. Father spotted me—as I've mentioned, I was the tallest Singer at the Hall—and brought me something that caught fire in the sunlight and patterned his black robe with reflected brilliance. It was my Champion's cup.

"Last night the judges sent Noia's trophy," he told me. "She was sure you'd want yours back before the tour. She wanted to thank you in person, but I told her there was no point in getting up this early if she didn't have to, and assured her I would give you the message."

As I clasped the chain around my neck, Father raised a paper that had been in his other hand. It turned out to be a list of the tour leaders and the Singers who would be on each tour. As he read each name, each person said "here" or "present". Each person, that is, but Zhia.

"Zhia?" Father said again. Of course, he couldn't shout. He looked around, then said to me, "Isn't she here?"

"She's by the wall," I said, pointing with my thumb.

Father looked. He tried to keep his face stern, but the corners of his mouth twitched when he said, quietly, "You know what she's done, don't you?"

"She's cut her hair."

"And why did she do that? She's complying with the letter of Aplin's instructions. He didn't give her permission to comb her hair. Now she doesn't have to."

I can't say it was encouraging to hear Father's thoughts agreeing with mine. "What should I do with her if she continues with this foolishness?" I asked.

"Ignore her," Father said, crisply. "When this foolishness, as you so aptly name it, becomes overly inconvenient, she'll stop doing it."

I nodded, though I couldn't help remembering that, while in prison, Zhia had feigned insensibility long after it had become inconvenient for her to do so.

"Duty compels me to add that, should she become a danger to the others, you must intervene," Father added.

"What if she becomes a danger to herself?"

He looked grim. "It might do her good to taste the fruit of what she sows." He looked again at the list. "She's obviously here and everyone else is present." After verifying that the tour leaders had their schedules, he invoked Nia Diva and asked protection for the tours. "Sing well," he said as the groups started for the gates.

Those that had the farthest to go left first. As a first-timer's tour—Zhia had yet to set foot on a stage, so she was still considered a first-timer—mine went last. Zhia brought up the rear, trailing behind even the pack tebecs, and there she stayed all day. When we stopped for our midday meal, she stopped, too; but I didn't see her eat. When we stopped for the night at a Quarter Rest, she quietly settled herself at the far end of the shelter. She didn't join in the conversation as we clustered around the fire when the rain began, conversation that included more than one comment on how great it was to be away from the Hall...and female Singers.

I didn't see her eat.

When I woke, she was already up and on her tebec. She said nothing while the rest of us ate and got ready to get back on the road. I didn't see her eat.

That day was an echo of the first. Zhia was present but not participating, traveling but not talking, the substance of the tour but choosing to be little more than a shadow on the road. That evening I couldn't keep my mind on the after-supper talk by the fire. My eyes kept wandering into the dark, cold corner where Zhia lay wrapped in blankets.

Ingbir finally said, in his deep bass, "Not very sociable, is she?"

In a moment, I thought of and rejected a number of possible replies, one of which was an unkind comment about Ingbir's unkempt, rather repellent appearance. He was a large man, not as tall as I am but with massive shoulders and shaggy black hair.

Trying not to sound overly concerned, I said, "She probably isn't feeling very good. Do you remember that when she showed up too late for the audition, her head was bandaged? That was because at the Festival someone threw a stone that hit her in the head. Aplin probably didn't want to her to tour at all. Making her go to bed early is the next best thing, I guess."

"So that's why Aplin told us we had to do everything for her but wipe her nose?" Fras asked, his red hair bright in the firelight. Both his appearance and his manner reminded me a lot of Dolin. He was one of the percussionists.

Tej chuckled. "I'm glad you said 'nose.'" Tej, the other baritone, was Taf's older brother. He had the same beaky face and the same levelheadedness. His hands didn't look suited for stringed instruments, but strings were his specialty. Remembering Zhia's comments when Eia asked if she would sew for her, I hadn't asked Tej to be in charge of the tebecs. He didn't offer, either; he took turns, like everyone else.

Derol, who sang the higher bass line with Fras, groaned. "Thank you, Tej. Can we change the subject? I'd like to keep my supper down." He made a face and clutched his middle, which was as round as the rimba he played.

Volan, whose craggy looks belied the range of his voice, said, "She can sing, can't she, Rois? I'm the only first tenor here, so I assume she sings soprano. I don't mind an occasional solo, but I'd rather not carry the melody by myself the whole tour."

"She can sing," I said. "She'll amaze you."

Fras looked skeptical. "I'll make my own judgment on that, thank you."

"And what instruments does she play?" was Azham's question. He was our wind man and looked it, being thin and reedy. When he wasn't playing, he sang the lower tenor line with Garit.

"The broom, of course!" I said, and was relieved when the others laughed. I wasn't ready to deal with their reaction when they learned that she played nothing.

"And the ax," Garit said, darkly, which made me think that he was the one who, the night before we left, had made the remark about surviving the tour.

Before I could say anything, Tej said, quietly, "As I've already told you, Garit, it's because of that ax my little brother is still alive. I'll thank you not to bring up the subject again."

After an uncomfortable silence, Oluzh asked, "So what are we singing tomorrow?" Oluzh was the other low bass. It was always startling to hear a deep voice come from him, because he was not very tall and was wiry rather than muscular. He and Volan should have traded voices.

I hope I hid my dismay. Choosing songs was what I had forgotten to do. As I've mentioned, the ability to improvise is essential to a Singer. I tried to look like I was considering the question, then replied, "I think I'll decide when I see what the nobodies look like. Some of the songs in our repertoire don't go over too well with more rustic audiences. We might have to dust off a couple of the bawdy ones."

I saw several of the men nodding. Ingbir rumbled, "Bawdy songs, when we're singing with a woman?"

Sounding as convincing as I could, I said, "She's a Singer. She sings what Singers sing, even if it's bawdy songs, or she doesn't sing at all."

Though that answer might have been more wishful thinking than any-thing else, it seemed to me that Zhia might not mind, as long as she wasn't the subject of the bawdiness. I remembered her comment, "I almost said 'It wasn't hard'", in reference to my late-night visit to her cubicle. She'd had a husband; she was no blushing maiden. I remembered the feel of her body, the softness that had filled my hand…

My thoughts were heading down paths I didn't dare let them go. I was glad when Derol asked, "Since she's a first-timer, will our performance include the usual?"

"Most certainly. If you have any ideas for which song it should be, let me know." I saw grins on the firelit faces, and hoped I hadn't made a mistake. "But don't tell me now," I added, hastily, as Volan opened his mouth. "I'm ready to call it a night."

In the morning, Zhia was once again up and ready to leave before anyone else. I still hadn't seen her touch a morsel of food or a sip of water, and was starting to worry. If she had been fasting since we left the Hall, she might very well pass out on stage. That would be less than desirable.

When we got on the road, I dropped back so I could talk to Zhia. "Today is our first engagement," I said.

"Good," she replied. "I'm looking forward to a bath." Then she frowned. "We do bathe before we perform, don't we?"

"Yes. Did you finish sewing your stage garb?"

"No, I'm starting a new fashion; I'm planning to sing naked," she drawled. "Yes, of course I did. Who wants to see me naked?"

Aware that was another question of the "Do you still beat your wife" variety, I said, "We'll begin after the midday meal. As usual, it's best if you eat only bread and water." I hesitated, then asked, "You have been eating, haven't you?" She nodded. "What have you been eating?"

"I have food in my pack."

"Why? Why not just eat with the group?"

"To answer the second question first, the first night, because my head didn't feel good. The motion of the tebec is a bit hard on it. Last night I didn't join you because you were all obviously enjoying being with only men. I would have been intruding. Why did I bring food in my pack? In case something happened like on TTTW. There's no reason a tour should be reduced to foraging. That's just poor planning, no matter who failed in his duty on that other tour." She sighed. "And I happen to believe that anyone who doesn't work shouldn't eat. I'm not supposed to cut or carry wood, fetch water, or cook. If I'm not taking a turn, I don't think I ought simply to enjoy the labor of others."

"Why does that bother you? You've followed Aplin's instructions to the letter on other things."

She frowned at me. "What does Aplin have to do with this?"

"The business with saddling your tebec and cutting your hair and not doing anything but eating, riding, and sleeping: aren't you trying to prove to Aplin that you can do precisely what he told you to do?"

Her laugh caused some of the others to turn and stare. "Aplin isn't here! Are you telling me you took him seriously? He's been around Singers too long; he was talking crap. Yes, he and I were disgusted with each other. I don't think I can be blamed if I was offended when the first words out of his mouth were, 'Can't you leave the Hall without getting hurt?', because I knew full well that I got hurt at the Festival because I was doing precisely what I'd been told to do, which put me in harm's way, as had been intended. I can assure you I'm not making that mistake twice."

"Then why did you saddle the tebec yourself?"

"I didn't; two of the stable hands saddled it for me. My decision to be mounted when the rest of you got to the courtyard had nothing to do with Aplin. I wanted to make clear to others on this tour that I am not baggage and that no one—or four—has to lift me onto a tebec." She saw my grimace, and said, "Yes, I heard what the men said after the audition. I've told you before, the only way to keep Singers from being heard is to keep Singers from talking."

"Then why did you cut your hair?"

"I expected you to have figured that out for yourself. Apparently, raiders abetted Gadig's escape from prison. He obviously has some way to communicate with them, even while in prison. I can think of no reason he would no longer want revenge, if revenge is, indeed, his motive. I kept wondering why he threw that rock at me, because it wasn't a deadly attack. Then I got to thinking that it might have been a way for him to identify me to any confederates—probably also raiders—who might have been in the Festival crowd. Since he could count on my head being bandaged, he knew I could also be easily identified even while on tour.

"The only thing I could think of was somehow to change my appearance. I had already decided I wouldn't wear the bandage, but I wasn't sure that would be enough. I was wondering what else I could do when your father returned my mirror, and it was as though the daemon spoke and told me what to do. I trust I no longer look like the woman anyone saw at the Festival."

"Not much," I admitted.

"Good. Are there any other misunderstandings we need to clear up?" Her tone was only slightly condescending.

"I don't know if it's a misunderstanding or just a question. Why are you riding way back here?"

"Not because of anything Aplin said," she laughed, then lowered her voice. "Several thoughts prompted that decision. First, it's fairly quiet; I'm reviewing the music. My second concern was safety. Were I to be recognized despite my efforts to look different and there was an attempt on my life, the rest of you might not be endangered. Similarly, were there to be an attack on the group as a whole, by being at the end, I might be able to fight back. I did bring an ax. Don't tell Garit.

"Third, I have nothing to contribute to long-winded boasts about exploits in bed. If I mentioned my most unforgettable experience, someone might think I was issuing an invitation. Of course, after exhausting more than twenty, entertaining nine would be nothing." There was something more hurtful than scorn in her voice.

At that moment, I decided we would sing no bawdy songs on tour, not because Zhia would have felt embarrassed, but because she would have felt accused; most of them were about women who didn't know when to say "no".

I decided to change the subject, and failed miserably. "Do you still dream about Pandir?" As soon as I asked the question, I wished I could have taken back the words.

She replied, even more softly, "I stopped dreaming about him after Pandizh was killed. But aren't you really asking whether I accepted your caress because I thought you were my husband?"

There was so much gentleness in her eyes I had to look away. "Yes."

She waited until I again looked at her to say, "I woke as soon as you lay down. As I told you the other day, I had no doubt about who you were. I knew you had to be acting blindly, on some impulse that had nothing to do with me because you would never willingly demean yourself with someone like me."

No, I willingly demeaned myself with someone like Eia, I thought.

"When I said 'You could have had me', I wasn't accusing you of rape. The truth is, that night you were the one in danger of unwanted advances."

Chapter Thirty-Three

I LAUGHED.

May Nia Diva forgive me, I laughed. It may have been from astonishment or even delight, but I laughed.

Zhia blushed a deep crimson. She managed a fleeting smile. Her throat sounded very tight when she said, "I'm sorry I offended your sensibilities. It won't happen again."

Then Volan, who was in the front, called, "We're here!", the town walls engulfed us, and there was no time to repair the damage I'd done.

Zhia was the only one who'd never been to that town. The rest of us knew where the stage was—we always stopped there first so we could drop off the instruments—where to leave the tebecs, where to bathe, and where to change into our stage garb. Even more like a shadow than before, Zhia followed the group.

Eager to bathe, have a bite, and get on stage, I forgot about her bad foot. I'm sorry to say it wasn't until we men were clean, dressed (with the usual chaffing about each others' stage garb), sparingly fed, and ready to go to the stage that I realized Zhia wasn't with us. I had no idea where to start looking for her. The town wasn't that big, but its winding streets were swelling with people coming for the performance. Finding one woman—who, I had to admit, might rightly be feeling rebuffed and might not care whether she was found—wasn't something we had time to do. While I didn't think Zhia would do anything to hurt the tour—her tour—dealings I'd already had with her that day had told me I didn't know her as well as I'd flattered myself I did.

Quickly and silently reviewing the repertoire, I chose songs that were mostly two or three parts, so Volan wouldn't have to carry the melody alone.

The expressions on the men's faces when I told them Zhia was missing were mixed. I saw glee, concern, relief, and annoyance, the latter from Volan.

"Shouldn't we at least try to look for her?" Tej asked.

I shook my head. "We still have to set up. Let's stow our packs, get to the stage, get ready, and start warming up. When she hears the music, she might find us."

As we took our packs to where the tebecs were penned, Ingbir remarked, "You're taking this rather lightly." His tone was just short of critical.

I kept my temper. "What would you do? We're Singers; we're at an engagement that's due to start very soon. Though we're missing someone, we have enough people to cover the parts of the songs I've chosen."

Though there was no further discussion, I was sure none of them was impressed with my performance as tour leader.

Derol was repositioning the rimba for the fourth or fifth time when a voice from in front of the stage said, "Are you missing something?"

Afraid I recognized the voice, I looked into the nobodies' area. The speaker was, indeed, Henz. Zhia was with him. She looked remote, which I should have expected. Considering we'd walked off and left her alone in a strange town, I was surprised she had been willing to come to the stage at all. Even if getting lost hadn't upset her, I knew she hadn't appreciated my thoughtless laughter. She probably loathed me. I did expect her to look nervous about her first performance. Surprisingly, she looked unruffled, perhaps because, with the other aggravations, she hadn't quite realized how soon she would be on stage for the first time.

I resisted the impulse to say something rude to Henz. No matter how much

I resented his involvement with Eia, he was a Festival Champion…of a sort. I said, "Yes, we misplaced Zhia. Thank you for finding her."

"I noticed how hard you were looking for her," was his sarcastic reply. "She was in tears when I happened upon her…"

"That's not true!" Zhia said, indignantly. "I was concerned that I wouldn't be able to wash and change before performing, but I was not in tears."

"She was nowhere near where she needed to be when I found her," Henz amended, "so, figuring you'd eventually get to the stage, I brought her here."

"Again, thank you." I hoped Henz would understand that I meant "Now get lost". I jumped off the stage—the four steps that went from it to the nobodies' area looked even more rickety than they had the last time I had performed in that town—and said, "Zhia, I hope you'll accept my apology for not noticing that we got too far ahead of you. Since we need to warm up"—I stared at Henz and he finally left—"can I offer you a hand up to the stage?"

"I believe I can manage on my own," was her dignified reply. She picked up her pack, slung it over her shoulder, and moved toward the stairs, going slowly so she wouldn't limp.

She climbed the stairs as a young child does, stepping up with her left foot and then bringing her bad foot up only to the same step. The planks were creaking horribly under her weight. The third one did more than creak; it broke. Zhia ended up thigh deep in the splintery wreckage, her careful dignity shattered.

Giving me an embarrassed smile, Zhia said, "Just think, if you'd been helping me, there would have been two of us in here."

"Are you hurt?" I asked, sharply, reaching the erstwhile stairs in one step.

She started to say "no", but said, "Something is stabbing my right leg. Good thing I'm wearing trousers, not my stage garb. Could you take my pack?"

I laid it on the stage, then looked into the hole. I saw one downward-pointing, wicked spike that had pierced her trouser leg. A dark stain was seeping outward through the cloth. "Crouch," I said. "See if you can get free of it."

That worked. I broke off the spear of wood. Seeing no others that posed immediate danger, I said, "Ingbir, come down here. I mean jump; don't use the steps. We can't be sure the other set is in any better shape than these were. Zhia, can you bend your arms and hold them tight against your sides?" She nodded. With our hands under Zhia's elbows, Ingbir and I lifted her out of the hole and lowered her to the ground.

She was pale, shaking, and biting her lower lip. "Thank you," she said, unsteadily. "That was an adventure." She noticed the seven men still on stage looking down at her, and said to them, "Don't you have anything better to do than stare?"

The stain on her trouser leg was spreading. "I've got to look at that injury," I said.

Zhia gave me a pitying look. "Why? All you can do is look. You have nothing for cleaning it, nor bandages to cover it once it's clean. Besides, I refuse to undress in front of everyone." Seeing me open my mouth, she added, "Rois, people are already arriving. Let's warm up and do the performance. The injury can be tended later."

"In case you hadn't noticed, it's bleeding."

"Is it?" Her sarcasm made Henz's sound polite. "Are you also going to tell me it hurts? Hand me my pack; I can take care of it for now." I helped her to her feet. She winced as she stood and slung the pack on her back. "It's a good thing it was my right leg; I still have one leg that works." She looked around. "Isn't there any privacy here?"

I indicated a side room on ground level. Zhia went away, walking very carefully.

Ingbir was looking at the broken step. "Rois, I think you'd better see this," he said.

When I went back to the staircase, he said, "Look. The splinters are all on the top side of the tread. The bottom edge of the break is clean, because there the board didn't break; it was cut."

"Are you sure?" I asked, fervently hoping he'd say "no".

He didn't take offense, but replied, mildly, "My family are carpenters. I know what a sawed plank looks like." He went to the other set of steps. I followed. He ran his hand slowly along the undersides of those boards. When he got to the third step, his face changed. I didn't have to ask what he'd found. I felt under that step, also. My family weren't carpenters, but even a Singer's son could feel the place where that tread had also been deliberately damaged.

Ingbir and I looked at each other, wondering who had caused the damage and why.

"We're expecting a performance here shortly. Who are you and what are you doing?" said a man who had come up to us. He had the sound and air of someone in authority. He wasn't in blue and gray, so I guessed he was the mayor.

After determining that he was, indeed, that town official, I said, "Sir, I'm the tour leader. One of my Singers has just been hurt falling through the steps over there." I pointed. "This man with me is part of my tour group. He comes from a family of carpenters and informs me that the tread which broke had been partly cut through, as is one of the steps on this side of the stage. While I don't expect all stages to be as lavish as the Festival stage, your stage is not only shabby, it's also hazardous.

"If my injured Singer is able to perform, we will sing today. If not, you may dismiss your people and tell them there will be no more tours here until Singers can reach your stage without suffering harm," I finished.

"And until the stage is a fitting place to invoke the daemon," Zhia said, joining us, pack in hand. Under the bloodstain, her right trouser leg was lumpy from what whatever she had used for bandaging her thigh. I was sure she had heard what I'd been saying when she went on to say, "My father, the lamented Ambassador Druzhin, often said that he could tell how a town regarded the daemons simply by looking at how that town kept its stage. I'm glad he's not here to see your stage; it's an insult to Nia Diva. Even the areas that only Singers see are filthy, dark, and musty."

The mayor wilted. "Ambassador Druzhin was your father?" he echoed. Zhia nodded solemnly. "I trust you took no lasting hurt." The mayor continued to cringe and fawn.

Zhia made a sound of disgust. "Quit groveling! What good is that doing?"

"A good question, a very good question, indeed," the mayor said, eagerly.

"What good can I do to make amends for this distressing mishap?"

Zhia, Ingbir, and I exchanged a glance. We managed to keep our expressions stern. I said, "I'm taking it as a given that the stage steps will be repaired and the stage cleaned and refurbished, though only the repair to the steps needs to be done before we perform. As I'd prefer that my injured Singer rest rather than travel after we finish our performance, it would be gracious if you would provide us with our evening meal and lodging for the night. There are, as usual, ten of us. As we hadn't expected to have to board the tebecs tonight, perhaps we could be forgiven that expense. Of course, it would be appreciated if, following the performance, you could send a doctor to make sure that my Singer's injury is no more serious than we believe it to be. Sir," I added as his smile became strained, "that is over and above our tour fees, you understand."

The mayor hid his dismay rather well. He assured us he would do all that and more. I soon shared Zhia's contempt for his obsequiousness. When I reminded him that the start of the performance awaited the repair of the steps, he left to get that work begun.

Ingbir and I lifted Zhia up to Volan and Tej, then climbed onto the stage.

"You will be able to sing, won't you?" I asked Zhia.

"Certainly," she replied. She looked down at herself with another sound of disgust. "I'm a bit the worse for wear. Since we're waiting for the steps to be repaired, I wonder if I'd be able to freshen up and change clothes."

"Let's find out," I said. Leaving the stage as I had before, I conveyed Zhia's wishes to the mayor, who sent people for water, soap, and towels.

"If I had a broom, I'd clean out the room I used a moment ago," Zhia said.

"You don't have a broom," I said. "Even if you had one, I wouldn't let you use it. You're a Singer. You don't have to regard yourself as better than the people who have come to hear us, but do remember that you're a servant of Nia Diva. You don't do the work these people have neglected to do. But I will say that bringing your father's influence to bear on the mayor was inspired."

"I appreciate the compliment, but I hope you don't think that was just a way to get the mayor to pamper us. My father actually said that. And he would have been heartsick to see the condition of this stage."

The sounds of sawing and hammering soon made conversation difficult. I saw Ingbir smiling as the smell of sawdust filled the stage area. Since I hadn't smelled sawdust before, he had to identify the smell for me. It was distinctive, and not unpleasant.

The mayor's people returned with what Zhia needed. She retired to a room on the same level as the stage.

"So we're touring with Ambassador Druzhin's daughter," Garit said, during a lull in the construction noise. Since we couldn't warm up, we were doing back rubs.

Azham asked, "Weren't the Ambassador, his wife, and his son killed by raiders?"

"Yes," I said, "but please don't mention it to Zhia."

Oluzh frowned. "Why? Doesn't she know?"

"If your head were any emptier, Oluzh, I could use it as a drum," Fras said in disgust.

Chapter Thirty-Four

After the steps were repaired, the stage was swept clean, Zhia was washed and garbed—in the reddish brown, not the golden green; I imagine she was concerned about bleeding on the better garment—and the ritual two sips of wine to Nia Diva were drunk (the mayor had to be reminded we needed wine and a cup), the performance began.

I don't recommend that any Singer attempt to perform shortly after construction has been taking place nearby; when we started singing, our ears were still ringing with the sound of hammering.

We began with a couple of two-part songs. Next, Azham, Tej, Derol, and Fras played a piece just for instruments, which was well received. By then our hearing was better, so we did one three-part song and one five-part song. I was being careful not to sing too loudly and thought our blend was good, but I couldn't hear Zhia. Even though I was upstage from her, I should have been able to hear her. I could hear Volan; Zhia was singing an octave higher than he was. Higher voices usually carry better.

We then did a drum-driven number that got the audience swaying, clapping, and nodding in time to the music. Zhia was swaying also, but not in time to the music. I knew her sense of rhythm wasn't the best, but it wasn't that bad.

I caught Volan's eye, pointed to Zhia, and gave the signal that means "Is something wrong?" Without losing the beat, he edged closer so he could look at her. When he missed a beat, I knew the answer.

The rhythmic song ended. I had the instrumentalists play alone, and signaled Volan to get Zhia off stage.

"What's wrong?" she demanded without much force when I joined them in one of the offstage rooms.

"Are you all right?" I asked, just as a courtesy. Clearly, she wasn't. The fact that she hadn't resisted Volan's leading her from the stage told me that more plainly than her colorless face and slack posture.

I think she meant to brazen it out, but suddenly she said, with a sob, "No. I'm sorry. I feel all shaky."

I said, "Lie down before you fall down. Volan, get the cup and the jug and give her some wine, then tell the others this will be our last song."

"We aren't going to do the usual?" Volan asked.

"The usual" is a ritual that every first-timer goes through but no first-timer is told about in advance. At some point in a new Singer's first performance, he or she sings alone. The only way to make this a surprise is for everyone to start singing and playing a song, and then drop out, leaving the first-timer without any voices or instruments to help. This sounds unkind; indeed, it's regarded as something of a point of no return for a Singer, for whether or not the person continues as a Singer can depend on how well he or she handles this surprise.

In view of Zhia's "distressing mishap", I had already considered postponing this often harrowing experience until another time. Seeing Zhia, I knew it would be not so much unkind as unwise. "Not today," I answered, and went back on stage.

When the instrumental piece was done, I announced that the injury suffered by one of the Singers shortly before we began compelled us to cut our performance short. Something—Zhia would say it was Nia Diva—prompted me to add that we hoped to find the stage cleaner and in better repair when we returned to it the next day to complete the performance a distressing mishap had kept us from finishing this day.

There was some applause, but it was unenthusiastic. I didn't mind; I felt better about the engagement. Not only imposing on the town's hospitality but also asking a full tour fee when we had given only half a performance wouldn't have been right, especially considering that even what we had done had been mostly short one Singer, and not just any Singer, but the Singer whose tour it was.

Having just made it sound like I was being noble and doing the right thing, I will confess that I was also aware that Zhia's being unable to finish the performance would allay any doubts the mayor might have had about her actually being injured. Not even I had thought she seemed hurt when she was lecturing the mayor on piety.

And, in fact, the mayor soon appeared in the room off the stage. "That Singer didn't appear to be too badly injured to…" he began, puffing up his chest indignantly.

I was with Zhia. I moved aside so the dignitary could see her, flat on the floor, eyes closed. Thinking to change the bandage, I had adjusted her garment so her leg was bared. The exposed bandage was liberally stained with blood.

"Oh," the mayor finished, immediately deflating. "You asked for a doctor."

"Please," I said. The mayor left.

Henz was the next one to drop in. "Did Zhia get a case of stage fr…" He, too, saw her bandaged leg. "What happened?"

Zhia opened her eyes. "Some Singers perform on stage; I tried to perform in it. Silly me." Her speech was a little slurred; the wine cup next to her was empty.

"The stairs on both sides had been tampered with," I explained to Henz. "One broke as Zhia was going to the stage."

"'Tampered with', how?" Henz asked.

"Cut most of the way through from the underside."

Henz cursed. "When you get to your other engagements, you'd better check the steps at those stages before you use them."

The rest of the tour had crowded into the room while he was speaking. Oluzh asked, "Why?"

"Figure it out, man," Henz said, impatiently. "What's happened here wasn't just mischief; it was malice, and it was aimed at Singers. You don't know if it was aimed at your tour specifically or at Singers in general, so it seems to me that it would be wise to take no chances. Speaking of taking chances, I used those steps. I take it they've been repaired?"

"Yes," I said. I was unwinding the cloth from Zhia's leg. "Zhia, do you have more bandages in your pack?"

"No. That's the one I took off my head." She grimaced. "My back hurts."

"You didn't land on your back when you fell," said Tej.

"The fall didn't hurt my back," was her pitying response, "the sudden stop did. I wouldn't turn down a back rub."

There was no immediate response, then Henz said, "If no one else will rub your back, I will." He smirked and added, "And anything else you want rubbed."

"Don't even think of touching me," Zhia warned. She closed her eyes.

Henz pretended to pout. "I know when I'm not wanted."

Shortly after he left, a man who identified himself as the doctor arrived. I tried not to stare; he was even more unkempt than Ingbir. I wasn't so naive as to judge a person's ability by his or her appearance, and the man did have the doctor's usual bag of supplies; but he inspired no confidence in me.

When he saw Zhia, he bent over her and pushed the hair from her forehead.

Even less impressed by the man, I said, "It's her leg that's hurt," and tossed aside the bandage I had removed.

"Don't tell me my business," he retorted.

Offended at his tone, I looked instead at Zhia. Her eyes were wide open; she looked thunderstruck. I started to speak, but she gave me a small but unmistakable shake of her head.

The doctor asked everyone to leave. Zhia said, "I'd like my husband to stay."

"Very well," the doctor said, and knelt by Zhia.

Puzzled, I pointed to myself. Zhia nodded. "Put the instruments in storage while you wait," I instructed the other Singers, knowing that would keep them close at hand. I also gave them the signal that means "Be ready". Some nodded; others looked confused. All went out.

The doctor stood. "She needs stitches. I'll give her something to make her sleep."

He picked up the wine cup and rummaged in his bag. I was watching him when Zhia caught my eye. She made a rocking motion with her crossed arms, pointed to her open mouth, then to the doctor. I stared, uncomprehending. Zhia pointed at the doctor, made a graphic, rude gesture, and then pointed at herself.

When I finally understood, it was all I could to keep my face from betraying what I now knew. What Zhia had meant with her signals was that, far from being a doctor, the man was one of the raiders who had killed her child and abused her.

Now he was here to kill her. Though she recognized him, it was plain that he hadn't recognized her; he'd needed to see where the rock had gashed her forehead before he had known he had the right person.

I clung to the thought that the man didn't know his pretense had been discovered. While he poured something into the cup, I said, "Shall I send for water so you can wash the injury?"

"Wash…" the false doctor began on a questioning note, then caught himself. "Yes, do that."

I went toward the door, wondering if leaving the room was a mistake. But the man was several steps from Zhia, and she was wary. I hoped I could do what I planned to do before the man did what he planned to do.

For a while I'd been aware of strange sounds from the stage, but hadn't really listened to them. Once outside the room, I saw that the stage and the surrounding area were full of people busy with brooms, mops, and tools. My Singers were still putting the instruments away.

I beckoned urgently to Garit. "Get a magistrate. Quickly!" I said in an undertone. He started to speak. "I'll explain later. Go!"

When I returned to the room, Zhia was propped on one elbow with the cup in her hand. I didn't think she would willingly drink what was in it; but the man might force her to do so, perhaps by threatening me. Indeed, he was even then taking a knife out of his bag. It was double edged, as long as my hand. The blade was dark. I doubted the darkness was just shadow. I knew the knife was no doctor's instrument.

I felt cold. How was I going to keep the man from killing or even harming Zhia, and avoid getting hurt or killed, myself?

Zhia was looking at me. I didn't think she was trying to give me any signals until I noticed that her lips were puckered as if for a kiss, and I remembered that I was supposed to be Zhia's husband. What would a husband do if his wife were injured?

I hurried toward Zhia, saying, "Let me hold you while he sews that wound." I went behind her. As I reached around her, I knocked the cup to the floor. It shattered. Looking up at the false doctor, I said, "I'm so sorry. I hope you had more of that." Moving between Zhia and the man, I crouched so I was facing him and began to pick up the fragments of the cup.

The man didn't know I hadn't asked for water, but he must have known that my Singers could return at any moment. His time was running out.

So was ours. Knife in hand, he advanced on us. When he was within a couple of steps of me, I lunged, ramming my shoulder into him. I wrapped my arms around his legs and stood. He fell backward onto the floor. The impact made the floorboards quiver and knocked the knife from his hand. He wasn't knocked out, but he was briefly stunned.

When I moved to stand by the knife so the man couldn't again wield it, Zhia rose and picked up the wine jug, which was, remarkably, unbroken. It was still fairly full. As the man recovered his wits, he started to struggle to his feet. He had risen to one knee when Zhia snarled, "You should have roasted and eaten me, too," and smashed the jug against his head. Wine sprayed him and Zhia, and puddled on the floor. The man fell forward into the wine, out cold.

I quit guarding the knife, picked up the discarded bandage, and used it to tie the man's wrists behind him. Enough length remained that I was able to bind his ankles, also.

Zhia turned the raider's head so he wasn't breathing in wine, then started to pull down his trousers.

"What are you doing?" I asked, wondering if she had taken leave of her senses.

"Looking for scars," she replied. "In the hope there might someday be justice for Pandizh, I tried to mark the men who killed him. While they were enjoying themselves with me, I dug my nails into them, somewhere they wouldn't notice." When his rear end was bare, she smiled grimly. "And there is my mark."

I had a brief glimpse of ten white, curved scars on the fleshiest parts of the man's buttocks before she pulled his trousers back up. "You weren't sure this man was a raider?" I exclaimed.

"I was very sure, but a magistrate is going to want more evidence than just my saying so." She eyed me. "When you left the room, it was to send for a magistrate, wasn't it?"

"Yes, I sent Garit."

"And I'm back," Garit said, entering. "I brought the magistrate."

Like Osrum, he was dressed in blue and gray and was accompanied by two functionaries clothed in gray. The rest of the tour group filed in behind them.

The magistrate's eyes swept the room, noted each Singer and the prone raider, touched the doctor's bag, and lingered on the knife. "Does anyone know this man?" he asked, indicating the bound man on the floor.

I replied, "He said he was a doctor, Your Honor."

The magistrate used his toe to touch the knife. "Where did this knife come from?"

"That man brought it, in that bag over there, Your Honor."

"Did you take it out of the bag?"

"No, Your Honor."

"Who did?"

"That man did, Your Honor."

"What did he do with it?"

"He held it in his hand and came toward this woman and me, Your Honor."

"How did he hold it? Demonstrate, please."

Assuming he didn't want me demonstrating with the knife, I picked up a fragment of the jug and held it as I had seen the man do. "Like this, Your Honor."

"What did you do when he came toward you with the knife?"

"I grabbed him around the legs so he fell backwards onto the floor, Your Honor."

"Then how did he come to be prone?"

"He tried to get up, Your Honor, and I hit him in the head with the wine jug," Zhia answered.

"You hit a doctor in the head with a wine jug," the magistrate repeated.

"Your Honor, he was no doctor," Zhia said.

"How do you know that? You're touring Singers; you don't know the people here."

"I could give you a lengthy explanation, Your Honor, including the fact that the man intended to stitch an injury without first washing it; but it would be more to the point to tell you that I recognized him."

"You recognized him as whom?"

"Your Honor, he is a raider, one of a band of raiders I had the displeasure of getting to know entirely too well a few turns of the star wheel ago."

A look of pity touched the magistrate's face. "Can you prove that he is that man?"

Zhia blushed. "I believe I can, Your Honor, though I'm reluctant to show the proof in your presence."

"What is this proof you are reluctant to provide?"

Her blush deepened. "Your Honor, if he is the man I believe him to be, you will find scars from my fingernails on his...his..."

"His what?" the magistrate prompted.

"Buttocks," she whispered, then added, "Your Honor." A tear ran down her cheek.

At the magistrate's nod, one of the functionaries bared the bound man's rear. The magistrate looked for a moment, then nodded. The scarred flesh was again covered.

One of the townspeople appeared in the doorway. Seeing him, the magistrate said,

"Yes?"

"Your Honor, we found a body behind the stage. It's the doctor. His throat was cut."

"Are you certain of the identification?"

"Yes, Your Honor. His son was helping clean the stage area. He found him."

The magistrate directed the functionaries to take the raider away. He collected the doctor's bag and the knife, said, "Thank you for your help," and left.

Nine pair of eyes were staring at Zhia. Mine was the only admiring stare. Zhia had played the magistrate of this town better than she had ever played Osrum. But then, the magistrate of this town hadn't impressed me as being as intelligent as Osrum.

Only one or two of my Singers' stares were compassionate. The others were a mixture of astonishment, lewdness, and curiosity.

Zhia looked around at us and said, "If you thought what you just heard was a revelation, keep listening.

"A Singer is a servant of Nia Diva; a servant of the truth. I'm weary of deception, evasion, short cuts, pretense. I don't want to have to be on guard every moment to avoid saying something someone else isn't supposed to know. So I'll tell you the truth, and let you decide what to do with it. When I was on that stage not so long ago, I was ashamed, not because I wasn't able to complete the performance—shameful though that was—but because I'm as much a fraud as that man who posed as a doctor."

She had to raise her voice to be heard above the outburst the statement provoked. "The nine of you are Singers. For that I admire and respect you. I wanted to be a Singer, but I'm not. I've never been to classes; I have no training; I don't know theory; I can't read music; I can't keep rhythm; I play no instruments. I don't know why I was sent on that first tour; but you know what happened to that tour. Please believe me when I say that when Rois' father told me he was going to send me on another tour, I begged and pleaded to be allowed simply to leave the Hall. I don't belong on a stage.

"If you'll allow me to take a tebec, I'll return to the Hall and have a real Singer sent to replace me." She swallowed, and added, "Or, if you prefer, I can stay with the tour in the capacity of a servant or…or whatever."

The silence that followed was long, cold, and grim.

Volan took a couple of deep breaths before he said, quietly, "Rois, you told me she could sing. Who's lying: you, her, Father, or all three of you?"

CHAPTER THIRTY-FIVE

Fᴜʀʏ ʟɪᴋᴇ I'ᴅ ᴋɴᴏᴡɴ the day I met Zhia filled me. After all Father and I had done for her, after I had just risked my life to save hers, she was now throwing it all aside. Was this her way of getting even with me for my laughter earlier in the day?

I curbed my outrage and tried to think calmly. To say the day had been challenging for Zhia would be a ridiculous understatement. She'd been lost; she'd fallen through steps and been hurt. She'd been on stage for the first time in her life, and had not made a good showing. Then someone had threatened her life. To ensure that the would-be killer, one of those who had brutally killed her child, would go to prison, she had told eleven strangers her deepest, most shameful secret, a secret she had immediately learned she wouldn't have had to reveal.

Looking at her averted face and downcast eyes, I realized she was waiting for someone to condemn her. It was going to be someone other than me; at the moment, I seemed to be in as much danger of condemnation as Zhia.

There was one effective way to answer Volan. "Choose a song," I said to him. "What?"

"Choose a song. Any song."

"Is this a joke?" he snapped.

"This is the answer to your question. Choose a song."

After the briefest of hesitations, he said, "The one you sang two Festivals ago."

I had to think for a while before I remembered it. I sang it—no trophy worthy performance, that!—and then asked Zhia to sing it. It wasn't just note perfect. She sang it better than I had, which told me that she wasn't simply echoing, she was putting herself into the music. Her low notes were warm and vibrant; her higher notes, shimmering. Her enunciation was clean. She improved on my dynamics. Her phrasing was weak; but she had been close to tears when I asked her to sing. I was amazed she sounded as good as she did.

Oluzh finally breathed one word. "Wow."

Volan was trying not to look impressed. "How long has she worked on that song?"

I gestured at Zhia. She met Volan's eyes and said, "I'd never heard it before today." Seeing disbelief on his face, she said, "Then sing a different song, but not one from the Hall repertoire, because I know those songs. Taf sang them for me."

Volan sang. Zhia sang what he did. Then Ingbir sang the low bass part of a song, which Zhia echoed in her own range. Azham sang the lower tenor part of the Festival song. I saw grudging admiration on his face when he heard Zhia sing it just as he had.

Tej touched my arm. "We have an audience," he whispered.

I looked. People were crammed into and around the doorway. They weren't trying to enter; they were just listening. When they saw me looking, many crept away. A few stayed. One youth said, "Your pardon, sir. We heard the wonderful singing and had to stop so we could hear it better. Is the lady going to sing tomorrow?"

Looking at the other Singers, I asked, "Is the lady going to sing tomorrow, or is she returning to the Hall?"

At once, Derol said, "I say she's singing." Oluzh nodded, emphatically.

"I've never seen anything like it," Fras said. "I say she stays with the tour."

"That's three," I said, "or, rather, four; Father sent her and I agree with why he did. Volan?"

He looked torn. "I don't deny Zhia sings well. Like Fras, I've never seen anyone do what she can do. But I think she's more of a soloist. We do group songs."

I looked at the young man in the doorway. "Be patient. We're still deciding."

"Isn't it for Nia Diva to decide?" he asked. Some of the Singers hid condescending smiles. "Did I hear that man say the lady is Zhia?" he went on. "The Zhia for whose sake the daemon defeated raiders and kept bodies from spoiling? How much more loudly does Nia Diva have to speak before you listen?"

No one laughed at his earnestness. Though I was offended that he was loosing verbal barbs at things that weren't his business, those Singers who hadn't yet spoken looked thoughtful.

Well, not Garit. "Kept what bodies from spoiling?" he asked, with obvious derision.

Tej said, "The Singers from TTTW. Taf was there. He can tell you it's true. Long past when the bodies should have been putrid there was no sign of decay. I'd forgotten that happened. Zhia tours."

"I don't like exceptions made for anyone," Azham said, "but I have to admit Zhia is exceptional. Yes, she tours. She sings."

"Six of ten," I said. "Ingbir?"

His deep voice reproachful, Ingbir said, "Are we still insisting on our own choices? The lad has the right of it. Nia Diva has spoken. Zhia is a Singer."

I looked at Garit and Volan.

"Since there are witnesses, I can hardly do other than concur," Garit said.

"Very well, she stays," Volan said. "But if things don't go well tomorrow, Rois, I'll be the one taking a tebec back to the Hall and sending a replacement."

I looked at Zhia and forgot what I meant to say. She was so angry she was shaking, but she managed to keep her voice low when she snapped, "How dare you? If you weren't going to allow me to return to the Hall because I wanted to, how dare you subject me to listening to these men's opinion of whether I should stay or leave? How dare you hold that discussion in the presence of the people for whom we came to sing? Your arrogance is beyond belief, Rois Isianrobil."

The people still clustered at the door stepped aside so she could leave. I managed to keep a civil tone when I said to the young man, "It seems the lady won't be singing tomorrow. I'm sorry."

The youth had one last barb. "I'm sorry, too. She was the best of all of you." He turned and left, as did the others who had remained.

I was still looking at the empty doorway, aware I had just doomed another tour and even more aware that this time I couldn't blame Darl, when Fras asked, "Since when are you and Zhia on a surname basis?" His tone said he was trying to improve my mood.

"We're not," I said, glumly. "I doubt we're on any basis."

"So you're going to let her leave?" Oluzh asked.

"Can you offer any suggestion for making her stay that won't make the situation worse?" I retorted. "I'm sorry, Oluzh. I apologize to all of you. I..." I composed myself. "We'll continue with the tour as planned. We'll do all two- and three-part music, to spare Volan's voice. We can either sing here again tomorrow, or collect the tebecs and head for our next engagement. I'll leave that decision to you. I don't seem to be making very good choices today. What do you think?"

Tej said, "I think I'd like to know why everything about Zhia has been so secretive. TTTW was strange from the beginning. There was the business with Rork, Dolin, and Chaz; then Zhia just went missing for days. Now this. It's like a stringed instrument: once the wood warps, you just can't keep it in tune. When did the wood start warping, Rois?"

Out of tune was how I felt. Just then I realized I also felt a little shaky. Tussling with an armed man has that effect on me. "Let's sit down," I said, "outside. It's close in here."

We went onto the now empty stage and sat under the roof. The clouds were starting to move in. I watched them for a while, feeling the freshening wind on my face. Then I looked at the other Singers and said, "Were all of you there the day Gadig was removed as Master?" Some nodded; more shook their heads. "I don't know when Gadig began receiving stolen property from raiders, but he'd been at it a while when a young widow who'd also been..." I stopped and shook my head. "I'm sorry. I shouldn't tell you."

Fras said, "If Zhia's told you her surname, I can't imagine her minding if you tell us less intimate things."

His expression made me say, "Since you didn't quite ask, Zhia and I have not been intimate. But as I was saying, a young widow who'd also lost her child appeared at the Hall and asked to be trained as a Singer. Gadig said all right, but that she had to work to pay for her training, only the training never began. She became a slave, not a Singer. Her chore was to sweep Gadig's office and the corridors nearby. She said he always left when she started working in his office. She thought it was so he could stay away from the dust. It was really simply to stay away from her.

"As all of you know, when you enter a Hall, you give the Master your full name. Zhia did that, and Gadig realized that the ring he always wore on his left hand belonged to her, the only surviving member of Ambassador Druzhin's family. He knew it was only a matter of time before she recognized it. She knew it had been stolen by raiders when her family was massacred. She would have asked how he came to have it, and why he hadn't returned it to her when he learned who she was. So he decided to send her on a tour, the tour that wasn't." I paused, wondering how much detail to provide. "I met Zhia right after I was first named Champion. The meeting was memorable in all the wrong ways. After my second Festival win, Gadig decided to make me her tour partner."

"Champions don't tour," Azham said.

"So I believed. I admit that some of what I'm going to say next is speculation. The only reason I'm telling you things I'm not sure of is because the story has too many gaps if I leave out the guesswork. Near as I can figure, I was sent with Zhia precisely because I was a two-time Champion. Everyone else on the tour was a first-timer. The tour was a disaster before we even left the courtyard, and got worse once we got on the road. If something could go bad, it did go bad, including my falling ill and Zhia's using rimba bodies as kettles for boiling water." I waited until the groans died before adding, "Our schedule had us going as far afield as Hollan's Town."

"This was a first-timer's tour?" Volan asked in dismay.

I nodded. "Zhia told me that, before we left, she saw another schedule on Gadig's desk, a schedule with her name on it, that had the usual first-timer's engagements. In view of what happened to that tour, I'm guessing that Gadig was prepared to blame me for leading the tour astray. Anyway, the only somewhat good thing about TTTW is that it didn't last long. You've all heard how we were attacked by raiders, and how Zhia pretty much saved the day, even though she couldn't save seven of the Singers."

Ingbir asked, "So why is it significant that a two-time Champion was on the tour?"

"Because when raiders attack, usually everyone dies. Had only Zhia died on tour, there would have been questions. Had only first-timers died, people would have wondered why so many first-timers were on a tour. With a two-time Champion as tour leader, when the raiders massacred everyone—as they should have—the attention would have been on the tragic loss of a Champion, not on the oddness of the tour.

"My suspicions of Gadig were pretty well formed by then, so I didn't let Zhia return to the Hall. Taf went back. When the rimba the raiders stole from TTTW, the ones Zhia had used for boiling water, showed up at the Hall, Taf told me. Derol," I said, "you heard that set at the Festival. What did you think of them?"

"They're marvelous. I was jealous that Egion got to play them," was his answer.

"Your turn will come, I'm sure. Taf had also been questioning the female servants at the Hall, and had learned that more than twenty of them believed they were working in exchange for being trained as Singers. Between our certainty that the rimba that had been stolen were the ones that had turned up at the Hall and the discovery that more women than just Zhia had been enslaved, we knew we had to call in a magistrate. Gadig might have gotten away with everything had Zhia not recognized her father's ring, and also a mirror which had been stolen from her on tour. Gadig couldn't explain how he came to have either item. He went to prison.

"Father became Master, which leads to how Chaz, Rork, and Dolin died. Apparently, their plan was to kidnap Mother and hold her until Father agreed to drop the charges against Gadig. Mother and Zhia managed both to stay alive and to keep the three Singers from ever threatening anyone else. But Zhia was hurt. Before she was well, she was taken from the Hall clinic, and put in the common prison."

"Why?" Oluzh exclaimed.

"The wealthy father of one of the dead Singers from TTTW brought charges that those seven were killed because Zhia had been entertaining Taf and me when the raiders attacked. The accusation, if anyone is wondering, was false. When the charges were brought, Taf and I were both on tour, so Zhia was kept in prison until the tours returned. The only way to satisfy the slain Singer's father was to go to where we'd laid the bodies, and uncover them. We were dreading it, but there proved to be nothing to dread; the bodies looked like they had just been put there. We brought them back. The Singer's father was required to pay a fine. Zhia, quite a bit the worse for wear, was released from prison, and spent a lot of time in the clinic recovering.

"Right before the Festival, Father received word that Gadig had escaped from prison, apparently with the help of raiders. We suspected he might want revenge against Zhia for her part in sending him to prison. And at the Festival, he threw a rock at her. Father and the magistrate had been prepared for such an event, so Gadig was captured and returned to prison. Even though Gadig didn't kill Zhia, it was enough that he damaged her, as today's events showed.

"We're a first-timer's tour. If Gadig is communicating with raiders from prison, as seems to be the case, he could tell them where a tour like ours would go."

"But how would he know Zhia would be touring?" Garit asked.

"He wouldn't have to. Now that Noia's a Champion, Zhia is the only woman from our Hall who might tour. All a confederate of Gadig's would have to know was whether a woman left the Hall with the tour groups. Zhia thought that not wearing the bandage on her head and cutting her hair might make her harder to identify. She was mistaken. If a woman left our Hall, her schedule was known. So at our first engagement we find stair treads tampered with."

Ingbir said, "But whoever did that couldn't be sure Zhia would be hurt."

"No, but he could be sure that someone, likely a Singer, would be hurt. Then, taking the place of the doctor who would certainly be summoned, as he did, he would have a chance to attack Zhia. You may have noticed that he looked at her forehead instead of her leg. He was making sure he had the right person."

I saw the others exchanging looks. Most of their curiosity had been satisfied. I wondered who would ask the question they most wanted answered.

Tej did. "Did you know she'd had…" he hesitated, "dealings with raiders?"

"Yes." After a moment, I said, "I'm with Zhia; I'm weary of pretense and evasion. Can I trust that none of you will ever repeat what I'm about to tell you, or even refer to it?" They nodded. I said, "I want a promise, not a wag of the head." When they had all complied, I said, "I told you Zhia was a widow, and that she had a young child, a son. After her husband's death, his family had collected his body for burial. She and the child were going to have to live with her husband's family. Raiders attacked their party. Her husband's family were killed in the general massacre.

"Zhia and her child weren't. They were taken to the raiders' camp, where the child was"—I decided the men didn't need every detail—"killed. Horribly. Then they began using Zhia. She let them think she was cooperating, hoping to wear them out, and using the opportunity to leave a mark by which she could identify them, if she got the chance. She did wear them out. And she escaped to our Hall, to slavery under Gadig."

Fras broke a long, appalled silence. "No wonder she was upset. Seeing that raider must have brought back the whole experience for her." He shook his head. "I'm never again going to complain about having a bad day."

"So I ask again, are you going to let her leave?" Oluzh said. "Especially in view of what you've just told us, how can you let her go off alone? You care about her. We all know that."

Indignantly, I began, "What makes you think…"

"We have ears, Rois," Derol interrupted. "We've heard how you say her name."

Chapter Thirty-Six

I KEPT QUIET TO LET them think I was annoyed—in fact, I was quite disconcerted—while I considered how to change the subject without sounding like that's what I was doing. Finally remembering what we'd been talking about before I'd laid bare Zhia's life to men not even I knew well, I said, "I never got an answer to my earlier question. Do we get the tebecs and go on to our next engagement, or stay here and perform again tomorrow?"

"You've just gone to great lengths to be truthful with us. I, for one, appreciate it," Tej said. "But now you're willing to lie to the people of this town? You've already announced that we'll perform tomorrow. I was taught that when a man gives his word, he does what he said."

I looked at the others. They were nodding. "All right. We'll get our packs off the tebecs."

"What about Zhia?" Oluzh asked as we stood.

"If a tebec is gone, we'll know she left. That's the best I can do, Oluzh," I added when he glared at me.

"What do you mean that's the best you can do?" Garit asked. "You're tour leader."

"Do know what that means?" I asked, managing to hold my temper. "Beyond making sure we get where we're supposed to be when we're supposed to be there and choosing what songs we sing, it means I'm responsible for anything and everything that goes wrong on tour, no matter whose fault it really is. That's rather amusing, because while I can tell all of you what to do, except on stage I have no real authority. Then I run into someone like Zhia, who…" I broke off. A man dressed in yellow and brown—since it bore some insignia, I took it to be livery or a uniform—was approaching the stage. "Yes?" I said.

"Do I have the honor of addressing the tour leader?" he asked. I nodded. "I have a message from the mayor, sir. The meal you asked for is ready, as are your lodgings. Follow me, please."

We were all ravenous; we didn't have to be asked twice.

I was glad we had a guide. My sense of direction is good, but even I would have been hard put to retrace our steps to where a lavish, delicious looking and wonderful smelling supper was spread. "Your lodgings, including bathing rooms, are up those steps," the man said, pointing to the far end of the low-ceilinged hall. He said nothing about the crowd of servants that were poised to do our bidding. We could hardly miss seeing them. Indeed, it was hard to miss stepping on them.

We were seated and had begun to eat when the man said to me, "Your pardon, sir. There was another message, for you only."

I rose from the table. "Keep eating. I'll find out what's going on," I told the others. The messenger led me back into an entrance hall and said, "Someone was caught trying to steal one of your birds, sir."

I groaned silently. "Is the thief being held where the tebecs are?" I asked. The man nodded. "Take me there," I instructed, daring to hope the meal would be at least tepid when I got back. How long could it take to make sure we still had fourteen birds and our supplies and belongings, and then have a miscreant thrown into prison?

Coming in from the gates, I knew where tebecs were stabled in that town. Finding the place from the building where the others were even now stuffing themselves was quite a different matter. At length, the windswept streets started to look familiar. The first cold drops of rain were falling when my guide said, "Here we are, sir. The stable hands thought it would be a good lesson for the robber to spend some time in the enclosure with the birds. I've heard tebecs are mean."

"They can be," I said, peering through the gloom into the paddock. It was encircled by a fence that was chest high on me. Its wide, closely-set planks stood on end both inside and outside the frame that supported them. The barrier would have been hard even for someone my height to climb. Nevertheless, I asked, "Isn't anyone on guard?"

"I'm on guard, sir," said a man, a stable hand by his dress, who came out of the feed and tack room. He held a covered oil lamp.

"Will you be needing my services any longer, sir?" the uniformed man asked.

"Yes, I'll need you to guide me back to where the others are, so please wait. If you don't want to get wet, wait inside." I really didn't care whether he got wet; my stage garb was another matter. If I could get to my tebec, I could get an oiled cloth cloak. I went to the paddock gate and lifted the latch.

The stable hand exclaimed, "Sir, you don't want to go in there!"

"Yes, I do. Please give me the lamp and close the gate behind me." Staying close to the fence, I started toward the clustered tebecs. My bird came to me. I got my cloak from behind the saddle and put it on, pulling the hood over my head. The wind became stronger. Something metal started blowing in the wind, adding a rhythmic, rusty creak to the sound of rustling leaves and pattering rain. Holding the lamp high, I kept going toward the other tebecs. As I walked, I counted the birds. All were there. No supplies appeared to have been taken from the pack birds. I thought I saw our bundles behind the saddles. Apparently, the theft had been discovered before the would-be thief could get away with anything.

My foot slipped in something squishy, something I doubted was mud. In trying to keep my balance, I wrenched my back. I made no effort to stifle my exclamation of pain. When the pain eased, I kept walking.

At first, I took the small sound to be another creak of the rusty, swaying metal. Then I heard it again, better. It was a voice saying, "Rois?"

"Zhia?" Trying not to bend, I looked lower, where the sound seemed to be coming from. "Where are you?"

"I'm against the fence. No, to your left."

Through the forest of tebec legs I saw a huddled shadow. "You're the thief?"

"Can we get out of here first and talk later?"

The birds wouldn't let me through, so I squeezed between them and the fence. "I'll help you up. Take my hand."

"I can't; my hands are tied behind me. My feet are tied, too."

"What?" My outburst startled the birds. I had to crouch in front of Zhia to keep their saddles from crushing me. I set down the lamp so I could undo the knots in the coarse, wet ropes. "Didn't you tell them you were a Singer?"

"They didn't believe me. I don't dress like one, you know."

"And I can tell you changed back into your trousers, so even if they'd seen you on stage, they wouldn't recognize you. All right, that's the last of the knots." I gave her my hand and helped her to her feet, groaning as her weight dragged on my back. "Are you going to be able to walk some distance, or should I have them get a cart?"

"I'll need a cart, I think. Even if it weren't far, my leg hurts and my feet are numb. It sounds like you also need to ride. What did you do?"

"Are you all right in there, sir?" came a shout. The voice was the stable hand's.

"Yes, I'm all right," I called back, "but there's been a terrible mistake. The person you thought was a thief is one of my Singers. Please get a cart so I can take her to where the rest of my group is." I could hear agitated noises from the feed and tack room. The mayor's messenger was probably afraid that, come morning, he would be out of work. To Zhia I said, "I wrenched my back when I slipped in...when I slipped."

She asked, "How bad is it?"

"I wouldn't say 'no' to a back rub."

"Maybe someone will give you one when we get...where are we going that's too far for me to walk?"

I kept myself from saying "The paddock gate, for starters," and said, "Somewhere you can get a meal—I hope it will still be somewhat hot—and a bath and a good night's sleep."

"And maybe a back rub for me, too? And bandages for my leg and my head?" She laughed, raggedly. "Did you know tebecs are attracted to raw flesh?"

My stomach felt like it was somewhere inside one of my manure-slimed shoes. I cursed. "How badly are you hurt now?"

"Not too badly. I can be sure there are no splinters in the puncture, at any rate. All in all, I fended them off well enough. I'm pretty offensive."

I knew she was referring to the odor of tebec that clung to her body and clothes, but the comment had also been a pun. I was fairly certain the pun had been deliberate, her way of reassuring me.

"Since we're here and will have a cart, we might as well take all the packs and cloaks with us." I hoped she could hear the smile in my voice when I added, "Speaking of being offensive and speaking also of cloaks, pardon my not sharing mine with you, but I'm still in my stage garb."

"That's all right; I need all the washing I can get. What I wore on stage today will need washing too." With a small moan, she added, "I hope the wine stain will come out."

That comment reminded me that she hadn't put her pack behind a saddle when the rest of us did. "Where are your things?"

"They're on my tebec. I could have been halfway back to the Hall by now, but my leg was hurting and I couldn't quite get into the saddle. The stable hands grabbed me."

"Did they mistreat you?" I asked, sharply.

She was silent so long I thought she was ignoring the question. I realized she had been considering possible replies when she answered, "Whatever they did to me, it's nothing compared to the anguish we've caused them."

"What anguish?"

Obviously making an effort to keep her tone mild, Zhia said, "Since we got here, Singers have been hurt and attacked on their stage. They've been scolded for failing in respect to Nia Diva. There was a raider inside their city walls. Their doctor was killed. May the Unknown pardon my part in all those things!

"Put yourself in their place. They're nervous, embarrassed, fearful, and sorrowing. It's not likely anything untoward happened here yesterday. Nothing bad happened until Singers arrived. I imagine they resent us; and if they do, they may feel ashamed that they do. They probably hoped that catching someone who apparently was trying to rob Singers would make us less upset with them; but that went awry, too.

"The songs you choose for us to sing tomorrow are going to be very important. We have a chance to bring healing to this town through Nia Diva's gift of music. We can bring these people assurance, hope, maybe even some comfort." She hesitated, then added, "And if touring men customarily amuse themselves at night, I would recommend that they be asked to control themselves tonight. After the loss this town has suffered, Singers using its women casually would make us look as callous as the raider. Pardon me if I'm speaking when I shouldn't." After another pause, she said, "And I'm sorry I was so awful to you earlier. I had no right to speak to you that way."

I remembered Father's observation that Zhia kept apologizing when he was in the wrong, and knew how he felt. Before I could reply, the stable hand shouted that the cart was waiting. I handed the lamp to Zhia and collected the tour members' cloaks and packs from the birds' saddles. Over my objections, Zhia carried her own pack and cloak.

As we started toward the gate, I asked, "Then I take it you also want to stay and sing tomorrow."

"No, I want to go back to the Hall. But Nia Diva kept me here, and now I know why."

"I wish I had your certainty."

"I wish I could give my certainty to you and give the stench back to the tebecs; but the situation that brought the stench is the same one that brought the certainty. You can't have one without the other."

With mock seriousness, I asked, "So if you bathe, you risk no longer being certain?"

Laughing, Zhia said, "That's a risk I am very willing to take."

We didn't speak on the way back to our lodgings, but only because I was driving the cart—with the messenger seated next to me, wearing one of our oiled cloth cloaks and giving directions—while Zhia and the odor that hung about her like a cloak rode in the cart's bed. When I wasn't gritting my teeth when the unevenness of the road jostled my back, I was reflecting on what Zhia had said.

I agreed with her opinion that it would be unwise for the other men to seek pleasure after supper, but didn't know how to broach the subject. However I managed it, I didn't think Zhia would mind if I presented the idea as my own. The men would be more likely to accept the request if it came from me.

Her comment about the importance of the choice of the music we sang the coming day was also true. I had no idea which songs would provide the healing Zhia believed they could. My mind felt thick and inflexible, like my voice so often did when I fell ill, which was probably because I was hungry, tired, and in no small amount of pain.

The piece of road that led to where we were being housed was the bumpiest. Zhia was moving better than I was when we got out of the cart. She looked at me in the light of the lamp that hung beside the roofed door of our lodging place, said, "A long soak in a hot bath is what you need," and forbade my carrying in anything.

When we entered the building, after making sure the rain had washed objectionable substances from our shoes, Zhia resisted well-meant attempts to take her pack and cloak, and instructed servants to bring in the packs and cloaks that were still in the cart. That done, she gave one of those servants my cloak and asked him to return the mayor's man to the mayor's office and the cart to the stables, and then return with the cloaks. She asked other servants to prepare two baths, specifying that one be as deep as possible and as hot as could be tolerated, and to prepare a tub for washing clothes. Then she told me to go into the hall and eat, and asked yet another servant to bring her a plate of food. (When I learned the servants didn't stop Zhia from eating outside I was irritated. She didn't smell that bad.)

The rest of the tour had finished their meal, but they had lingered to find out where I had gone and why. While I ate—the food was delicious and still hot; either it had been freshly prepared or it had been returned to the kitchen to be kept warm—I explained what had happened to Zhia. Even those who were dismayed couldn't help being amused. Now that it was over, it did seem funny in a cruel sort of way.

I didn't tell them what Zhia had said, either about the songs for our upcoming performance or about their activities for the evening, so when I said, "I appreciate your keeping me company while I eat, but you don't have to hang around if you have other things to do", I was surprised when Derol replied, "Tej pointed out that the people of this town suffered quite a loss today, and that our usual evening pursuits could rightly be viewed as unfeeling, at best. We'll hang around here."

With a silent prayer of thanks to Nia Diva, I commended Tej for his thoughtfulness.

I don't believe in enduring more pain than is necessary. I'd drunk quite a bit of wine with my meal, and took a jug and cup with me to the bathing room. The supper wine was already helping relieve the pain; hot water and more wine took care of much of the remaining discomfort. I don't know how long I soaked, but the tips of my fingers were quite wrinkled when I finally climbed out and toweled off.

With a dry towel wrapped around my middle and another one around my shoulders, I stepped into the chilly corridor. A man servant awaited me. "Your chamber is this way, sir. I trust your back feels better?"

"Yes, thank you."

"Then you won't be needing my services, sir?" I probably looked puzzled, for the man hastened to add, "The lady said you'd hurt your back, sir, and needed a good rub down. I have some skill in that area."

"A back rub wouldn't hurt," I said, marveling at Zhia's concern for my well-being and wondering if she had arranged for someone to rub her back. I asked, "Could someone attend to my clothes? They're my stage garb; I'll need them tomorrow."

"Yes, sir. I'll see to it."

"Thank you. Did the lady get her bath?"

"Yes, sir. She washed her clothes, too, even though we told her that was our job."

"Pardon her. She's new to being a Singer."

"I wouldn't speak ill of a Singer, sir."

So why did you tell me she washed her clothes? I thought, but was too relaxed and weary to pursue the subject.

The room to which the servant led me was warm, comfortably though not lavishly furnished, and softly lighted by lamps that burned sweet timi oil. Sniffing the aroma, I suddenly wondered how much the meal and the evening's lodging were costing the town. This was not a wealthy place.

I shed the towel around my shoulders and stretched out on the bed. When the man began kneading my back, I managed not to groan much. The benefits of the hot water and the wine were already wearing off. The ill effects of the amount of wine I'd drunk weren't yet manifest. As the pain in my back eased, I began to doze; I wasn't aware of the man's pulling the bedclothes over me and leaving.

I dreamed of our upcoming performance. We were singing a wonderful song, a song I shouldn't have been able to sing because I'd never heard it before. It was tender, uplifting, hopeful. The faces of the people listening were rapt, aglow with the joy and comfort the song had brought them. When the dream song ended, so did my sleep. The song was fresh in my mind, but I had no way to write it down. I needed Zhia's gift.

Hastily pulling a blanket around myself, I stepped into the corridor and stumbled over my newly-cleaned shoes, which were outside my door. My freshly washed and dried clothes were next to them. Looking both ways in the dimly-lit passage, I saw Zhia's shoes and clothes outside a door at the far end.

Hurrying down the chilly corridor, I opened the door and crept into the chamber. The form curled under the light-colored bedding was certainly Zhia's; none of the men had hips like that. I touched her shoulder and softly called her name.

She woke with a start and sat up, then gasped. I heard the slither of cloth as she pulled up the bedclothes. There was no need for concern; the chamber was quite dark. "Rois, what is it?" she whispered.

"I've just dreamed of a wonderful song. I can hear it in my head, but I have no way to write it down."

"Sing it to me."

I did, then said, "Sing it back. I want to hear how it sounds, too."

She did. We were both silent when she finished, then she breathed, "Rois, it's..."

"Yes, isn't it? I'm sorry I woke you; but I think it's the song we need tomorrow... or today, depending on how close we are to daybreak."

"It's a gift. Nia Diva gave you a song."

"I guess so." And with my stupidity at supper, I had given myself a headache. Suddenly, all I wanted to do was go back to bed. I turned at the door. "Thank you for arranging for the man to give me a back rub."

"You're welcome. Is your back better?"

I moved it, slowly. "Yes, I think between the hot water and the rub down, it is."

"Good."

"I don't suppose you got a back rub, too?"

"I forgot."

"Does your back still hurt?"

"It's bearable."

"I take that as a 'yes,'" I said. "Lie down."

"Rois, you need your sleep."

Sharply, I whispered, "What do you think I'm planning to do? I said 'back rub'. I didn't say and I didn't mean anything else."

"I'm sorry. I'm not used to men visiting my chamber at night."

"Would you rather I leave?"

All at once, she was weeping. "No. Please don't laugh at me, but I want a man to hold me and caress me and to do all the things men and women do together, in bed and everywhere else. And I want the man to be you, but I know you don't feel that way about me; so yes, you'd better leave."

I was halfway back to my own chamber when I finally realized that what everyone else had been telling me was true: I did feel "that way" about Zhia. I wanted her, not Eia, and not just in bed but in every part of my life.

I knew I didn't deserve her. Even though I had wanted someone else, I had gone to Zhia for comfort the night of the Festival. That she had welcomed my touch didn't make it any less presumptuous. Though less than a day ago I had humiliated her with my laughter, all day she had shown me unmerited kindness. Now, for the third time, she had made it plain that if I wanted her, she was mine. Somehow, I knew this was my last chance. If I went back to my chamber now, I would regret the decision the rest of my life.

I went back into her chamber. I knew from her breathing that she wasn't asleep.

She sat up when I knelt by the bed. Again, she pulled the bedclothes up to cover her bosom.

I put my hands over hers. "Rois Isianrobil hopes you will accept his offer not only to rub your back but also to do whatever else will please you for the rest of your life."

She was smiling; I could hear it in her voice. "Zhia Vediandruzhin would love a back rub, and would be honored to spend the rest of her life being pleased by and pleasing you."

She dropped the bedclothes and moved her hands so that nothing was between my hands and her curves. Leaning into my caresses, she put her arms around my neck and kissed me, hungrily.

As for what happened after that, I will say only that I learned the truth of the saying, "If it feels that good, you waited too long."

By the way, she did get a back rub, too.

CHAPTER THIRTY-SEVEN

THE OTHERS WERE BREAKING their fast when we went into the dining hall arm in arm the next morning. Zhia looked radiant. In the golden green garb, she outshone me; the joy in her face outshone her attire. I hope I also looked pleased. Except for a well-deserved headache, I was pleased.

Zhia blushed as the men stared but didn't look away. She looked up at me with a smile that made me want to take her back to her chamber.

Ingbir cleared his throat. "I take it congratulations are in order."

"Yes. Zhia has done me the honor of becoming my wife." I kissed her.

Fras said, "It took you long enough."

Volan summoned a servant and asked for wine. He casually let slip that Zhia and I had just become husband and wife, at which news the servants brought not only wine, but a veritable feast (which led me to believe they already knew what had gone on during the night). We were eating and drinking our way through the delicacies when Zhia quietly reminded me that we had to sing later that day, and that the other men needed to learn the song.

"Do you remember it?" I asked, softly.

"Though you would be more flattered if I said 'no'; yes, I do."

"While I agree that knowing I'd made you forget would be flattering, I'm glad you remember it."

"So am I. You can make me forget it tonight," she whispered, and kissed me.

I almost laughed aloud for sheer delight. I had never before known this close-ness, this certainty in a relationship with a woman. In the past, my awareness that a woman was mine only for a night had added spice and urgency to what we shared. I had never imagined that knowing with whom I'd be spending the night—and the days—could be so exciting, so fulfilling.

Garit said, "Either go back upstairs and get it over with, or calm down. This isn't fair."

Then I did laugh. "I won't apologize; but you're right. Can any of you still sing? We have a song to learn."

I arranged for a cart. Zhia could possibly have walked as far as the stage, but after doing so she wouldn't have been able to stand for the length of a perfor-mance. As all Singers know, music is sung best when the Singers are standing. We threw our packs into the back of the cart and crowded in wherever there was room.

"So what's with making Zhia your wife?" Azham asked me. "Since she told the raider you were her husband you had to make an honest woman out of her?"

"That's a possible reason," I replied, without taking offense; it was going to take a lot to put me out of humor that day. "But not the right one."

Fras said, "Pardon if I'm intruding on your personal arrangements, but we'll be staying at a Quarter Rest tonight. Some of us might want to sleep."

I'd forgotten that. As far as I knew, Zhia and I were the first husband and wife to tour together. Fasting so soon after a feast was a dismal prospect. Sternly reminding myself I had managed a good many nights without Zhia and could certainly do so again, I said, "We didn't sleep much last night, so we'll prob-ably want to sleep, too."

Zhia added, demurely, "But if we can't sleep, I'll try to not to scream too loudly."

The others laughed and took the comment for what it was: an invitation to indulge in the good-natured ribaldry that is customary when a man asks a woman to be his wife. They hadn't been able to tease us at the time; they made up for it now. I realized the chaffing also had the benefit of allowing the men to relieve some of the urges they had agreed not to satisfy the night before.

Our arrival at the stage put an end to most of the bawdiness. The man from whom I'd hired the cart had assured me he would be at the performance and would collect his property afterwards, so I parked it out of the way and put it out of my mind. When I tried to help with moving the instruments back onto the stage, the others suggested I was worn out from my exertions during the night and told me to rest. I gave them the usual reply to that kind of comment (which I won't repeat), and went to sit by Zhia.

She was on the edge of the stage with her legs hanging over. The cloth of her garb was taut over her thighs. I could see a lump on her right thigh, a bandage, that hadn't been there the night before. Belatedly, I remembered what she'd said about the tebecs.

"I forgot to check how much damage you suffered in the paddock," I said.

"As I told you, I wasn't much harmed. However, our activity last night, though delightful, was perhaps ill-advised."

I smiled and said, "Don't blame me. I was willing to stop long before you were."

"I know." She drew a voluptuous breath. "I could start again right now."

With mock consternation, I exclaimed, "We have a performance coming up!"

She glanced down. "I can see that."

I was grinning; I knew it. Every man wants to think he's wonderful in bed. Knowing that Zhia wanted me as much as I wanted her was good for me. Even so, we had a performance—a stage performance—to do. I wanted to be able to concentrate. Much as I hated to allow reality to intrude into our dream, I had to say, "As Garit said, calm down. If you keep looking at me like that—yes, like that!—and making sly comments, I'll likely stand up in front of everyone this afternoon and forget the words or make some other obvious mistake." I kissed her and added, "Remember what we were doing when we stopped."

Knowing it would be easier for me to think about the music if I weren't next to Zhia, I stood up and went to where the others had nearly finished setting up the instruments.

Before I could say anything, Volan remarked, "I never thought I'd say this, Rois, but you and Zhia are embarrassing me."

"You're just jealous," I said.

"Even if he is, he's right," Tej said. "Your being so cozy…"

"To put it mildly," Azham put in.

Tej nodded and went on, "Isn't fair to the rest of us. I'm not saying you shouldn't have asked Zhia to be your wife—we've been waiting for that to happen ever since TTTW—but you would have done better to wait until we were back at the Hall. I believe you gave Taf just that advice not so long ago."

"I did," I said. I was starting to feel guilty.

Ingbir picked up where Tej left off. "Out of consideration for those of us who can neither get away from you two nor get what you're getting, could you control yourselves? I, for one, am glad that Zhia doesn't seem to be one of those women who has to have her hands all over her man all the time; but what she does to you with her eyes is nearly as bad."

I thought of a number of joking replies, none of which would have done justice to the men's valid objections. "You're right; but you're asking a lot, you know," I finally said.

"We know that," Derol said, looking up from polishing the rimba. "But a tour asks a lot of every person on it. We want to know that you and Zhia are going to be giving the tour your best. If you're not sleeping at night and are distracted when you're awake, you're cheating us and our audiences."

Zhia spoke from behind us. "You forgot to mention that we're also cheating Nia Diva. Allow me to apologize. I'm still new to touring; I didn't realize how my selfish actions were hurting the rest of you. If Rois won't take it too unkindly—and he'd certainly better not take it personally!—for the remainder of the tour, I'll try to conduct myself as though I have no husband. And may I request that if, at any other time on this tour, my actions become a problem to the good of the tour, you tell me to my face." She waited for a moment, then asked, "Are there other things I need to amend?"

Oluzh said, "Can we have your word you won't run away any more?"

Zhia was no longer radiant. She looked like she was trying to hold back tears.

"I have been a trial to all of you, haven't I? It's not too late for me to take a tebec back to the Hall. That would make things easier for all of you, especially Rois."

"No, it wouldn't," I said, bluntly. "Just so the subject doesn't have to come up again and again, you're not leaving this place or any other on the tour until all of us are ready to leave. Now please sing that song so we can learn it before this afternoon."

"Wait a moment," Fras said. "Did you say 'sing that song'? There's no music?"

"Not yet. I'll write it down when we get back to the Hall. Just listen. Zhia?"

As she sang, I watched the other Singers' faces, and saw reluctance turn to guarded enthusiasm.

"Where did that song come from?" Fras asked.

"A dream. Do you want to listen to it again, or are you ready to try it?"

Garit asked, "Are we doing it in unison, or parts?"

"Let's learn it in unison first. If we can do it in parts, that would be great."

The first run through wasn't encouraging. Derol, Fras, Ingbir, and Oluzh all claimed the melody went too high for them, so we started lower. Then the tenors had to strain to reach the low notes. When we started on a higher note with only the baritones and tenors singing, it sounded thin.

"Let's take a break," I said, and walked off stage. I was out of humor, and not only because the song wasn't coming together. I knew that, for precisely the reasons the men had cited, Tej had been right in saying I should have waited to ask Zhia to be my wife until we were back at the Hall. I still believed that, had I waited until then, Zhia would have convinced herself that I wanted nothing to do with her. In the bustle of Hall business, likely no opportunity would have presented itself. Had one arisen, Zhia would probably have turned me down and thought she was doing me a favor.

It had been so like Zhia to accept all the blame for the embarrassment the other men were feeling. I knew what she didn't: if she and I had been intimate on tour without being husband and wife, the men would have had no objection. It wasn't our intimacy, but our altered relationship, that made the others uncomfortable.

To be honest, I was a little uncomfortable, too. While I knew I had given

Zhia all the pleasure a woman can have, she'd never seemed satisfied. I had
found myself thinking of her comment about exhausting twenty raiders, and
felt guilty when I wondered if that event had left her unable to enjoy only
one man. Or had it been that the memory of the abuse she suffered at their
hands had made her appreciate tenderness that much more? Whichever—and
I deemed it best not to raise the subject until the tour was behind us—she and
I now faced several days apart. It would be good for the tour; it might be devastating to us as a couple.

Volan approached. Quietly, he asked, "Can I bother you, Rois?"

"What is it?"

"About you and Zhia…"

I held up a hand. "Please, any subject but that. I'm not angry or anything;
but doing what's best for the tour will be easier if I can just focus on the tour.
Or isn't that what you were going to say?"

"That's one thing," he admitted. "The other thing is this song. It's a great song;
but as a group, we sound terrible singing it. It's your decision as tour leader,
but I wondered if that song should be the one Zhia sings alone. You asked our
opinion; that's mine."

"How would we make it work? There's no accompaniment."

"Tej and Azham are working on that right now. We could practice it a couple
more times with whatever they manage to come up with, so it seems like we'll
be doing it together and Zhia will know when to start."

I almost said "Zhia doesn't know when to stop", but caught myself. It was
hard to believe I'd been so elated at breakfast. That the sun was shining seemed
like an affront. "That's a good idea, Volan. Maybe we should do that song last,
so Zhia…" Again, I caught myself.

"I think I know what you were going to say, Rois." His regard was pitying.
"Do you think Zhia has the temperament to be a Singer? The only thing she
seems to know how to do is run away. Singers can't do that."

Once again, the image of Zhia holding the blood-dripping ax rose in my
mind. "She runs when she doesn't know how or whom to fight. She's already
told you and everyone else what her shortcomings are. Today she's been made

aware that she's even more detrimental to the tour than she already believed herself to be. Worse, she now thinks that she's detrimental to me. I certainly don't think so; but once Zhia gets an idea in her head, it's hard to get it out of there.

"I'm asking you and the others to give her all the support you can. Father thinks she should be a Singer; Father sent her on this tour. I'd like him to know his confidence wasn't misplaced."

Volan was shaking his head. "So now the reason we're touring is to prop up both the confidence of someone who isn't really a Singer and your father's, who isn't really Hall Master?"

I could only stare at him, wondering how many others questioned my father's right to be Master. Finally, I said, "If you're that dissatisfied with the tour, you're free to go. I ask only that you stay for this performance. You're a strong tenor with a good voice. We'll need you."

"I've already said I'll sing today," he said, curtly, as he walked away.

Shortly after that, I heard Zhia call that our midday meal was ready. It wasn't midday, but the familiar sight of the pre-performance snack of bread and water helped us focus on our job. I hadn't arranged for any food to be brought to the stage; Zhia must have been thinking that far ahead. I also saw wine and a cup in their usual place, at the back of stage under the symbol Nia Diva.

For some reason Zhia had changed into the reddish brown garment. The color matched the wood of the wall behind the stage so well that only her face and hands were distinguishable from a distance. There were dark circles under her eyes that I hadn't noticed at breakfast.

After we ate—none of us was especially hungry; we'd eaten too much at breakfast—we did as Volan had suggested and practiced the new song as if intending to sing it as a group. Though Azham and Tej had put together quite a passable accompaniment, the song just didn't sound good. Everyone looked glum.

"That's enough," I said, "let's save our voices for what we do well. Those of you who need to change, do so. We'll finish warming up with that drum number."

I looked for Zhia, intending to ask her to wear the golden green garb, but didn't see her. I assumed she was at one of the public conveniences. I was already in my garb and so had nothing to do until the others returned to the stage and we did our back rubs. Right before a performance is always the hardest time for me. I'm not usually nervous, which is not necessarily a good thing, but I'm impatient.

"So you are doing a repeat performance."

I didn't groan aloud, though I wanted to. Henz was the last person I wanted to deal with right before a performance. I turned and saw him standing, as he had the day before, below the stage. Trying to think of something casual to say, I settled on, "Why are you still hanging around?"

"I haven't heard Zhia sing. For all I know, she may be competing next Festival. I want to know how hard I'm going to have to work to win again." His smile was cocky.

"I think you can drop the word 'again,'" I said. "We both know the truth. If you employ the same methods next Festival you used at this one, I'd say it's likely you'll again be Champion. Zhia won't stoop to seducing the judges."

"I didn't seduce anyone," Henz protested. Then he leered. "Maybe if Zhia seduced me…"

"She's my wife, Henz."

Now his smile was mocking. "Thoroughly tamed, are you, Rois? Domesticated, caged, decent: no fun at all. I'll have to work extra hard to take care of the women you'll be missing out on."

I tried to sound haughty and indifferent when I said, "I have all the woman I need," but I wasn't as cool as I sounded. Henz's taunts stung, especially since I knew I'd be sleeping alone for the remainder of the tour.

My Singers were taking their places. The nobodies were starting to fill the area in front of the stage. Zhia missed back rubs, but was there when we warmed up with the rhythmic song that had been so well received the day before. I noticed that when they heard music, the nobodies came in more quickly. I would have to remember to mention that to Father; delaying a performance to accommodate latecomers is high on most Singers' list of gripes.

We saluted Nia Diva, then began our performance. I don't know if the audience could tell, but it was obvious to me that we were singing in our sleep, as Singers put it. There was nothing wrong with our singing and our playing; there was nothing really right, either. We were going through the motions. We weren't a group; we were ten individuals who happened to be on a stage together. We weren't doing anything that even vaguely resembled our best.

During the feeble applause at the end of that song, I beckoned to the Singers. Keeping my voice low, I said, "Is this really the performance we want to give, especially considering that Henz is in the audience?" I saw some puzzled looks. "Henz is one of the Festival Champions, not by virtue of a performance I considered lackluster, but by virtue—which is entirely the wrong phrase—of bribing the judges. Let's show him how Singers with integrity perform, even on tour."

My Singers rose to the challenge. The music began to come alive, and the wonderful interplay of skill and emotion that make performing such a thrill started and grew. Each song was more vibrant than the one before. The nobodies were so lost in our music I debated even doing the new song.

Then I remembered the surpassing joy that had followed my receiving the new song, and remembered also the crushing disappointment of the morning after. Though at the moment my situation with Zhia looked bleak, I still had hope; some who even now were absorbed in the music would have no hope once the music stopped. For now, the townspeople could forget the fear and loss of the previous day; but the fear and the loss would still be there when the performance was over. I refused to believe that I'd been given just that song at just that time for no reason, or so I could choose not to use it.

When we had performed everything in our repertoire we hadn't done the day before, I said, "New song," gave the others the signal that means "the usual", and listened to Azham and Tej play the first few notes of the accompaniment.

I hadn't planned to sing at all. I don't know if the other men had made their own plans without telling me, but no one else was singing when Zhia began the lyrics. After an almost unnoticeable hesitation she went on, her voice caressing the low notes that opened the song. She sang the words more slowly than we had practiced, and with utter conviction, as though she'd written them herself. If she noticed when the instruments stopped playing, she gave no sign. The melody line rose gradually as the song progressed, climaxing with a note that, though high, was well within Zhia's range. It shimmered in the rapt silence before descending back into Zhia's warmer range. Since there was no accompaniment, she let the final note fade out.

There was a profound hush when she finished. She was in front of me, so I couldn't see her face, but I could see her tense when the audience didn't respond. I was afraid she'd leave the stage, but she didn't. Finally, the applause burst forth, thunderous, echoing back from the curve of the stage wall.

I saw Zhia start as the noise rose. Collecting herself, she acknowledged the acclaim with an inclination of her head. Then she turned her back on the audience.

Had the audience not been clapping so loudly, the collective gasp from the rest of us on stage would have been audible a stone's throw away. We exchanged looks of dismay. No one had thought to tell Zhia that a Singer never turns his or her back on the audience. None of us had any idea what she meant to do.

Straight and poised, Zhia faced the back wall. With a motion of her right hand I would call a caress except that the back of her hand was toward the wall, she indicated the symbol of Nia Diva. Her left hand came up, also, then both hands swept out and down. Curving only the upper part of her body, she bowed to the symbol of the daemon. She straightened, looked again at the symbol, then faced the audience and gave them a bow that wasn't as deep.

Just when the rest of us were starting to think of things to do to relieve her of a swollen head, she stepped back, extended both arms wide to remind the audience that she wasn't the only Singer on stage, and looked at the rest of us with a smile. She wagged her hands to tell us we should bow, too, so we did.

Then she raised her hands in the gesture that is a request for silence. "We extend our thanks to all of you. We thank you, first, for your understanding yesterday when we weren't able to complete our performance; second, for your prompt attention to the stage. You can be proud of the work you did; it's become truly lovely. Third, we thank you for your gracious hospitality last night; and last but by no means least, we thank you for returning today.

"We would be remiss if we failed to express our concern at the distressing things that happened here yesterday. We ask the mayor to give our tour fee to the family of the doctor who was killed, both to show our sorrow at their loss, and to help them get by during these first difficult days. I know the rest of you good people will do all you can to comfort and support them as they grieve."

The applause was even louder. Zhia just stood there. No one had thought to tell her how to get off stage, either. Volan looked at me. I nodded. He took her hand and led her away. The rest of us left as we usually do, carrying our gear with us. The speed with which a tour can finish a performance and be on the road is something in which Singers take pride.

We men had changed out of our stage garb and were collecting our packs when a swollen-eyed woman rushed up, fell to her knees, and grabbed Zhia's hand and kissed it. "Thank you," she sobbed. "I didn't know how I would provide for my children now that my husband is dead. Thank you." She kissed Zhia's hand again.

Flustered, Zhia said, "Please don't thank me. I know what it's like to lose a husband."

At my nod, Derol helped the woman to her feet, pried her hand from Zhia's, and escorted her back to the nobodies' area. Zhia bit her lips and disappeared into one of the rooms to change into her shirt and trousers. Garit and Oluzh left to fetch our pack tebecs so we could load the instruments.

Volan said, "I'll stay with the tour, Rois, if for no other reason than because I'd rather you were the one who has to tell Father that Zhia turned down a tour fee."

"Thank you," I said and added, gloomily, "I'm beginning to understand the appeal of running away. Father will have my hide."

CHAPTER THIRTY-EIGHT

WHETHER ZHIA WAS AVOIDING me, I don't know; but that day I didn't get a chance to talk to her about what she'd done wrong at the performance or, more precisely, its aftermath. When we left that town, she again rode at the very back of the group. When we reached the Quarter Rest, in plenty of time to cut wood before it rained, she again ate food she had brought with her. Again, she chose a place to sleep well away from everyone else. Again, she was asleep long before the rest of us were ready to call it a night.

In a way, I was glad; her solitariness meant I didn't have to deal either with my doubts about the wisdom of my late-night, half-drunken decision or with the resentment Henz's taunts had sparked. Sitting with the other men, talking around the dying fire, I could almost believe I was as free as they.

We didn't talk about the performance. People often look at me in disbelief when I say that. They're even more incredulous when I tell them there's no need for Singers to rehash a performance. Each of us knew if and where he had fallen short, and knew what to do to improve, as well. It's part of our training. I suspect that night there was an additional reason no one mentioned the performance: they were reluctant to criticize Zhia in front of me; Zhia, who had made it so obvious she had no training.

I remembered my recent tour with Noia, who had given the rest of her tour group no reason to gasp or cringe or curse. She hadn't been mistaken for and apprehended as a thief. Never once had I been required to rescue her from angry stable hands or raiders or anyone else. She had done her job professionally, competently, thoroughly. She had been good company when not on stage, flashing that delightful smile and rarely voicing complaints. Taf was blessed in his choice of a wife.

Ingbir, who was sitting next to me, elbowed me. "You asleep?" he rumbled. "Twice Azham has asked if we're doing the new song at our next engagement."

"No," I replied, without thinking. Then I did think about the question, and added, "I doubt I'll even bother writing the thing down. It's served its purpose."

"And what about…" Garit pointed with his thumb at the corner where Zhia slept.

"Were it up to me, she'd never tour again, not because she can't sing, but because we're supposed to improvise music, not procedures. It's not fair to ask trained Singers to deal with those kinds of surprises."

There was a lessening of tension I hadn't been aware of until it diminished. I should have been gratified that I'd improved the men's mood; instead, I felt like a traitor.

Our talk turned to other subjects. Since we were healthy young men, I won't elaborate.

Zhia was again awake, fed, and in the saddle when we men awoke. Again, she rode at the back. Dropping back to talk to her never occurred to me. She didn't join us for the midday meal; she didn't join us for supper at the Quarter Rest where we stayed that night. I wasn't sure whether I appreciated her remoteness or resented that she was keeping so much distance. The next day was a repeat of the previous one, until midmorning when we reached our next engagement.

With Zhia out of my sight—and, by then, pretty much out of my mind—I could pretend it was a normal tour, and just follow the routine I knew so well: going to the stage to drop off the instruments; stabling the tebecs; finding where to bathe, change, and eat; returning to the stage to warm up and prepare to perform.

I was relaxed from back rubs, which again Zhia missed, and looking forward to doing what I knew I did well when I saw Henz coming up the steps to the stage.

"So what's your excuse now?" I said by way of greeting. "You've heard Zhia sing."

"I don't recall being made accountable to you," he replied, "but I thought that since you're going to be let off your leash only long enough to sing, I might pass along what I heard while hobnobbing with the riffraff two days ago."

"What might that be? And make it quick; we need to start soon."

"The nobodies were very taken with Zhia: her singing, her antics with the Nia Diva symbol—if a Singer on one of my tours pulled a stunt like that, I'd personally kick him off the stage—her little speech, and her giving away Hall money. In short, they liked all the things a real Singer would rightly despise. I hope she's not going to tour again."

Though I had said pretty much the same thing two nights earlier, Henz's saying it offended me. "That's not up to me, as you know. Now how about you go hobnob with the riffraff so we can sing."

He grinned and said, "I saw one of the riffraff I intend to hobnob with at length. I'll bet she has a friend." When he left the stage, I watched where he went. The woman he ended up next to was attractive. The woman next to her was just as appealing.

I made myself look away, but knew I hadn't recovered my focus when I almost forgot the wine ritual. Fras grimaced and gestured, and I managed to get my head together.

I thought I had my head together. It wasn't until the middle of our third song that I realized the melody sounded weak. Then I noticed that Zhia wasn't on stage. Not until we were another two songs into the performance did I notice her, standing just offstage. When that song was done, I asked for an instrumental piece and, seething, went to where she hovered. I saw no remorse on her face, which made me angrier.

I grabbed her arm and pulled her farther off stage. "You have a lot of nerve,"

I snarled. "Even without Singer training you should know you don't show up late for a performance. You rely entirely too much on the fact that you're Ambassador Druzhin's daughter. I have news for you: he wasn't a Singer, and neither are you. Don't you dare set foot on a stage ever again." I turned to go back to the performance, then turned back. "By the way, you don't know my name."

I didn't see what she did; I didn't care. The rest of the performance went as it should. There were no antics, no surprises. We were warmly applauded. We collected our gear and our tour fee, and left the stage.

Oluzh was the one who asked about Zhia. "She's gone," I said. "I repudiated her." Before anyone else could speak, I went into the nobodies' area and found Henz, who was easy to spot because of his colorful clothing. "I'm short a tenor," I said, without explanation. "Could I borrow you for the rest of the tour?"

I could see he was brimming with questions, but he simply patted the rump of the woman he was embracing, sent her off with a kiss, and said, "All right. This will be a first: two Champions from two different Halls on the same tour. Ought to be interesting."

The instruments were loaded and we were in our traveling clothes, ready to claim the other tebecs and leave, when a man came up to me. "Your pardon, sir. The lady said you would pay me for my services."

"What lady? What services?"

The man looked troubled. "She said she was a Singer, sir. I'm a doctor. She came to me with a festering wound in her leg. I'm sorry she was late for the performance, but I couldn't treat it as quickly as she wanted. I gave her something for the pain, so she'll likely fall deeply asleep fairly soon."

I paid the man. I turned to see the rest of my tour group looking at me. Most looked concerned. A few looked angry. "Yes, I messed up," I said. "No, we're not going to look for her. At any time in the last two days she could have told me she needed a doctor. She couldn't be bothered. She's not my wife any longer. We have a tour to complete. Let's get on the road."

When I saw that all the tebecs were there but that Zhia's packs were missing from hers, I didn't know whether to be angry that she had gone wherever she had gone on foot, or relieved that we wouldn't have to find another tebec for Henz. I decided relieved was easier, but as I climbed onto my bird, I found myself muttering, "Idiot woman."

The rest of the days on the tour seemed to pass quickly, with performances that were all they should have been. It was the nights at the Quarter Rests that were strained and seemed interminable. No one dared mention Zhia. We soon tired of Henz's tales of his exploits but had little else to discuss, so we listened, or pretended to. By the time the tour was over, most of us were ready to swear off women or, at the very least, talking about intimacy.

We had left Henz at his Hall and so had a riderless tebec when we returned to ours, some eight days after we'd left it. Father came out to the courtyard to meet us and to offer prayers of thanks for our safe return. I followed him to his office and handed him the tour fees. He pushed them aside as if they meant nothing, and asked, "Where is Zhia?"

"I kicked her off the tour," I replied, evenly. "She made a fool of herself on stage in Owlin's Run and then was late for the performance in Knollwood. Henz happened to be in Knollwood, so I asked him to fill in as the other first tenor for the rest of the tour."

"Where is she now?"

"I have no idea." When I saw he was angry, I said, "If she were a man, Father, would it matter where she is now? Would you ask, or even care?"

"Yes. I am answerable for the Singers at this Hall." He picked up a paper from his desk, looked at it, and set it aside before asking, "Did Zhia's offenses at Owlin's Run include singing a song that moved the mayor to tears, doing obeisance to the symbol of Nia Diva, and offering your tour fee to the widow of a doctor who was killed by a raider who, I assume, was trying to finish what Gadig didn't?"

"Yes, sir."

"Which of those actions did you find objectionable?"

"All of them, sir. They aren't what Singers are accustomed to doing."

"That doesn't make them wrong." He regarded me coldly. "There's something you're not telling me. If it concerns Zhia, I need to know what it is."

I looked away. "At Owlin's Run I asked her to be my wife. We had just one night. The others on the tour didn't like the way we acted when we were together, so Zhia said she would act like I wasn't her husband. When I got angry with her for being late for the performance at Knollwood, I told her she wasn't a Singer, and I...I repudiated her."

Father sank into his chair and covered his face. When he looked at me again, he said, "You now have the record both for the shortest distance covered by a tour on its first day and for the shortest union ever entered into by a Singer. I hope you aren't proud of either one." I said nothing. What could I say? Father asked, "Did you bother to find out why Zhia was late for the performance?"

"I did find out, but not until I'd sent her away. She'd been hurt in Owlin's Run. Some of the steps up to the stage had been tampered with, cut most of the way through from underneath. Zhia fell through. A piece of wood pierced her thigh. She wasn't able to finish the performance that day—we sang there two days in a row, since I stopped the performance the first day—and there were things said that shouldn't have been, and Zhia lost her temper and tried to take her tebec to come back here. The stable hands thought she was stealing it, tied her up, and threw her into the paddock with the birds. She said that tebecs are attracted to raw flesh, so I assume they bit her and made her leg injury worse, though she said they didn't."

"Was this before or after you asked her to be your wife?" Father asked.

"Before, sir."

"And later you weren't able to see for yourself how badly she was injured?"

"It was dark, sir."

His face relaxed briefly, but his voice stayed hard. "So she was injured and in a paddock with tebecs and, one must assume, tebec manure."

"Yes, sir. After the performance at Knollwood, a man came up asking to paid for services rendered to Zhia. He said he was a doctor and had treated her for a festering wound."

Father cursed. "I can perhaps understand your decision to continue the tour without her. I cannot understand your not even trying to find her."

"She could have told me she needed a doctor. She could have told me the wound was going bad."

Father drew a long breath. "Tell me, Son, when the men from your tour objected to what they saw between you and Zhia, what did you say or do?"

I thought back. "I don't recall that I said or did much of anything, sir. The men were kind of all complaining at once, then Zhia came up and said she was the one who was in the wrong. She offered again to leave. She said it would be for my good." To my horror, I could feel tears gathering.

Father's rasping voice was gentle when he said, "It's easy to mistake knowing how to give pleasure to a woman with knowing women. No matter how skilled you think you are in bed, you don't know women at all, Son. Zhia kept waiting for you to put her first. When you didn't, she assumed—rightly, I would guess—that you cared less about her than about the tour." Again, he picked up the paper. "This is a letter from the mayor of Owlin's Run. It came with your full tour fee. In the letter, the mayor can't say enough good about your second performance there. He praises Zhia's singing and her piety, but more, he praises her humility and decency. He says—where is it?—he says, 'The kindness, courtesy, and generosity of that one Singer make up for much of what my townspeople have had to endure in the past from arrogant Singers to be able to enjoy their music. The men didn't even take advantage of any of the women, which showed uncommon sensitivity...uncommon for Singers, at least. The last song, the one the woman sang alone, was both a comfort and a beacon of hope to my people, who were reeling from a series of events unprecedented in my quiet town.'"

Again laying aside the letter, Father said, "Before the Festival you were wondering how your songs sound from somewhere other on than on stage. Now you know how your Singers are regarded from somewhere other than on stage. I must confess that, despite the praise it lavishes on Zhia, this letter was not pleasant reading. You may take it as a given that some tour practices, habits we've take for granted, are going to be changed. Tell me, whose idea it was it to restrain the men?"

"Zhia suggested it to me, sir. Tej had the same thought."

Father nodded. "And what is this song, this 'beacon of hope'? I've perused all the songs in the Hall repertoire and found nothing fitting that description."

"It's a song I heard in a dream, sir."

"In a dream?" He sounded startled.

"Yes, sir. I had no way to write it down, so I woke Zhia and sang it for her. In the morning she sang it for the others, but the range is such that, no matter where we started it, either the basses couldn't reach the high notes or the tenors couldn't reach the low notes. Volan suggested it be the song Zhia sang by herself."

"So because you needed Zhia's gift, even though knew she was injured, you woke her. Was this before or after you asked her to be your wife?"

"Before, sir. And no, we weren't in the same chamber; but right after I left her chamber to return to mine, I realized I wanted her to be my wife, so I went back and took care of that matter. I should have waited until we were back here to ask her."

"Since you say you repudiated her, you could have the opportunity to do so, if you still care about her. I trust you're prepared for the likelihood that she'll say 'no.'"

I was silent. I didn't know whether I cared about Zhia. I didn't know if I'd risk asking her again to be my wife. I didn't know if I'd care if, this time, she refused me.

I did know that I was weary, hungry, dirty, and thoroughly ashamed of myself, but probably less ashamed of me than my father was.

Father stood. "I want to hear Zhia sing that song. Tomorrow you're going to look for her. Don't come back until you find her."

"Yes, sir."

When I was at the door, he said, "By the way, Son, it's 'Father.'"

CHAPTER THIRTY-NINE

I HAD BEEN DREADING TELLING Mother that Zhia hadn't returned from the tour with me, but Lisia was ill with something all children get and most children survive; so the next morning when I told Mother I had to go back for something I'd forgotten in Knollwood, she simply nodded, told me to be careful, and went back to cooling Lisia's feverish face. I was asking for a tebec to be saddled when Father came into the stable and told me to take the cart and desdal, explaining that if Zhia's leg was so bad that she willingly went to a doctor, she shouldn't be riding a tebec. My pride was still blistered from things Father had said to me the day before; that I hadn't realized a cart would be a better choice didn't salve it at all.

"Where do you plan to go?" Father asked as I prepared to leave.

I shook my head. "I have no idea where Zhia might be—probably halfway to Hollan's Town, knowing her—but I thought I'd start looking in Knollwood, where I last saw her."

"That's wise. What was she wearing?"

"It wasn't her stage garb, so it was probably the reddish brown thing she wore to the Festival. If not that, the shirt and trousers she wore the day we left on tour. She doesn't have much choice."

"And her hair is now short, which isn't usual for men or women. Was I right about why she cut it, or don't you know?"

"She said she cut it to try to change her appearance. She was concerned that anyone at Festival who had seen the rock hit her could too easily identify her. That's also why she wasn't wearing the bandage on her head."

Father smiled. "I misjudged her. I'm glad." His smiled faded. "If you can't find Zhia in, say, ten days, come back. But I know you'll find her."

"How do you know that, Father? No one knows who she is. Unless they saw her in Owlin's Run, they won't even know she's a Singer. Even the stable hands there didn't recognize her when she wasn't on stage."

"Nia Diva wouldn't have given you a song without making sure there was someone to sing it. Zhia will sing it again, and not just for me."

As I urged the desdal into motion and headed for Knollwood, in my mind I could hear Zhia singing that song, and knew hope.

I didn't get as far as the first Quarter Rest before it was too dark to travel, but when I knew I'd be taking a cart, I'd added two tents to my provisions. The muted plop of raindrops on the fabric of a tent is much more calming than the sharper patter when they hit the roof of the shelters. Though I was anxious, I was able to sleep. The second day and night were the same. Since I wasn't first stopping at Owlin's Run, I reached Knollwood in the afternoon the third day after I left the Hall. I left the cart where we usually stabled the tebecs, and went in search of the doctor.

He was surprised to see me, but when he learned why I was there, his surprise became indignation. I didn't try to defend myself; I simply asked whether he'd seen or heard anything about Zhia since the day he treated her. His brusque "no" assured me only that I had taken as much of the doctor's time as I dared.

I went to a stall and had a cup of wine and a light meal while I tried to think. I was fairly certain Zhia didn't know the area around the Hall. The next town on a first-timer's tour, Ketridge, was a full day's tebec ride farther. Since every time Zhia had become upset or discouraged she had mentioned returning to the Hall, I couldn't imagine that she would go farther away from it, instead, and especially not on foot.

But, I reminded myself, what I imagined Zhia doing often fell short of reality. She continued to surprise me. Who would have expected a woman being misused by a band of raiders to have the presence of mind to scar their buttocks as a way of identifying them later? I wondered how many, if any, of the raiders who had attacked TTTW had borne Zhia's "mark".

Thinking about raiders made me realize I'd heard nothing about large-scale attacks since TTTW. Festival was usually a-buzz with horrifying accounts of raider activity, and small towns are notorious for rumor and gossip. Save for what was said in dealing with the raider who had posed as the doctor at Owlin's Run, at no time in any of the towns we'd been in on tour had I even heard the word mentioned. Was it possible that, rather than the numberless, widespread horde rumor and panic had made them out to be, the raiders had never been more than a small, widely-ranging band? Had fear and the lack of first-hand accounts of their methods magnified the popular perception of their threat?

Zhia had said that more than twenty raiders had used her. Others had been too drunk. If there had never been more than thirty or forty—I favored the lower number; were I the head of a band of raiders, I wouldn't tolerate half of my men being too drunk to function—how many remained since TTTW? Zhia had killed eight. The tebecs and swarmers had finished off nearly that many, and injured even more. Another one was now in prison in Owlin's Run. If my guessing was even close to right, more than half and possibly as many as two-thirds of the raiders were dead, badly hurt, or in prison. I had to assume there was a minimum number of attackers needed for their kind of attack to be successful.

I wondered if magistrates communicated with each other. Even if Osrum didn't have more information about recent raider attacks—why I thought he'd share it with a Singer, I don't know—he might be interested in hearing what I'd learned on tour. I reminded myself to try to see him when I returned to the Hall.

The clouds weren't yet gathering when I finished eating, so I decided to head for Owlin's Run. To get to where I'd left the cart, I had to pass the stage. I'd told Father I'd start looking where I'd last seen Zhia. I realized that the precise last place I'd seen Zhia had been on the stage at Knollwood. It wasn't a large structure, but I looked in all the rooms. There was no sign that anyone had used any of them since my tour had left.

I collected the cart and rattled through the town gate. I divided my attention between the road and the area on either side of it. Had Zhia tried to start walking back to the Hall after the doctor gave her something for pain, she may have fallen asleep out in the open. Of course, I reminded myself, that was several days ago. Had that happened, she might have been attacked by an animal and scattered bones might be all I found. But there was always the chance that she'd found some shelter, perhaps a cave or an abandoned hut. Feeling like an idiot, I realized the terrain was too flat for caves. The trees didn't grow thickly enough to hide a hut, though I noticed one tree that looked like someone had tried to chop it down so a hut could be built.

Still, when it began to be dark and the rain was approaching, I stopped for the night. I preferred a longer journey to taking a chance of overlooking some sign, either of Zhia's still being in the area or of her having traveled the route.

As I journeyed the next day, the land between Knollwood and Owlin's Run became even less conducive to concealment. Even without the added height a tebec offered, I could see long distances to either side. The road was empty; the land was empty; I felt empty. I didn't want to think about Zhia, but couldn't think of anything else.

Dare I again ask Zhia to be my wife? Were I in her place, I would regard that night in Owlin's Run as nothing more than a ploy on my part to get what I couldn't get otherwise—from Zhia, at least—or even as a ploy to get what the other men had agreed to do without that night. That I had so quickly repudiated her she could easily take as a sign that I had been dissatisfied with her... or that I had sobered up.

How drunk had I been that night? Drunk enough to forget the injury on her thigh? Drunk enough to be unaware of it when I was touching as much of her as I could? And how badly had her head hurt that night, if the tebecs had been picking at the gash on her forehead as well as at the puncture in her leg? I didn't have a lot of grounds for sneering at Henz; at least he didn't use injured women.

I was fairly certain I hadn't hurt Zhia. Her actions, her words, her glances the next morning had given no indication that she was in undue pain or that she had resented our joining.

I chuckled, remembering. If that was what she was like when she was unwilling…

My amusement quickly faded as the image of her callously using herself as a weapon against the raiders again filled my mind. The raiders had been drinking; I had been drinking: by now, Zhia must surely believe that she was appealing only when a man was incapable of reason or judgment.

Again I saw in my mind Zhia sitting in the big chair, cradling Lisia and singing her to sleep. Again I felt the welcoming softness of Zhia's bosom as she comforted me the night of the Festival. I remembered that there had been no words of judgment, only of solace.

Impatiently, I thrust the memories aside. I already had a mother; I wanted a wife.

Didn't I?

All the things that had sent me back to Zhia's chamber in Owlin's Run— her kindness, her thoughtfulness, her care, her patience with my moods and temper—were motherly traits. Except for the fact that she wanted me, something I was accustomed to encountering from women, had I seen any wifely traits in her?

But what was a wifely trait? Zhia was fertile; she had given birth. To judge from her leadership on TTTW when I was ill, she was fully capable of organizing a multitude of chores, and of doing more than her share of them. She knew how to sew. I assumed she could cook. But servants could handle all but the first of that list. Whenever I thought about being a father, I would tell myself, "Not yet", which meant only that I wanted to be free to continue having casual relationships without responsibilities, no matter what the consequences.

Were those casual relationships the reason I didn't know what I wanted in a wife?

Then I remembered Father's telling me that I really didn't know women at all. Even were that true, what would Father have said had I put Zhia first, as he had said I had failed to do, and angered the other men on the tour to the point that our subsequent performances were poor? Or even to the point that they left the tour? I hadn't told Father Volan had threatened to do just that.

But wasn't I now putting, not a tour, but my pride ahead of Zhia? Did the possibility of a poor performance or the chance that I might not end a tour looking like a wonderful tour leader justify my repudiating my wife? Hadn't I told her I would do whatever pleased her for the rest of her life? Did I think anything I had done since that night had pleased her much, if at all? Was it possible that the one the others on the tour had been avoiding criticizing after our second performance at Owlin's Run had been, not Zhia, but me?

And did it really matter whether those eight men approved of my dealings with my wife? Had I promised to please them? My duty to them was to get them to engagements on time, and to tell them what to sing. I had done that. I could have done those things without abandoning Zhia when she became an inconvenience, an embarrassment.

But I hadn't regarded Zhia as an inconvenience until Henz had started poking fun at me, using taunts that wouldn't ruffle even a child. In what way was "domesticated" a taunt? Didn't the word ultimately mean "useful"? Did I want to spend the rest of my life as a womanizer, bringing shame not only to my parents but also to my profession?

Father hadn't been the only one who had found the letter from the mayor of Owlin's Run unpleasant reading. Especially hard to take had been the mayor's statement that sensitivity was something uncommon to Singers. That the mayor hadn't found fault with Zhia's embarrassing antics on stage meant nothing. Zhia played people; as Father had once said, her honesty made her that much more able to manipulate others. But Father seemed to have admired what she had done. Father, the stickler for custom, hadn't condemned a series of actions that weren't customary for Singers.

Or perhaps Father had simply admired that Zhia's eccentric actions, her finely-calculated honesty, had squeezed a tour fee out of Owlin's Run, after all.

I couldn't believe that, not of Father and not of Zhia. Father's first concern had been for Zhia, not for how much money the tour had brought the Hall. And Zhia didn't know the mayor had sent the Hall the tour fee. I doubted she'd even stopped to consider what Father would say or do when he heard she gave away a tour fee to ease suffering, just as she'd never stopped to consider the value of the rimba when she needed them to save my life.

To say that Zhia hadn't known the value of the rimba would be quibbling. Somehow, I knew that, even if Zhia had known their cost and, more, had known she would have to bear the cost of replacing them, she would have sacrificed them. I would have liked to flatter myself that she had been willing to make so great a sacrifice for me, but I was sure that Zhia would have made just as great a sacrifice for any of the men on that tour, risking not only the rimba but also herself.

What had I risked for her? If I hadn't been able to face Henz's derision or the unease of the other men, what would I be able to face? "It's not fair" had been the men's main complaint; a childish one, now that I thought about it. Unwilling to risk being unpopular with company I would be keeping for only a few days, I had broken promises made for life and had made things unfair for Zhia, instead.

How much time had I spent worrying whether Zhia had the qualities I wanted in a wife without once wondering whether I had the qualities Zhia wanted in a husband? What qualities did I have? Zhia knew I functioned in bed. I didn't know whether I was capable of fathering a child.

For the first time, I wondered if there were any children who would never know their father, because he was a self-indulgent cad who'd never looked beyond one night of impulse, of reckless abandon, of irresponsible thrill-seeking. No matter what magistrates had ruled, had I, indeed, fathered children, I now accepted that I had a duty to them.

I thought of Lisia and the use to which her mother had been put. Though I had never raped a woman, I can't say I'd ever given a woman a second thought once I'd had my pleasure. Not until Eia, that is.

What kind of fool am I? I thought. How much time had I wasted panting after that woman? The only good thing that had come of my infatuation with Eia was that I'd been introduced to the idea of being true to one woman, even though that woman hadn't been true to me.

Being true, being faithful: likely that was one thing Zhia, or any woman, valued in a husband. Probably strength, as well; and tenderness, when it was called for. Patience, too; though I didn't think I could ever be as patient with Zhia as she was with me. Remembering Zhia's saying that when Pandir had died, she had been left without a home, I knew a husband should be a provider. As long as I was a Singer—as long as Zhia and I were Singers, I corrected myself, sternly—that wouldn't be a problem. As long as there were tours, Singers were provided for.

In thinking of qualities a husband should have I hadn't considered love, because I was no longer sure I knew what it meant. For too long, it had been for me just a word, part of a technique, a way to cajole a woman into giving me what I wanted. With Eia, what I had thought was love was lust. I was beginning to think that love wasn't so much a quality—a thing or a feeling—as a way of living, one that didn't necessarily have anything to do with intimacy.

Zhia's giving our tour fee to the doctor's widow and children was undeniably an act of love; but it had nothing to do with physical joining. Mother's taking responsibility for Lisia was an act of love, while the activity that had brought Lisia into being had not been an act of love. Taf's conduct toward Zhia on TTTW, though at first motivated by his desire to make her his wife, had been loving even after she turned him down. Most recently, Oluzh and Ingbir had shown the kind of genuine, loving concern for Zhia's welfare that Zhia invariably showed for mine...and I so often failed to show for hers.

How could I have refused to look for her when I learned why she'd missed the performance?

CHAPTER FORTY

My mood was darker than the gathering clouds when I reached Owlin's Town and stabled the desdal and cart. Pack over my shoulder, I started to walk through the town.

It was late enough that the shops were closed; like the other townspeople, the merchants would be at home: eating with their families, talking with their families, sharing with their families. Loving their families. No matter how urgent my errand, I wasn't about to start knocking on unfamiliar doors and bothering strangers.

I was resigned to having to postpone my inquiries until morning when a youth appeared at my elbow. I thought he asked me if I was looking for a lady, and frowned. I wondered if business had been that slow since the tour left. Pimps weren't usually so aggressive...or so young.

When I just kept walking, the youth spoke again. "Are you looking for the lady, sir?"

"The lady?" I echoed. Then I recognized the youth as the one who had asked the all-too-apt questions after our first performance. "Do you mean Zhia? Was she here? Did you see her?"

"Yes, sir. She's here now. I saw her going toward the stage."

I thanked him and hurried that direction.

Since the rain was close, I assumed Zhia would seek shelter in one of the side rooms, so I looked in them first. Those that weren't empty contained nothing out of the ordinary. I looked in the public conveniences. None was in use. I looked in the lush undergrowth behind the stage, where the murdered doctor had been found. She wasn't there, either, alive or dead.

I checked my impulse to panic, took a breath, and thought. The youth had said Zhia was going toward the stage. It was possible she hadn't actually gone to the stage, although there wasn't much else in this part of the town. I was sure that, had she left the town, I would have seen her.

I took the four stairs to the stage itself in two steps and looked across the nobodies' area. Nothing two-legged and limping moved anywhere I could see.

I turned toward the freshly-painted symbol of Nia Diva on the back wall, intending to ask the daemon for her help. She helped me without my asking. Directly under the symbol Zhia was crumpled on the floor. In the deepening shadows, with the reddish brown of her garment and her hair blending into the color of the wall, I hadn't seen her. I knelt beside her and touched her face. It was cold, as was the hand I next touched. Again I had to hold off panic. I stilled my own breathing and listened for the sound of hers, at the same time anxiously feeling her throat for a pulse. Though she was cold as death, she had a pulse. She was breathing.

My blankets were on the cart. I saw her packs in the shadows and opened them. The one that had held food was empty save for a small jug. In the other, the one with her personal possessions, I found a blanket. I wrapped it around her, then lay beside her and drew her into my arms to add my warmth.

The rain was beating an intricate rhythm on the stage roof when Zhia stirred. She didn't wake, but she shivered and snuggled closer to me. Trying to move only my arm, I reached into her pack. After some rummaging, I felt and pulled out the golden green garment, which I managed to spread over both of us. It didn't come close to covering my legs; but Zhia was fully covered. She sighed and again nestled into the warmth.

I may have dozed. It was quite dark when Zhia woke with a start and a gasp.

"It's all right," I said, quickly, before she could free herself from the blanket.

"What are you doing here?" she whispered.

"I've come to take you back to the Hall."

"What if I don't want to go back to the Hall?"

"You're going anyway. My instructions were, 'Don't come back until you find her.'"

I could hear laughter in her voice when she said, "You've found me. But your instructions said nothing about taking me back with you."

I'd have to mention that loophole to Father. Amused, I asked, "Since you're being so finicky, why are you on this stage? Didn't I tell you never to set foot on a stage again?"

"I didn't set foot. By the time I got here, I was crawling."

I stopped being amused. "Is your foot that bad, or does your leg hurt that much?"

"A little of both. Mostly, I'm just worn out. That's a long walk for someone who's pretty much one-legged."

"Are you saying no one offered you a ride?"

"Yes, but only because I saw no one between when I left Knollwood and when I arrived here."

I remembered the doctor at Knollwood saying he'd given her something for pain. "Did the medicine make you sleep?"

Her voice became hard. "It certainly did. I wish he'd told me it had that effect. I must have slept for two days."

I said nothing. If she'd spent more than one night in the rain, it was entirely possible she'd take a chill before we reached the Hall.

"Do you happen to have bandages with you?" Zhia continued. "The one on my leg should probably be changed."

"Yes, I actually thought to bring some; but I can't do that in the dark. Just a moment." I went to one of the storage rooms, where I'd seen a lamp. It had some oil in it from its last use. I had firestone in my pack. In the flickering light I uncovered Zhia's injured leg and unwrapped the bandage, which was none too clean. "Don't tell me you've been wearing the same bandage all this time," I pleaded.

She hesitated, then said, casually, "It got washed more than once."

I knew she didn't mean she had removed it and washed it; she meant it had been rained on, which was obviously the only washing she'd had for several days.

I cursed silently when I saw the wound. The tebecs had made the puncture much larger. It wasn't festering, but it wasn't healing, either. The jug in Zhia's food pack held only a few swallows of wine. I poured the wine over the raw flesh, then wrapped a clean bandage around it. She didn't argue when I looked at the gash on her forehead, as well. It had been enlarged by the cursed birds' beaks, but not as much, and was closing well.

Zhia said, approvingly, "Stay around me and you'll end up being a doctor as well as a Singer. Since I'm being a nuisance, could you get my right shoe off me?"

As had been the case after the attack in the hollow, the shoe was entirely too tight. I didn't have a knife that would cut the leather, so I had to worry the shoe loose. Zhia, who moaned twice, softly, during the ordeal, fainted before I succeeded in freeing her foot. I wrapped the coverings around her and took the now-empty jug to the stage cistern, where I rinsed it and filled it with water. When I got back, Zhia's eyes were open. I offered her a drink. She drained the jug. I went back to the cistern and also drank a jug of water before I refilled the jug and returned to Zhia.

"Do you want me to try to wrap your foot?" I asked.

"No. I think it would be better just to leave it alone."

I sat next to where she lay. "When did you run out of food?"

"A day ago, maybe two days. I wasn't trying to keep track of time. Mostly I was trying to keep going." After a moment, she said, "Would you hold me again? I'm still chilly."

I blew out the lamp and obeyed. We lay in silence. Zhia may have been relaxed; I wasn't. I kept waiting for the inevitable accusation. I'm not good at waiting, especially not for the inevitable. When I could wait no longer, I said, "Don't hold in your anger on my account. Go ahead and tell me how cruel it was for me to leave you in Knollwood. I might as well hear it from you; I've been chastising myself all day."

Zhia was silent so long I thought she had gone back to sleep. Finally, she said, gently, "It sounds like you've been punished enough. I doubt anything I could say to you would hurt as much as the things you've probably been telling yourself."

The mild answer made me lose my temper. "Are you trying to say you aren't angry? Because I'm not going to believe that."

Her voice ragged, Zhia said, "I was angry. I was furious. Didn't you believe me when I told you not to set me up as a touchstone, as some ideal? In fact, I was more than angry. I went to the room off stage where my pack was and got the ax." She felt me start. "You'd forgotten I had it, hadn't you? I was sitting, honing it—I didn't want to hurt you, just kill you—when the medicine took effect. I fell asleep holding the ax and, as I said, I slept for probably two days. By the time I woke, the tour was long gone, and I had no idea where. When I realized you hadn't just left me behind, you'd left me with no money, I got angry again. I went outside the town, found a tree, and hewed it until I was rid of my anger. Then, because I didn't trust myself to have the ax, I left it embedded in the tree and started walking. I shouldn't have left it; it would have been useful as a walking stick."

"It would have been useful for protection," I said, quietly.

Zhia snapped, "My protection seemed to be of no great concern to anyone, least of all to me." After a moment, she went on, "As for whether I'm still angry, I don't think so. My father used to say that anger is the least useful emotion. It's no help when something needs to be done; in fact, anger usually makes doing what's needful that much harder. Once what's needful is done, anger just prevents moving on to the next thing.

"I knew as soon as I saw your face that day I should have told you I needed a doctor, but you were already so wrapped up with tour details I didn't want to add to your concerns. I'm now of the opinion there would have been no right way to handle that situation."

I knew there would have been, but it was nothing Zhia could have arranged. Had I put her first, had I asked even one caring question, I'd have learned why she'd been delayed. Now that I thought about it, I should have known that a woman who had insisted on performing while bleeding from a puncture wound in her leg wouldn't have missed even part of a performance without a very good reason to do so.

Then I realized simply thinking that answer would leave Zhia believing she had erred.

"Using that ax on me would have been a mercy," I said, "because then I wouldn't have had to endure the flaying Father gave me when the tour returned without you. He made it very clear that I was in the wrong. He told me I had failed to put my wife first."

Zhia took a deep breath. "Pardon my asking, but I have to know. Did you tell me what Father said because you think he was right, or because you want me to know how misunderstood you were?"

Heatedly, I asked, "Didn't I tell you I spent all day chastising myself?"

"If you're going to lose your temper, we'll stop talking until you have it under control. That might take fifteen turns of the star wheel, but..."

"All right. So your question was whether I think Father was justified in scolding me?"

"Yes."

I couldn't seem to find words for my thoughts. Finally, I said, "I don't think what he said would have stung so badly had it been unjust. Not only could I not convince myself that he was wrong, today I thought of so much more he could have said, and didn't. He wasn't unjust; he was too kind. I took a long look at myself while I was coming here, and I didn't like what I saw. It was like cutting into a piece of fruit that looks sweet and juicy, but when the halves fall apart you see that it's rotten in the center, and all you can do is throw it out."

"That's true for fruit," Zhia said, softly. "Unlike fruit, you have a choice. You can be different. And I've already seen you changing, becoming more the man you want to be. For what comfort it is, we're all rotten in the center, but that doesn't mean we need to be thrown out, or that we just allow the rottenness to spread into what isn't yet tainted. There's a lot of sweetness and goodness in you. Don't let anyone, and certainly not yourself, tell you otherwise." She cleared her throat. "And since we're both avoiding the subject so strenuously, let me say that I wouldn't have agreed to be your wife had I not thought you would have been not only a good husband but also a good father for our children, had we been blessed with any."

"But you're not my wife; I repudiated you," I said, glumly.

"I know. That wasn't one of the better moments on TSTTW."

"TSTTW?"

"The Second Tour That Wasn't."

I had to laugh, but was serious when I said, "It wasn't a tour for you. I'm sorry."

"It wasn't your fault. I would have had to leave the tour anyway. As I found out, with my leg hurt, I can't get into a tebec saddle." Suddenly anxious, she asked, "You didn't bring a tebec for me to ride, did you?"

"No. I brought a desdal-drawn cart."

She nodded. "Even had I not been injured, I'm not sure the tour would have been very successful. I think it's time all Singers acknowledge that big changes are going to have be made. It's obvious to me, a woman who has twice toured with only men—or tried to tour, at least—that a female Singer can't simply be substituted for a male Singer. You can't put a tebec in a desdal's harness, not because a tebec isn't strong, or because it couldn't carry a rider or some other burden, but because it just doesn't fit. You're not going to cut off the tebec's wings or anything like that, because that's not what needs to be changed. Once the harness has been changed to fit a tebec, the tebec can do very much the same job as a desdal.

"Tours were designed by and for men. I think we're way past the point at which we can say let's go back to having only men as Singers. The more than twenty women at just our Hall who are even now being trained make that clear. I heard you toured with Noia. You haven't said anything about it, but was it the same as touring with only men?"

"Of course not," I said without thinking. Wondering how long it would be before the utter weariness that was revealed by Zhia's talkativeness caught up to her, I had been only half listening. Then I did think, and said, "No. Noia never complained, but I noticed that much on the tour—the Quarter Rests, the design of the tebec saddles, the accommodations on the stages, even the lyrics of some of the songs—made things less pleasant for her."

"I'm glad you said that," Zhia said. "Actually, I'm glad you said anything. You were quiet so long I thought I had bored you to sleep. Anyway, this isn't simply a case of 'male Singers have to be more accepting' or 'female Singers can't expect so much,' because that loses sight of why any of us are Singers. Ideally, we're all here for the same reason. We should all be willing to do whatever needs to be done to meet the goal of serving Nia Diva and sharing with others her gift of music. If it means, for example, that female Singers will tour only with other women, and that an entirely new tour system will need to be devised, then that's what should be done. Or if there's some way to adapt the present tour customs—not to favor women but at least to recognize that tebecs aren't desdals—then that's what should be done."

My comment, "There's a lot to what you've just said," was sincere. I added, "You may not be aware that other Halls have had women touring—at least, I think they've had women touring; they've had women being trained as Singers— far longer than ours. Father may want to talk to the Masters of other Halls to find out if they've had any of the problems you've been mentioning and, if so, what they did to address them. And I think you and Father ought to sit down and have a long talk when we return."

"Not until I've had a bath," she said, firmly. Then she yawned. "What do you know? I've bored myself to sleep."

I laughed and kissed her forehead. "Sleep well."

She was asleep almost at once.

Reflecting on what she'd said, it occurred to me that if raider activity had, indeed, stopped or even dramatically diminished, Quarter Rests could again be supplied and furnished so they were comfortable accommodations for Singers of either gender, which would go a long way toward making touring more pleasant for everyone.

Just before I fell asleep, I reminded myself to talk to Osrum.

Chapter Forty-One

ZHIA'S RETURN TO THE Hall should have marked the beginning of a long-overdue time of recovery, peace, and quietness. In time, she did recover. That peace and quiet were delayed wasn't entirely Zhia's fault.

Aplin was the first to share the blame. Actually, it was a continuation of something that had started earlier. I doubt that anyone from TSTTW but Zhia remembered what he'd said the day before we left. Both remembering and resenting his comments, Zhia was at her most unreasonably stubborn.

"Never," she said firmly when I tried to persuade her to let him examine both her foot and the wound in her thigh. "He said he didn't want to see me in his clinic, so I won't go there. It will do him good to see where his little pronouncements can lead." She gave Father the same answer, adding that Aplin knew where to find her, if he was at all concerned.

I'm certain Aplin knew Zhia had again been injured, for the others from TSTTW had been both free and lavish with details of the tour, especially the damaged stairs. I'm just as certain he was waiting for her to come to the clinic so he could turn her away.

The battle of wills, which not only quickly attracted the attention of Singer and servant alike but also—and even more quickly—divided the Hall into pro-Aplin and pro-Zhia factions, continued a good day and a half and would probably have gone on longer had not Mother asked Zhia to watch Lisia. The child was recovering from whatever she'd been ill with when TSTTW left and was just well enough to be fractious. Mother's patience was in tatters. As before, I had brought Zhia's supper to the nursery. Though the plate was empty, I was keeping Zhia company when, purely by chance, Aplin stopped in to check on Lisia.

Lisia was resting on Zhia's bosom, soothed and nearly asleep. Aplin knew better than to undo what Zhia had achieved, so he didn't examine the child. However, he planted himself in the doorway, so once the slumbering baby was in bed, Zhia was trapped. I decided I'd better remain to keep the altercation from becoming too loud.

"No," Zhia whispered before Aplin could even finish a sentence. "You said you didn't want to see me after the tour was over. Have it your way. Don't see me."

Aplin said, through clenched teeth, "I have a responsibility to this Hall."

"Then I'll leave the Hall and your responsibility concerning me will be discharged."

Still visibly controlling himself, Aplin asked, "Would you allow me to summon another doctor? Capis, perhaps?"

"The doctor from town? You don't share Father's opinion of him?" Zhia inquired.

"And that is?"

"I believe the phrase he used was 'squeamish fool.'"

Aplin's face relaxed in silent laughter. "He is, too. May we start afresh? First, allow me to say that I was not acting wisely or professionally when I addressed you slightingly in front of your tour group. Second, I must apologize for calling you an idiot woman. Mind you, that doesn't mean I've changed my opinion, only that I'm acknowledging I gave offense."

Then Zhia was grinning. "The truth can hurt."

"Third, may I request that you permit me to examine your injured leg and the foot that you probably reinjured. I will do so here and now, if you wish; or later, in your cubicle, if that is more to your liking. I'm sure you would prefer not to walk as far as the clinic."

"I walked from Knollwood to Owlin's Run."

The doctor shuddered. "Don't remind me."

"Here and now is not the place or time; I have a responsibility, too. My cubicle would be acceptable. When Mother returns, I'll meet you there."

From the look on Aplin's face as he left the nursery, it was clear that he believed that he had prevailed, which I knew was what Zhia wanted him to believe.

I was torn between amusement and admiration. Zhia had played people again, and had won, again. "I think you'll need a witness or a referee or something when you and Aplin clash later, so let me take this plate back to the kitchen now," I said.

She looked smug. "Thank you."

"Why the grin?" Father asked me as I passed their table on the way to the kitchen.

"The combatants in the great battle of wills seem to have achieved a truce."

"The word 'truce' is entirely too accurate," Father said. "Who gave in first?"

I lowered my voice. "Aplin did. He even apologized for calling Zhia an idiot woman. Of course, he made sure she knew he hadn't changed his opinion."

Then Father was grinning.

Mother, who had been preoccupied with Lisia and had missed much of the preceding days' drama, looked confused. "What's this about, Son?" she asked.

"I'll tell you later," Father said to her, chuckling, and patted her hand.

After I returned the plate, I stopped again at their table. "Father, I've been intending to mention that when we were getting ready to play our make-up performance at Owlin's Run, we warmed up with a song rather than with just scales and bits and pieces. It was amazing to see how quickly the nobodies managed to assemble when they thought they were missing something. We didn't have to delay the performance at all."

"A pre-performance number? That's something to think about," Father said.

"Do you know what I'd like you to think about?" Mother asked. "Having our Singers, all our Singers, do a performance for the people of our town. Our townspeople never get to hear what we do here. Only some are able to go to the Festival, where there they hear only the Singers from this Hall who are competing for Champion, and the Festival song. They don't hear all our Singers by themselves."

"So we'd do a tour to our town?" Father asked. "That's a very interesting idea. I'll think about it. For now, Isia, don't you think you should relieve Zhia?"

Immediately flustered and apologetic, Mother hurried to the nursery.

I followed. I could tell from Zhia's expression that she would have preferred to keep Aplin waiting longer. Since she had set the terms of the truce, she was honor-bound to keep them. She allowed me to help her to her cubicle. To her even greater chagrin, Aplin was waiting in the corridor. Zhia let go of my arm, edged past Aplin, and lit the lamp in her cubicle.

In the meager light, Zhia's reddish brown garment looked black. I knew that was what she'd been wearing the day she missed the performance at Knollwood. It was what she'd had on when I found her at Owlin's Run. I didn't remember seeing her in anything else since her return. I wondered if she'd taken it off for anything but sleeping. Though it was rumpled, it wasn't smelly. She'd probably been washing it in the evenings so it could dry during the night.

She'd been wearing it when Aplin had taken care of the gash in her head before TSTTW began. He stared at her for a moment before asking, "Is that the only clothes you have?"

Zhia replied, "If you're here to discuss fashion, you can leave."

Aplin pointed at the bed. "Sit down." Remembering their truce, he added, "Please."

When he first saw the large, half-healed injury on her leg, he said, sounding puzzled, "I heard this was a puncture wound."

"That's how it started out," Zhia confirmed.

Aplin waited for her to elaborate, but she didn't. A flush of anger rose in his face. He said, shortly, "This needs no attention."

Zhia folded the skirt of her garment back over legs as Aplin bent to look at her foot. I saw him stiffen as he probed and prodded it. Zhia stiffened, too.

A hiss escaped her.

Aplin looked up at her. "It hurts here?" He pressed. "And here?" He pressed another spot. "And here as well, I believe?"

Though Zhia's face was drawn with pain, she was glaring at him. "Yes."

Aplin straightened. "There's no damage beyond what you'd done to it before, and no damage I can repair. You've simply overused it. If you'll rest—by that I mean stay off it—for even three days, you'll probably find it won't hurt as much."

When it looked like he was going to leave without doing anything to ease the pain, I asked, "Aren't you going to give her something to make it feel better?"

"I won't unless she asks for it." He looked at Zhia, who looked away. "You know where to find me." He left, again convinced he'd prevailed. This time, he was right.

When I started to say something, Zhia glared at me, so I left, also.

I didn't see much of Zhia for a few days after that. A tour returned and, as before, Father had me do the paperwork. I understood why Gadig had been content to ignore that chore. It was time consuming and quite thankless. When I was finally done, Father asked my help in planning the tour to our own town that Mother had suggested. When we got to the point of choosing which songs to do, Father said he wanted to close the performance with my dream song.

"That seems to be the most appropriate place for it, Father; but how are our Singers going to learn it? There's no music for it."

"That's being taken care of," he replied. "In your dream, was it sung in parts?" I nodded. "All right. Neron ought to have it to where you can look at what he's done and advise him on the harmony. He knows you have the final word on it."

"But how…" I began, then figured out the answer. "Zhia sang the melody for him?"

Father nodded. He didn't see me cringe. I couldn't think of two less compatible people than Neron and Zhia. "His classroom or his office?" I asked.

"Classroom," Father said, and returned to planning the hometown tour.

I could hear the argument long before I reached the classroom where Neron taught Theory and Composition. Neither Neron nor Zhia was shouting, but their statements were very emphatic. As I approached, I heard Zhia say, "As I told you yesterday, that's not right, sir. That's not how it sounded."

Neron retorted, "You have no business telling me how to compose music. You've never taken a day of instruction from me. I listened to you only because the Master said I had to."

"Then why aren't you listening, sir? Who told you to rewrite Nia Diva's song?"

"Nia Diva?" he echoed, laughing derisively.

"Sir!" Zhia exclaimed, sounding appalled. "Do you refuse to acknowledge the one who gives us songs? Where do you think they come from?"

"From inside my head, woman." I was sure Neron was tapping his thinning black hair as he said that. "Now leave."

"No. If I leave, you'll ruin that song." There was a pause, then I again heard Zhia's voice, this time sounding alarmed. "Don't you dare lay a hand on me."

I ran the remaining distance, stopped at the open door just long enough to slow my breathing, and entered the classroom.

Neron, who was massive, had raised one of his plate-sized hands. His contorted face was purple. Zhia was holding a broom poised; whether to fend him off or to strike, I didn't know. I thought it better to act before they came to blows.

I stepped between them and said crisply, "Zhia, please sit down. Instructor Neron, Father said the music was ready for my review."

"It isn't," he said, peevishly. "It would have been ready had this nobody posing as a Singer left me alone."

"Had I left you alone, sir, the song you wrote wouldn't be the one the Master wants," Zhia snapped.

Zhia was right, but I knew Neron wouldn't relent as long as she was in the classroom. "Would you excuse us?" I said to her, hoping fervently she would simply comply.

Her mouth set in a tight line, she limped toward the door. She was almost in the corridor when Neron snarled, "And don't come back."

Zhia turned and drew a breath. Then she exhaled, slowly. "You have nobody's pity, sir," she said. "This nobody's." She went away.

I was fairly certain that anything I said right then would be wrong, so I picked up the score from Neron's desk and looked at it. I shook my head.

"Well?" Neron said.

"As are all of your compositions, this one is superb. This would be a wonderful Festival song," I said. I waited until his face had resumed its normal hue to say, "However, this isn't the song you were asked to arrange."

His face returned to purple so quickly I feared for his health. Hoping I sounded objective, I asked, "Had you given me the assignment of arranging the melody Zhia sang for you, and I turned in this composition, would you consider the assignment properly done?"

Clearly, he wanted to say "yes". His pride in his reputation as a strict instructor made him say, "No." Then he added, "I don't remember the melody as it was sung; but I won't have that woman in my classroom again."

"Then either I can sing the song, or I can write down the melody."

"Sing the song. Composition was never your strength," he said, rudely but truthfully.

The process took a while, because we had to start over; Neron didn't want to make changes to his version of the song. I would sing a phrase, sometimes more than once, and he would write it. When we were finally done, I verified that the melody line was accurate. Even though I'd asked Neron's permission before doing that, his face was again purpling when I headed for the classroom door. I would have preferred to stay while he worked on the arrangement, but, like many composers, he did better in solitude. I was concerned that, his pride having been hurt, Neron's next effort would be quite a bit less than his best.

Thinking both that I didn't want to have to reject another arrangement and that Neron might welcome a chance to shirk the assignment while appearing to do it, I said, "I don't think I told Father, so he couldn't tell you, that two men from my tour, Azham and Tej, improvised accompaniment on the day that song was first performed. I considered that quite a testimony to your skill as an instructor. You may want to listen to what they did."

The way he said, "I may do that," suggested I'd done the right thing.

Feeling much more confident about Neron's cooperation, I decided to tell Azham and Tej what had just gone on in case Neron asked to see them.

Figuring the percussion classroom was a good place to start looking for them, I closed the door to the Theory and Composition classroom and went that direction.

I saw Zhia coming slowly toward me. Watching her walk was painful. I greeted her and asked, "Did you notice if Tej or Azham is in the percussion classroom?"

"Neither of them is. It's time for the midday meal. They're probably in the dining hall."

The bell that marked mealtimes must have rung while I was singing for Neron. I hadn't heard it. "I'll look for them there," I said. "If you're going there, may I help you?"

"Yes, thank you; but I'll have to stop at Instructor Neron's classroom."

"Why are you going there when you know it'll only make him angry?"

"I left my broom."

"So you're sweeping again?"

"No, I'm using the broom to help me walk."

"There are other brooms."

"I know, but I've managed to get the end of the handle of that one roughened enough so it doesn't slip on the floor. You wouldn't think this floor is as slippery as it is." She sighed in frustration. "Believe it or not, I'm trying to rest my bad foot, but the hopping is very hard on my other foot. The broom handle has already rubbed my hands raw." She looked at them and grimaced.

I winced. "Those have to hurt."

"I don't know why I blister so easily. You'd think by now my hands would be tough as tree bark."

"Are you going to be able to eat?"

"My fingers are almost usable, I think." She curled them and made a face. "Gripping anything bigger than utensils isn't going to be pleasant."

Mildly, I said, "Maybe you should quit trying to hop around with a broom for support and just rest. I've heard some people do that by lying on a bed."

She grinned. "That's true; but Father needed me to sing your song for Instructor Neron. I wasn't about to invite the instructor into my cubicle."

"He's not about to invite you into his classroom. Why don't I fetch the broom?"

"No. Even if Instructor Neron hasn't yet gone to the dining hall, he can't forbid my presence in any part of this Hall. My training has been paid for. Besides, I imagine he'd appreciate my removing any reminders of this morning's unpleasantness."

Wondering, not for the first time, why I bothered trying to reason with Zhia, I helped her back to the Theory and Composition classroom. The door was closed. I knocked. There was no answer. I opened the door and stepped back so Zhia could go in.

At once I heard a sharp inhalation, then she said "Rois" in a tone of utter dismay.

I rushed into the classroom. Neron was slumped on his desk. His eyes were closed; he was motionless. I found no pulse, felt no breath. He appeared uninjured.

"I killed him," Zhia said in a tremulous voice.

"No, you didn't," I said, firmly. Contradicting myself, I added, "Don't say that to anyone else. Collect your broom and go sit in the corridor. I'm going to find Aplin."

Aplin was in the dining hall at a table with Father, Mother, and Lisia. Between bites of food, the child was babbling happily, winning smiles from everyone around her.

Quietly, I said, "Pardon my interrupting your meal, Aplin, but please come with me."

"Is it Zhia?" he asked, wearily.

"No," I said, rather too sharply. "Father, you'd better come, too." When we were outside the dining hall, I said, "Instructor Neron is dead."

"How?" Father and Aplin asked together.

"I didn't see anything that suggested a cause of death, so I guess he just died. Father, you know I'd gone to his classroom to look at the song he'd arranged. Zhia was there when I got there. They were at odds, because he'd written quite a good song, but not with the melody he was supposed to use. Zhia left, and I had to sing the song again because he said he didn't remember what it sounded like. When he had the melody down, I left. Zhia was in the corridor and coming toward the classroom, returning for something she'd forgotten. I knocked on the door and got no answer, so I assumed Instructor Neron was in the dining hall. Zhia went in and saw him. She called me. I saw him slumped over the desk, his eyes closed. I found no pulse; he wasn't breathing. I went to the dining hall to find you."

"Aplin?" Father said.

The doctor shook his head. "He might have suffered a stroke or his heart might have failed. Either is quite possible for a man of his size and temperament. However, I'm making no firm statements until I examine the body."

But when we reached the classroom, we saw an ax embedded in Neron's skull.

Father looked at me and asked, grimly, "Where's Zhia?"

CHAPTER FORTY-TWO

Not until then did I realize that she hadn't been in the corridor. "She was sitting just outside the door when I left," I stammered. Father went with me to look. Zhia wasn't there.

Father said to Aplin and me, "Touch nothing. Discuss nothing." He went out of the classroom and was gone for a short while. When he returned, he said, "I've sent someone to fetch the magistrate."

We were waiting in somber silence for Osrum to arrive when we heard shrieks in the corridor. "Now what?" Father exclaimed. Before he could leave the classroom, a serving woman burst in. "Sir!" she cried. "Someone has fallen down the stairs! I think she's dead!" Then she saw Neron's body, and fainted.

Aplin started toward the woman, but Father said, "Leave her. Come with me."

"Where are we going?" was Aplin's practical question. At Father's gesture, he revived the woman. She was still distraught, but we were able to learn that the site of the accident was the main stairway from the classroom area to the part of the Hall where most of the cubicles were, and also the corridor to the courtyard.

Since we knew the victim of the latest mishap was female, none of us was surprised to discover that the form sprawled on its back at the foot of the stairs was Zhia's. A broom lay nearby. Aplin knelt beside Zhia. "She's not dead; she's out cold. She's hurt."

"Don't change her position," Father warned. "The magistrate will have to see this."

"You don't think it was an accident?" I asked.

"We're discussing nothing until Osrum arrives," Father said.

It probably wasn't as long as it seemed before Osrum, flanked by the usual gray-clad functionaries, arrived. Father had asked Aplin to stay with Zhia, and had told the serving woman to remain there, also. He'd repeated the injunction to touch nothing. I'd returned to Neron's classroom. Father had gone to his office for the Hall records and then joined me in the classroom. That's where Osrum was escorted, presumably by the person who had been sent to summon him.

The sight of Neron's body saved Osrum asking several questions. By consulting the Hall records, Father was able to provide Osrum with Neron's full name.

"Who discovered the body?" Osrum asked.

"Zhia did, Your Honor," I replied. "If I may presume to volunteer information, I was only moments behind her."

Osrum nodded. "Why isn't Zhia present?"

Father said, "Because she's lying at the foot of a staircase, insensible, Your Honor."

"You don't make my job easy," Osrum remarked. "Rois, describe what you saw when you came into this room."

"I saw Zhia, Your Honor, stopped just inside the doorway. I saw Instructor Neron, slumped over his desk, his eyes closed. I checked him for pulse and breathing; he had neither. I saw no injuries. I was fairly certain he was dead. I know he didn't die from a split skull, because when I saw him, there was no ax embedded in it."

"Why were either of you in the classroom?"

I told Osrum everything I'd told Father, and the details Father hadn't heard, including how purple Neron's face had become during his confrontations with Zhia.

"Was that typical of their interaction?" Osrum asked.

"No, Your Honor. Zhia first met him only a day or so ago."

Father said, "You forgot, Son, she met him at the audition."

"No, Father. She missed the audition. Remember? She was in the clinic so Aplin could look at the gash she got in her forehead at Festival."

Osrum said, "I must ask that you confine your remarks to those addressed to me."

"Your pardon, Your Honor," I said, though I was glad I'd been able to remind him of the part Zhia played in returning Gadig to prison. "After the melody was written, Your Honor, I left the classroom. I saw Zhia coming toward the classroom. She'd returned for the broom she was using as support to help her get around." After repeating our conversation about her blisters, I said, "When I knocked on the door and there was no answer, Zhia went in. Just a moment later, I heard her gasp. She called my name. I went in and saw Instructor Neron, dead of no visible cause, Your Honor."

"So Neron was alone in the classroom when you left, and no one else was in the classroom with the victim until Zhia went in."

"To the best of my knowledge, yes, Your Honor. I wasn't yet far from the classroom when I saw Zhia. I would have seen if someone had gone in after I went out."

"Zhia's hands were empty when she was coming toward you in the corridor?"

"Yes, Your Honor. In fact, when we were talking about her blisters, she showed me both hands."

"You said they were raw."

"Yes, Your Honor."

"Isn't this the same woman about whom I have previously heard testimony that on tour she was chopping wood with badly blistered hands?"

"Yes, Your Honor," I said, feeling ill.

"What did you do after you examined the body?"

"Your Honor, I told Zhia to collect her broom and sit in the corridor. That's where she was when I went to the dining hall to summon the Hall doctor and Father."

"Where is the doctor?" Osrum asked.

Father said, "I asked him to remain with Zhia, Your Honor."

Osrum asked me, "Why did you tell Zhia to stay behind?"

"Because, Your Honor, the foot that was giving her trouble when you were looking into the charges against the former Master of this Hall hasn't healed properly," I replied. "She limps all the time. Despite that, only a handful of days ago, she walked from Knollwood to Owlin's Run, which aggravated the existing damage so badly that by the time she got to Owlin's Run she could only crawl. Even now, she has to use a broom to keep from putting any weight on that foot."

"The Hall doctor has re-examined her foot?"

"Yes, Your Honor," I said, grateful that the battle of wills wasn't still raging.

"Do you know what he found?"

"Yes, Your Honor, I was present when he told Zhia that there was no new damage, that the old damage couldn't be repaired, and that she should stay off her foot."

Osrum was silent for a moment before saying, "So the last place you saw Zhia after you saw the victim, who you say was dead from no visible cause, was outside this classroom."

"Yes, Your Honor."

"Tell me why I shouldn't draw the obvious conclusion: that a woman who is known to have killed using an ax—granted, the victims were raiders and self-defense has been established—isn't the person who planted an ax in Instructor Neron's skull."

"Why would Zhia do that to a man she and I already knew was dead, Your Honor?"

Osrum appeared to be thinking. Then he said, "Show me where Zhia is."

In reply to his question whether anyone had moved Zhia, Aplin said, sharply, "No, Your Honor. And I'd like it to be noted that failing to treat an injured person is counter to the requirements of my profession."

"Your complaint is noted," Osrum said, evenly.

The serving woman's testimony was unhelpful. She had found Zhia at the foot of the stairs. She hadn't seen Zhia fall, but that must have been what happened. The poor woman had already fallen so many times hopping around with just that broom for support…

Osrum interrupted the spate of indignation to ask whether the serving woman had seen anyone else in the area. After a mercifully brief "no", she added that most people were eating when the mishap occurred.

"So was I," was Osrum's comment. "You're dismissed. Speak of this to no one else." He had the functionaries examine the steps. There was nothing on them that might have caused Zhia to fall. There was no blood on them, either, even though there was plainly blood under Zhia's head. "Examine her," he said to Aplin.

"Here? Your Honor," he added, hastily.

"Might I a suggest a curtain of some sort?" Father said. When Osrum assented, Father sent me to get some blankets. The functionaries, Father, and I held the blankets. Osrum remained inside the enclosure with Aplin.

Zhia's reddish brown garment was more rumpled than I'd ever seen it, but at least it was clean. The significance of the thought hit me. "Your Honor," I said, "when Zhia used an ax on the raiders, her clothes, face, and hair were spattered with blood and bits of bone, flesh, and brain. I'm sure you've noticed that her clothes, face, and hair are clean."

Aplin had been working to get the garment off Zhia. He handed it to Osrum, who looked at it closely before setting it aside. I could see Aplin frowning as he checked Zhia, limb by limb, and ran questing fingers over her pelvis, ribs, and collar bones. With Osrum's help, he turned her over and repeated the process. "Something's not right," he muttered.

"And that is?" Osrum prompted.

"If she fell down those stairs, she'd be bruised, at the least. Despite the damage you see, Your Honor, I can assure you she has no new injuries or bruises." When Aplin ran his fingers slowly over her head, his hands suddenly stopped moving. "But there's a lump here the size of a tebec egg." He finished examining her skull. "That's the only damage I find. She didn't fall down stairs, Your Honor. She was already at the foot of them when someone knocked her senseless."

"Are you certain?" Osrum asked.

"Quite certain, Your Honor."

"May I cover her now?" I asked, angry that she was exposed to so many pairs of uncaring eyes. When Osrum nodded, I wrapped the blanket I was holding around her unmoving form.

"More to the point, may I transport her to the clinic?" Aplin asked.

The functionaries lifted Zhia onto another blanket. They took two corners and Father and I took the other two. Aplin kept cautioning us not to jostle her and bemoaning that he'd moved her without determining the extent of her injuries. When she was settled on a bed, Father, Osrum, the functionaries, and I headed for Father's office.

"May I have a meal sent up for you?" Father asked Osrum. He accepted with thanks.

"Can we make that two meals?" I said, plaintively. "I haven't eaten."

Father said, "Let's go to the dining hall. It should be fairly empty by now."

It was. Father chose a table farthest from the kitchen. The functionaries sat at a table nearby.

Father said, "May I summarize what little we know? One, Neron is dead, apparently of a stroke or heart failure. Two, someone who either didn't know he was dead or who hoped to lay blame for his death on an obvious suspect cleft his skull with an ax. Three, Zhia, the obvious suspect, was attacked in a way that suggests she fell down a flight of stairs." He shook his head. "It makes no sense. I said we know little. I should have said we know nothing."

"Why those stairs, Father?" I asked, after a while. "Unless the whole thing was an attempt to make it look like Zhia killed Instructor Neron, and then fell down the stairs while trying to get away."

"At the end of the classroom corridor is an outside door," Father reminded me.

"Then maybe it was supposed to look like she was trying to go to her cubicle, only the person who attacked her didn't know her cubicle isn't in that area."

"But why?" Father exclaimed. "That's what makes no sense. Why implicate Zhia? And why attack her? As you said—may I now be less formal? Thank you—as you said, Osrum, Zhia's guilt is the obvious conclusion. As far as I'm concerned, attacking her casts doubt on her guilt."

"Knowing who is behind today's events would shed light on why. I wonder if she saw who struck her," Osrum said, as Father poured more wine for him. He thanked Father, and added, "It would be good to know who was struck first, Neron or Zhia."

Father added, "And whether the same weapon was used on both. Son, would you say there was enough time while you were coming to the dining hall and returning to the classroom for someone to get Zhia away from the classroom, attack her, and return to leave the incriminating weapon in Neron's skull?"

Before I could answer, Osrum asked, "Why do you think Zhia was struck first?"

"Because I can't imagine Zhia simply sitting in the corridor while someone with an ax entered the classroom. Had she been struck where she was sitting, there would have been a trail of blood between there and the foot of the stairs. Also to be considered are the facts that dragging a person Zhia's size that far would be difficult, and that Aplin said she hadn't fallen down the stairs. I imagine there would also have been some visible damage had she been dragged rather than pushed down them.

"I think she walked from the classroom to the foot of the stairs, perhaps thinking she was responding to a summons from one of us. For simplicity's sake, let's assume there was only one weapon, and that Zhia was struck with the blunt end of the ax, of course. Osrum, you might want to look more closely at that ax before anything happens to it."

Osrum nodded, and sent one of the functionaries. "Don't touch the head of the ax," he instructed.

Father continued, "Then the assailant returned to the classroom, left the misleading evidence, and went away before Rois, Aplin, and I got there."

"Might we want to look in today's laundry before everything is washed?" I asked.

Again, Osrum nodded. Father summoned a servant and asked her to guide the other functionary to the laundry area.

"While your idea of what happened has merit, what it fails to answer is where the ax was before Zhia was struck; if, indeed, she was struck with the same weapon," Osrum said to Father. "As you said, Zhia wouldn't simply sit while someone with an ax entered the classroom. Neither can I imagine her leaving the classroom corridor with someone holding an ax—I'm assuming she would've had to go willingly, or someone would have heard her resisting—or going down stairs toward someone holding an ax."

"Maybe there were two people," I said, heavily.

Osrum regarded me for a moment before remarking, "I considered that, also."

Before we could begin another discussion that would likely prove as fruitless as those we'd already had, the first functionary returned with the ax. He'd wrapped it in blank composition paper. I was glad he'd used neither the pages with Neron's last song nor the ones with the melody of my dream song.

Osrum pushed his plate aside so the ax could be placed in front of him. Father averted his eyes as Osrum unwrapped the gory weapon. After a close examination he said, "I would say the blunt end has also been used." He pointed, and I saw finger length, reddish brown hairs stuck to drying blood.

"Now what do we do?" Father asked when the ax was again wrapped in paper.

"I'm going to finish my meal," was Osrum's composed reply as he replaced the ax with his plate.

Before he was done eating, the second functionary returned. He shook his head when Osrum looked at question at him. Osrum said, "Apparently whoever did this was clever enough not to put blood-spattered clothing in the laundry. At this point, I've done all I can. I accept that Instructor Neron was dead before someone tried to make it look like he was murdered. I accept that, though the evidence suggests her involvement, Zhia isn't the one who left the ax in the classroom. She certainly didn't use it on herself. Without more information, I'm going to return to my chambers."

"Thank you for your help," Father said, and rose to escort him out. I rose also, intending to go to the clinic. Father had other plans for me. "Please fetch a sheet and some stable hands and remove the body from the classroom. Take it to the stable. I'll send a messenger to Neron's widow. We'll lay him to rest this afternoon."

I wanted to protest, but Father looked so harried I simply obeyed. Then I went back to the classroom to get Neron's last song and the page with the melody, which I took to Father's office. He was giving instructions to the messenger, so I waited. When the man was gone, I set the pages in front of Father. He looked at Neron's last composition, then asked me to gather a group of Singers and have them learn the song so it could be sung when Neron was laid to rest. (Impossible as that sounds to a non-Singer, Singers do that kind of thing all the time.)

To make things easier for myself, I chose to be one of those singing the new piece, so I was, of course, present when Neron was laid to rest. The song was well received. Father agreed with me that it would be a good Festival song, but said he would rather present it during our hometown tour. Not until Neron's weeping family and the dry-eyed Singers were gathered did I realize that Father had wanted that song included so the Singers could say something complimentary about the otherwise unlamented instructor.

Father had to sit for a while and console Neron's widow. Then her children, the oldest of whom was almost of an age to come to the Hall, took her home.

Father breathed a sigh of relief. After some perusing of the Hall records, he told me to take the melody page to Ganit, an older Singer skilled in composition, and ask him to arrange it. I had sense enough to find Tej and Azham and take them with me so they could at least tell Ganit what they had done on TSTTW.

By then it was evening. I knew Aplin wouldn't let me into the clinic. I moped through supper. I won't try to deny that I did my best to drown my anxiety. Wine only made me more anxious.

Mercifully, Father let me sleep off my overindulgence. As soon as I had eaten—the midday meal, not breakfast—I headed for the clinic. To avoid passing Father's office, I went down the main stairway. I groaned when I heard a familiar commotion in the courtyard. Another tour had returned. Father also heard the commotion, and came out of his office to welcome the returned Singers, so I couldn't get away even for a moment.

I spent the rest of that day and part of the next doing paperwork. The last two tours returned, one the evening of the second day after Zhia was attacked, the other in the afternoon of the next day. The paperwork and the myriad other after-tour duties weren't done until the afternoon of the fifth day that Zhia had been in the clinic.

I took the paperwork to Father's office, intending to tell him I was doing nothing else until I had seen Zhia. As soon as he saw me, he said, "Aplin says Zhia is awake."

Aplin stepped out of the way when I ran through the outer room of the clinic, but followed me when I went to the bed where Zhia lay, eyes dull, face as pale as the bandages that swathed her head.

Her blistered palms had also been bandaged. I lifted her hands and gently kissed her fingers.

Zhia smiled—the tiny upturn of the corners of her mouth was supposed to be a smile, at least—and asked, weakly, "What hit me?"

Chapter Forty-Three

I THOUGHT FAST. THERE WAS no doubt in my mind that she wasn't strong enough for the truth. "It looked like you fell down the stairs," I said, which was true enough.

Zhia tried to shake her head. She moaned, then said, "No. I remember walking down the stairs." Her eyes closed for a moment. "Aplin won't tell me how long I've been here."

Aplin signaled "no". I wanted to argue, but I said, "That's not important now. What's important is that soon you'll be better. I should go so you can rest."

"Stay with me a while," she said, reaching toward me.

Aplin nodded and brought a chair. I sat next to the bed and took Zhia's outstretched hand. "How do you feel?" I asked, and regretted the question when I saw tears slide down her cheeks.

Aplin was already pouring something into a cup. I helped him lift Zhia's head so she could drink it. She made a face. "It's not supposed to taste good," Aplin informed her as we lowered her head. We were being careful; but Zhia's hand clenched in mine and she drew a sharp, short breath. It wasn't long before her hand relaxed and her eyelids first drooped, then closed. Aplin motioned for me to follow him to the outer room, which served as a kind of office. I guess I wasn't hiding my distress very well; he pushed me into a chair before sinking into another one.

He said, "This isn't quite what I had in mind when I told Zhia to stay off her bad foot. Darl will have his laugh. The good news, beyond the fact that she's awake, is that she hasn't lost her memory and that she shows no sign of either double vision or paralysis. The less good news is that I have no idea how long it will be before she can leave the clinic. I have to be honest with you, Rois; as hard as she was hit, I didn't expect her to live five days. I certainly didn't expect her to regain her senses."

"If you'd been able to bring her here right away," I began, finding it hard to talk.

"It would have made no difference," he said, quietly but firmly. "All I've been able to do is change the dressing on her head."

"We didn't hurt her carrying her?"

"No, Rois. Whoever and whatever struck her did all the damage that was done."

I stared a moment before I remembered that Aplin had already been in the clinic when we discovered the answer to "whatever". I said, "What struck her was the blunt end of the ax that was left with Neron."

Aplin wilted into his chair. "An ax? That makes her regaining her senses even more astonishing. You saw evidence?"

I nodded. "I saw blood and hair that looked like Zhia's on the blunt end. It must have looked like Zhia's to the magistrate, too." I made some sound of exasperation and stood. "I suppose the magistrate will want to know she's awake. I'll send a messenger."

"Let me recommend you take the message yourself," Aplin said. "And don't tell anyone else she woke up."

"Why?"

"Because in the past five days, when I wasn't praying and worrying, I was thinking. I think the attacker was a Singer, and not just any Singer, but someone she knew and trusted. Perhaps someone she'd toured with."

I sat down again without willing to. Aplin's words struck me as true. The attacker being someone Zhia knew from a tour answered a lot of questions, but raised even more. Besides me, only Taf had survived TTTW. Obviously, I hadn't harmed Zhia. The only reason I could think of for Taf's hurting Zhia would be that she had refused to be his wife. But Noia was now his wife, and he seemed entirely content.

Though I knew that several of the men from TSTTW had been irritated with Zhia at various times in the few days she had stayed with the tour, I remembered no incident, no exchange of words that suggested enough aggravation to lead to an attempt on her life. The men had all had many days on tour without her presence, and nearly as many days between when the tour returned and when Zhia was attacked. I would have considered that more than enough time for any lingering annoyance to fade. Clearly, I was wrong.

"She asked me what hit her, not who hit her," I said slowly. "She may know who."

Aplin was nodding. "Which is why I suggest you tell no one that she's able to communicate."

"Did you make the same suggestion to Father?"

"Yes."

I left the clinic, then went back in. "Now that she's regained her senses, will she continue to recover?"

After starting to speak several times and stopping before he'd said more than a word or two, Aplin finally said, "I wish I could give you the assurance you want. For what comfort it is, I will say I'm more hopeful."

I nodded. "That helps. Thank you."

"Rois, if you can't sleep, see me. I'll give you something. Don't get drunk again."

Wondering who told Aplin I'd been drunk, I went to Father's office to let him know I was going into town to see Osrum. I must have looked distraught; Father asked if I was all right, then asked if I wanted him to accompany me.

"I'm all right," I lied. "The walk will do me good. I need time to think."

Father's expression told me he knew I was lying. "You aren't planning to linger in town, are you?"

"No, Father. There's no longer any reason for me to linger in town. But if I want to see Osrum, I'd better go."

Telling Father I wanted to think hadn't been a lie. I'd been so busy since the day—indeed, the moment—Zhia had been attacked, I hadn't had time to reflect... or to pray.

Prayer had never before been very important to me. When I wasn't regarding it as ultimately futile bargaining with capricious daemons—the sort of thing I did with Darl before tours—I was scorning it as a "can't hurt; might help" type of exercise, the real purpose of which was to impress other people. Since I met Zhia, I had found myself invoking Nia Diva rather than using the name as an expletive, but still with little actual belief behind the words.

Now that I needed to believe there was a power beyond mine, though not necessarily one that cared about anything that mattered to me, I found myself regretting the self-sufficient attitude I had regarded as sophistication, an attitude I finally realized was formed of pride and distrust. I had thought it evidence of strength to need and trust no one, to rely on myself, to look with amusement on the claims others imagined they had on me for affection and consideration. Then I had met Zhia, and I came to understand that the very things I had considered admirable in myself were what made her so aggravating.

When had I stopped loathing her and started loving her? She was far from perfect. She both exasperated and elated me. She was unyielding and unreasonable, and she was amiable and wise. She was comely, but certainly no beauty. But when I first saw her cradling Lisia, I knew I had never seen anyone more beautiful.

Though she'd been bruised and bloodied and terrible that day in the hollow, she'd also been beautiful, because she'd risked her life for me. Was that when I'd first known that, even if I needed and trusted no one else, I needed and trusted her? Would I have let down my guard had I known that if I allowed her to see where I was weak, I had to take the same chance with others?

Zhia's life was at stake; I needed and had to trust Aplin. I was old enough that I could now admit I also needed and trusted Father and Mother. Since I was walking into town to see Osrum, I couldn't deny that I needed and, possibly, trusted him, as well.

If I could admit my need for those five people, why balk at admitting my need for the Unknown?

Was there an Unknown? I still wasn't sure. I'd seen things for which I not only had no reasonable explanation, I had no explanation at all. I'd told Osrum it was a miracle that the bodies of the Singers from TTTW hadn't decayed. Why had I said "miracle" if I didn't believe in the Unknown, or in Nia Diva, Darl, Henia, and the other daemons? Before I tried praying, I would do well to decide whether I believed anyone was listening.

If I prayed that Zhia would recover and she didn't, would that prove I'd been a fool to pray? If I prayed and she did recover, would I acknowledge that my prayer had been answered? I knew that if I didn't pray but Zhia recovered, I would be quick to thank Aplin for his part in her return to health. But if I didn't pray and Zhia didn't recover, would I feel guilty for failing to do everything possible for her? Would I dare to blame the Unknown for not answering a prayer I hadn't prayed?

Was I willing to allow that "no" might be an answer?

How demanding was I going to be? I knew that none of us, Zhia included, should have survived the attack in the hollow. Zhia shouldn't have been alive to be struck by an ax; the slashed blood vessel she had suffered when Dolin, Rork, and Chaz tried to kidnap Mother should have killed her. Couldn't I admit that prayers—prayers I hadn't even known I'd prayed—had been answered?

Was I willing to put aside both my sophistication and the scorn for the daemons I'd learned both at home and at the Hall, admit I was powerless to do anything for Zhia, and come empty, a beggar, to the Unknown?

If I weren't empty, how could I ask to be filled?

My prayer, if it could be called that, wasn't eloquent. I'm not even sure it was an expression of trust. Even to me, it sounded desperate. How could the Unknown be anything but offended by my saying, "I've tried everything but you"? If the Unknown took offense, I could only pray the punishment would fall on me, not on Zhia. Zhia had been punished enough.

I remembered to thank the Unknown that Osrum had accepted Zhia's innocence in Neron's death. He hadn't hesitated to put Zhia in the common prison when she'd had an injured arm. I doubted he would have spared her for the sake of a cracked skull.

The concern on Osrum's face when I was shown into the cold, black chamber made me wonder whether I had misjudged him. Then he sent for wine; and I realized his concern was for me. I must have looked quite distressed. I certainly felt distressed.

"Zhia is awake?" he asked, filling my cup.

I was startled; wine sloshed. "Yes, Your Honor. How…"

"This is not a hearing, Rois; we can be informal."

"Thank you. How did you know she's awake?"

"Because you came in person. Had she died, you could have sent a messenger. Has she spoken?"

"She asked what hit her."

"What hit her? Not who?" he asked.

"Yes. She also said that she walked down the stairs. Then Aplin gave her something for pain and she fell asleep."

Osrum nodded. "Who besides you, Aplin, and—I assume—your father knows she's awake?"

"I'm not aware of anyone else."

"Good. I'll go to the Hall with you and find out if she can answer questions."

I curbed my impulse to exclaim "No!", and said, "You're welcome at the Hall any time; but you may not be able to question Zhia today. If what Aplin gave her is the same medicine a doctor in Knollwood gave her, she may sleep for two days."

"I hadn't thought of that. Then I'll send some soldiers to guard her until she wakens."

"If you think that's needful; but won't that tell everyone that she's already been awake?"

"Not if they remain in the clinic. She is in the clinic, is she not?" When I nodded, he went on, "The soldiers will bring their own provisions so no one can slip something into their food or drink."

I know I was staring. "Do you believe the danger is that great?"

"Yes," he said, emphatically, "and not only because of this latest attack on Zhia. I've had a letter from the magistrate of Owlin's Run with the details of the capture of a raider there. There have now been raiders in our town, and at least one in Owlin's Run."

I remembered what I'd wanted to discuss with Osrum. "On the subject of raiders, at the Festival, there's usually a lot of talk about the most recent raider activity. This Festival, I heard no talk on that subject. Do you know, or is there a way you could find out, whether there has been an overall drop in the number of attacks?"

"I could find out. I gather there's more behind the question than what you've said."

"Yes, there is. If the magistrate of Owlin's Run told you everything he learned when the raider was captured, then you know some of Zhia's history. She didn't tell the magistrate that there were perhaps only thirty or forty raiders in the band that... that held her captive." I went on to tell him the reasoning which led me to believe the raiders were all but finished as a large-scale threat.

"An end to the raiders is something I, for one, have long desired. I can assure you I'll make inquiries," Osrum said when I finished. "Of course, I won't have replies for many days. In the meantime, soldiers will be guarding Zhia. Send me word by one of them when she next wakens."

"I will. May I ask that you delay just a bit in sending the soldiers so I can warn Aplin they're coming?"

"That's a good thought. Last time some of my men showed up in the clinic, they took Zhia away. I'd hate to upset the good doctor needlessly."

The supper bell was ringing when I reached the Hall. I told Aplin what Osrum would be doing and why, relayed the request that Osrum be notified when Zhia woke, checked on Zhia—who, as I expected, was asleep—and went to the dining hall. I sat with Father, Mother, and Lisia. After Mother took Lisia away for her bath, I quietly told Father of Osrum's plans.

"Had I been there, I would have asked him to reconsider," Father said, "but it never occurred to me that he might decide that Zhia needed protection, so I gave you no instructions. You did the right thing in asking for a delay so Aplin could be advised."

Since I couldn't quite decide if Father was pleased or annoyed with me, I changed the subject. "How much are you going to need me in the next few days, Father?"

"As much as usual, I should think. Why?"

"I'd like to stay in the clinic with Zhia."

Father gave me a measuring look. "In what capacity, Son? You're not her husband. It would hardly be proper. Besides, if there were another attempt on Zhia's life, you might interfere with the soldiers, or even give them someone else to protect." I'm sure I looked mutinous, for Father added, "I'm worried about her, too, Son. Neither of us can give Aplin the skill to repair the injury she suffered, or to speed her healing. All we can do is be patient. And pray."

Resignedly, I asked, "So what do you need me to do next?"

"Nothing else today. You look like extra sleep wouldn't hurt you at all. Tomorrow, check with Ganit and find out how your dream song is coming. If or when it's done, copies will have to be made of it. Neron's last composition needs to go to the copyists, as well, so my Singers can start learning it before our hometown tour. Speaking of which, that won't be until Zhia can sing with us."

In a haze of weariness and discouragement, I went to my cubicle. While I knew and appreciated that Father was trying to give me hope, I also knew that if Zhia had run out of miracles, we'd still give a hometown tour, and we'd close with my dream song.

Sentimentality has no place on stage; but I knew that if Zhia didn't recover, I'd never sing my dream song again.

CHAPTER FORTY-FOUR

GANIT DID HAVE THE arrangement ready for my hearing and approval. Though what he'd written used much of what Tej and Azham had worked out at Owlin's Run, it didn't sound quite right. He and I labored over it most of the morning, until it was more like what I remembered from my dream. Assuring me the copyists would have it as soon as the score was readable, he went away. I found Neron's composition and took it to the copyists, and told them a second piece would soon be coming. They grumbled, and even more when they learned the first piece was from Neron, who had been fond of displaying his technical prowess. Most of them had heard the song when Neron was laid to rest and, like nearly everyone else who heard it, had recognized it as one of Neron's best works. They were glad to see that it was also one of his least complicated.

That chore done, I went to the clinic. I'd already forgotten Osrum's plan to send soldiers and so was startled to see six grim-faced men: two at the main door into the clinic, two at the door into the area where Zhia was, and two at the door that opened on the grassy area.

Zhia was asleep.

"I hope you had nothing to do with the guards being here," Aplin said to me in a low voice. When I assured him they were Osrum's idea, he added, "I need to have some kind of framework built so I can put curtains around Zhia's bed. Patients' modesty has never been a big concern of mine; but that's because in the past I didn't have female patients. And having the guards here makes for a different situation entirely."

I talked with him a little longer about the curtain idea, finding out approximately what size he'd like the framework to be, then, after a hurried midday meal, went to Father's office to tell him the copying was in progress. I also informed him I was going into town and inquired whether he needed any errands run.

"Buy more paper," he said as he gave me money. "Check with your mother, as well."

Mother had number of errands she said I could do for her. I got paper and made a list, then had the desdal harnessed to the cart. Watching the stable hands work made me remember Henz's comment about my being on a leash. I wondered how soon I'd be able to get back into the harness I'd so briefly worn.

As the cart jostled toward town, it occurred to me to wonder whether Zhia would again accept my request that she be my wife. I could hardly blame her if she refused me. I hadn't exactly proven to be steadfast. But if she did accept me again, would I be willing to tour without her, or to have her tour without me? I wondered whether Taf had considered that question. Granted, he had a full turn of the star wheel before Noia would again be touring; but he'd be a fool not to have given the matter some thought. I toyed with the idea of asking him when I got back from town, then decided I'd better wait until I knew whether I had a wife.

Once again, I wondered whether the custom of having only men as Singers hadn't been founded on something more than scorn for women. Accommodations at the Halls for couples, scheduling tours that were respectful of the needs of husbands and wives, and female Singers with child (and, of course, bearing children) were just some of the concerns Halls traditionally hadn't had to deal with. Would the children live at the Halls? Would children tour with their parents? At the moment, the answer to that question was certainly "no". Quarter Rests were scarcely usable by adults; they were certainly no place for children.

I was reflecting that Halls weren't much better when I realized that children who, like Lisia, knew no other life would find a Hall as good a place to grow up as any. I wondered whether Lisia would be a Singer when she was older. Whoever her father was, he had been a Singer, and her mother, whoever she was, was training to be one. I wondered whether Mother and Father would still be alive when Lisia was old enough to begin training, and whether her name would be entered into Hall records as "Lisia Isianrobil". Then I wondered what would happen to Lisia should my parents die while she was still young.

I knew the answer to that problem, at least, almost before it occurred to me. Should Father and Mother not live until Lisia was old enough to take care of herself, I (I was, of course, thinking "Zhia and I") would care for her.

I laughed, inviting looks of surprise from the people with whom I was now sharing the road. I didn't even know whether Zhia would again be willing to be my wife, and here I was arranging a family for her!

Telling myself I'd do better to arrange my errands so I could finish them before the rain came—I had, as usual, neglected to bring an oiled cloth cloak—I pulled out the list and decided which to do first. What Mother needed was mostly things for Lisia, which I had no idea where to purchase, so I started by buying paper, because I knew where to get that. A woman passing the paper seller's shop was kind enough to direct me to my next stops.

Mother's purchases were soon handled. I headed next for the shops of the various cloth merchants. I remembered one Eia had scorned even to enter, saying the man sold poor quality cloth, suitable only for the meanest of uses. I couldn't imagine that bed curtains for the clinic needed to be made from fine fabric, so that's where I went. The selection of colors didn't impress me; but Aplin had asked for white, which the merchant had in abundance.

My last stop was in the carpenters' section. I had to look for a while to find someone whose specialty seemed to be things other than furniture. At one time, I would have stopped at the first woodworker's shop I saw, knowing the townspeople were loath to say "no" to a Singer. Thanks to Zhia, now I knew better. I wouldn't purchase stuff like Zhia's golden green fabric for clinic bed curtains, nor would I ask a craftsman who made fine furnishings to construct a free-standing curtain frame.

As the shops became rougher and the unmistakable fragrance of sawdust more in evidence, I glimpsed someone dark, shaggy, and massive under a roofed area beside a shop. It could only be Ingbir. When I called his name, he looked up with fear on his face, then turned and disappeared. I jumped out of the cart, tethered the desdal, and went after him. I found him trying to hide in the shadow of an untidy stack of roughly cut wood behind the shop.

He wasn't in Singers' colorful attire. He smelled of hard work. That evidence together with the sawdust that coated his drab clothes and his hair and that clung to the sweat on his face and bare arms told me he wasn't just shopping.

"Ingbir, what did you do, decide you don't want to be a Singer?" I asked, smiling.

His eyes were those of a cornered animal. "I couldn't stay at the Hall. Not after what I've done."

He wasn't joking. I stopped smiling. "What have you done?"

"Something terrible. Please, just go away and forget you've seen me."

Sternly, I said, "This isn't getting us anywhere. Tell me what you've done, so we can find out if it can be undone."

"It can't," he said, his voice breaking. "She's dead."

Hoping he didn't mean what I suspected, I echoed, "She? Do you mean Zhia?"

He nodded. "I'm sorry, Rois."

I took his arm. "Come with me."

"Where?"

"Just come with me."

Osrum didn't keep us waiting long. After the usual formalities, Osrum started asking Ingbir questions. Ingbir said that he'd asked Garit to help him find Zhia, because he—Ingbir—had a gift for her. He'd asked Garit to search the classroom area while he looked on the main level and, if he found Zhia, to ask her to meet him at the foot of the main stairway after the midday meal.

He himself had arrived at the meeting place earlier than arranged, only to see that Zhia was already there, having apparently fallen down the steps. He'd seen the blood under her head and had assumed she was dead. When he'd heard someone approaching, he'd panicked and fled the Hall.

"May I ask what the gift was?" Osrum asked, gently.

"A proper walking stick, with her name and the symbol of Nia Diva carved on it," was Ingbir's choked reply. "I made it for her."

Osrum's gesture invited me to put the distressed man's mind at ease. "Ingbir, Zhia is alive," I said. "At least, she was alive as of midday today. She's in the clinic. Aplin is hopeful about her recovery. And he says she didn't fall down the steps."

Of several things I'd rather not see again, one is Ingbir weeping. After he was more composed, I told him that if he would wait, I would go with him back to the carpenter's shop, then Osrum had one of the functionaries escort him from his chambers.

"Now what?" I asked Osrum.

"You know whom to watch. Beyond that, I can take no action; there's not enough evidence."

I thanked him and left.

"Zhia is really alive?" Ingbir asked when I joined him outside Osrum's chambers.

"Believe me, Ingbir, I wouldn't make jokes about that," I said. "Since we didn't see the walking stick when we found Zhia, I assume you took it with you." He nodded, not meeting my eyes. Suddenly I asked, "You didn't destroy it, did you?" He nodded again. Mildly, I said, "I can't say I blame you, either for that or for coming to the conclusion you did. The person you heard approaching was probably the serving woman who alerted Father, Aplin, and me. She came to the same conclusion you did. Am I correct in thinking you made the walking stick because you'd seen Zhia fall trying to walk with the broom for support?"

"Yes. I'll make her another one."

"I'm sure she not only will like that, but will also need it. Aplin says that one foot will always be bad. But there's something else you could make that would be of help to her, as well, and sooner." I told him about Aplin's desire for curtains around Zhia's bed, and described the frame I had envisioned.

Ingbir was nodding even before I finished talking. "I can make that today. If you're in no hurry, you can take it with you when you return to the Hall," he said.

"I'll wait for it," I said. "I'm starting to appreciate the smell of sawdust. Besides, the Hall is missing a low bass. I'd also like to take him with me when I return to the Hall."

Ingbir again looked troubled. "Not yet, Rois."

"Why not?"

"Two reasons, I guess. One, I have better tools here; I can make a better walking stick. Two, I'd rather not return until whoever hurt Zhia is in prison. If I'm at the Hall when his identity is discovered, he might not get to prison."

I hadn't before considered prison a place to go to be safe. Now that Ingbir mentioned it, whoever hurt Zhia might need to be protected from me, as well.

The sounds of sawing, smoothing, and hammering made further conversation with Ingbir difficult, so I perched on the end of the cart bed to watch Ingbir, and to think.

Zhia had spent part of at least two days with Neron. A snippet of the conversation I'd overheard the day Neron died told me that their disagreement about the tune of my dream song was ongoing rather than new. Anyone in the classroom corridor within a stone's throw of the Theory and Composition classroom would have heard not only their voices but also their topic of conversation, so it would have been known that Zhia and Neron were at odds.

Garit could have been one of those. I knew from TSTTW that Garit was distrustful of Zhia. He hadn't wanted her to continue with the tour. It was possible—assuming, of course, that he was the one who struck Zhia with the ax before leaving it embedded in Neron's skull—that Garit hadn't actually planned to harm Zhia; but three circumstances combined to give him an opportunity to rid the Hall of her.

The first circumstance was that Zhia was again in Neron's classroom, and that their differences were as marked as ever. The second was that Ingbir asked for his help in finding Zhia. Since Garit already knew where Zhia was, he didn't have to waste any time looking for her. He couldn't have seen me go to the Theory and Composition classroom. He must have reached that classroom to give Zhia Ingbir's message right after I left it. Seeing her in the corridor, plainly upset, he'd asked what was wrong. If Zhia had told him, she had probably not mentioned either my knowledge of the event or the fact that I was bringing Aplin. Neron's sudden death was the third circumstance. Garit couldn't have planned on it; but Neron's death likely suggested to Garit a modification of his plan that would get Zhia out of the Hall, either dead or alive.

He probably told her only that Ingbir wanted to see her at the foot of main stairway without telling her the time of the meeting was after the midday meal. He may have offered her his help. Since she had the broom, she would have declined (this detail involved no guesswork on my part). In the time it took her to get from the classroom corridor down the staircase, Garit could have found an ax and waited for Zhia to reach the foot of the stairs. Once he'd used the ax on her and arranged things to give the appearance that she'd fallen down the stairs, he'd returned to Neron's classroom to leave the ax where it would incriminate Zhia.

The beauty of Garit's plan—if Garit was, indeed, the one who attacked Zhia—was that if Zhia survived, he could be fairly confident that a woman who was known to have killed with an ax would go to prison for murder. If Zhia died from the blow, Garit would pretend to mourn. The biggest thing that could have gone wrong with his plan did go wrong, and that was that someone else had seen Neron dead, not murdered; and had reported his death before his "murder" was arranged.

Darl must have been enjoying himself that day. The timing of the events had to have been such that Garit (or whoever) had been close to being discovered more than once. Once Zhia had been struck, the attacker would have had to hurry up the stairs and to Neron's classroom. He'd probably narrowly missed encountering Ingbir, who'd narrowly missed encountering the serving woman. I doubted much time had elapsed between when the attacker left the classroom and Father, Aplin, and I reached it. On our way there, the three of us must almost have run into the serving woman, as well. Had the events not been so tragic, they might almost have been humorous.

I was congratulating myself on my reconstruction of the events when I remembered Osrum's saying there wasn't enough evidence for him to act. A clever guess wasn't evidence, either. A further consideration was that, even if the attacker was Garit and he was caught, he wouldn't go to prison for murder... not Neron's murder, at least. Since it appeared that Zhia would recover, whoever attacked her, if discovered, wouldn't go to prison for her murder, either.

I wondered whether the law had a provision regarding attempted murder.

Further reflection convinced me that Osrum's soldiers weren't needed. The attacker wouldn't likely make another attempt on Zhia's life. He couldn't know that both the cause of her injury as well as her innocence in Neron's death were known. He would still be counting on her going to prison if she survived the cracked skull. Of course, I was in no position to ask that the soldiers be removed from the Hall.

Zhia was safe as long as the facts of the event weren't known. I smiled grimly. Once again, lies had to be told to safeguard the truth.

Chapter Forty-Five

THE QUALITY OF THE work Ingbir did on something as simple as a wooden frame for curtains suggested how fine the walking stick had been. Improving on my suggestion, he made the frame not just three sections, but three hinged sections, both so it would more easily fit into the cart and so it could be used in the clinic in more ways.

After it was loaded and we finished arguing about whether he would accept payment for his work (I finally was able to persuade him), I again asked if he would return to the Hall with me. Again, he said, "Not yet." We weren't on tour; I had no authority over him. I thanked him and headed the cart back to the Hall.

I left it in the courtyard and went directly to the clinic, the folded frame in my hands. Zhia was still asleep, but was beginning to stir. I asked that, in addition to sending a soldier with a message to Osrum, Aplin notify me as soon as she woke.

Though he resented being reminded of the soldiers' presence (as though he could have forgotten them), Aplin was pleased with Ingbir's work. Once I brought in the white material, which he found satisfactory, he sent for servants so they could measure the frame and begin sewing the curtains.

I again looked in on Zhia, then went back to the cart for Mother's parcels, and back again for the paper Father had requested. Then I drove the cart to the stable so the workers there could groom and feed the desdal and put away the cart.

The day had grown unusually warm. I was considering bathing before supper when Ganit came to my cubicle. He looked grave.

"May I talk to you, Rois?"

I invited him in and asked him to sit, but he chose to remain standing. Well, fidgeting. When he didn't start talking, I said, "You appear less than pleased about something. I trust no one spilled wine on the completed score or anything like that."

"No, the score is with the copyists. It's my brother. I think he's done something wrong."

"Your brother?"

"Garit. You toured with him, didn't you?"

I nodded. I didn't dare start speaking for fear that Ganit would stop speaking.

"He came to my cubicle while I was working on the song. When he saw what it was, he started complaining—ranting, actually—about how it was performed on tour. He said Zhia sang it alone and then turned her back on the nobodies and did some uncalled-for business with the Nia Diva symbol. He said he'd made sure she wouldn't embarrass the Hall again. I tried to get him to tell me what he'd done, but he just said I'd know when everyone else did." Ganit hesitated, then asked, "Rois, has anything bad happened to Zhia? Since the tour, I mean?"

I had to chuckle. "With Zhia, one does have to be precise in asking that question." Then I became as grave as he. "The answer to that question is 'yes'; but I can't tell you more than that."

Looking even more troubled, Ganit said, "I'm assuming she's still alive, because we haven't laid anyone to rest since Instructor Neron."

"May Nia Diva speak for him," I added, when Ganit showed no sign of saying the usual words. "Yes, Zhia is alive."

Ganit cursed. "You're being careful to say as little as possible. She must be

ument— document

badly hurt." When I said nothing, he cursed again. "Rois, I'm talking about my brother! I have a right to know what's going on!"

"Yes, you do; but I don't have permission to tell you."

"You don't have permission? Did Father say... No, wait. The magistrate has been called in, hasn't he?" He waggled a forefinger at me. "I'm warning you, Rois; if a magistrate is asking questions, I'll deny I ever spoke to you."

"Were that situation to arise, that would be one of the choices open to you," I said evenly.

He started to leave, but turned in the doorway. "What's come over you, Rois? I thought you'd understand."

"I do understand, Ganit; you're worried about someone you care for." I caught myself before I said "as am I".

He stormed away. Wondering if I could have handled the situation better, I freshened up with the tepid water in the basin in my cubicle and went to supper.

I sat alone. I felt like I would burst from trying to hold in both what Ingbir had said and what I'd just learned. I had no choice but to hold it in. If and when Osrum next came to the Hall, Ganit's information had to be fresh. I wondered what penalty there was, if any, for withholding information pertinent to an investigation, should Ganit carry out his threat to deny what he'd told me. Would my recitation of the exchange suffice? Or was what Ganit revealed not evidence? Could Osrum compel either Ganit or Garit to speak?

I felt torn. I wanted the one who hurt Zhia punished, but I didn't want a Singer in the common prison. But hadn't that person forfeited his right to be a Singer by attacking another Singer? Could a person forfeit the call of the daemon? Could it be considered forfeit if, as it seemed, he thought he was acting to protect the dignity of that call?

Father hadn't censured Zhia's actions in Owlin's Run. It was Henz, Garit, and the other touring Singers who objected. Since Ganit said Garit was still upset by what Zhia did after she sang my dream song in Owlin's Run, I decided I wanted to know what Father's view of the matter was.

After Mother left with Lisia, I took my plate and went to Father's table.

"I wondered which of us forgot to bathe," Father joked as I sat. "Or is there some other reason you're avoiding my company?"

"The latter," I said. "I can't tell you even now, so please don't ask."

Father studied my face, then nodded. "Then why did you decide to be sociable?"

"When you had the letter from the mayor of Owlin's Run and asked me which of the things Zhia did I found objectionable and I said all of them because they weren't..."

"If I may interrupt, Son, I remember the conversation," Father said.

"I didn't mean to be repetitious. You said the fact that her actions weren't what Singers are accustomed to doing didn't make them wrong. I need to know if that means you approve of what she did."

"I didn't see what she did," Father said. "Was she making a mockery of things?"

"Far from it. It was one of the most graceful things I've ever seen anyone do on stage. There was no question she was sincere. I think even the nobodies understood when she turned her back on them..."

"She did?" Father gasped. "Why?"

"That's when she bowed to the symbol of Nia Diva. Then she turned around and bowed to the audience, though not as deeply. Then she beckoned to the rest of us and had us bow, also."

"She'll have to show me just what she did. If it appears respectful, I may make it a practice at our Hall."

Then I nodded. "I think that answers my question. Thank you."

As I was rising from the table, Father said, "I haven't seen Ingbir for the past few days. Do you know where he is?"

I hesitated. "May I simply say 'yes'?"

Father's shoulders slumped. "Not Ingbir."

Answering what I assumed Father's concern to be, I said, "No, not Ingbir. He said he will return to the Hall. Later."

It looked like "later" might be "sooner", for a servant was waiting just outside the dining hall with a message that was simply, "See Aplin".

Osrum and his functionaries were already there when Father and I reached the clinic. Zhia was awake. That the bandages on her head and hands were not as heavy and that she was propped on several pillows were all I could see in the light of the single lamp that burned; but I knew she was recovering when she remarked, "You've all come to see the new baby being fed?"

Father laughed and said, "The seeing is more like guesswork. Aplin, could we have more light in here?"

"No; light makes her head hurt worse," was his answer. He held a plate in one hand and a spoon in the other. "Zhia, do you want more to eat?"

"Yes, but not right now. Since everyone's here, let's get this over with."

Osrum dispensed with the formalities, either because he already knew Zhia's full name or because he wished to avoid wearying her.

"It is my understanding that the first thing you said to Rois when you awoke was, 'What hit me?'. Do you know who hit you?"

"Garit was the only other person in that part of the Hall when I was hit, Your Honor."

"You didn't actually see him strike you?"

"No, Your Honor. I assumed that since he'd given me Ingbir's message, he was on his way to the dining hall. I was looking for Ingbir."

"And what was the message Garit gave you from Ingbir?"

"That he—Ingbir—wanted to meet me at the foot of the main staircase because he had a gift for me, Your Honor. Shouldn't Ingbir be here, Your Honor?"

"I've spoken with Ingbir."

Zhia nodded, winced, and closed her eyes. Her head drooped. Her breathing slowed. Aplin removed the extra pillows from under her head, blew out the lamp, and shooed everyone into the outer area.

Osrum spoke quietly to one of the functionaries, who left. He returned after a while with Garit, whose nervousness was betrayed by the fact that his face was almost as pale as his hair.

After learning Garit's full name, Osrum said, "I have heard testimony from one Ingbir Iriangebir that some days ago he gave you a message to give to

Zhia. What was the message?"

Though Garit cleared his throat several times, his voice sounded harsh when he replied, "The message was that he had a gift for her and she was to meet him at the foot of the main staircase, Your Honor."

"Is that precisely the message he gave you?"

"Yes, Your Honor."

There was a sound of scuffling in the corridor outside the clinic. One functionary went to investigate. When he returned, he and a soldier were holding Ganit by the arms. Disheveled and as pale as Garit, Ganit was trying to break free.

When he saw me, he stopped struggling and, before anyone else could speak, said, "Curse you, Rois."

Osrum said, "Tell me your full name, or go to prison unidentified. You're disrupting an official proceeding."

Ganit glared, first at me, then at Osrum. "I'm Ganit Cominantagir. I'm his brother."

"You will address me as 'Your Honor,'" Osrum informed him. "Why are you here?"

"I'm here to find out why my brother is here, Your Honor."

"Why did you curse Rois?"

"Because I warned him..." Ganit began angrily, then stopped, realizing his error. "I've nothing to say, Your Honor."

"Yes, you do. Since you intruded and clearly have information pertinent to this proceeding, you will answer my questions. What was the gist of your warning to Rois?"

With great reluctance, he said, "That if a magistrate was called in, I would deny speaking to him." The "Your Honor" he added was far from respectful.

"By 'him' you mean Rois?" At Ganit's nod, Osrum asked, "What did you tell Rois that you don't want me to know?"

When Ganit hesitated, Father said, sternly, "Answer."

Ganit repeated what he'd told me. When he finished, Osrum looked at Garit. "How did you make sure Zhia wouldn't embarrass the Hall again?"

Garit said nothing. Osrum said to the functionaries, "Take his brother to prison."

"No!" Garit exclaimed. "He did nothing!"

"You will address me as 'Your Honor,'" Osrum repeated, with more edge to his voice. "Answer my question."

"I hit her in the head with an ax, Your Honor," he replied, miserably.

"Did you know whether you killed her?"

"I thought I had, Your Honor."

"What did you do then?"

"I made it look like she'd fallen down the stairs, then hit Instructor Neron in the head with the other side of the ax so it would look like Zhia killed him, Your Honor."

"Were you aware that Instructor Neron was already dead?"

"Yes, Your Honor."

"Garit Cominantagir, you have admitted attacking a Singer and an instructor. The instructor was already dead; you can't be charged with murder. The Singer survived."

"Zhia's alive?" Garit exclaimed, whether in relief or dismay, I couldn't tell.

"Shouting like that you'd wake her even if she were dead," Aplin said, angrily.

"Doctor, calm yourself," Osrum said. "As I was saying, the Singer survived, so you're innocent of murdering her. According to what you told your brother, you acted as you did in the interest of the dignity of this Hall. How you could imagine that attempting to murder a Singer and then implicating her in the death of the instructor would achieve that is beyond my comprehension. I am aware that you've lied to me in the course of this proceeding, which is an actionable offense. My judgment is that you leave this Hall. You will never again be a Singer.

"Ganit Cominantagir, you attempted to withhold evidence, which is also an actionable offense. You will also leave this Hall. If some other Hall will have you, I put no restriction on your continuing to be a Singer. You can be thankful I'm not putting both you and your brother in prison. Should either of you return to this Hall, you will go to prison."

Garit and Ganit looked stunned. At Osrum's direction, the functionaries and the soldiers accompanied the brothers as they left the clinic, ostensibly to help them with their belongings, but actually to make sure they left the Hall.

Father, Osrum, and I left the clinic and went to Father's office. Once there, Father shook his head. "I had been considering Ganit as Neron's replacement," he said to me. "I don't think any Master has ever lost as many Singers from his Hall in his first turn of the star wheel as I have. Unless I miss my count, those two make fourteen."

Osrum asked, "Twelve Singers have died since you became Master?"

"No. Two others were sent to other Halls. Ten have died."

"I know of the seven Singers on Zhia's tour. Why didn't I hear of the other three?"

"Because they died in my home in an attempt to kidnap my wife."

"You said 'they died', but you mean they were killed, don't you?"

"No. One died by accident. Zhia killed the other two while defending my wife. I told you that when Zhia was in prison."

"How did she kill them?"

Father regarded him coldly before saying, "I'm not going to answer if you're going to take Zhia to prison again. You can take me, but not her."

"You will answer, Robil. If I'm satisfied that Zhia did, indeed, act to defend your wife, then she won't go to prison. How did the men die?"

"Isia said…"

Osrum interrupted. "I'd prefer to hear the account from your wife."

"With all respect, Osrum, she can't oblige you. We've become responsible for a young child and this is the child's bedtime."

"Can someone else put the child to bed?"

"Zhia is the 'someone else' the child is accustomed to," Father said, quietly. "May I continue with what I was saying?" At Osrum's gesture, he went on, "The men began the violence when they tried to grab Isia and take her from the house. She and Zhia were running, with the men in pursuit. They couldn't run out of the house, because Isia is deathly afraid of going outside, so she and Zhia were trying to go upstairs. As they went through the kitchen, Zhia threw a pot of boiling water in the face of one of them, then smashed his head with the pot. The second one was burned to death when she dropped a jug with firestone on him. The third one, the one who died by accident, slipped on the stairs and fell on the knife with which he had slashed Zhia's arm. She suffered a cut blood vessel. If you wish to see the bodies, I buried them outside my house. I can't promise they're as fresh as the ones from the tour."

I couldn't identify all the emotions that crossed Osrum's face during this recital. He finally said, "The three were Singers?" Father nodded. "What motivated them?"

"By the time I reached my house—that was shortly after I became Master and was still trying to make sense of the confusion Gadig had left, so I was here when the trouble began—none of the three was able to answer questions. I surmise that by kidnaping my wife they hoped to pressure me to drop the charges against Gadig."

"How did Gadig inspire such loyalty?"

Father sighed deeply. "It seems he, those three, and the two I mentioned who were sent to other Halls were demanding intimate services from some of the female slaves. There's no way of knowing which of them fathered the child Isia and I have taken into our care."

Osrum shook his head. "That sheds light on what prompted Gadig to tell Mirlov that Zhia was providing intimate services for Rois and Taf. And since I don't recall having said so before, I must apologize for putting Zhia in prison when she was injured. My failing to do would have cast doubts on my impartiality."

"I understand," Father said. "But you haven't said whether you're going to put her in prison again."

Without the slightest hesitation, Osrum said, "No. But may I ask, Robil, how things at this Hall became so bad?"

"People began serving themselves, not Nia Diva. When people lose sight of their purpose, they can find reasons for doing anything."

"And yet Garit thought he was serving Nia Diva."

"No," I said, "Garit was serving his own pride. He was embarrassed by Zhia's respect for the daemon, respect he didn't share."

"How can a Singer not respect Nia Diva?" Osrum asked.

"Have you ever known of a magistrate who didn't respect the law?" I asked in return.

As Osrum nodded, Father said, "If I may change the subject, Osrum, I've been meaning to mention that I'd like to have my Singers do a performance for the people here, who, as my wife pointed out, have for the most part never heard them sing."

"You're advising me so I can put into place measures such as are employed at Festival?"

"Yes. It won't be until Zhia can sing with us."

"All right. Just give me a few days' warning," Osrum said, "and pray nothing further goes wrong."

Chapter Forty-Six

Thank the daemon, nothing further went wrong at my Hall. Nothing serious, anyway.

Father kept me busy for the next double handful of days going to other Halls to try to find someone to replace Neron. Traveling alone and quickly—rather than having a pack bird in tow, I had loaded the tebec I rode almost as heavily as the one Zhia had ridden on TSTTW—I had visited all but two Halls when a Theory and Composition instructor recommended his most gifted student, one Atera.

Yes, a woman. I looked at some of what she had written and was impressed, so the instructor called her to his office. Had I not been told her age, I would never have believed she was some turns of the star wheel older than I. She was quite short and painfully thin, with a serious, studious demeanor and a childish voice, which made me wonder what her singing sounded like. Her eyes were pale blue; her hair, so fair it was almost white. It reached to her knees. I wondered how she would do teaching men, most of whom would be much taller than she; and how she would make herself heard.

I reminded myself—and also made clear to her—that mine was not the final word on her selection, and informed her that, in the event that Father chose her as an instructor, she would be the only woman instructor at my Hall. That didn't seem to bother her.

She packed her belongings, collected a tebec and, with both her Hall Master's and her Theory and Composition instructor's blessing, left with me. She had, of course, toured, so she handled most of the challenges on the return trip quite well. She did take exception to our using tents, claiming she couldn't believe they wouldn't leak. She was not reluctant to tell me she would have preferred to spend nights at Quarter Rests.

She was even less reluctant to let me know that she expected me to keep my distance, which I found rather offensive, because my conduct had been nothing but respectful. In view of her stated preference for Quarter Rests, I also found her attitude odd, because tents afforded a far more tangible separation than did a Quarter Rest. She kept me at a distance verbally, as well, so we journeyed in almost total silence. Though the weather continued to be unusually warm, it felt chilly where I was. By the time my Hall was in sight, I was hoping that Father wouldn't employ Atera, even if it meant I would have to escort her back to her Hall. In terms of personality, she wasn't much improvement over Neron. I could take comfort in knowing that, if Father did make her an instructor, I wouldn't have to take any classes from her.

(And, in fact, Father did make her the first woman instructor at his Hall. She never became a popular instructor; but any Singers who studied with her knew their music theory. Thank the daemon, Father spared Zhia taking classes from Atera, though perhaps he was sparing Atera trying to teach someone who had proven as impervious to music theory as Zhia.)

By the time I returned from that protracted errand, Ingbir had returned to the Hall. Zhia was out of the clinic, and was getting around rather well using the walking stick Ingbir had crafted for her. Aplin had been having Zhia eat what seemed like six times a day, so she was regaining her strength; but she had little stamina and suffered from frequent headaches. In view of her slow recovery, Father held off scheduling the hometown tour. He did have all the Singers learning both Neron's last work and my dream song, and had asked me to be present whenever the latter piece was being rehearsed.

Those rehearsals often took place late in the afternoon, when the untyp-ical heat was at its highest and the practice room was rank with the smell of closely-packed, overly-warm bodies. Even without the smell, drawing a good breath in the hot, moist confines was difficult. Most Singers left the rehearsals feeling queasy.

One afternoon, Noia fainted during rehearsal. Kneeling at her side, Taf looked like he might pass out, as well. I went to fetch Aplin. He and Taf car-ried Noia to the clinic. Taf and Noia returned before the rehearsal was over. Noia looked like she was trying not to smile. Taf made no such attempt.

"I'm going to be a father," he announced, as Noia dimpled and blushed.

"Congratulations! That calls for a party," I said, and the rehearsal ended abruptly. On my way to the dining hall, I stopped at Father's office to tell him the news and to invite him to the celebration.

"Your mother will want to come, as well," he said, and went to the nursery. Lisia was asleep, cradled on Zhia's bosom. Zhia was also asleep. Mother was sewing something for Lisia.

Mother put down her work and rose at once. When we were in the corridor, she said, anxiously, "I think Aplin should look at Zhia again. I don't think she should still sleep as much as she does."

"If he's at the party, I'll ask him to look at her," Father said. "She didn't wake for five days after she was attacked, you know. We can thank Nia Diva she's still with us."

When Mother heard what the party was about, she at once began making plans for providing a nursery for Noia's baby. "And we ought to keep a mid-wife here, because once the baby starts to be born, it's too late to send for one from town."

When Mother walked away to congratulate the parents-to-be, Father said wryly to me, "Women shouldn't be Singers."

Just as I laughed, a crack of thunder shook the Hall and rain poured down: not the usual evening rainfall, but a torrent. Lightning rarely accompanied the evening rain; tonight, it was as though the sky was ablaze. The thunder was so loud it drowned out voices. People began to cringe and flinch as the storm's fury increased. Some headed for the doors.

Father said to me, urgently, "Tell everyone to remain. This is the safest place in the Hall to be."

I raised my voice above the crackling and booming and gave Father's instructions. There was fear on many faces as people obeyed. The party was forgotten, but wine—false courage—continued to be consumed.

Mother, who had been cowering in Father's arms, suddenly clutched my arm. "Lisia and Zhia!" she exclaimed.

Father said to me, "Go!"

I heard Lisia's cries before I reached the nursery. Zhia was coming toward me. She couldn't manage the screaming, struggling child and the walking stick, so had left the stick behind. I helped them to the dining hall. Mother relieved Zhia of Lisia and went off to try to soothe her.

Another clap of thunder shook the Hall. "Quite a storm. It won't last long," Zhia said, calmly. Then, just as calmly, she began to sing my dream song. As she lifted her voice above the storm's rage, one by one the other Singers joined in, in parts, until our combined voices drowned out the fearsomeness without and the fearfulness within. When we finished singing, Zhia said, "Let's sing it again," and we did, more strongly, more confidently. The storm ended before the song did. Without the accompaniment of thunder and lightning, the high note close to the end shimmered, a sound of defiance. There was silence, then someone laughed.

The party resumed.

Carrying Lisia, who was again asleep, Mother left the dining hall. Father stooped to kiss Zhia's cheek and say, "Thank you," before following Mother.

I went to get wine for Zhia and me. When I turned, cups in hand, I saw that she was standing, head bent, eyes closed, her forehead resting on the tips of the fingers of her right hand. She lowered her hand when she heard me approach and gave me an unconvincing smile. "Thank you," she said as she took the cup.

"You're welcome. Have you eaten?"

"Only about four times today." The reply was accompanied by a wry expression.

"They should be serving supper soon."

She started to nod but changed her mind. "So what's the occasion for the party?"

"We've just learned that Taf is going to be a father."

There was amusement in Zhia's voice when she said, "Which means either that Noia is going to be a mother, or that she's going to kill Taf."

I laughed (it didn't thunder). "Noia passed out during rehearsal. I think Taf is safe."

Zhia smiled. "It's going to be lively around here. First Lisia, then baby Noiantaftan, then..." She sipped her wine. "I ought to congratulate them. Where's my stick?" She made a sound in her throat. "It's in the nursery."

"I'll fetch it for you," I said. "Anything else you need?"

"A chair."

"But if you sit, won't you fall asleep?"

"Possibly. But if I don't sit, I'll fall down. Take your choice."

I brought her a chair. As she sat, I noticed that the reddish brown garment was starting to look frayed. "I thought your foot would be better after being off it... so long."

"Yes, the rest did my foot good. However, my knees are a bit wobbly. The storm frightened me."

"You? You didn't look frightened."

"Of course not. I had Lisia to consider. Had I given in to my fear, she would have been even more upset. You have to put the needs of the children first."

"I'll try to remember that," I said. It looked like Zhia started to say something. When she didn't comment, I went to the nursery.

Mother was again sewing, now by lamplight. Lisia was in bed, deep in the sweet sleep of the young. "What is it, Son?" Mother asked, softly.

"I'm looking for Zhia's walking stick." I also spoke softly.

"Isn't it next to the big chair where she was sitting?"

In fact, it had somehow gotten partly under the big chair. It was made of dark wood, so in the shadows I hadn't seen it. I picked it up, kissed Mother's cheek, and headed back to the dining hall.

I hadn't had a good look at what Ingbir had done, so I examined the stick as I walked. As he said he'd done with the stick he destroyed, Ingbir had carved Zhia's name and the symbol of Nia Diva into the stick, etching the wood so deeply that the much lighter inner wood showed. The stick was smoothly finished, save for an area near the top, which I assumed he left rougher to keep Zhia's hand from slipping, and the part that came into contact with the floor. The upper area was circled by bands of leather, which would also serve to improve Zhia's grip on the stick. It was a fine example of the woodworker's craft, and a tribute to how much Ingbir cared about Zhia.

The business with Garit had left me uneasy about Zhia's dealings with the other men from TSTTW. Seeing the care that went into Zhia's walking stick helped put my mind at ease… about Ingbir, at least.

Supper was being served when I reached the dining hall. Zhia was still awake. When I saw how Zhia was looking at me, I refrained from commenting on the fact. I gave her the stick, and she at once went to speak to Taf and Noia. I collected plates of food for Zhia and me. When she joined me at the table I had chosen, she asked, "Does your mother need me for Lisia?"

"The baby was sleeping when I left."

The tender look was on Zhia's face again. "I think she would have slept through the storm had that first crack of thunder not made me jump."

"Deeply as you appeared to be sleeping, I'm surprised you heard it."

"I told you, mothers learn to wake when there are strange noises. I haven't heard thunder like that in a long time."

I nodded. "I don't remember another storm that violent. I hope it did no damage."

"There wasn't much wind, which is a mercy." She took a breath, but rather than speaking began to eat.

Again, I had the feeling that she was avoiding saying something. I didn't think it had to do with the storm, though that was a topic of conversation at the tables all around us. After I returned the empty plates to the kitchen, Zhia said, "Could I talk to you?"

"You are talking to me."

The breath she drew verged on exasperated. "Someplace quiet?"

I can't say I wasn't apprehensive. My first thought was that we should go to my cubicle, but remembered that it was on a fairly well-used corridor. "Your cubicle?"

She started to shake her head, grimaced, and said, "No. The courtyard."

The courtyard was quiet and full of deepening shadows. The torrential rain had left puddles, which we walked around. The storm had broken the grip of the unusual heat. A light breeze ruffled Zhia's hair, which had grown since she cut it for the tour. She needed either to cut it again or to find some way to keep it out of her eyes, for it appeared to be at an awkward length, too short to pull back but too long to be allowed to hang loose.

She pushed it out of her face, turned to me, and asked, "How long was I in the clinic before I awoke?"

I avoided the question. "Didn't Aplin tell you?"

"Had Aplin told me, I wouldn't be asking you."

"Why do you want to know?"

"Why shouldn't I know? At the risk of sounding rude, I haven't the strength for these games. Please answer my question."

She had a point. I said, "Five days."

She was silent for a while, then said, "Something strange happened."

Unwisely, I said, "Your not dying was strange."

She didn't lose her temper. In a voice charged with emotion, she said, "That's just it. I think I did die, or at least came as close to it as one can without dying. I was walking and my foot didn't hurt at all. I was walking toward this light. It was a bright light, but not a dazzling one. It didn't hurt my head or make me squint. It was like the light from a lamp in a window that you know is there to help you find your way home." She rubbed her arm across her eyes. "I was getting closer and closer to the light, and I was so happy, and then I heard a voice that said, 'Go back'. And it was like your father's voice when he's really stern and you know you better do what he said; but it wasn't an angry voice. It was a gentle voice; but I didn't dare disobey. And the light went away, and

I was sad." I could see tears gleam in her eyes when she added, "I didn't want to come back."

I didn't know what to do. I could think of nothing to say. When she asked, "Can you forgive me?" I was even more at a loss for words.

"For what?" I finally stammered.

"Because I didn't want to come back, even though I'm carrying your child."

It seemed to be my night for saying stupid things. "Are you certain?"

Her voice suddenly edged, Zhia asked, "What are you asking? Whether I'm certain I'm carrying a child, or whether I'm certain it's your child? I am with child. I have been with no man but you in at least two turns of the star wheel."

"But we were together only once."

Her laugh was pitying. "If you're virile and I was fertile, once is all it takes. I just wasn't sure I was fertile any more. Not since..." I heard her stifle a sob, then she said, "What I need to know is whether I'll be raising this child alone. I understand that the law says you don't have to do anything for this child, so I want you to know I'm making no demands. This is your choice."

Of all the emotions I was feeling at that moment, I think gratitude predominated. I was grateful that the Unknown had sent Zhia back. I was grateful—I was delighted—that she was carrying my child. I was grateful that she had given me the opportunity to ask her to be my wife again without making a Hall-wide event of the occasion. I didn't know whether word of our short-lived union on tour had spread. I knew and Zhia knew that we were husband and wife when that new life within her was planted. Before the night was over, we would be husband and wife again.

I was silent too long. Zhia said, bleakly, "As you wish," and started to walk away.

I stepped in front of her. "That's not what I wish. I hadn't said anything because I was thanking the Unknown that you're still here, and that once again you can be with me as my wife. I've known all along I was a fool for repudiating you. I'm delighted about our child. I must be truthful; I didn't know whether I could father a child. As you said, the law doesn't require me to take responsibility for my antics, so I've never heard whether I've left some woman with a child she wasn't expecting to raise at all, let alone by herself. But even if you weren't carrying my child, I'd want you as my wife." I knelt—in a puddle—took Zhia's free hand, and said, "Rois Isianrobil asks that you forget what an utter fool he can be and again do him the honor of being his wife."

Weeping, she said, "I'm sorry, I get like this when I'm with child. Rois, remember that this toy is old and worn out and broken, and can't ever be made new, and that you can still choose any other toy you want."

"This is… no, not this. You are the toy I want. And I must mention that I'm kneeling in a puddle and the water is starting to creep up my trouser leg and I'm going to have to go change clothes before we can tell Father and Mother the good news. Or is there no good news?"

"Yes, there is." She laughed. "Stand up. I can accept you as my husband even if you're on your feet."

I stayed where I was. "No, let's do this right."

"Stubborn. You've been around me too long. Zhia Vediandruzhin doesn't know any utter fools, but is honored and delighted to accept you again as her husband." Then her voice became mischievous. "Since you have to change your trousers anyway, why don't we go to my cubicle first?"

We did.

Afterwards, I went to my cubicle to wash and put on dry clothes. When I returned to Zhia's cubicle, I saw that she'd again cut her hair. She was wearing the golden green garment. She looked lovely, and I told her so. She said, "I'm glad I came back."

"As am I." I kissed her, slowly, thoroughly.

Somewhat later, newly freshened up, we went in search of Mother and Father.

Mother was still sewing. She looked up when we came into the nursery. A smile of sheer delight spread across her face. "Congratulations! I always wanted a daughter." She put down her sewing and enfolded first Zhia, then me, in her arms. "When did you decide?"

Zhia looked at me, so I said, "Actually, Mother, she became my wife when we were on tour. Then, foolishly, I repudiated her. She became my wife again tonight. In view of the fact that she already knows she's with child, I wanted you to know we were husband and wife when she quickened."

I didn't think Mother could look any happier. She hugged Zhia again. "The Hall will need a nursery for certain!" Then she hugged me again. "I'm so proud of you, Son."

"Thank you, Mother. Do you know where Father is?"

"In the dining hall, I imagine. The party must still be going on."

We said goodnight. As we headed that direction, I said, "I wonder what I did to make her so proud. Did you know she's been after me to make you my wife since TTTW?"

"Maybe she's proud that you finally took her advice," Zhia said. "I have a request, though, which is that you stop insulting my husband. He's not a fool."

"Then I need to request that you stop insulting my wife, who isn't even as old as I, and—in view of what just went on in your cubicle—is certainly not a worn-out toy. I wasn't sure I could keep up with you."

"You certainly rose to the challenge," was her saucy reply. "But I must point out that 'Toy' is Noia. I hope you can tell us apart."

"I'll try," I said.

"You'll do more than try," Zhia warned, with mock severity. "By the way, when do I get a stage name?"

"When someone thinks of a good one for you. I'd like to be the one to give you a stage name, but the only things that come to mind at the moment are a bit too personal."

"Like what?"

I whispered them to her and was pleased to see her smile and blush. She pulled my head down and kissed me. "Don't start that again… yet," I said, smiling, already regretting that we were so far from her cubicle. Then I thought of something, and my smile faded. "If at any time during intimacy your head hurts, will you tell me?"

After a moment, she said, "I'm glad you didn't ask that until now."

I groaned. "I hurt you?"

"No. Garit hurt me. And if you think I'm going to give up the pleasure you give me to avoid a little bit of pain, you can think again." She looked up at me with a smile. "Or you can kiss it and make it better. If you'll do that, I'll find lots of things that hurt."

"Find them later."

"My place or yours?"

Laughing, I said, "I'd better bring my things to your cubicle. Remind me to tell Father."

Father was in the dining hall. The party was still going strong. I knew Zhia was glowing. I must have also looked satisfied, because when Azham and Volan saw us, they both said, "Not again."

At this, Tej turned and also saw us. He grinned and said, "This party's going to last all night!"

"Go right ahead," Zhia said. "We're leaving early." There was a chorus of laughter.

That's when Father noticed us. He came over, saying, "I take it more congratulations are in order?"

"Yes, Father, Zhia is again my wife. I stress the 'again' because, as we've already told Mother, Zhia is with child from… from before."

Noia and some of the other female Singers clustered around and drew Zhia away from my side. With their giggles and happy chatter muffling our voices, Father said, unsmiling, "Son, are you certain this is what you want? You didn't ask her to be your wife only because she's with child, did you?"

"This is what I want, Father. I want Zhia, and I want our child. I'm moving my things into her cubicle tonight."

Father nodded. "Then accept your father's blessing. May you be happy… and wiser than you've been in the past."

"That wouldn't take much, Father."

Chapter Forty-Seven

In the morning, Zhia was asleep on the floor next to the bed.

I wasn't sure whether I felt offended or confused. I didn't want to waken her. Though we'd left the party early, we hadn't slept until much later. I lay half-dozing until she stirred, then turned on my stomach and leaned over the edge of the bed to kiss her and say good morning. She joined me in the bed and ensured that it would be a good morning.

Later, as I was contentedly stroking her body, I asked, "Why were you on the floor?"

She kissed me and said, "Because there's scarcely room for you in this bed, let alone both of us. Did you know that you sleep diagonally?"

"No."

She grinned. "I didn't think so. You kept shifting in your sleep and I kept trying to take up less of the bed. I finally decided it would be better for me to get out of the bed rather than fall out of it. We really could use a larger bed, or even two beds; but this cubicle isn't big enough for either."

"I don't like the idea of two beds," I said. I stood and reached for my trousers. Half-dressed, I went into the corridor, peering into each doorway I passed. Four doors down I found a cubicle that was considerably larger. When I returned and told Zhia about it, she pulled on the reddish brown garment and padded, barefoot, down the corridor, leaning on my arm.

After she looked around the cubicle, she said, "It's certainly big enough for a larger bed, but where would we get one? Would we have to order one specially made?"

"Unless you and Mother destroyed it beyond saving, my bed at my parents' house should hold both of us, and should also fit in this cubicle."

"Truthfully, I don't remember whether we left enough of it to be called a bed. It may just be kindling. Even if it's at all usable, after so long in an empty house, it's going to need a lot of cleaning before it's fit to use; but it won't hurt to see if it can be salvaged."

We washed and dressed quickly, Zhia in her shirt and trousers. After breaking our fast, we went to tell Father what we had in mind and ask if we might use the desdal and cart.

For a long while he said nothing. I was starting to wonder if we had somehow offended him when he said, "Rather than bring your bed here, Son, why don't you and Zhia move into that house? You could use your mother's and my bedchamber, and your chamber could be a nursery. You'd still be close enough to the Hall to be reached by messenger, if need be; but you'd be far enough away to have the privacy I know you want and need."

I was about to agree when I realized that I'd better ask Zhia first. When I turned to her, I saw her face alight.

"Do you mean it?" she said to Father. "You'd allow Rois and me to live in your house? That's very generous."

"Actually, it's very calculating," Father said, though I could tell he was pleased. "Isia has been worrying about what kinds of undesirable things might be living in the house, since as far as we know, no person is living in it. She'd be happy knowing the place was being cared for."

Zhia turned to me. "May we, Rois?" she asked.

"I was hoping you'd want to," I said.

"That's settled, then," Father said. He opened the locked box and gave Zhia her father's ring and me quite a staggering amount of money.

"What's this for?" I asked.

"This is part of what Mirlov paid for Zhia's training. You might as well use it for what you'll need to get the house the way you two want it."

Tears were shining in the corners of Zhia's eyes when she dropped her stick, threw her arms around Father's neck—he was, of course, sitting—and kissed his cheek. "Thank you," she said, weeping. "May I tell Mother?"

At Father's nod, Zhia picked up her stick and left the office. Father looked at me, his brow furrowed. "Is she all right? I don't remember ever seeing her weep."

"You haven't seen her with child before."

Looking relieved, Father nodded. "It affected your mother that way, too." As I was leaving his office, he said, "Son, take what time you need to get the house livable. The hometown tour won't be for ten days or so. Assuming that at some time in the next few days you'll be in town making purchases, you might purchase your own cart and animal, since I'm sure you won't be wanting Zhia walking to the Hall, and I'll need the Hall's cart back at some point."

I thanked Father, collected Zhia, and had the cart readied.

It took us a full day to scrub and sweep the house and get the larger bed-chamber ready for our use. I was able to put my bed back together. Wisely (for a change), I reassembled it in the larger chamber so it didn't have to be moved once it was again usable.

We must have made more than thirty trips up and down the stairs. Zhia, of course, couldn't use her walking stick and manage both the stairs and cleaning supplies, so she climbed the steep steps without its help. So involved was I in what we were doing that it wasn't until Zhia finally limped to the divan, sat, carefully put her right heel on the floor, and said, "This isn't going to work, Rois," that I realized what a toll the day's exertions had taken on her.

"I wanted so much for this to be our home," she went on, tears shining in her eyes, "but I can't manage the steps. How vexed will your father be if we return to the Hall?"

We had opened the shutters to air out the house. Through the window above the divan I could see the clouds gathering. "We won't be returning tonight," I said.

With a small grimace, Zhia said, "Good." Then she said, more plaintively than I'd ever heard her speak, "I'm hungry." She leaned back against the cushions and fell asleep.

Finding nothing with which to cover her, I pulled down the curtains from the shutters on the windows in the front room and used them. Then I closed all the shutters and hitched the desdal to the cart. I already knew there was no food in the house. Mother had left food behind, but vermin had invaded the larders and fouled it. Killing the creatures or chasing them from the house—I favored the latter; Zhia, the former—had been one of the more exciting parts of the day.

I drove to the Hall. When I went to the dining hall to get food to take back for Zhia and me, Father was there. I had been thinking about Zhia's problem with the house, and had come to a possible solution. I didn't want to suggest it to Zhia until I had Father's permission to pursue it.

Father looked surprised when he saw me. "Is Zhia here, too?" he asked.

"No. She was exhausted. I actually came to beg some food for our supper, and to ask your permission to make some changes to the inside of the house."

"What kinds of changes?"

"For one thing, we need a door on the front room. Zhia was in tears this evening because she's not going to able to manage the steps. I thought that if the front room could be closed off, it could be our bedchamber, instead. There's plenty of room in it for my bed and a baby's bed."

"Then what would you do with the chambers on the second level?"

"Perhaps Taf and Noia would prefer a little more privacy."

Father nodded. "Are you going to ask them?"

"It's your house, Father; I think you should make the offer. I would suggest that, if they're agreeable, they wait a day or two to make the move. All we got done today was cleaning."

"Four more hands and four good feet would spare Zhia," was Father's comment.

"That's up to you and them, Father. I can't leave the cart and desdal tonight, though. I imagine we'll be going into town tomorrow for food and whatever else we'll need right away. We'll stop here and see what Taf and Noia have decided."

"That's a good plan," Father said.

I collected food and wine from the kitchen and a lamp and our things from Zhia's cubicle, piled everything in the cart and, since it was already raining, covered the pile with a couple of oiled cloth cloaks. I drew another one around myself before heading back to the house.

Zhia was still asleep when I arrived. I lighted the lamp and woke her so she could eat.

"Thank you," she said, as she attacked the food. "You didn't drive into town for this, did you?"

As my mouth was full, I shook my head. After I swallowed, I said, "Just to the Hall, but that was far enough for me to do some thinking. Would you consider making this room our bedchamber? That would keep you from having to climb stairs."

"But you'd have to take your bed apart again to bring it down here."

"That's no problem," I assured her. "I just don't know where we'd put the divan."

"Anywhere but in the house," Zhia said, flatly. At my look of surprise, she added, "Don't tell me you haven't noticed that it smells like vermin have been living in it."

Now that she mentioned it, I did detect a disagreeable smell. I had thought it was just our sweat. "We'll have to leave it in here tonight and maybe even sleep on it, both because it's too big for me to move by myself and because I don't intend to move my bed tonight."

"That's all right. If I crawl, I think I can manage the stairs one more time," Zhia said, with mocking laughter. "But after tonight, what will we do with the chambers upstairs?"

I told her my plan. She liked the idea of sharing the house with Taf and Noia, if they found the arrangement to their liking. She had some misgivings about sharing the kitchen, but was willing to work with Noia to avoid disagreements. "Of course, we may find she doesn't even like to cook," she said.

"That's possible," I said. "Promise me one thing."

"What's that?" she asked, warily.

"You won't serve tebec."

She laughed. "May I serve shellort stew?"

"If you can find a shellort."

I didn't bother mentioning something Zhia knew as well as I: we hadn't gotten around to arranging the kitchen or bringing in firewood, so she couldn't even boil water. We washed ourselves and our clothes with cold water before heading upstairs. Walking stick in hand, Zhia crawled up the stairs. She made me go up first, claiming she was embarrassed enough without knowing that I was watching her from below.

It's some indication of how worn out I also was that the first night in our new home I was content to do nothing more than sleep.

I woke before Zhia and was considering starting the day pleasurably when I heard voices downstairs. I had to dig in the pile of things I had brought with me from the Hall and carelessly dumped on the chamber floor to find shirt and trousers. (It's some indication of how worn out Zhia was, despite her nap, that she neither mentioned the heap on the floor nor made any attempt to tidy it before climbing into bed.)

Tense, I crept downstairs as quietly as possible. The voices sounded like they were coming from the dining room. I stopped in the kitchen and peered into the dining room. The tension left me. The intruders were Taf and Noia.

I must have been holding my breath, for when I exhaled, they turned and saw me. "Good morning," I said, opening the shutters on the dining room window. The sky was still quite dark. "It is morning, isn't it?"

Taf laughed. "Barely. Noia was so excited about coming to live here that she hardly slept, despite my best efforts."

"Taf!" Noia chided, blushing.

"What?" he asked with mock indignation. "You're my wife, aren't you?" She blushed more deeply, and Taf quit teasing her. "When Father mentioned our living here with you and Zhia, he said something about there being no food in the house, so we brought breakfast for you."

"Thank you," I said. I was also grateful the table and chairs hadn't gone to the Hall with Father and Mother. "I'd better wake Zhia."

"Zhia is awake, thank you," said my wife to me from the doorway. She had her walking stick and was wearing her trousers and shirt. From the way they fit, I could tell they weren't completely dry. To Taf and Noia, Zhia said, "Good morning. Did you walk out here from the Hall?"

"We rode tebecs," Taf said.

Zhia made no comment, but the expression on her face made Noia laugh and say, "I'll fit a tebec saddle for a while yet."

Smiling, Zhia said, "The place is reasonably clean; but it isn't quite ready to be lived in. Since you're out here already, I'm assuming you do want to move in, so it's just as well that we haven't bought utensils or furniture. I'm sure you'll want to select your own furnishings, starting with a bed. Once Rois moves his bed into the front room, the upstairs chambers will be bare. You'll be able to arrange your quarters just as you please. We can start buying furniture today, if you're agreeable."

They were. They had left the bundles of their belongings on the tebecs. While Noia and Zhia set out the food, Taf and I brought them in.

We ate, then Zhia showed Taf and Noia the rest of the first level and I showed them the second one. Zhia and Noia discussed what things other than furniture would be needed right away. I asked Taf if Father had given him any money. He nodded.

We all rode into town in the cart. The first thing I did was follow Father's advice and purchase a cart and desdal so I could return the Hall's animal and conveyance. Taf suggested I delay doing so until we saw how much we had to carry back to the house, since it was quite possible we would have enough to fill two carts. It was a good idea, one I should have thought of myself.

That done, we bought a bed for Taf and Noia, and other furnishings they and we would need for our respective bedchambers. Since we were in that part of town, we went the woodworker's shop that belonged to Ingbir's family. A man I suspected was Ingbir's kin—who proved to be Gebir, Ingbir's father—asked what we needed. When I told him, he nodded and said he could come out to the house and take measurements.

"Take measurements?" I echoed. "For a door?"

With laughter in his eyes, Gebir said, "A door needs a wall. Also, I assume you'll want a door you can walk through upright. Or do you want to have to remember to duck whenever you go into your bedchamber?"

Chuckling, I said "no" and added that we would stop by his shop before we left town and take him to the house with us.

"Thank you, but I have a chero," he said.

"How hard would it be to enlarge the front door of the house?" Zhia asked Gebir.

"Why would we want that done?" I asked.

"Because you have to duck when you go into the house," she replied.

"Is the house wood?" Gebir asked.

"Stone," I said.

Gebir shook his head. "I don't work in stone, but I can recommend a man who does. He's good."

"That you recommend him assures me of that," I said. "We'll see you at the house later, then."

Taf and I visited the wine seller's stall while Zhia and Noia purchased bedding, cloth for curtains, and kitchen items. They loaded their purchases into the carts, leaving no doubt that we'd need both conveyances to get everything back to the house. Then the women announced they were ready to start shopping for food, though by then Zhia, who had been using her walking stick the whole time, was again limping badly.

Taf and I exchanged a concerned look. He squinted at the sun and said, "It's past time for the midday meal. I knew there was some reason I was so hungry. Let's find a place where we can sit and eat."

By the way Zhia pressed her lips together when she sat, I knew she was trying not to sigh with relief. While we waited for our food, Taf and Noia excitedly discussed their new living arrangements. Zhia was silent, her eyes closed, her forehead resting on the fingertips of her right hand, a posture I recognized as meaning her head was hurting. When her breathing deepened and that hand began to fall toward her lap, I caught it and lowered it gently, then moved my chair closer to hers and drew her against me. She didn't waken.

Taf noticed what was going on. "What's wrong with Zhia?" he whispered, frowning.

Not until then did I remember that Father, Osrum, Aplin, and I had managed to keep Zhia's most recent brush with death a secret. Also whispering, I replied, "A man from her second tour knocked her in the back of the head with the back of an ax."

"Why?" Taf and Noia exclaimed in a hushed unison.

"He thought she was embarrassing the Hall."

"And he thought his murdering another Singer wouldn't embarrass the Hall?" Taf asked, his outrage plain even though he continued to talk quietly. "Who was it?"

"It doesn't matter now. He's been sent away and forbidden to be a Singer."

"He got off lightly," Noia said, with icy anger. "Zhia must have been badly hurt."

I nodded. "She was insensible for five days. Aplin is satisfied with the way she's recovering; though, as you see, she falls asleep at odd times, even when we haven't worked as hard as we did yesterday."

"Then it's a good thing Noia and I will be helping you from now on," Taf said. "I don't suppose Zhia can be persuaded to let us do the work?"

I didn't have to answer. Taf and I both knew better.

When the food was served, I woke Zhia. From her expression, I thought at first she was annoyed with me, but her words proved otherwise.

"Not again!" she exclaimed as she straightened in her chair. She looked across the table at Taf and Noia. "I'm so sorry. What must you think of me?"

"That you worked very hard yesterday," Noia said, smoothly. "Knowing how long that house has been unoccupied, when we arrived there this morning I was prepared to look only at the arrangement of the house and to overlook its condition. It was a welcome surprise to see it in such good order."

"That's very gracious of you," Zhia said. "I find it's easier to keep a house in good order when there's almost nothing in it."

We all laughed and began eating. It didn't surprise me that during the meal Zhia raised the subject of cooking. Noia confessed to being inexperienced in the kitchen.

"My family employs a cook," she explained. "If you'd be willing to do most of the cooking for a while, Zhia—and, of course, teach me the basics—I'd be grateful."

"Basics are all I can teach," Zhia said, modestly. "I don't do fancy cooking."

"It's a shame our wives are so inadequate, isn't it?" Taf remarked to me as the polite disclaimers continued.

"I can't imagine what we saw in them," I said by way of agreement.

Noia and Zhia laughed. "You were just lusting after our beauty," Noia teased.

"Yes," Taf said, emphatically, and kissed Noia's cheek.

Smiling, Zhia looked at them. When she looked at me, her smile was sour. "Don't bother," she said, quietly.

"I want to bother," I said, and kissed her full on the mouth. "I've asked you once to stop insulting my lovely wife. Must I ask you again?"

"Point out your lovely wife, and I'll try to desist." Tears were again in her eyes. She stood and picked up her walking stick. "Excuse me. I need to find a…" She swallowed. "Excuse me."

Noia excused herself, also.

Taf sat looking at me with what was plainly pity. "Don't take this wrong, Rois, but I'm glad Zhia's not my wife."

I hoped my smile didn't look as false as it felt. "She's moody because she's with child, also."

In carefully casually voice, Taf said, "Really?"

That was when I realized the group from Zhia's second tour hadn't spread the word that I'd made Zhia my wife on tour, so Taf was probably thinking either that Zhia was carrying someone else's child, or that she and I had been carrying on. I told Taf what had happened on TSTTW. He shook his head and said, with feeling, "Congratulations. You know, if what you just told me was a song, no one would believe it."

"No one would believe what?" asked Noia, who just then was returning with Zhia.

"How blessed Taf and I are in our choice of wives," I said. (As I've mentioned, improvisation is one of the skills a Singer must have.)

"That's flattering, but not true," she said with a smile. She ate the last of her food and added, "I'm ready to finish our shopping. Zhia, how about you?"

Zhia hadn't eaten even half her food, but she pushed her plate away. "Yes. We have a lot yet to do if you and Taf will be staying at the house tonight." She stood and again picked up her walking stick.

Looking at her plate, I started to say something, but Noia caught my eye and shook her head. As we went toward the part of town where foodstuffs were sold, she managed to have a private word with me. She told me that when she and Zhia visited the public convenience, Zhia had lost what little food she had eaten. "I hope she's not falling ill," she finished, sounding worried.

"She's with child," I said. Before Noia could entertain mistaken ideas, I explained, "She was my wife for maybe two days during her second tour. That must be when she quickened."

Noia frowned but nodded. "Aplin told me to eat porridge. That works for me."

"I'll tell Zhia," I said, thinking she likely already knew. She'd carried a child before.

Even though Noia, Taf, and I were trying to walk slowly, Zhia kept falling behind. I could see people looking at our group—three persons who by their bright clothing were plainly Singers, and Zhia in her plainly well-worn dark green shirt and dun trousers—and wondered whether they thought Zhia was our servant. Once the hometown tour was over, they would know the truth.

As we went from miller to greengrocer to vintner to butcher, Taf kept glancing back at Zhia, who had insisted on carrying her share of the parcels and so couldn't use her walking stick. Finally, he said, "This already looks like enough food for a tour. I don't know about you and Zhia, Rois, but Noia and I will probably eat some of our meals at the Hall. As long as there's something in the house with which to break our fast, we'll be happy. Let's get what we have back to the house and make sure we have places to sleep tonight."

I muttered "Thank you" as we loaded the parcels into the carts. I helped Zhia climb onto our cart—Taf and Noia were driving the Hall's cart—and we returned to the house.

When both Taf and Noia joined their voices to mine in forbidding Zhia to carry anything but her walking stick into the house, she capitulated. I told her to sit on the divan and put her foot up. Surprisingly, she did. Not surprisingly, she fell asleep. Not even the racket Taf and I made carrying in furniture or my discussion with Gebir, who arrived at the house shortly after we did, disturbed her. Gebir said he'd be back the next day with what was necessary for closing off the front room, and assured me the work would be done that same day.

Taf helped me dismantle my bed and bring the pieces into the front room, then we carried his and Noia's bed and the rest of their furniture up the stairs and into the larger bedchamber, no mean feat. While Noia started putting their belongings away, Taf hitched the tebecs to the back of the Hall's cart, which he then drove to the Hall. I followed in my cart so he could ride back to the house.

Zhia was awake when we arrived. She had stored the foodstuffs and was arranging the kitchen. I brought in a load of firewood and filled the water jars, then Taf and I hauled the divan outside and burned it. By the time my bed was again put together, Zhia had supper ready.

Since she hadn't helped with the cooking, Noia insisted on washing the dishes. Zhia didn't argue. Instead, she went into the front room to arrange our furniture and make the bed. When the rain started and the shutters were closed, Zhia and Noia measured windows and, sitting in the dining room, started sewing curtains by lamplight. It was evident that Noia hadn't done much sewing, either. Patiently, Zhia coached her.

Taf and I were standing in the entry with the door open to admit the evening breeze. Watching the women bent over the work, Noia's long blond curls contrasting with Zhia's short brown hair but their faces equally intent, Taf said quietly to me, "The reason there aren't any songs about this kind of thing is that there's no way to express how satisfying it is. Had someone told me I wouldn't miss what other male Singers are probably doing right now, I wouldn't have believed it. This seems so right."

"That's because it's a home," I said. "We lived at the Hall, but the Hall was never home. And it isn't just a home; it's your home. Yours and Noia's."

With a Darl-like grin, Taf asked, "Then are you and Zhia renting that room from us?"

I laughed. "No. You'll have to tour for your money, like every other Singer."

Chapter Forty-Eight

We had two more days to ourselves, days in which we continued to make the house even more our collective home—which included Gebir's building the wall across the former front room and installing a door; our hanging new curtains as they were finished; and the purchase of comfortable chairs, lamps, and a low table for the entryway, which Zhia and Noia had decided would be the front room—before another reality intruded.

We were lingering over our morning meal when a Hall stable hand knocked on the door with a message from Father. Zhia and I were to pack whatever was needed for several days and come at once.

"He didn't say why?" I asked the man.

"No, sir."

"Taf, would you hitch the desdal…" I began.

"The Master sent tebecs, sir," the stable hand said, interrupting. The interruption as well as the fact that we were sent tebecs told me the matter was urgent.

Zhia was wearing the reddish brown garment. She changed into shirt and trousers, packed the reddish brown and the golden green garments and her brush and mirror, slid her father's ring onto her right thumb, and picked up her walking stick. "I'm ready."

My packing took only slightly longer. With the help of the stick, Zhia was able to get into the tebec's saddle. I secured the stick behind the saddle with the rest of her things, then climbed onto my bird.

Taf and Noia stood in the doorway to see us off, calling assurances that they'd take care of the house.

"It's not the house I'm worried about," I said quietly to Zhia. "It's what's waiting for us at the Hall."

Zhia said, "Even if it's something bad—Nia Diva forbid!—we know this time it doesn't involve me."

Darl must have been listening, for it was something bad, and it did involve Zhia.

We went at once to Father's office. Father wasn't wearing the black robes of a Hall Master; he was wearing shirt and trousers. He thrust a piece of paper at me and began to pace. I held the paper low enough so Zhia could read it, as well.

It was from Arion, Master of the Hall where Henz was. The storm that had caused such distress the evening I'd made Zhia my wife for the second time had devastated Voestrand, where Arion's Hall was. The lightning had caused numerous fires, one of which had damaged the stage. More than a score of lives had been lost. The mayor and the townspeople were paralyzed by despair. Henz had told him, Arion, about the song Zhia had sung at Owlin's Run. Arion was asking—pleading, actually—that Zhia come and sing that song at Voestrand.

Zhia looked up from the letter. Seeing an inquiry on Father's face, she said, crisply, "If food and other supplies are ready, we can leave immediately."

Father's face relaxed into a smile. "I was hoping you'd say that."

I was looking forward to a couple of nights completely alone with Zhia when Father hoisted a pack from his chair. "You're coming with us?" I asked.

"I've never heard Zhia sing on a stage," he replied. "Let's go."

When Zhia fell asleep on her tebec in the middle of the morning, Father said, "I'm not sure this was a good idea."

"This was an excellent idea, Father," I said. "Don't fuss about Zhia; she won't thank you for it."

"But she is recovering."

"Yes. She just falls asleep when she needs to."

Father shook his head. "Osrum was too easy on Garit."

I said nothing. While I shared Father's opinion, I was more than ready for the cycle of retribution to end.

After a long silence, Father suddenly asked, "Has Zhia sung since she was hurt?"

"The night of the storm, remember?" I replied. "And she and Noia have been singing duets while they fix the house."

Father looked thoughtful. "She and Noia could sing a duet at our hometown tour."

"Will we be back by then, or are you going to have to reschedule it?"

"I don't expect to do more in Voestrand than express our sympathy, have Zhia sing, and return."

"Then why am I here?"

"You're her husband; where else would you be?" Father asked, a bit sharply. "Besides, since there's no accompaniment, you'll need to give her a starting pitch."

I doubted Zhia needed a starting pitch, but there was no point in arguing about it with Father. Our conversation turned to details of the hometown tour, which by then Father had fairly well planned; then to Zhia's comments about putting tebecs in desdal's harnesses. Before that discussion could go very far, Zhia woke and we had to stop so she could lose her breakfast. Since we were stopped, we ate our midday meal. Zhia refused everything but bread and a small amount of wine.

"We're not so far from our Hall that we can't turn back," Father said to Zhia.

"Please don't fuss, Father. I'm a woman with child; this is to be expected. No blessing is unmixed, especially this one."

"Did you bring your stage garb?" Father asked, by way of honoring her request.

"Yes; though I'm not sure that would be appropriate for this engagement. Do I want to get on the stage—whatever is left of it—looking untouched by what the people of Voestrand have suffered?"

"They know you haven't suffered what they have," he observed.

Zhia started to say something, stopped, then said, "I promise I'll wear something."

Father laughed.

A long and winding road runs between my Hall and Voestrand. The land is wooded and fairly hilly. The road skirts the densest parts of the woods and the higher hills, which makes the journey longer than the actual distance. As we neared a place where the road ran between hills, I felt myself tense. Reason told me the raiders' numbers had been reduced to the point that they were no longer a threat. Fear doesn't listen to reason. I saw Zhia was also keeping an eye on the higher land.

Father finally noticed our watchfulness. I saw his expression change as he realized the possible threat. It had been many turns of the star wheel since he'd toured; but the shape of the land hadn't changed. He knew, as did I, that farther along the hills weren't quite as high. We urged our tebecs to a faster pace, and were able to reach the lower hills well before the rain started. From much travel on that road when I was still indulging in escapades with Henz, I knew where the Quarter Rest was. The trees around it grew so thickly that it couldn't be seen from the road.

Father had us back on the road before daybreak. We reached Voestrand by midday. Atop a hill that overlooked the town, we reined in our tebecs. Zhia caught her breath and began speaking softly. Hearing the word "Unknown", I knew she was praying. Suddenly I wondered what possible help a song could be to the people of this town, even a song I believed I'd been given by Nia Diva. Nothing I'd imagined had prepared me for the sight of the destruction Voestrand had suffered.

Most of the buildings in town were of wood. The fires had spared only a few houses. Of those, many had the black-draped doors that betokened a recent death. The mercantile area had suffered even more. The stage was now roofless. Even from a distance, I could see debris on the parts of the floor that, though blackened, were still intact. All that remained of its curved back wall was the part with the symbol of Nia Diva. For a moment, I wondered whether I was seeing the daemon's punishment on Henz for cheating at the Festival. I quickly dismissed the notion. Henz had survived the ruin of the town. More, Henz's offense hadn't occurred in Voestrand; the people of this town didn't know of his wrongdoing. If daemons were allowed to punish, surely any daemon worthy of worship could manage to penalize the guilty rather than the innocent.

At Father's gesture, we rode slowly on. As was customary, Arion's Hall was some distance from the town, right on the bank of the creek from which the town took its name. The woods between the town and the Hall were scorched; soot streaked the gray stone from which the Hall was built. The gate into the courtyard was open; its wood had been partly consumed. Otherwise, the Hall appeared to be untouched.

Arion, a stooped and frail old man, awaited us in the courtyard. His black robes were smudged with gray ash. A very somber Henz was with him.

"Thank you for coming," Arion said to Father as soon as we dismounted. Turning to her, he said, "And you must be Zhia."

Leaning on her walking stick, Zhia inclined her head and said, "Yes, sir."

"This is Zhia's husband, my son, Rois," Father said, indicating me. "Arion, I have no words to express our dismay at the magnitude of the tragedy you've suffered here. May the daemon forgive me if I express my doubts that a song will make things any better."

Arion said, "I think it's safe to say that a song can't make things any worse." No one laughed, but the mood was lighter when he asked, "Would all of you join me for the midday meal?"

Zhia declined at once. I think she would have refused food even if she weren't going to be singing. Though that day she hadn't lost her breakfast, just then she looked both queasy and nervous. Father also declined, so I had no choice but to follow his example.

When Arion affirmed that Zhia would be singing on the stage and that the song would be as soon as word had reached everyone that Zhia had arrived, Father said we would go to the stage and start getting ready.

Arion informed us that he had been on the stage since the fire and had found it to be quite safe, but he was slightly built. Even if Father didn't plan to find out for himself whether the stage was capable of supporting someone of Zhia's weight, I wasn't going to allow my wife set foot on it until I had checked it thoroughly. Voestrand's stage wasn't as high off the ground as the Festival stage, but it was higher than Zhia or anyone else needed to fall, should the charred floor break.

As we were talking, several tebec-mounted Singers left the courtyard, presumably to summon the surviving townspeople to the stage. I heard Zhia swallow and looked at her quickly.

She gave me an unconvincing smile and said to Arion, "Sir, could I trouble you for a jug of water and a basin to take with me so I can freshen up before I sing?"

"It's no trouble," he answered, immediately. "Indeed, I'm remiss for not offering you a bath. I'll fetch what you need."

"Might I come in with you for just a moment?" she asked, hesitantly.

Arion looked puzzled, then he nodded. "Certainly. I'll show you where it is." He offered her his arm, so she handed me the walking stick. Father decided to go inside with them.

"Doesn't she know the word 'pee'?" Henz remarked, with a trace of his usual grin. "So how are you liking your cage, Rois?"

Knowing I'd be seeing Henz, and suspecting he wasn't finished needling me, I had spent part of the trip thinking of answers to possible gibes. Comments having to do with cages or leashes were ones I most expected. Satisfied at having guessed correctly and confident that I believed the answer I had prepared, I said, "I don't consider having a wife being in a cage. What I have is a foundation. Unlike you, I'm building for the future."

He was shaking his head. "No one can talk crap like you, Rois."

"It's not crap, Henz; it's the truth. When I'm gone, there will be someone to carry on my name. If you're remembered at all, it'll be as the Champion who cheated."

Henz seemed not to have heard my last statement. "Zhia is with child?" He laughed. "So that's why you made her your wife."

"Zhia and I weren't intimate before I asked her to be my wife."

"Which just shows you're a fool," was his sneering rejoinder.

I couldn't afford to lose my temper, so I changed the subject. "Since you're at this Hall, I assume your family lives in Voestrand. Were they affected by the fire?" (The question probably seems strange. Though it's true I'd known Henz for some time, I knew nothing about his family. He never mentioned them.)

"They don't live here; they live in Yster Ridge," he said, carelessly. "I haven't seen them in probably nine turns of the star wheel. And no, I don't miss them. My father disowned me when I got the mayor's daughter with child." He smacked his lips coarsely. "She was a choice morsel."

When I said nothing—Henz's choice of words had made me remember the fate of Zhia's son—Henz snatched the walking stick from my hand and looked at it. "This is nice." He ran one finger down the carving. "It has her name on it. Zhia. Zhia Diva."

"That's not what it says," I chided.

"That's how I read it. Did you make this for her?"

"No. One of the men from her second tour did."

"Her second tour?" he echoed. "What second tour? Your wife still hasn't completed a tour, Rois. She's still a first-timer."

Before our bickering could degenerate into another argument, Zhia, Father, and Arion returned. Arion was carrying a jug and a basin. He had changed into shirt and trousers. Zhia and Father mounted their tebecs. As before, I secured Zhia's walking stick before climbing onto my own bird. A stable hand brought a tebec for Arion. Henz told him to bring another, so there were five of us riding to the stage.

The fire had damaged the side and lower rooms of the stage. Choosing one that afforded the most privacy, Zhia handed Father her walking stick, took her pack and the jug and basin Arion was holding, and went in to wash and change. Father and Arion stood nearby to ensure that she wasn't disturbed.

Testing each tread, I went up the steps to the stage and walked slowly on every board that wasn't obviously unsafe.

"I did that," Arion called to me.

"With all respect, sir, I'm doing it again. I value my wife."

Several of the boards that appeared to be whole sagged dangerously under my weight. I picked up a piece of charred wood and marked them.

"Do you want help with that?" Henz asked from the ground.

"Thank you, but no. I need to be certain the stage is safe. If it's not, it's better that only one of us take a risk."

"All the more reason it should be me," was Henz's serious reply. Startled, I looked at him. "You don't want to leave the child fatherless, do you?" he added.

"Don't tell me you're going decent on me," I joked.

His usual grin back in place, Henz said, "Not a chance. Had you worried, though, didn't I?"

"Not a chance." As I bent to mark another unsafe board, I thought I saw Henz's grin droop a little.

Zhia came out, dressed in the golden green garment and looking lovely but anxious. Father returned her walking stick. I saw him smile and say something, probably reassuring, because some of the tension left her face.

I knew a back rub would further calm Zhia, but my hands were filthy with cinder and ash. I considered the alternatives, then said, "Henz, would you be so kind as to give Zhia a back rub?"

It was his turn to look startled, but he nodded and complied. I confess I did keep an eye on him. As far as I could tell, he did only what had been asked of him.

People were starting to gather. Some were bandaged. Most looked like they had recently been weeping. All had the appearance of being utterly defeated.

From the stage I could see tears in Zhia's eyes as she watched the townspeople arrive. Hoping to distract her, I jumped down from the stage, pointed out the marked boards, and told her what they meant. Looking dubiously at the scattered marks, she said, "I never was very good at dancing. I'll be careful." As she surveyed the stage again, the tension returned to her face. She looked away and asked, "What do I use for the wine ritual?"

Arion hadn't remembered about it. He suggested we do without it, but

Zhia said, "With all respect, sir, no. For this performance to be of any help to the people of this town, it can't be just a song done any old way. It has to remind them that there are constants in life. What I do here and now has to be familiar. It has to be right."

There was no arguing with that. Father got a wine jug from the supplies our tebecs carried. I removed my Champion's cup from its chain and held it so Father could dribble the two sips of liquid into it. I set it on the stage, went back up the steps, picked it up, and hesitated. I needed something on which to set it. It wouldn't be fitting to put it on the half-burned boards.

Henz went away and came back with the basin, which was still full of water. "Turn it upside down," he suggested. "It's nowhere near tall enough, but it's better than nothing."

Before I emptied the basin, I washed my hands. When the cup was sitting on it, in its proper place under the Nia Diva symbol, I steadied Zhia as she walked up the steps. She went to the back of the stage, where most of the sound planks were, and stood, stick in hand, poised and unmoving, as the last of the townspeople arrived.

A harried-looking man I took to be the mayor greeted us and bowed to Zhia. She returned his bow. A great hush fell on the gathered people, a silence that to me seemed less one of anticipation than of hopelessness.

Picking up the tiny gold cup, Zhia faced the symbol of Nia Diva, raised the cup, and said, "Nia Diva, we come to you in fear, sorrow, and despair. Pour on us the balm of your music. Grant us healing, courage, strength, and comfort. Even so." She drank as those of us on the ground echoed "Even so".

After replacing the cup, Zhia turned to face the people. Seemingly without looking at which boards I'd marked, she stepped forward. I was holding my breath and forgot that I was to give her the starting pitch.

She didn't need it. As the first low, warm notes caressed the hearers, I saw tentative smiles appear on faces that likely hadn't smiled for days. Every sure note and every clear word Zhia sang affirmed the prayer she'd offered. The music was a balm. That the daemon was present could not be doubted.

There was no applause when Zhia finished; the people were too moved to respond. Zhia turned again to the symbol of Nia Diva and made the same graceful salute she had used in Owlin's Run. Next to me, Father caught his breath and muttered, "Even so."

Zhia again faced the people and said, "I'd like all of you to sing with me now. Rois, Henz, you know this song." She gestured widely. "Singers, you can do it, too, I know."

Startled, Father, Arion, and I turned. Ringing the townspeople were men and women dressed in gaudy clothing. Every Singer from Arion's Hall must have been there.

Zhia started again. Henz and I were singing from the first note. The other Singers were all with us within a few measures. Slowly but surely, the townspeople raised their voices, as well. I can't say the song sounded good; but the unison became more than musical. A new spirit filled the ruined stage area. Without being told, we sang the song together a second time. Zhia left the stage briefly and came back wearing the reddish brown garment. When the song was again over, she applauded the people. Then she pointed to a woman near the front of the crowd and said, "May I borrow your broom?"

She began to sweep the stage. As the townspeople watched, dumfounded, someone next to me began the song again. It was Father. He could sing again. As the music spread and swelled, Zhia finished cleaning the stage. When the last note died, again she bowed to the symbol of Nia Diva.

I hugged Father, something I don't remember doing since I was a small child, then went on stage to hug Zhia. Though tears were in her eyes, she was smiling. She cleared her throat and dried her eyes on the fabric over her arm before saying to the people, "You have received the gift of healing. Continue the work that has begun on this stage. Your Singers will be joining their efforts to yours in rebuilding what was lost. May Nia Diva and the Unknown bless you as together you make a new beginning."

With a cheer, a man shouted, "Zhia!" One or two voices echoed him.

Another man—I knew it was Henz—called, "Zhia Diva!"

I heard Zhia curse softly; I don't think anyone else heard her.

Cursing did no good. The name spread through the crowd faster than the fire had spread through the town. Soon everyone was calling "Zhia Diva" and applauding.

Her face bright red, Zhia left the stage, broom in one hand, walking stick in the other. She returned the broom to the woman from whom she'd borrowed it. I'm certain she thanked the woman, but the acclaim was so loud I could scarcely hear myself think.

The crowd parted to let Zhia through, though people were reaching out to touch her as she passed. She was smiling and speaking to the people around her, but I could see that she was tense.

When the mayor appeared in front of her, the noise abated. With a bow, he said, "Accept our thanks. Today you have given Voestrand a gift beyond price. When the stage is rebuilt, it will be given your name in honor of this day."

"Please don't, sir," Zhia said, her voice thick with emotion. "I did nothing. If the daemon chose to act through me, to Nia Diva be the glory. The stage is hers, not mine. To be able to serve—to see smiles where there were tears and hope where there was defeat—is all the honor I need or deserve."

The mayor bowed again, more deeply. "It shall be as you wish." He managed to attract the attention of the townspeople and exhorted them to continue the clean-up Zhia had begun, however symbolically, on the stage.

I went back on stage to collect my Champion's cup and the basin, which I returned to Arion. As we were going to where Zhia had left her shirt and trousers, Henz came up, all smiles. "How do you like the stage name I gave you?" he asked.

"I should have known it was your idea," she said, so mildly that Henz should have been wary.

"Why? Because it's clever?"

"Because it's blasphemous," was Zhia's cold reply. "I'll do without a stage name before I allow that to be my stage name."

CHAPTER FORTY-NINE

As I KNEW ALL too well, a stage name often sticks whether a Singer likes it or not.

Just how a stage name becomes public knowledge is a mystery. Knowing that Zhia had cursed when she first heard her stage name (and for some time thereafter winced whenever it was spoken) I had told no one what it was. I'm certain Father told no one. The townspeople and Singers of Voestrand were too busy to travel. Taf suggested that workmen summoned there to help with the repair and rebuilding spread the story and the name, which is quite possible.

My personal opinion is that, as a petty sort of revenge, Henz took it upon himself to make the name so well known that Zhia had no choice but to accept it.

Regardless of how Zhia's stage name became known, it was already widely known by the time of the hometown tour, which took place less than a handful of days after our return from Voestrand.

The return trip had been much faster than the journey there because Zhia had slept much of the way back. That the performance at Voestrand had exacted a considerable toll on her was evidenced by her almost nonstop talking between when we left the town and when we reached the Quarter Rest where we again spent the night.

When I asked her why she had swept the stage, she said the gesture had occurred to her only when she'd noticed the woman with the broom. It had been her thought that wearing her less fine garment would show her willingness to share the people's tasks.

In response to questions about how Arion's Singers came to offer their assistance to the townspeople, Zhia explained that the contrast between the devastated town and the relatively unscathed Hall had suggested the idea to her. When she'd gone into the Hall, a Singer who appeared familiar, who she learned was her lamented husband's brother, recognized her and spoke with her. She'd mentioned the idea to him, expecting him to dismiss it scornfully. Immediately impressed by the sheer graciousness of the idea, he had told her he would persuade the other Singers and bring them to the stage.

"In other words," Father had said, his restored voice every bit as compelling as I remembered, "what you did was simply improvise."

By then we were eating supper at the Quarter Rest. Zhia should have been hungry, but her head was hurting, so she wasn't eating much. I'd almost had to force her to accept a morsel of bread, some fruit, and a cup of wine. Trying to choke down the bread, she nodded in confirmation of Father's comment.

"It was brilliant improvisation," Father said. "And in answer to your question of some days ago, Son, henceforth Singers at my Hall will be saluting the symbol of Nia Diva." He looked again at Zhia. "May I depend on you to demonstrate how it's to be done?"

She blushed as she sipped wine to help the bread down. "If you wish." Suddenly, she started so violently that the wine sloshed. "You have your voice back!" she exclaimed. "When did that happen?"

"When you were sweeping the stage. I wondered when you'd notice." Father laughed heartily. "My Singers are so used to ignoring me, I wonder if anyone else will notice."

"Another miracle!" Zhia whispered. "Praise the Unknown."

"Even so," Father and I said together.

Just then the breeze that was bringing in the evening rain began to explore the shelter. Though far from cold, it was noticeably cooler than it had been only a few days earlier. Zhia began to shiver. Father put more wood on the fire. I drew Zhia against me. Only moments later, she was asleep. I caught the wine cup before it fell from her hand, and set it aside.

Father regarded us from across the fire. I must have looked disheartened, for he said, gently, "She'll recover, Son."

I nodded, but said, "Maybe I'm being ungrateful, Father, but it seems to me that since the Unknown was working miracles, he could have spared one— or two—for Zhia."

"I would gladly give my voice if thereby Zhia's head or foot or both could be mended; but I don't think the Unknown works that way. I doubt even an Ambassador can explain the working of the Unknown. No doubt you've realized how miraculous it is that Zhia is still with us." Again, I nodded. Father added, "You've had a hard day. Get some sleep."

In the morning, Zhia claimed her head felt better. Nevertheless, she slept most of the day. Father and I took turns leading her tebec which, lacking her guiding, kept trying to stray. The sun was just setting when we reached the house. I woke Zhia and sent her inside. Taf came out to ask if I needed help bringing in anything. I had Zhia's and my packs in one hand and the walking stick in the other, so I said "no".

When Father bid us farewell, Taf stared. "Your voice!" he said. "What…"

"Come to the Hall the day after tomorrow and you'll hear all about it," Father said, grinning.

Taf continued to stare until Father's tebec and the two he was leading were out of sight. "He can talk!" he said to me.

I was also grinning. "He can sing, too."

"How…"

I shook my head. "Father wants to tell the story. Trust me; it's worth waiting for."

When Taf, Noia, Zhia, and I arrived the Hall at midmorning on the day specified, it was to find the Singers and the instructors gathered in the dining hall, which was filled with a buzz of excitement and speculation. Father entered, once more clad in his black robes and with a rolled paper in his hand, and the conversations stopped abruptly.

Father said, "Good morning," his restored voice easily carrying to every corner of the large room.

The silence lasted scarcely a moment longer. Cheers broke out. When order was restored—clearly enjoying the moment, Father was in no hurry to interrupt the outburst—he related what had happened in Voestrand. I was watching faces as he spoke. Some were soon wearing the expressions of disbelief or even scorn I had expected, but most were rapt. Then Father said that obeisance to the symbol of Nia Diva was to be part of our Hall's practice, and there was a thin, secretive muttering.

Father raised his hand for silence. "I'm not asking your approval of this decision. Indeed, it grieves me that we have so long neglected to show proper respect to the daemon we claim to serve. The salute will be made by all Singers at this Hall at the end of every performance on tour. Any who choose not to do so may make their choice known to me, and will be free to find a Hall where their lack of obedience will be tolerated. Please note that I speak of obedience, not piety. I cannot compel your belief; my request is simply that you comply with the instructions of your Hall Master." Looking directly at her, he asked, "Zhia, would you demonstrate the salute?"

As she made her way to where he stood, Father unrolled the piece of paper. On it was the symbol of Nia Diva. He held it against the wall at the height at which it was seen on the back wall of most stages.

Zhia leaned her stick against the wall. Coloring slightly under the mixed regard of the Singers, she cleared her throat and said, "Before I do as Father asks, I must ask you to remember two important things. One, move deliberately. You have to look like you aren't making a mistake. Two, don't bend from the waist, because then you'll bend over too far. The audience doesn't want to see a stage full of Singers' rear ends."

"Not your rear end, anyway," someone called. Laughter dissipated some of the strain Father's words had caused. When the Singers were again silent, Zhia faced the symbol on the paper and made the obeisance. She seemed to be moving stiffly. When she again faced the Singers and I saw anger on her face, I knew why. I had to give her credit for keeping her voice even when she added, "And then you can bow to the audience, but never as deeply as you bow to the symbol of the daemon." She looked at Father. "All right?" He nodded. She escaped into the mass of Singers.

"Since we'll all be saluting the daemon's symbol at the conclusion of our upcoming performance on the Festival stage, you might practice it now," Father said, in a tone that made clear that it wasn't just a suggestion. He watched as the group attempted to copy what Zhia had done. He was less than pleased with their effort and asked Zhia to come forward and again demonstrate it. Though she said nothing, her face likely betrayed her resentment, for he said, "Yes, you must." Then, to the entire assembly, he said, "The sooner you learn this, the sooner I can stop embarrassing Zhia."

Again, there was laughter, more than slightly colored with derision. The salute—both Zhia's and the group's—was better the second time. Father thanked the group, then shared the details of the hometown tour, which was to take place the next day. Both because I had already heard what Father had in mind and because wonderful aromas were issuing from the kitchen, I was only half listening. I must confess that, after what happened in Voestrand, I expected the event to be, at best, an anticlimax.

Darl wasn't going to allow that to happen.

Father finally said, "That's all. Are there any questions?" When no one spoke, he said, "Then let's give thanks to the Unknown and enjoy the delicious meal that's been prepared for us." He bowed his head, saying, "Once again you bless us with bountiful food. As we offer our thanks, keep us mindful of those who have recently suffered loss, and of our fellow Singers who are working with them to repair and rebuild, that not only their homes and their livelihood but also their joy may be restored. Even so."

"Even so," came the somewhat tentative echo.

I turned to Zhia, intending to ask whether she'd like me to bring a plate for her. The question died on my lips. Her face was stormy. "What's wrong?" I asked instead.

"I won't sing alone tomorrow," she said. (Part of Father's plan was for Zhia to sing my dream song as a solo and then have the entire group sing it again, in parts.) "Volan was right: Singers sing in groups. There's no need for me to show off."

"Let's not argue until after we eat, all right?" I said.

"I'm not hungry," Zhia snapped. She snatched up her walking stick and left. Taf, Noia, and I got plates and sat at one table.

Soon Father joined us. "Where's Zhia?"

"She said she wasn't hungry," I answered.

"Is she still upset about demonstrating the salute?" Father asked, shrewdly.

I shook my head. "I don't know if she's upset about anything in particular, or if it's just that she's moody because she's with child."

To my surprise, Noia said, "That's not true, Rois. You know why Zhia is upset. If you're afraid to tell your father the real reason, I'm not." She turned to him and said, "Zhia would rather not solo tomorrow. In view of the reaction of some of your Singers to what she was required to do today—and you yourself acknowledged that you were embarrassing her—it would be kind if you excused her from further showing off, as she put it." She took the edge off her voice and added, "I think it would be wonderful if you sang that solo, Father. Think of the surprise and delight that would give the people of this town, to be among the first to hear High Note sing again!"

"Do, Robil." Mother and Lisia had come in while Noia was talking. "Noia's right; that you can again sing is worthy of a celebration." Mother deposited Lisia in my lap and went to get a plate.

The child started to fuss and squirm, probably looking either for Mother or for Zhia. One flailing arm caught the edge of my plate and flipped it off the table, spraying both Lisia and me with food.

Arms clad in badly frayed dark green cloth reached over me and picked up the messy child. Zhia's voice said, dully, "I'll do whatever I'm told to do tomorrow, Father." She tucked the child under one arm and again left the dining hall.

When Mother returned with her food, I told her what had happened. With an exclamation of dismay, she set down her plate and turned toward the door.

Father put a hand on her arm. "Please stay here," he said. He looked at me. "You stay here, too." Then he rose from the table and left. When he returned sometime later, in one arm he was carrying Lisia, who was bathed and in fresh clothes. His other arm was around Zhia, who looked like she had been weeping. He gave Lisia to Mother, fetched a plate and wine for Zhia, and returned to his own meal.

No one dared ask what had been said. Not until both he and Zhia were finished eating did he say, "Zhia will sing the solo on Rois's song. I will also sing a solo."

I started to say something, but Zhia said, curtly, "Let's go back to the house. If I don't wash your clothes right away, I'll never get the stains out of them."

Taf and Noia wanted to remain at the Hall, so Zhia said, "We'll stop for you on our way back from town."

She left the dining hall before they could do more than tell me where the cart was. "I thought we were going to the house," I said as the cart left the Hall courtyard.

"We are. I'll put your clothes in to soak, then I'm going into town."

"You don't want me to come?"

"You don't have to. I'm perfectly capable of driving a cart, you know. I'm not a baby."

Then I understood, or at least thought I did. "Is that what Father said to you?"

She wouldn't meet my eyes. "I told you once I value the truth. If I later say I don't want to hear it, then I was lying to you, wasn't I?" was her oblique reply.

"Why do you have to go into town?" I asked, mildly.

"I have to purchase fabric."

"You certainly could do with a new shirt. Those trousers are also looking well worn."

She looked at me in surprise. "Are they?" She looked at her clothes as though seeing them for the first time. "Yes, I guess they are. But that's not what I need the fabric for."

"Since we'll be in town, let's also get you some changes of clothes."

Then she was weeping. "Are you ashamed of me?"

"Did Father suggest that, too?" I asked, reminding myself not to be angry until I knew the answer.

"No. I was just asking."

She needed more than words. I put one arm around her and persuaded the desdal to shamble faster. Zhia didn't object when my hand slipped into the neck of her shirt. We were already kissing when we entered the house. Not until later, when we were lying, fully satisfied, across our bed did I say, "No, I'm not ashamed of you."

By then, her smile had returned. She kissed me once more and slid out of bed. Hastily pulling on the reddish brown garment, she went out of the room. I slipped into a contented doze, so don't know how much later it was when she shook me and said, "Your bath is ready."

When I saw that the clothes the food had stained were hanging to dry, I knew I'd been fully asleep, and for quite a while. Zhia's was wearing her shirt and trousers, but her hair was wet, so I assumed she'd already freshened up. I washed hurriedly. As I stepped out of the tub, Zhia's arm appeared around the door and dropped a fresh shirt and trousers on the floor. "Thank you," I called, amused at the contrast between her present modesty and her earlier unrestrained passion. "May I go to town with you?"

"If you wish." I might have been a little miffed had I not heard a note of teasing in her voice.

Shopping with Zhia was much less stressful than shopping with Eia—which is not to say that Zhia wasn't particular about what she bought, only that she wasn't so careful to let the merchants know her opinion of their goods—and considerably faster. It took her no time at all to select two new shirts and two pair of trousers. I hardly need say all four garments were of dark, one-color cloth. When I expressed a desire for some wine and asked if she was also thirsty, she said "no". In the time it took me to get to the wine seller's stall, drink a cup of wine, and return, she had purchased the fabric she needed.

Her secretiveness was doing nothing to quench my curiosity. While I went into the Hall to fetch Taf and Noia, Zhia climbed into the back of the cart with her parcels. At my suggestion, on the way back to the house Taf drove the cart and Noia sat in front with him. I rode in back with Zhia.

"So what's the big mystery?" I asked as we gripped the sides of the cart's bed to steady ourselves as the cart bumped and lurched over the rutted road.

"There's no mystery," Zhia replied, with unconvincing innocence.

"Then why can't I see your fabric?"

"Did I say you couldn't see it?" When I continued simply to look at her, she said in obvious annoyance, "All right. Your father and I made a deal. I said I'd sing the solo as long as I didn't have to stand in front of the other Singers. He said that, provided I could be heard, I could stand where I wanted as long as I was dressed like the other Singers. So I bought this." She unwrapped a parcel and displayed cloth that, while brighter than what Zhia usually wore, was quite subdued by Singers' standards. "Will it be suitable, do you think?"

There was, of course, no doubt that Taf and Noia could hear our conversation; but Noia didn't turn around until after I'd approved Zhia's selection. Then, with well-feigned surprise, Noia said, "Zhia, what lovely fabric. What's that for?"

Zhia laughed. "You have the best manners of anyone I know. You know that I know that you know what it's for, which is good; because I might have to ask your help to get it sewn before tomorrow."

"I'd be happy to help, if you need it. I hope you aren't too particular about whether it holds together for the duration of a performance."

"Your sewing is already better than mine, in case I haven't mentioned it," Zhia remarked, "but if you want to pretend otherwise, you can sew the hems."

From the curtain-sewing sessions, the rest of us knew Noia disliked hemming. She laughed. "What are you planning to make in so little time? Surely not a skirt and shirt!"

"No, just one of my shapeless things. That way I'll be able to use it until the baby comes."

"I haven't thought that far ahead," Noia confessed, "though I expect to continue to tour as long as possible. I might have to make a couple of those for myself."

I don't know how late Zhia sat up sewing. I know her head hurt the next morning, but knew also there was no point in my saying anything about what she'd had to do to keep her part of the bargain she'd made with Father. She seemed to be losing her touch; this was the second time she'd failed to play people to her own advantage.

The new garment fit Zhia—indeed, save for length, it would've fit just about anyone, including Father—but it didn't suit her as well as either the golden green or the reddish brown one did. However, when she was on the Festival stage with the other Singers, she blended in so well that Father didn't see her when he was making sure all was in readiness for the performance. He beckoned urgently to me. I handed the tiny cup of wine in my hand to the man next to me and left the stage.

"Where's Zhia?" he asked.

I pointed her out to him, then asked, "Where's your wine?"

"That's what I forgot!" he said, and went to where the cups for the ritual were being distributed.

Perhaps unkindly amused to see that my father was as prone to pre-performance nerves as any other Singer, I returned to my place on the stage.

The highlight of the performance was, of course, Father's return as a Singer. The crowd gave him a rousing ovation both before and after he sang. I'm not ashamed to say that I was in tears when he finished singing. I saw many other Singers, men and women alike, drying their eyes. Father had recovered from his pre-performance jitters enough to call for an instrumental piece to give all of us time to regain our composure.

That piece was followed by Egion playing the improved rimba, then several choral pieces from our Hall repertoire.

Neron's last work was our second to the last song. Before we started to sing, Father told the audience that it was being presented in memory of its composer, a man who had been an instructor at the Hall for twenty-three turns of the star wheel, a man whose dedication to the Hall was so great that he actually died at his desk in his classroom.

Singers may not always act properly when offstage, but as Father's encomium wore on, not one Singer snickered… not loud enough for the audience to hear, anyway. The eulogy was a fine example of Singers' ability to talk crap. Without saying anything false, Father managed to make Neron sound like a beloved and much-lamented instructor. Wisely, Father ended his comments before any of us did anything that would reveal to the crowd that Neron was not that lamented.

The muscles of my cheeks were aching from trying not to grin during Father's introduction to the song, but singing quickly loosened them. Perhaps to make up for the fact that we'd all been thinking ill of the dead, we put ourselves into the song, and did it very well. In fact, I thought we should have ended the performance then. I couldn't imagine that even my dream song could top what we had just done.

Tej, on strings, started playing the accompaniment of my song. Just one voice—Zhia's—emerged from the massed Singers. Excepting her performance in Voestrand, I've never heard her do that song better. Then the massed voices began, and even Zhia's solo was surpassed. With the excellent acoustics of the Festival stage, the effect was awe inspiring. It was a shame Ganit wasn't there to accept acclaim for his arrangement; it was superb.

As in both Owlin's Run and Voestrand, there was a profound hush when the song was over, a hush that is actually a greater tribute to the musicians than immediate applause.

In the silence, we turned as one and made our salute to the symbol of Nia Diva, then turned and bowed to the audience. Zhia did not take an individual bow; Father did.

No one among the listeners could have known who sang the last solo; no one in our town had heard Zhia sing. The silence at last was broken by a man shouting, "Zhia! Zhia Diva!"

What Henz was doing at our hometown tour when he was supposed to be helping with repairs and rebuilding at Voestrand, I didn't know. Actually, I did know; he'd just shown what he'd come to do. What I didn't know was why Arion had let him shirk his part of the task. The answer to that was moot; Henz had succeeded in stealing from Zhia the anonymity she had until then succeeded in keeping.

The crowd had heard her name, of course; tales of TTTW were already legendary. Soon everyone on the ground in front of the stage was applauding and calling her name—her stage name, to be precise.

Father had little choice but to draw Zhia forward and have her take a bow. She acknowledged the unwanted attention with the merest inclination of her head. Then she stepped back, extended both arms wide and, as in Owlin's Run, invited applause for everyone else on the stage.

Recognizing the graciousness of the gesture, most of the audience stopped calling Zhia's stage name but cheered and applauded more loudly.

Zhia was edging back among the Singers when Osrum climbed onto the stage. He spoke briefly to Father, who held up his hands for silence. Father stepped aside, motioning Osrum to center stage.

"As your magistrate, I have the honor and privilege of reporting to you that I have for some time been communicating with the magistrates of other towns. Save for two minor and quickly-contained episodes, there has been no raider activity. We are daring to hope that raiders are ended as a threat. Credit for that goes to…"

"The Unknown," Zhia called, safely concealed both by the other Singers and by the fact that she was speaking, not singing. "Praise the Unknown!"

"Even so!" came a thunderous roar from the crowd.

I was certain Osrum knew who had upstaged him; Zhia's speaking voice was very familiar to him. He knew better than to continue with what he had planned to say. "Even so," he echoed, and quickly left the stage.

It took the massed Singers quite a bit longer to finish leaving the stage, load the instruments into the cart and onto tebecs, and return to the Hall, where Father had promised an extravagant party. Though I kept looking for her, I didn't see Zhia in the brightly-clad crowd queuing to use the steps to the ground. I didn't see her in the dining hall, where the party was being held. Taf and Noia hadn't seen her since she interrupted Osrum's comments. Father hadn't, either; but he soon brought me a folded piece of paper that had been left on one of the tables. On the outside it said "Eventide". On the inside it said, "My head hurts. I've gone home. Don't worry about me. Enjoy the party."

I did; Zhia wouldn't have. Everywhere I went I heard her name, both her given name and her stage name. Most of the Singers seemed to share her opinion that her stage name was inappropriate. Many believed that she liked her name and had enjoyed being singled out. No one could adequately explain why someone generally agreed to be attention-hungry had prevented Osrum's giving her well-deserved and very public credit for routing the raiders.

Taf wasn't listening as closely to the talk as I was, but he heard enough to make him say to me, with a grin, "Even if Zhia didn't want Osrum to mention her name, he could have mentioned you and me!"

"And the rocks and tebecs and swarmers," I added. The silliness helped me ignore the unkind comments about my wife. After that, I enjoyed the celebration more.

We got to the house very late, in a pleasant haze of weariness and wine. As we went through the kitchen to use the convenience in the far corridor, Noia suddenly stopped and pointed to a stack of neatly-hemmed towels and wash rags that hadn't been there when we left that morning.

They were made from the garment Zhia had worn to the performance.

CHAPTER FIFTY

ASK ANY PERSON OF fewer than thirty turns of the star wheel to name a Singer. Nine out of ten, non-Singer and Singer alike, will say "Zhia Diva". Non-Singers will speak the name with respect, even awe. There are still some Singers who regard Zhia with scorn and derision.

Father couldn't help but be aware of what had been said about Zhia at the party. Having little authority over what Singers said, and none at all over what they thought, he gave them something else to talk and think about. He sent them on tour.

Indeed, Father is the Master who started the practice of having his Singers tour during the entire turn of the star wheel save for the cold spell, when weather made travel too dangerous and there was too much risk of illness.

Two days after the performance on the Festival stage, Taf, Noia, Zhia, and I were all on tour, though not all on the same tour. Taf and Noia were on a tour led by Oluzh. I was leading a tour that included Zhia. My tour didn't include any of those who had been her most vocal critics at the party but did include Ingbir and a first-timer named Madia, whose tour it was. Despite what tales have circulated, I must make clear that Zhia in no way attempted to distract audiences from Madia. That the crowds clamored to hear Zhia

Diva cannot be blamed on my wife. (Since before the next Festival Henz was killed by an outraged husband, there's no point in blaming him, either.)

As the tour progressed and Madia continued to be ignored or even spurned by those who had presumably come to hear her sing, she became increasingly morose, until she was scarcely able to face an audience. The best I can say for that experience is that we finished the tour. No one really enjoyed it. (Father later told me that Madia had become so discouraged she'd given up being a Singer and left the Hall.)

Since I had become so good at it—only because Father kept giving me the task—I again had the job of all the post-tour paperwork. That kept me away from Zhia, who was staying away from the Hall as much as possible. Evenings that I could spend at the house, especially before Taf and Noia returned, were that much more satisfying. Zhia often remarked it was a good thing there was no one living nearby.

Scarcely had all the post-hometown performance tours returned than Father was sending out another four or five groups. Taf and Noia didn't tour, for which they and Zhia and I were thankful. I hadn't before realized how much having a home but not being in it could occupy one's thoughts.

Zhia and I toured more often than anyone else, though never again with a first-timer. Looking back, I'm fairly certain Father was thinking that putting as many Singers as possible on tour with Zhia would help them see that she didn't seek acclaim. In this, he was partly successful. I say "partly", because Zhia didn't have to seek acclaim; acclaim sought her. Even older Singers resented when audiences at places they'd never before been asked for Zhia Diva.

Eventually, Father did the only sensible thing: he sent Zhia out with Singers who were strong instrumentalists rather than strong vocalists. Though I'm not a strong instrumentalist, Father knew I could take my turn on drums, at need, so Zhia never toured without me.

Zhia developed a distinctive style on these tours. She was the first one to invite the children onto the stage. She would sit down with them and teach them a simple song, often one she'd composed over the long stretches of road that, with the threat of raiders over, weren't nearly as empty as they'd been during the days of TTTW. As far as I know, she was the first to set to familiar tunes absurd new lyrics that she made up while traveling between towns. It wasn't uncommon for her musicians to be laughing so hard while she sang these songs that they couldn't play.

Soon, composers were writing songs for her. Since she never did learn to read music well, Father and I would review them, then I would sing the ones we considered most suitable for her voice so she could learn them.

As the child grew within her, we had to start traveling with a cart rather than with tebecs. Our first child, a boy we named Rozhil, was born backstage after a performance, which earned Zhia and me a break from touring, though not a break from my paperwork.

Baby Noiantaftan, a girl named Toia, had been born only a handful of days earlier, so two bleary-eyed mothers, two babies and baby beds, and a clothesline that never seemed to be empty of diapers became usual sights at the house.

At first disgusted that both his female Singers who could tour were unable to tour at the same time, Father quickly became reconciled to the situation when the group of tours that left shortly after the babies' births returned with reports of flawless, on-time engagements. When audiences saw no one on the tours even remotely identifiable as Zhia Diva, they had settled for and even enjoyed what the tours had to offer.

"I told you, Son, women shouldn't be Singers," he remarked to me yet again one evening after welcoming and speaking with the last of the returning all-male tours. The cold spell was upon us; no more tours would leave until the weather was warmer. By then, Toia and Rozhil would be old enough to accompany their parents on tour. "All these changes we've had to make to the Quarter Rests, the extra conveniences that have had to be added at the stages: it all makes a man feel old."

"Father, I can assure you that the changes to the Quarter Rests are appreciated by everyone who tours. And though I know touring isn't about money, you can't deny the Hall is now making money."

Father nodded, though he was likely thinking that one reason he'd had to resort to sending out so many tours so often was because quite a number of his older Singers, those who had started at the Hall when Nia Diva was still taken lightly, had left after the hometown performance. Some of them had found places at other Halls, more had ceased to be Singers in anything but name when the practice of saluting the daemon's symbol became widespread. Many of them, blaming Zhia for disrupting their lives, circulated malicious half-truths about her and kept alive the assertion that she craved attention.

Some even tried to revive rumors about how dangerous Zhia was; but after Osrum surprised Zhia at the first Festival after Rozhil's birth with a specially-struck medallion to commemorate her single-handedly bringing about the end of the raiders' reign of terror, no one listened to such talk, let alone believed it.

Strange though it may sound, Zhia was never Festival Champion. As I mentioned, I won the honor several more times, as did Noia. Zhia did compete. I always thought her performance was worthy of a Champion, and Father usually agreed. We also agreed that her stage name was one thing that probably kept some judges from choosing her. Like Zhia, they believed it blasphemous. Like so many other Singers, they couldn't believe that Zhia hadn't been behind Henz's very intentional attempts to spread the melodic but ill-advised name. I was known to be Henz's friend; Zhia was my wife. The conclusion was obvious to anyone with half an eye. Our insistence that the conclusion was wrong seemed only to embed it more deeply in everyone's thoughts.

Her never winning the Championship didn't trouble Zhia as much as it did me. As she'd said on the day of the tragic end of TTTW, we weren't Singers so we could decide who was best and give ourselves prizes, but so we could give others the gift of the joy of music. At doing that, no judge, however biased, could deny Zhia excelled.

She also excelled at producing children. Rozhil was followed by Druzhil. After him came Risia; then another girl, Diria; then another boy, Boril.

During the cold spell after Boril's birth, Father took a bad chill and died.

Mother died shortly afterwards of no apparent cause. Zhia said it was a broken heart, which is entirely possible. I became Master of the Hall, so Zhia and our children moved to the Hall. (Taf and Noia continued to live at the house with Toia, their only child.) I kept touring if Zhia was on tour. And Zhia continued to tour, even though Lisia, who had seen by then some seven or eight turns of the star wheel, joined our growing family.

Zhia's fame continued to grow. More and more women became Singers.

I was the one who started sending out all-female tours, as well as the usual all-male and mixed male-female tours. Composers and arrangers began rewriting many of the songs in the Hall repertoire for only women's voices. Atera's skill in doing this proved Father's wisdom and foresight in employing her as Theory and Composition instructor.

I had thought Atera might also be of help in advising the growing number of female Singers at the Hall; but she remained as cold and distant with the young women as she had been with me when I first escorted her to the Hall. In fact, in all the time she was an instructor, she never made any friends, close or casual. I finally employed some older women, widows of Singers, who knew what it meant to be a Singer and could advise the young women and answer questions I couldn't.

Everything seemed to be going well until one day, when Boril had seen almost four turns of the star wheel, Zhia came into my office at the Hall and announced that she was done touring.

"Why?" I gasped, mopping up the wine that, in my surprise, I'd spilled on the Hall records.

"We have children who need a mother, not a legend. And the legend is out of control. I'm starting to wonder whether Father wasn't right all along when he said women shouldn't be Singers. Everywhere I turn, there's some female Singer trying to be a better Zhia Diva than Zhia. Quite truthfully, many of them far surpass me in singing. They can all read music. Many of them can play instruments.

"They're Singers, Rois. I never was. You know it. I know it. Your father knew it. The Festival judges have always known it." This last was spoken softly.

"I'd rather stop touring now by my choice, than later when people start saying, 'Who told her she could sing?' or even, 'Doesn't she know when to quit?'"

I stood up and came around the desk to draw her into my arms. "You have a lovely, unique voice, and you know it."

"All the more reason to leave people with that memory rather than to continue until my voice is unlovely and ordinary." Though she nestled in my arms, her voice was hard when she added, "But that's not the main reason. I never have a day without pain. I stand on stages trying not to wince noticeably when my foot gets tired, which it does sooner with every performance. My head still hurts…"

I held her away from me and looked at her in dismay. "You told me it doesn't hurt any more."

"That's true: it doesn't hurt any more; but it doesn't hurt much less, either."

I bit back a sharp reply. Zhia had given me that so-clever assurance shortly after I became Hall Master. Glad to be able to give my full attention to a task I already knew so well yet found so overwhelming, I'd quit watching for the signs of pain I'd come to know all too well. I knew now that Zhia had said what she had to allow me to focus on the working and needs of the Hall. But I also knew I'd failed to put my wife first. Again.

"Zhia," I began.

"Please, Rois, don't try to talk me out of this. Don't tempt me with talk of one last tour or by telling me about special requests for the dream song. There are a hundred Singers out there who can sing that song better than I ever did."

"Nia Diva never worked miracles through any of them."

"Once I stop touring, maybe she will. Or maybe the miracles aren't as needed as they were. Show me a Hall where the daemon isn't invoked both at meals and when tours leave and return. Show me a Singer who, in saluting the symbol of Nia Diva, doesn't look like he or she truly means it. I've served the daemon, Rois. Surely she'll allow me now to serve our children, who may someday be Singers like their father and his father." Tears were in her eyes.

Again, I held her away from me. "Zhia, are you with child again?" I asked gently.

"Yes."

Knowing there was more behind the torrent of tears that followed than I could possibly understand, let alone find answers to, I simply held my wife close.

Somehow, I knew that was all she'd ever really needed from me.

By the way, the name of the girl who at eighteen became the youngest Singer to win the Champion's cup is Vezhia Zhianrois.

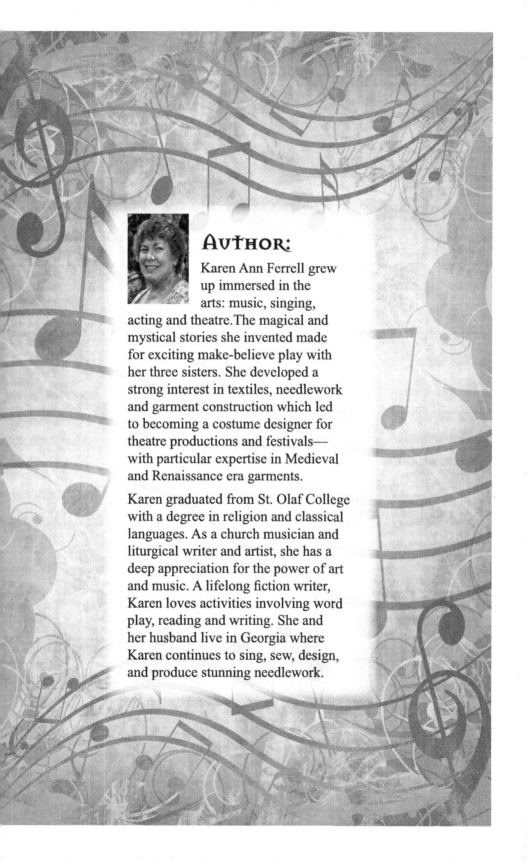

Author:

Karen Ann Ferrell grew up immersed in the arts: music, singing, acting and theatre. The magical and mystical stories she invented made for exciting make-believe play with her three sisters. She developed a strong interest in textiles, needlework and garment construction which led to becoming a costume designer for theatre productions and festivals—with particular expertise in Medieval and Renaissance era garments.

Karen graduated from St. Olaf College with a degree in religion and classical languages. As a church musician and liturgical writer and artist, she has a deep appreciation for the power of art and music. A lifelong fiction writer, Karen loves activities involving word play, reading and writing. She and her husband live in Georgia where Karen continues to sing, sew, design, and produce stunning needlework.

Made in the USA
Monee, IL
20 March 2022

93195937R10262